Sherif Meleka was born in Alexandria in [...] doctor, he emigrated to the United States ir [...] fiction and poetry in 2000, publishing his [...] in 2003. He is the author of nine novels and several books of poetry and short stories. He lives in Jacksonville, Florida, USA.

Raymond Stock is senior instructor of Arabic at Louisiana State University. He holds a PhD in Near Eastern Languages and Civilizations from the University of Pennsylvania (2008). A former resident of Cairo (1990–2010), he has translated seven books and many short stories by Naguib Mahfouz (1911–2006), including *Before the Throne, Khufu's Wisdom, The Coffeehouse* (all AUC Press).

Suleiman's Ring

Sherif Meleka

Translated by
Raymond Stock

hoopoe
AN IMPRINT OF AUC PRESS

First published in 2023 by
Hoopoe
113 Sharia Kasr el Aini, Cairo, Egypt
420 Lexington Avenue, Suite 1644, New York, NY 10170
www.hoopoefiction.com

Hoopoe is an imprint of The American University in Cairo Press
www.aucpress.com

ISBN 978 1 649 03204 1

Library of Congress Cataloging-in-Publication Data applied for.

1 2 3 4 5   27 26 25 24 23

Designed by Adam el-Sehemy

CHAPTER ONE

WHY TODAY?

This thought gripped Daoud Abdel-Malek as he mulled over the events of the hours just past. A feeling that he could not shake held him fast for a long time thanks to this day unlike all others. Time and the seasons blend together; people come and go, and we don't know where they have come from or where they have gone. And every few years, there comes a man unlike the others—one with a distinctive character who grabs us by the lapels and dazzles us for a spell. But soon he disappears along with all those who had vanished before him. The days pass after him as they had before: neither joyful nor sad, neither exciting nor monotonous, but simply ordinary. The sun rises in its accustomed way. Folks rush to their jobs as ever, then return to their homes as always. They are content with their wives and husbands, with their children, with their fathers and mothers. They joke a little, are merry a little, eat a little, and talk a little. Then they split up, or go to sleep, or depart from us, and the smiles with the sorrows all fade away as all these "normal" days merge until once again there comes along an unusual man. Most people think of all that happens in this life as either chance or irony while others call it fate or destiny. What folly!

O God, what is this accursed cold weather?

He was still walking on the Corniche with confident steps, far from the ruckus of Ramla Station, drawing comfort from the repetitive tread of the heels of his shoes on the surface of

1

the pavement amid the calm that shrouded the street around him in an unusual silence. Under his left arm dangled an oud—the Arab lute—that never left him. Before today he had been merely an oud player who performed in an ensemble at parties for the underprivileged people in Moharram Bey and Maks or the most affluent in Azarita or Ibrahimiya, where the foreigners lived, with their opulent tips. True, they called him "the King," but that was only talk—just joking around to have fun with those who brought him money. In any case, the pay—for weddings, birthdays, celebrations during the first week after a birth, and circumcisions—was rather paltry.

His friend Sheikh Hassanein al-Basri, impresario of weddings and Qur'an reader at wakes and funerals, would come to the old house in Moharram Bey, where he had his flat on the third floor. "Hey, *Khawaga* Daoud!" the sheikh called from the entrance in his loud, ringing voice. And Daoud realized at once that there was a job for him somewhere, with thirty piastres attached.

He stopped, turning to look up at the sun setting behind the Silsila quarter stretching out before him, its low buildings heaped up along the horizon before becoming the magical line separating the spreading blue sea from the sky red with its turning, burning, plunging sun. The sun's lower third had disappeared, signaling for Daoud the departure of an eventful day and promising that, for his sake alone, a completely new sun would rise tomorrow at dawn. He pulled in the sides of his woolen coat, whose gleaming black color from the day he bought it in the Ladies Alley market had changed to a deep mousey hue from long use and neglect. He had wrapped the wine-colored scarf around his neck and adjusted the dark red *tarboush* (the Egyptian fez) stained with black at the bottom—it had never been cleaned or pressed, solely for lack of money— that sagged on his head. He pressed it down to ward off the February cold blowing from the rebellious sea waves, which tumbled and broke wildly, spraying in the wind over the line of cube-shaped rocks covered with a green carpet of plants and algae that became exposed when the water receded from them. These rocks lay compressed down the length of the Corniche in Alexandria—Daoud's sweetheart, his refuge, his home, and the place where he was born.

He filled his chest with the bracing smell of the sea, swimming in his thoughts as he contemplated the scene around him and those succeeding events that had made up his day until now. Quickly he put his chilled hand into the right-hand pocket of the coat to feel its warmth, fingering the silver ring abandoned in its depths as he hummed:

My heart wept for the wound that my lover left in me.
To whom shall you complain, my heart
Now that my lover has left me?

In those days, Daoud Abdel-Malek was called "*al-Khawaga* Daoud" despite the fact that he wasn't a foreigner who had come to Alexandria from another country, for example. Nor had he ever left her or even the district of Moharram Bey, where the apartment that he had inherited from his deceased father was located. Except, of course, the rare times when work or immediate necessity compelled him to leave for a few hours or days at most for nearby cities or to Cairo: *Masr*, as the Alexandrians called it. And even that had happened just a few times. Despite the fact that he did not know any other country and spoke only Arabic, he was still called "*al-Khawaga*" because he wasn't a Muslim like the others. He was called such also even though he had been dubbed "The King of Crooners" in moments of revelry for the number of tunes and songs that he had memorized, his skill in playing the oud, and his strong, sweet voice, to which all would testify. An Alexandrian like his father, grandfather, and great-grandfather before him, born and raised in its streets and alleys, he was educated in its schools until he earned his baccalaureate, but he never chased after a government posting. He was like a bird who loved his freedom; he would boast of it among his peers.

The days fluttered past until he reached middle age, on the brink of fifty. He was of medium build and modest height, yet he was handsome, with delicate features. Brown-skinned with a bronze cast wrought by the wind, water, and sun of his radiant city, with close-set, honey-colored eyes that always burned brightly. His curling, symmetrical mustache gleamed black like his hair, in which the white roots showed on his side-burns and forelocks, all oiled and combed neatly at all times. He walked haughtily with a broad gait, holding himself higher with each step, always taking care of his clothes and appearance as his material circumstances allowed. He was a vigorous man who loved life, singing, and good cheer.

He liked everyone, but he adored women! He had married three times over the course of the years gone by, losing his first two wives—the first, Budur, to tuberculosis and the second, Sophie, who was of Turkish–Jewish stock, when she ran away. Sophie was the only non-Egyptian woman he had ever been with. She had fled from Egypt in the upheaval of the Second World War when the news spread that the Nazi forces were approaching the town of al-Alamein. Sophie had suddenly packed up her suitcase and, with her child, Margo, in her arms, sailed to Marseilles onboard a little steam ship carrying a small group of European—Ashkenazi—Jews from Alexandria, running away from the coming Germans. Daoud had sired thirteen children, seven of whom were lost in infancy or adolescence while six remained. The dearest to his heart was Suleiman, the eldest son from his current wife, Elaine, who also had borne him Mona and Makari, though the last was carried away by the cholera epidemic of the previous summer. There was also Fouad, the oldest of all his sons, as well as Musa and Layla, whose mother was Budur.

As for Elaine, she had been an orphaned Coptic girl living under the protection of the church in the Sanctuary of the Virgin in the Kawm al-Dikka district. She was pretty, with wide dark eyes that dominated her face and made people look at her. Her jet-black hair was braided in a ring atop her head, which was extremely round like that of a baby; her wheat-colored skin was soft. But what truly set her apart most was her ceaseless, burning energy. She always used to jump out of bed before all the other girls in the little dormitory and rush off to the church, which was really the last room in the passage that stretched like an artery connecting the rooms of the house.

Against the dormitory's eastern wall they had built a shrine for the Virgin Mary. This, in fact, was but a small wooden table covered with a brightly colored cloth that fell to the flagstones on the floor. The cloth was embroidered with an image of the Christ Child in the arms of the Virgin Mother of God, called the *Theotokos*, a Greek word rendered in Coptic. The word was written in Demotic letters, then in Arabic, on the sign at the church's entrance. Covering the floor in front of the shrine or altar was a simple red *kilim*, a peasant rug, on which Father Mikhail stood to say mass on Sundays, Wednesdays, and Fridays at 5:30 in the morning. After this, he would head for the Church of the Virgin in Moharram Bey to share with the Archpriest Morcos Abdel-Messih in saying the mass there, as well.

Elaine tirelessly practiced the rituals of her life with discipline and endurance. She would kneel to say the Matins prayer, the tears running down her cheeks, at dawn each day, before anyone had awoken in the house. Then she would hurry to the kitchen as she sang hymns to the glory of God or even the popular songs of *Si* ("Sir" or "Mr.") Abdel-Wahhab or *al-Sitt* ("The Lady") Thuma (short for Umm Kulthoum), which would reach her ever-sharp ears through the windows, for the radio in the coffeehouse on the pavement across from the home played music both day and night. She would prepare tea and breakfast for Mother Irene, the director of the orphanage for the girls, who would sneak by, one by one, to the dining room, and spend her day afterward chanting to herself as she worked until sunset. Then all the girls would gather in the little reception hall to hear lessons from the Bible and the hymns that Mother Irene would teach them every day but for Mondays and Fridays, when Father Mikhail would lead the meeting instead.

One day, the house was ready to throw a special celebration for the first-ever visit by the bishop when Master Daoud, the famous oud player from Moharram Bey, came to perform at the hour at which the girls were chanting. As it turned out, he wound up admiring the voice of the young Elaine even before he was drawn to her appearance. Her moving singing with its ravishing tones was at least as good as that of Layla Murad, he had thought at the time. He had just lost his wife Budur and wound up with three children under his roof.

He thought of marrying Elaine and brought up the idea with the priest, who first asked him about his faith to be sure he was an Orthodox Christian. When Daoud said that he wasn't, the priest refused to marry them, of course, unless he obtained the blessing of baptism according to the rites of the Coptic Church. And so Daoud asked, what would he have to do to receive this blessing? The priest explained that he would have to be immersed in a water-filled baptismal basin in one of the halls of the church in which the Holy Spirit resides. Daoud, for his part, was not opposed to this, given that he was urgently in need of a wife at the time. His official religious identity as recorded on the marriage certificate did not matter much to him. Nor was Elaine opposed when she, in turn, learned from Sister Irene of the church's commitment to wed her to Master Daoud Abdel-Malek, a man she didn't know at all, for in principle it was, first and foremost, a matter of submission. Moreover, she saw him as both handsome and respectable regardless of his status as a widower with three children and of the clear difference in age between them. He was thus acceptable if marriage was her only way out of life in the sanctuary.

He was still playing with the silver ring in the pocket of his overcoat. He grasped it in his hand, then drew it out and put it on his ring finger. He was seized by that obscure feeling of hidden inner power to which he had grown accustomed whenever he wore the ring. He raised his eyes before him in the direction of the rocks and stared at apparitions striding between the waves, which came one after another in close succession. He thought he recognized among them the form of Dinocrates, the Greek engineer of whom he had seen a portrait in the *Encyclopedia Britannica* that he inherited from his father, in his diaphanous white robe. This man had drawn the plans for the city of Alexandria on the order of Alexander the Great more than twenty centuries ago. He transformed it from a mere coastline of white sand around a tiny fishing village into a giant metropolis of its age, crammed with palaces and grand buildings. The city of the astounding lighthouse and the awesome library, the capital of the Egyptian state for nearly a thousand years. Yes! A thousand years that stretched from roughly three centuries before the birth of Our Lord until Amr ibn al-As founded the city of al-Fustat as the country's new capital in the middle of the seventh century BC.

On that February evening in 1951, Daoud Abdel-Malek's journey down the pavement of the empty Corniche in Alexandria, while everyone else was savoring the warmth of their houses in the cruel Alexandrian winter, was nothing more than an attempt on his part, in his own way, to share with the limitless sea his private thoughts and feelings. In return he hoped to gain the calmness and clarity of mind that would lead to a full understanding of what had happened to him that morning.

He had awoken at eleven o'clock, as usual after a long night out. While smoking a cigarette he had rolled hurriedly himself, he drank a cup of coffee ground with fragrant nutmeg, prepared for him by his wife. He usually crumbled the tobacco into a piece of cigarette paper. Next, he would roll the paper and lick its edge until the whole of the cigarette stuck together. Then he would light it and begin smoking, spitting out bits of tobacco that leaked onto his lips. Quickly, he got back into the clothes that he had thrown off onto the chair next to his bed the night before. Then he grabbed his oud, speedily put on the silver ring and his wristwatch, which he kept on the bedside table, and—as he turned the knob on the apartment door—called out, "I'm going out, Elaine!"

This was the time for his rendezvous with Sheikh Hassanein al-Basri, who had spoken to him about a work engagement that might be for three or four nights per week. They had agreed to meet at the Khalil Agha Café in Moharram Bey. And, indeed, he found the sheikh waiting for him when he arrived. Yet he was not alone. With him sat a young man in military uniform whose features seemed instantly familiar. The presence of the young officer surprised him, but Daoud thought that perhaps he had something to do with the job that he had come to discuss.

Sheikh Hassanein was a heavyset, powerfully built man, vain of his Turkish descent with his white skin and sleek black hair that covered his head without the least sign of graying or thinning despite his being in his fifth decade. He always dressed in a *jubba*, caftan, and red turban—the *kakula*—testifying to the two years he spent at al-Azhar, the great center of Islamic learning in Cairo, nearly twenty years earlier. He was a bearded, beturbaned colossus, whose massive form concealed the mind and spirit of a ten-year-old child. With a cheerful face, he was easily delighted and always mirthful to the point that he had none of the grave solemnity of the clergy. His bellowing guffaws rarely left him. He spoke little on the whole, and even more seldom was he serious when he did. Guileless most of the time, indeed, yet he had the instinctive shrewdness of the common people, and their likeability. *Al-Khawaga* Daoud was the only friend who drew him of out of his enclosed little world, meeting him virtually every day either for work reasons or as a companion from his own neighborhood. He sat down facing them, proffering his hand in greeting first to the officer, who gripped it so enthusiastically that it almost hurt.

"Welcome, *Khawaga* Daoud!" he exclaimed. "Don't you remember me?

His high-pitched voice did not match his hulking frame, making it seem as though a mischievous waif were hidden within the officer seated before him. Daoud, with a flattering smile on his face—or perhaps one that merely expressed relief at his fingers' escape from the young man's violent grip—answered him, "I thought I recognized you, like I knew you a long time ago. Isn't that so, captain, sir?"

He had cast a surreptitious glance at the three gold stars on the captain's shoulders before turning toward Sheikh Hassanein, his hand extended in greeting and the words flowing out between his laughs.

"Peace be upon you, Sheikh Hassanein," he spouted. "Your face is bright and round like the moon, as though you hadn't been up last night till dawn. I got up by sheer willpower today—if it weren't for the cup of coffee that *Umm* Suleiman made for me, I wouldn't have been able to come see you for another two hours. But isn't it amazing that I'm sitting here like this, all fat and sassy like a turkey, as though nothing had happened!"

These gibing words brought back their laughing and joking together for the more than thirty years of their friendship. Daoud then swiveled toward the officer.

"I'm sorry, Your Excellency the *Bey*," he told him. "We just like to rib each other sometimes."

They had spent most of the night, as they always did, talking as Daoud played the oud and sang the songs of Abdel-Wahhab, consuming half an *qirsh*'s worth of hashish that Sheikh Hassanein had taken as *baksheesh* after presiding over a wedding the day before.

"You're telling *me*, Khawaga Daoud?" the officer said. "I've been witnessing this since I was little. Look, let me remind you of who I am because it's obvious that you don't remember me. *Sidi*, I am Gamal, son of Abdel-Nasser Hussein, the postal employee who was your neighbor in Moharram Bey in the twenties. Do you know me now? My father was your friend—you used to stay out late together, and I would listen to you sing the songs of Thuma and Abdel-Wahhab. Our apartment was in Fleming, and you were the sultan with your oud there."

He gestured toward the instrument that was laid loosely over the chair next to *al-Khawaga* Daoud.

"Ah, Abdel-Nasser Hussein," sighed Daoud, throwing back his head, wandering absent-mindedly down the corridors of memory opened by these words. He took off his *tarboush* and stroked the hair combed back on his head with his hand. His friend, the respected man who had shared his zeal for patriotic work after the Revolution of 1919 and with whom, before moving to a flat in Moharram Bey after the death of his father, he had exchanged visits for a while in Fleming to plan—secretly, of course—little operations here and there aimed at upsetting the English presence in Alexandria. And he remembered, as well, their happy late nights together on the balcony with the oud and song and the plates of liver *Iskanderani*—Alexandria-style—flavored with hot pepper, cumin, and other spices, the lamb kabab, the *kufta*, and the *tahina* salad, all of which they used to buy fresh at *'Amm* Sayyid's meat shop in summer.

"Excuse me, but you mean, then," he said, his memory coming back to him, "that you're the little boy that they sent to your uncle's place in Cairo after the demonstration in Manshiya? Right, I remember—you're the son of Abdel-Nasser Effendi—a man with a truly fine ear."

Then Daoud turned toward the other man with them.

"Sheik Hassanein, you remember Abdel-Nasser Effendi, who was living in the house of Dr. Qanawati?" he asked. "But right—I didn't know you in the days we were in Fleming."

The sheikh shrugged, still smiling his radiant smile. If he didn't remember the man or his son, he still did not want to appear like a stranger to them both, even if the one called Abdel-Nasser Hussein wasn't his friend to begin with.

"And where is he now?" Daoud asked the captain. "I haven't seen him for about twenty years. Have you moved to Cairo, or what? Welcome, dear son of a dear one!"

Then he straightened apologetically for speaking so familiarly with someone whom he hardly knew, in fact.

"I'm sorry, captain, sir, if I said something out of line," Daoud added hastily, "it was just our long acquaintance speaking. Forgive me for saying it, but the last time I saw you, you were like this," he said as he held his hand in front of him to a indicate a half-meter in height.

"Of course, of course, *Khawaga*," the officer rushed to reassure him. "My father is fine." Then, in a saddened tone, he added, looking away into the distance, "But my mother has passed away. The most important thing, how are you all doing? We've been talking like this, and you still haven't asked me why I wanted to meet with you."

Daoud thought of all those years that went back between these friends. Each one had lived a long life on his own path, but time, which had separated them, had also now reunited him with his friend's son. He had not expected this encounter. Yet he smiled as he contemplated the confused teenager that had become, as if only between night and morning, a young man full of passion and vitality, who had come back to Alexandria once more to meet with him. He thus revived those memories that Daoud had thought had passed into the beyond and perished.

CHAPTER TWO

Captain Gamal Abdel-Nasser, in his mid-thirties, was tall, handsome, youthful, and brown-skinned, with a winning personality—though he liked to control all that happened around him. Words came out of his mouth like bursts from a machine gun. Despite his obvious seriousness, one was utterly unable to resist him within just a few minutes of meeting him. His expression was stern, with a piercing gaze under thatching eyebrows. His neat black mustache rimmed a majestic nose. He seemed wrapped in a halo of simple elegance that belied his middle-class origins, without any hint of the affect or pretension found among most officers in those days, when it was difficult to enroll in the War College if you weren't the son of somebody important or at least recommended by a person of that kind, as often happened at that time. This prompted some of them to brag about their exalted origins or their elite social status as proven by their attaining high positions as officers in the Egyptian army.

Gamal sat up in his chair and reached into the pocket of his military jacket with its gleaming gold buttons and pulled out a packet of cigarettes. He lit one of them and then looked at *al-Khawaga* Daoud, who had gone off in his mind, meandering through many long-ago evenings with Abdel-Nasser Hussein when he was still young.

Daoud thought not only of their taking part together in the demonstrations against the treaty of 1936 and in writing and handing out leaflets against the king and the British, but also of their clandestine trips to the British barracks in Abu Qir when they planted sticks of dynamite that Daoud had acquired from one of his friends in the Cavalry Corps. He was amazed at how they had kept these memories secret from their families. Twirling the silver ring on his finger, he marveled equally at the extraordinary resemblance between father and son. But soon the officer's words brought him back once again to the Khalil Agha Café. He stared straight ahead over the café owner's desk with its marble covering upon which sat the only telephone in the entire residential block. His gaze continued over the officer's shoulder to the prominent portrait of Farouk I in its gold-plated frame, featuring the king's vacant gaze and suspicion of a smile that labored under a curling mustache. The stream of his thoughts was interrupted by the sound of Gamal asking, "Does the situation in this place please you two?"

"Which place do you mean, effendi?" queried the sheikh quickly. "Do you mean Alexandria? What's wrong with her, do you think?"

"Why just Alexandria?" wondered the captain. "I'm talking about all of Egypt, Sheikh Hassanein. I know that you are interested in patriotic work as you are a member of the Society of the Muslim Brothers here in Alexandria."

Here the sheikh suddenly seemed embarrassed. His torso bent forward and he placed his hand over his mouth, moving it back and forth rapidly to signal that the officer should stop talking.

"*Ayyu!*" he blurted, using an Alexandrian expression to demonstrate his dismay. "Enough, enough—the walls have ears, Captain, sir."

Hassanein then turned toward Daoud apologetically, for until that moment he had concealed from him that he secretly belonged to the Brotherhood despite their long friendship. Perhaps that was because he did not fully believe in the principles of that association, which he would not have joined but for the insistence of Sheikh Foda of the Ramla district, whose long arm he feared should he not obey him. He had not known anything about political Islam before, but he learned during his few meetings with Sheikh Foda and his companions the creed of the Brotherhood—that Islam was both a religion and a state. He likewise learned that this was the case in the age of the Rightly Guided Caliphs and that it was obligatory for the ruler of the land to be a Muslim who followed God's law and the traditions of his Prophet and to apply these laws and traditions in practice in his management of the country's affairs.

"Look, men," Gamal Abdel-Nasser added in a sharp whisper, thus pulling them back into his speech once again, "I have just now returned from the war in Palestine and am working as an instructor in the War College in Cairo. But Alexandria is a part of me, so I must come and smell the scent of her sea and see her people once in a while. To be frank, I and a few of my friends among the Brothers in the officer corps have formed a nationalist organization. That is, we don't like the situation in the country, and we dream of change."

He shifted a little, looking around to gauge the effect of his talk upon his two companions as well as to make sure that what he was saying was not being overheard by the other patrons in the coffeehouse.

"You are people I trust," he continued, "because I'm sure that there is no one in Alexandria who loves this country more than you men, isn't that true?"

Daoud was disturbed somewhat by the mention of Palestine. But the dusky youth, who was leaning forward on his haunches against the marble-topped table, did not wait for anyone to respond to his question. Rather, he tried to detect their reaction to his words as it showed on their faces. As he smoked one cigarette after another, it seemed as though his statements emerged from between his lips shrouded in a cloud of smoke. Both his listeners were enjoying it, so he elaborated at length.

"I'll tell you a story that really affected me, but maybe nobody knows about it," he said. "All my life, I dreamed of becoming an officer. That is why, when I first got the results of the final secondary school exam, I rushed to my father to plead with him to find one of the important people he knew who would help me get accepted to the War College—for this was something, as you know, that required the intervention of someone with real influence. By God Almighty, it tore my heart to ask my father to do this for me, but what could I do? My poor father told me that he knew a big shot's driver, and he promised he would talk to him for me. Two days later, the driver asked me to meet him at the gate of the mansion belonging to the pasha responsible for admitting the new students in order to take me to him. I just couldn't believe it—I thought that for sure I was dreaming. And for sure I didn't sleep a wink that night. Instead, I stayed up the whole time, wearing the only suit I owned, standing straight up, afraid that if I sat down, it would get wrinkled. And at dawn I flew to the pasha's villa and waited by the gate in the iron fence that surrounded the beautiful, well-ordered garden until someone came out in a black Cadillac.

"The driver, Lam'i, saw me and stopped the car. The pasha opened the window and motioned for me to get in. So, I went around to do so—from the other side, of course. As I opened the door the pasha barked at me, 'Hey, boy, what is this thoughtlessness? Are you going to sit next to me? Get out and sit up front next to the driver!' At that moment, I longed for the earth to open and swallow me. What was all this contempt? And why? Why do people treat each other this way? And why did I need 'His Excellency the Pasha's' intercession to get into the War College and become an officer in the Egyptian Army? Isn't Egypt my country, and not some other people's country? So as long as I live, I will never forget this episode."

Then he turned to address Daoud.

"My father told me a lot about you, *Khawaga* Daoud," Gamal resumed. "He advised me to make you our arm here. We want men with us here in Alexandria to help us print and distribute leaflets and to organize demonstrations—in total secrecy, right to the end. We must regain our country's freedom and the dignity of our people. You men, what is your view of what's happening with the British High Commissioner? Or with the Palace?"

Their faces blanched as he spoke these words. But as it seemed neither of them would resist or stand in the way, he concluded the soliloquy that he was determined to complete.

"Sheikh Hassanein," he said, "I was sent to you directly by Sheikh Foda himself. He is one of our brethren—from the group of officers that I told you about. But the most important thing is discretion. That is, we work very hard in secrecy and silence, even from our families—as though there is nothing going on."

Here Gamal crumpled the empty packet of cigarettes and threw it on the table in front of him.

"I'll tell you what, you guys," he exclaimed. "Isn't there a tobacco shop around here? These smokes are done."

"Take the second street to the right, and at the top you'll find *al-Khawaga* Ballo, the tobacconist," said Daoud, entranced by the talk that he had just heard.

Gamal stood up and made to go out of the coffeehouse. He walked with steady steps, following the directions given to him by Daoud. Meanwhile, Sheikh Hassanein, the white giant who had been sitting in front of him, raised his cup of tea to his mouth for the first time since their meeting, as though he were waking from an afternoon nap. Then he put it back down on the table and said, as if speaking to himself in a delirium, "What is this crazy discussion? *Ayyu!* Demonstrations, and leaflets, and a palace! And a high commissioner!

"What is that juvenile officer talking about, *Khawaga* Daoud? Is he an agent working against us? Is he an informer

17

from the police? Isn't he operating undercover, trying to get us in trouble when they find out about the story of those Brothers' associations? May God forgive you, Sheikh Foda! Wait till I see you! *Ayyu*! You're done for now, Sheikh Hassanein! I never attended even two of those meetings. Will they throw me in jail just for that? Wait till I see you, Sheikh Foda! Oh boy, will no one speak up for me?"

The sheikh drew his cloak up on his shoulders, shivering as he stood gripped by the agitation that was part of his Turkish makeup—all this to the astonishment of Daoud, who suppressed a laugh with difficulty. But he took control of himself before speaking.

"Sit down, Sheikh Hassanein," he urged. "Just sit down. Be calm and say a prayer for the Prophet. What police, about what? The point is about these beautiful young people full of zeal who want to do something for Egypt. They're like the rest of them, my brother Hassanein—do you think they are the only ones doing this? And what's the story with you and the Muslim Brotherhood? Later, later—you can tell me later. Just sit down and we'll see what *Si* Gamal wants exactly! This is the son of Abdel-Nasser Effendi, my neighbor and my dear friend, that patriotic man—and on my guarantee!"

The sheikh returned to his seat, still grumbling, as always was his habit in finally yielding to *al-Khawaga* Daoud's opinion. It did not take long before the officer returned with a light-hearted expression, a smile replacing the seriousness that had covered his face. He felt that he had discharged the official duty for which he had come and as though he had stepped out of his military uniform, which he filled with such gravitas and resolve. There returned the fiery young Alexandrian that had been hiding behind that formal mask. He pulled his chair toward him and gave it a half-turn with a joyful twist, mounting it like a knight on his steed.

"Hey, *Khawaga* Daoud, aren't you going to play something for us today—how about from Thuma's list?" he asked playfully.

Sheikh Hassanein's furrowed brow relaxed, and he looked toward Daoud Abdel-Malek to show that he wished he would agree to the strange young officer's suggestion. After all, it wasn't possible for a spy from the political police to want to listen to the songs of "The Lady!" So he raised his arm and cried, "A glass of hot fennel and a water-pipe with molasses tobacco!"

Daoud picked up his ancient oud and cradled it as he adjusted its strings for some minutes while plucking a series of tunes. Then he looked up and called out to the waiter, as though he owned the place, "Turn down that radio a couple of notches, will you, brother? Don't you want me to tune this thing?"

He began to play loudly at first, then softly in the mode known as the *kurd* until he was sure that he had gotten everyone's attention. Gradually the clacking of the backgammon chips on the tabletops, the slap of the cards on marble surfaces, the shouts of the winners, and the laughter of the people around them grew fainter. Even their orders for more drinks grew quieter as he launched into singing the latest masterpiece of *al-Sitt* Thuma:

> *You spite me and you abandon me*
> *When my heart begs acceptance you deny me*
> *You torture me and you burn me*
> *You confuse me and you weaken me*
> *And when I complain you berate me*
> *And when I say, "My oppressor, you'll get yours one day,"*
> *You get angry.*

The appreciation was etched on Gamal's face as his eyes closed and his head bobbed in rapture with each stanza. As for the sheikh, his fear of this youthful officer had left him completely. He beamed as though he were dancing in his seat, his fat belly bouncing ecstatically before him in rhythm with the music.

Shame that you leave and do evil to me
That you forget all that happened to me
I spend my whole life waiting for the day
When you will favor me

Absentmindedly, Gamal leaned back, his knees thrusting forward until they bumped into the table in front of him, shaking the drinks laid upon it as though they, too, were intoxicated by the song. He muttered an apology and straightened in his chair as Daoud continued singing entrancingly:

I was patient for years when you rejected me
Endured cruel grief when you avoided me
So one day you might pity me
You forsake me and forget me
And in my distress you have left me
And when I complain you berate me
And when I say, "My oppressor, you'll get yours one day,"
You get angry

When the flowing melody had finished, life returned to the café as normal in mid-afternoon. Once again, voices rose among the delighted customers, and Daoud asked for a cinnamon tea to soothe his throat after its exertion. After two sips he found himself meandering in a dream in which he saw his country, Egypt, an independent nation once again. No longer would the foreigner be able to impose his will on her soil. Daoud would once again take part in the patriotic labor that he had left behind with the years of his vanished youth. Tomorrow looked down upon him dimly, staring at him from the world of the Unseen. Daoud had watched the faces of Sheikh Hassanein and Captain Gamal Abdel-Nasser as they sat lost in reverie in front of him, and he had kept wondering curiously, what lay hidden for them all in the days to come?

*

Daoud Abdel-Malek thought a lot upon these ideas for the rest of the day until that evening, when his feet led him to the district of Ibrahimiya. On that freezing night, he had not intended to walk so far, so he stopped. He turned right and left, seeing no living things down the length of the Corniche, its streetlamps surrounded by that faint halo of light. He turned right at the next corner toward *al-Khawaga* Antonelli's Tavern, wandering into the nearly darkened hall that was warmed by the breaths of the drunken patrons and their convivial guffaws. Western music wafted feebly from a gramophone set upon a table of medium height next to the bar. Antonelli was delighted to persuade Daoud to offer his refined entertainment, which captivated all his patrons. As a result, their requests for drinks went on until at dawn. And in return, *al-Khawaga* Antonelli refused to let him pay for what he had consumed.

Daoud took off his checkered scarf and overcoat after drawing the ring from his finger and putting it back in its pocket. He then laid both garments on the chair next to him. He rested his oud against the nearby wall, wanting nothing more than to return to the singing he had done that night. And he never stopped thinking—yet again amazed—about the effect of that magical silver ring.

CHAPTER THREE

WHEN HE WAS JUST AN ordinary oud player, he used to wear the cloak of normalcy as most people do. But Daoud Abdel-Malek felt that he was invisible—that others could look right through him. They would hardly notice him, would hardly distinguish him from the rest of his peers in the companionship of song. Nor would they really distinguish him from the other residents of Moharram Bey or even from his fellow Jews who had lived in Alexandria for hundreds of years and who were completely mixed with all the city's people except in three things: marriage, the practice of worship, and burying the dead. Then the Jew, the Muslim, and the Christian would all part company from their neighbors who lived around them, each into their own final place of rest in their own community's tombs. It was as though it had been decreed that no matter how people mingled during their lives, they could not linger together past the threshold of death.

The days had droned by one after another until that day in January 1950, nearly a year before Daoud's meeting with Gamal Abdel-Nasser. He had been heading out to meet Sheikh Hassanein al-Basri. There was still one hour left before their appointment as he dawdled along down al-Suq Street, which stretched all the way to the distant Cairo Station. He had nothing on his mind but to kill time until his meeting. As usual he greeted people here and there on both sides of the street with the customary exaggerated compliments to the owners of the little stores lined up all in a row. He had known these shop owners when he was a child, through school and into young adulthood. But *al-Khawaga* Zaki Fariha, the wealthy jeweler, stopped him. He was stationed in front of the door of his shop, warming himself in the rays of the winter morning sun. He was tall and trim, his hands wandering up and down the length of his suspenders over his beige shirt surmounted by an elegant red necktie, his right leg wrapped around his left. He wore his *tarboush* perched at a jaunty angle. This look matched his distinguished financial status among the people of the quarter. Zaki seemed to rejoice at this encounter, calling out to him first in French, the language of Alexandrian high society.

"*Bonjour*, Daoud! Come in, I want to see you!"

Since there was plenty of time to kill, Daoud accepted the invitation without hesitation. *Al-Khawaga* Zaki turned around with purpose and went into the shop. Daoud followed him, enjoying the scent from a stick of burning incense that stood at the corner of a glass-sided display table. Doffing his *tarboush* to put aside any formality, Zaki motioned for him to sit down and went toward the rear side of the table. He pushed a key into its lock, pulled open its door, and withdrew from it a blue, velvet-covered box.

"*Bonjour*, dear friend!" he said, "I have an incredible gift for you, my brother Daoud, just because you are a man of destiny and good fortune."

At the word, "gift," Daoud felt a jolt of curiosity and caution at the same time. *Al-Khawaga* Zaki was a dealer in jewelry and objects wrought in gold. He did not achieve all his wealth and luxury by giving away jewels and trinkets. To the contrary, he was famous throughout the district for his tight-fisted circumspection.

Nonetheless, out of nothing more than civility, he answered, "You've always been a gracious man, Monsieur Zaki."

"Really, brother Daoud," said Zaki, "from the moment that this masterpiece came to me the day before yesterday, I said, this belongs to you—I swear to you on my father's memory!"

He then opened the box with a delicate movement of his fingers and held it out to Daoud. In it was a silver ring with a piece of red jasper mounted at its center. On its four corners were obscure engravings that Zaki had to use his magnifying glass to see. An ordinary-looking ring, or even less than ordinary, so worn out was it that it seemed dilapidated. Daoud now understood the secret of this unexpected magnanimity. When a look of joy did not appear on the customer's face, Zaki carried the box in his palm, stretching his slender forearm out in front of him. With the other hand he played with the end of his mustache. Then he turned back toward the table and took the chair facing Daoud. He settled in his seat, smiling in preparation, for he was about to strike the decisive blow that he was sure—with the instinct of a skilled businessman—would, without the slightest doubt, conclude the commercial transaction in his favor.

Clearing his throat, Zaki told him, "This, of course, is a used silver ring—silver from a long time ago. But that isn't what's important. You won't believe, Daoud, to whom this ring once belonged."

He paused for a moment, then delivered the *coup de grâce*.

"On my life," he swore, "that used to belong to Sheikh Sayyid."

Then he added quickly, stressing with force each syllable as he spoke, "Indeed, like I'm telling you—Sheikh Sayyid Darwish himself! And why did I choose you, exactly? That is, how many musicians in our quarter are worthy of something like this, brother Daoud? You know, if I said these same words to anyone else, they would immediately reply that Sheikh Sayyid died thirty years ago. Look, then, at how aged this ring really is! I'm telling you this because I know that you will understand what I mean."

Then he stepped backward, proud of the delivery of this statement and of his cleverness, though he regretted a little—to himself—having used the word "aged," which might have detracted from the object's value. But he said nothing as he anticipated the reply to his persuasive words.

He didn't have to wait long for Daoud to ask, "Great, *Monsieur* Zaki. That 'aged' ring—how much would this 'gift' cost me?" He pronounced these words with a deliberate note of sarcastic nonchalance, hoping to reduce the price if it appeared too expensive. Also out of thriftiness, for he barely earned enough for himself and his children and could not afford any luxuries.

"You're going to be satisfied, Daoud, my brother," Zaki exclaimed. "I would give it to you even if it were worth a million pounds! But I know your sense of honor—you would not be satisfied knowing that I took a loss. And by the way, the man who sold me this ring said that it was magical—that it has amazing powers! But take care, Daoud! Don't rub it, don't clean it, and don't polish it—so as not to thwart its effect! Fifty piastres—my final offer!"

Indeed, Daoud Abdel-Malek did buy the enchanted ring, after haggling it down to thirty-three piastres. Still, fearing her reaction, he did not tell Elaine. As soon as he put it on the little finger of his right hand, he was gripped by an overwhelming feeling that this silver ring—without a doubt—was the principal reason for Sheikh Sayyid Darwish's reputation and success. From then on, it would accompany him, supporting and lifting up his cause. He felt that day for the first time a sense of exception—that he could excel far over his peers—but he did not know the source of this power. For that reason, he was neither pleased with nor disapproving of Gamal Abdel-Nasser's visit that day when he came to him in Alexandria, though Sheikh Hassanein, for his part, was not happy at the time. He was not really surprised then nor did he feel unworthy. Neither was he surprised later when he truly began his clandestine activities with the group of officers. And nor was Daoud taken aback by Gamal's visit to him in the summer following his first visit. He seemed not only happy and energetic but to actually revel in the secret work that he and Sheikh Hassanein were both doing in Alexandria.

Daoud stood cautiously behind the marble column, listening to al-Nahhas's speech announcing his pledge to abrogate the 1936 Treaty, which he himself had signed with the English fifteen years before. The agreement allowed the British Army to remain in Alexandria and Port Said and on the banks of the Suez Canal to protect that nation's interests in Egypt. But then a few days ago came the provocative incidents at Ismail-iya that led to the death of many Egyptians. This had greatly angered the people, so the head of the Wafd Party demanded the agreement's cancellation.

Daoud had organized—with Sheikh Hussanein, who was hiding at the other side of the hall—a huge popular demonstra-tion to erupt at the end of the meeting and al-Nahhas Pasha's address. Daoud had watched with his own eyes the troops of the British Army and its commander as they surrounded the hall, placing themselves in strategic locations to prevent the planned demonstration. He traded looks with the sheikh from across the hall. He saw clearly that he had to do something to seize control of the situation, or their mission would fail. His eyes ran over the tautly muscled, slender-framed British sol-diers spread everywhere about the place, and he realized that their only chance to carry out their action was for him to put their commander out of commission at whatever cost.

To him, the English commander, with his ruddy complex-ion on extremely white skin, his reddish blond hair under his brown military cap, and blue eyes that glared out menacingly from his face, was like a monstrous giant. In Daoud's eyes, his mixture of loud, screaming colors made him appear inhuman while his tightly muscled body made him seem like the trunk of a towering sycamore that stood between himself and the success of his plan. The Briton was not only a giant but a malevolent genie like those that filled the stories told in the streets and back alleys of Alexandria, the kind one could only overcome with a magical spell that would shake his foundations and make him collapse in front of you without a trial of strength. Daoud looked contemplatively at his silver ring with its setting of red jasper, and his doubt and trepidation about the fulfillment of his mission were transformed into an absolute belief in his certain victory.

A derisive smile rose on his face as he paced with confident steps to where the mighty demon stood at the side of the hall. Al-Nahhas Pasha was nearing the end of his speech as the excited crowd's hubbub filled the place like the rattle of a boiling pan's lid on the stove. Daoud's slight build did not suggest danger to those who were watching the hall, so he was able to stroll unopposed until he stopped just in front of where the commander stood. At this moment al-Nahhas wound up his speech and the hall resounded with applause. Daoud stared at the Englishman, eye to eye, still smiling at him. The genie lowered his gaze toward him and returned his smile with an air of superiority and condescension as befitting the difference between his immensity and the tininess of the middle-aged man who was trying to pass by him. The crowd was clapping and calling ecstatically. Daoud balled his hand into a fist with all the power he could summon, drawing courage and resolve from the audience's cheers. In a flash he cocked his arm and punched his ring into the red nose of the Englishman, and blood gushed everywhere.

The masses were still shouting and stomping when the giant staggered and fell to the floor. While the demon's soldiers, with their red, yellow, and blue faces and their hardened muscles, scurried toward their leader, trying to succor him, Daoud raised his hand to tell the sheikh of his triumph. Calls for independence rose from across the hall as the people chanted wildly with zeal, "Long live Egypt! Long live Egypt!"

*

He remembered that he and Sheikh Hassanein were up late together after this event during a visit by Gamal Abdel-Nasser and his friend, Kamel Fayyad, who he introduced as the one responsible for the movement's affairs in the northern region, which included the Delta, Alexandria, and her coasts. He also recalled that they met in the Hotel San Stefano on the Corniche in Alexandria in celebration of Gamal's attaining the rank of lieutenant colonel. After they finished the dinner in his honor, Gamal asked Daoud to perform some songs by Umm Kulthum, extolling his voice to his friend Kamel and exaggerating to the point of claiming it was more beautiful even than that of *al-Sitt*—"The Lady"—herself. Daoud, hoisting the glass of whiskey from which he was sipping, replied by singing for him a monologue that was five years old or even more, but which was still close to his heart:

> *The one who is dear to me*
> *Kept his promise to me*
> *He yielded after being long away from me*
> *With a smile he met me*
> *Making me long to be with him.*
> *After he greeted me,*
> *"You told me words*
> *That made my heart dance,"*
> *He said to me.*

That night, after his third drink, Daoud told Gamal laughingly about the story of the magic ring—that ring that had raised Sayyid Darwish to the firmament. Daoud sensed, possibly with the fatherly spirit that he had begun to feel toward him, that Gamal needed the silver ring—the cause of his own happiness and success—more than he did then for a reason he did not fully know at the time. He offered to lend

29

it to him and Gamal laughed along with his friend Kamel. Yet without a word Gamal put the ring on his finger and left for Cairo after embracing *al-Khawaga* Daoud. And despite the effects of drunken euphoria, he was amazed that the ring, which was roughly the right size for his rather thin little finger, slid so easily onto Gamal's pinkie.

Daoud wondered what had driven him to give Gamal the ring at that time. How could he give away the object that had caused luck to smile on him? And why had Gamal agreed to take it from him? Only a few weeks passed before Daoud knew the reason. For on the morning of July 23, 1952, after a group of officers seized control of the radio building, the following proclamation was broadcast in Cairo:

"Egypt has passed through a critical period in her recent history—a period of bribery, corruption, and unstable rule. All these factors have had a great impact on the army. Those who work for bribes and their own selfish interests caused our defeat in the Palestine War. In the period after the war, the agents of corruption came together and the traitors conspired against the army. The ignorant and corrupt were in control to the point that Egypt had no army to protect her. Thus, we have undertaken to purify ourselves. Our mission was carried out within the army by men whose ability, morality, and patriotism we trust. There is no doubt that all of Egypt shall greet this news with welcome and jubilation."

Truly, Daoud and Sheikh Hassanein received this news with tremendous joy. They were aware that their participation in patriotic work for a full year had aroused the suspicions of the police and led to their being followed by informers, especially when they returned to their homes at the end of the night. They had decided to meet each other less often so that each one was able to carry on their activities should the other fall into the hands of the authorities. And on top of that, they continued their artistic endeavors, organizing weddings and other occasions in addition to evenings of Sufi chanting and condolence services, which were Hassanein's specialty. They were thus carrying a double burden in all they undertook—until that event that changed the face of Egypt in a way that no one had ever dreamed of.

Three days later, Daoud expected Gamal Abdel-Nasser to come to Alexandria in the company of Brigadier General Mohammed Naguib, the leader of the Free Officers' organization, to oversee the departure of King Farouk from the country. Naturally, Daoud went to the harbor to meet him, but the presidential guards forbade his approach. Despite his insistence, a huge praetorian guard blocked his way, and Daoud was not fortunate enough to make out the person of Mohammed Naguib. Nor, of course, was he able to meet with Gamal Abdel-Nasser or even to confirm his presence, though he thought he saw him from a distance by the side of Farouk I, who had stepped down from the throne. Even from far way, he appeared to be turning his face toward the former king like a lion about to pounce on his prey.

Daoud lingered until he watched the royal yacht, the *Mahrusa*, vanish across the sea. Yet he'd been unable to meet with Gamal Abdel-Nasser.

CHAPTER FOUR

THE SUDDEN HEAT OF DAY that filled the room forced Daoud to wake up early once again. Yet, in any case, he was prepared for that. He had not stayed out late at all during the last two weeks. For almost a year now, he had noticed Sheikh Hassanein distancing himself, from the first days after the Free Officers' Revolution. Despite the circumstances of work, the bonds of friendship, and the evenings with hashish together over the years, they had gradually grown apart—especially during the cold nights of winter, which had inevitably shut down the usual parties and soirees. This loss of closeness was not much corrected by the arrival of spring, and it now came to a complete halt for several weeks even though it was the peak of summer, which customarily brought a surge of work.

What led Daoud to visit the sheikh now, in his apartment on this Friday morning, before the time for prayer? Firstly, to see how he was faring, for he was not used to him disappearing for so long. Secondly, he wanted to scold him for the shortage of work, as the cash reserves he needed to take care of both Elaine and his creditors were dwindling.

It was now mid-summer, its heat and humidity at their highest in Moharram Bey. Daoud found it suffocating. Masses of Cairenes had come to Alexandria, and the streets and alleys were jammed—and so, of course, the beaches were as well. It was as though armies of rabble had invaded the city, with her well-known goodness, beauty, cleanliness, and serenity, and swallowed it up. He thought to himself how much he hated those wandering vacationers from the much dirtier Cairo. Yet he was glad that only a few days from now they would go home to where they had come from, leaving him alone with his darling Alexandria. Daoud stood catching his breath in front of the apartment's door, giving it several quiet knocks. Afterwards he removed his *tarboush*, which was soaked with sweat, wiping his head and forehead with his handkerchief and listening to the sound of steps inside approaching the door. Then a hand pulled back the bolt and opened the door a crack. Daoud put the *tarboush* back on and bent his head in respect. His eyes looked into those of a child staring out from a head oblong like a sweet melon, who opened the door without saying a word. Then came the sheikh's wife, who had covered most of her face with a cloth, which she held by its edge over her nose.

"Who is it, little boy?" she asked.

Doaud was still catching his breath, and he bowed his head down further lest his eyes fall on the voice's owner. He therefore focused his gaze on the bare feet of the boy, who was still stood there watching the guest that came to visit them. His dainty toes were dancing to the rhythm of his innocence and curiosity.

"Is Sheikh Hassanein here, *Sitt* Umm Lutfi?" he asked without raising his head.

The woman swiveled her head to look inside, then called out loudly, "*Al-Khawaga* Daoud is here, Sheikh Hassanein."

Then his voice rang out from within. "Okay, tell him that I'm coming out right away!"

Daoud was astonished by this sudden, spontaneous embarrassment that came over *al-Sitt* Umm Lutfi, whom he had gotten used to seeing with her face uncovered for many years, though he really had never noticed her features before.

In a few moments, Sheikh Hassanein walked quickly toward the coffeehouse after appearing suddenly in front of

Daoud at the doorstep of the apartment, muttering some words that Daoud took to be a *salaam* or a greeting. But in a flash the sheikh had shot past him and was flying down the steps as though trying to avoid facing him. He headed toward the street as Daoud followed him doggedly despite the heat, quickening his pace until he had nearly caught up with him. The pair of them looked—at least to those around them— as though they were walking together as panting Daoud wondered what the cause of all this hurry could be. But the sheikh walked in silence, his scowling white face flushed red in the sultry air, until the café loomed in front of them in the great square at Misr Station. But then he began to encounter the crowds, and as the voices of the street peddlers, the car horns, and even the whistles of the trains leaving the station rose about them, so too did the tension between the two of them as well as with those around them rise to the point of pure incitement.

Then, without warning, the sheikh turned toward Daoud.

"Come with me by the sea," he said. "Some fresh air would be better."

He walked away to the right without waiting for even a comment on his suggestion. When Daoud caught up with him, he was huffing and puffing behind him until they arrived at the Corniche. Sheikh Hassanein chose one of the empty stone benches that were closely set down the length of the street. He plopped down on it, his head and turban dripping with sweat. The sheikh was in a pitiable state: his big belly bounced up and down rapidly, his *jubba* and caftan soaked as well about his chest and armpits. Daoud's anger grew as he saw his contemptible condition.

Nonetheless, sitting down next to him between gasps for breath, he demanded, "What's the story, Sheikh Hassanein? I haven't seen you for all this time. When I go to your house to see you, you drag me away at breakneck speed until we get all the way over here, and without even saying hello."

The sheikh, still breathing hard, could not reply; he seemed about to take his last breath. Daoud began to feel sorry for him and ceased his rebuke. He pulled a handkerchief from his jacket pocket, lifted his *tarboush*, and wiped his hair and forehead before returning the handkerchief to its place. He waited for Hassanein to catch his breath and for his belly to stop inflating and deflating like the bellows in Hamza the blacksmith's shop. After a while, the sheikh's breath began to slow down as a soft breeze from the sea swept over them, bearing the delicious scent of the salty air; the heat lessened around them. The pure blue of the sky and its blazing disc of gold held no hope that even a single straying cloud would cover them and that the scorching heat of the sun would abate at all.

At that moment, a seller of cold refreshments jangled by, calling in a soothing voice, "Drink, oh thirsty one!"

Daoud took a chance by saying, "Get us two bottles of Spatis, Sheikh Hassanein. On the life of your father, I'm as parched as a stone, and all I've got in my pocket is one piastre."

The sheikh smiled at the corner of his mouth, for the idea pleased him, but he was still unable to speak. His chest was still heaving as he recalled his first acquaintance with *al-Khawaga* Daoud, who was no doubt a small child when he was a young man. After his return from Cairo wearing the sheikh's turban, a married man with three children moved into the district to occupy the apartment owned by Daoud's father, *al-Khawaga* Issa Abdel-Malek. The Jewish neighbor—husband of *al-Sitt* Rachel, Daoud's mother's friend—had just passed away. Daoud and the sheikh met at the tram stop one morning when the thin man standing next to him as they waited asked him if he knew a *ma'zun*—someone who performs Muslim marriages. Daoud had a friend who had divorced his wife, and he wanted to take her back without outrageous expense. Sheikh Hassanein demurred, denying that he was a *ma'dhun*, but took advantage of the opportunity to tell the man that he was a beginning Qur'an reader on the road to success and fame and that he drew customers with the beauty of his voice and his melodic chanting. He then let out a disarmingly innocent laugh, putting Daoud at ease. Daoud remarked in turn that he likewise sang and played the oud. They arranged their first meeting for that night, and it lasted nearly till morning. By the end of that encounter their friendship was born.

These memories passed through his mind at lightning speed. Smiling a little, he raised his arm toward the drink peddler with difficulty. The man rushed over, opening two cold bottles of sparkling water that were among many others he kept in a bucket full of ice that he carried on his shoulder. He then sat down nimbly on the wall facing them, surveying the passersby in search of a new customer and waiting for them to finish drinking so that he could collect the money along with the empty bottles and be on his way. The sheikh hesitated to begin talking, not only because of his distress at the confrontation that he knew was coming but also because of the stranger's presence. But after a few moments, he cleared his throat loudly, then belched before turning his face toward Daoud to signal that he was going to answer his questions. Then he turned it the other direction, far away from his friend, avoiding his gaze as though another person were speaking strange words from his lips, removing his responsibility for their meaning. He began muttering in a faint voice at first, which quickly became a hectoring sermon filled with loathing.

"I have a question for you, *Khawaga* Daoud," he said, falling silent for a while to prepare his next utterance as Daoud's eyes followed him eagerly.

"Honestly, brother" he asked, "what has kept you in this country for so long? Wasn't it enough what you all did in '48, eh? What else are you waiting for? Aren't you all, please, going to leave us?"

These very accusations had long bored into Sheikh Hassanein's heart until he felt he would explode with the vast amount of censure and criticism he had heard—particularly from Sheikh Foda—not only of the work relationship but also of the friendship that bound him to this Jew named Daoud. To have such a friendship was to forget what the Qur'an says about the Jews because of their treachery toward the Prophet Muhammad, peace and prayers be upon him. And the fact of their friendship likewise ignored the Jews' rape of the land of Islam and the Muslims and their setting up a Jewish state on it over the past few years. Even some Egyptian Jews had emigrated to it, merrily proclaiming their loyalty to it! Sheikh Foda clothed some of these insinuations in the garb, not only of scolding and blame—"Is all that okay with you?"—but he also at times made outright accusations against Sheikh Hassanein: "What's holding you back? Does this Jew have something on you?"

Sheikh Hassanein for his part had insisted on keeping all this to himself until today, not wanting to confront Daoud directly with it. For first and last Daoud was his only friend, so he just tried to avoid him. He thought that this would stop the blaming mouths and embarrass his critics. Instead, the torrent of angry thoughts and words continued to gush over him. Then Daoud came to his house, which gave witness to the eyes and ears of all that their friendship continued, as his hangers-on confirmed! So Sheikh Hassanein surprised Daoud with an outburst of fury—with words that landed like successive blows upon him, and against which Daoud found no opportunity to defend himself. He then realized that the sheikh's meetings with the members of the Society of the Muslim Brothers had begun to bear fruit. Yet he replied as one terrified, because these words were coming from his only friend.

"What are you telling me, Sheikh Hassanein? Now you want me to leave my country—to go where? Do I have any other home but here? Come on, then. Who are these people that are 'doing,' and 'waiting,' that you're talking about? Who do you mean? Start making sense!"

The sheikh looked far away towards the sea. He was no longer able to say such things while facing *al-Khawaga* Daoud eye to eye—for whatever else was true, he was his best, lifelong friend. Yet he gathered his strength and resumed.

"I'm saying that a lot of others like you have left since '48," spat Hassanein. "Don't you now have a country, Daoud, in the land of Islam, and among its people? Or am I wrong?"

Daoud was unable to respond, so strong was his own reaction. Rather, he clenched his fist on the armrest of his seat, resolved to stand up and leave the sheikh alone. But instead, he took hold of himself and turned in his friend's direction, his tears welling up.

"You have no idea, Sheikh Hassanein, how much that talk wounds me!" he said, his voice shaking. "Especially coming from you. Are you satisfied to say things like this? And to whom? To me, Sheikh Hassanein? I'm one of *them*? Those who left might really be *khawagas*—coming from Europe or the Levant or Turkey fifty or sixty years ago. They stayed for a while, made some money, and later left when things were no longer good for them. And now you're asking me, 'What's keeping you in this country?' That's not what I expected from you! That's it—this is the last thing I ever thought I'd hear from a friend like you!"

Again he pulled out the handkerchief soaked with sweat to swab the tears that flowed over his cheeks for the first time. His voice still shaking, he added, "If I leave Alexandria, where will I go, Sheikh Hassanein? When I go just down the road to Damanhour for work, I feel like I'm going abroad. This is not what you get from a friend—this is not what friends do to each other! This is my country, Sheikh Hassanein! My country, and I don't know any other one. The land of my father, my grandfather's grandfather, and his grandfather too—it's the land of my sons, of my wife, friends, and dear ones. Just like it's your own country to you, too, Sheikh Hassanein. Fine—if I leave her, where will I go? And if I left her, would she leave me? Will she ever leave me? That would be impossible! This is not friendship, by God all mighty—this is not how friends behave!"

This time Daoud turned around and left the sheikh behind him. He took off walking, not paying attention to anything. He cared nothing about the burning heat as he walked and walked until he came to an opening in the low wall alongside the Corniche. He wiped away his tears with the back of his forearms as he stepped down onto the sandy beach, trudging with difficulty as his shoes kept sinking with each step, straining each time as he pulled them out, still walking slowly toward the smooth, level sands that met the waves of the sea. Like the waves themselves, he didn't know if they came to stay, or if they made this whole journey simply to touch the sands of the Alexandrian shore and embrace it for an instant, afterward to leave searching for the sands of a new beach. His tears continued to flow as he walked a tortuous route along the edge of the strand where it met the sea, the pounding waves driving him more and more toward the dry land. The suction of the sand on his shoes impeded his steps and made him walk closer to the water where the shore was hard and flat while the sea pushed him farther and farther away again.

He proceeded this way until he came across a young boy whose back was bent as he leaned down to play with a pile of sand in the shape of an overturned bucket. First the boy looked at Daoud's shoes as they approached. Then he peered upward at that older man who had appeared fully dressed, complete with his *tarboush*, on the shore. As Daoud passed by with his hands folded behind his back, the boy was frightened when he saw the man was crying. Reflexively, the child rose and ran toward him.

"Mister, Mister," he cried. Daoud stopped and turned toward him, and the boy told the man pedantically, "*Baba* told me that men don't cry. Isn't that true?"

Suddenly he was yanked out of his grief. He looked at the innocent child with his wide, smiling eyes. He wiped away the tears and walked toward him, leaning down and tenderly stroking the child's head of short black hair, then kept going.

As he trod with difficulty over the soft sands of the beach, Daoud reflected on his own origins as a Jewish Alexandrian from many generations back, and his heart overflowed with sorrow. The ghost of Dinocrates, who had returned to him, motioned to him with his arm outstretched toward the sea, eastward in the direction of al-Azarita, to show that here, over numerous centuries, Jews had lived at the city's eastern portal when it was known as the Gate of the Sun (opposite the Gate of the Moon in the west).

"No, I'm not leaving," he said, pondering what Sheikh Hassanein had told him.

Daoud again thought about what he had read of his beloved city in the encyclopedia set with such care on the shelves in the library that he kept in the salon of his apartment. Phantoms appeared to be dancing on the white foam of the waves, swaying around him as if they were disputing with him as he passed over the sands, surrendering to these contradictory feelings of anger, sadness, and estrangement from his home and his homeland. These feelings were mixed with the pride that swept over him now of one who carried in his heart and mind that long history—for he was an Alexandrian, from a direct line of forefathers who lived here in this city.

In that long-ago time, in the epoch of Dinocrates, Alexandria was not only the capital of science and learning in the world; she was also the city with the largest community of Jews on earth. Her reputation among seekers of knowledge and culture in the world was the reason that so many Jews from Europe and the countries around Egypt emigrated to her.

The specters moved along in front of him as he walked on his way, taking full rein of his imagination. The words skipped in front of him as if they had leapt from the pages of books. They seemed to hold onto each other, their audible voices reaching his ears as though they were coming from a deep abyss. It was the army of Ptolemy I—one of Alexander the Great's commanders, who eventually became the first ruler of Alexandria—comprising mercenaries drawn from every part of the world. Naturally, among them were Jews who settled in Alexandria in its earliest era. And then later, Ptolemy II enslaved many Jews before freeing them and allowing them to remain in Alexandria. Daoud was astonished by the amount of this information he remembered despite the intense hatred he had acquired for the subject of history thanks to *Ustaz* Ahmed al-Ma'adawi, who had taught it in Daoud's childhood school with the brutal application of the stick that never left his hand. Al-Ma'adawi's name remained stuck in his mind when he could not recall those of his other instructors—except for Munir Mursi, of course, who had taught him music. In truth, the Jews of Alexandria, including many philosophers and theologians, such as Artabanus, Philo, Suleiman Abu Ayyub, and others, had, throughout history, taken part in the cultural enrichment of the city. Ptolemy II was mad about knowledge and learning. It was he who ordered the building of the famous Library of Alexandria, which over time became the greatest world center for the arts and letters, attracting thinkers and wise men from all parts of the world. And it was Ptolemy II who ordered the coming of seventy-two senior Jewish rabbis from Jerusalem to Alexandria to undertake the interpretation of the Torah for its Alexandrian Jewish translators. They had translated the five books attributed to the Prophet Moses into Greek. This rendering of the Torah—referred to as the Old Testament by Christians later on—became known as the Septuagint. Daoud felt pride in this expansive history handed down to him through generations; he preserved it in his heart and was committed to handing it down to his own children after him—especially to his son, Suleiman, in whom he saw promising signs of that voice that would transmit this heritage to his sons after him.

Defiance seized him and he said once again, "No, I'm not leaving!"

Daoud entered his house, the anger and sorrow etched on his face. This convinced Elaine to leave him alone. He changed his clothes and took his favorite seat on the little balcony, wearing an undershirt and pajamas and raising his head to look at the buildings facing him, packed with occupants. The familiar evening clatter arose from below: the calls of the men selling figs and grapes, the shouts of the boys kicking a rubber football by the light of the streetlamps, and the flaming gas lanterns of the wandering vendors. And there was the distinctive metallic clanging of the trams' wheels coming from the direction of al-Suq Street in addition to another, fainter sort of uproar whose origins were unclear—a blend of pedestrians' conversations, the neighbors' nightly chattering, and the sound of radios, the clamor of cars, motor scooters, and motorcycles, of horse-drawn buggies and carriages, coming and going in all directions.

Daoud wondered if his voice, too, was a part of this tumult. His thoughts stirred with childhood memories of his classmates in the compulsory grammar school whispering among themselves, "Daoud is a Jew, everybody—I saw him going into the synagogue with his father last Saturday." Yet he acted like he didn't hear them. Elaine came out with tea on a tray, putting it down in front of him on the flat top of the balcony railing and then took her seat on the old *fauteuil* in the corner under the braids of garlic and nets of onions hanging on the wall to the right.

"Who am I, Elaine?" he asked her.

"What's wrong, Daoud? What is it?" she replied fearfully.

"Sheikh Hassanein has told me that I must leave Alexandria, and Egypt altogether, like the rest of the Jews that have gone."

"May his knees rot, that Sheikh Hassanein of yours!" she gasped. "Where are you going to go? Besides, you've been an Orthodox Christian from the time you married me!"

"You mean, that's it?" he reeled. "Now I'm an Egyptian because I became a Christian when I married you, Elaine? Before that I was a foreigner—like a tourist, that is?"

"How do I know—whatever you see fit," she replied. "But you and I are not leaving this country."

Daoud recalled the distress of his oldest son, Fouad, who was raised in the arms of not only one but two nonbiological mothers and in the relative absence of his father, who was busy with his art and his work on one side and with both his subsequent wives after the death of Budur. Moreover, Fouad had grown up on his own accord, always doing what he wanted to do. He left secondary school when he was not even fifteen, first to work in a *pasterma* factory, then in a plant that produced the Spatis brand of bottled sparkling water, rising until he became the foreman for a shift of workers at merely nineteen. He would never forget when he learned that Fouad had joined the Communist Party. Not only did he regularly attend weekly meetings but in the summer of 1948, after the declaration of the establishment of the State of Israel, Daoud was caught off guard when his son informed him that he would be leaving Egypt. Along with his younger brother, Musa, he would be going to Israel. Daoud was aghast, but the two of them left the next day. Daoud did not feel as lonely even after the death of his two first wives as he did after the departure of his two sons.

Did not the same hot blood flow in their veins? How did they come to uproot themselves like this from their homeland and their own home to go somewhere to create for themselves a new country? How could they go and leave their family and their people behind them, searching for a new family and a new people to become a part of instead?

He could never understand it.

CHAPTER FIVE

THE BURNING HEAT OF THE summer's day quickly dissipates and dissolves as soon as the sun dips into the sea to take the place of the bathers who jammed it before. Then the air fills with the smell of grilling fish wafting from the restaurants spread all the way down the Corniche. Strolling families swarm the length of it after dinner to enjoy treats of sweet corn roasted over charcoal fires while children crowd around the wagons selling Alexandrian *granita*—made of mango and strawberries—or pistachio ice cream. Sellers of oysters and sea urchins, with their platters of seafood garnished with sliced lemon, pass among the patrons of the cafes who spend their evenings chatting and sipping cold beer and buying fresh little salads as snacks while the invigorating sea breezes dance about them. Meanwhile, among the customers move the indefatigable legs of the Greek waiters who serve their drinks and light fare mixed with their laughter and their famous witty repartee in their peculiar dialect that distinguishes the summer nights of this city.

This was how it was for those coming to spend the summer and for those Alexandrians who made their living by hosting them. But the rest of the people of Alexandria hid inside their skins and behind the walls of their houses for the whole summer season. They would be busy with their routine daily jobs during the day and at night frequent their accustomed haunts, away from the eyes of the noisy tourists in the heart of the city, usually far from the Corniche.

And that is how Daoud spent many nights in *al-Khawaga* Antonelli's bar in Ibrahimiya until the early hours of dawn. Then he would walk to the empty Corniche, caressed by the soft zephyrs of the sea which whispered to him the answers to the riddles he could not fathom about his life's affairs: on Sheikh Hassanein, and on Fouad and Musa, on Suleiman, and what the days were yet concealing from him—and from them. Then he would retire to his home, where he would pull himself in like the head of a tortoise until the next evening arrives and gently rescues him from the confines of his morning prison. Sometimes he would stop by the low stone wall alongside the Corniche. There he would contemplate the last frail filaments of night as they receded bit by bit under the newborn day's advancing rays, spilling out completely over the surface of the water to clothe it in a gleaming silvery delicacy that would steal his heart away. He would pull his oud from its case, taking a seat high atop the wall, or go into one of the silent bungalows—*cabinas* as they were called—that lined the shore. Turning his back to the city, with his fine playing and singing, he would commune with the yellow sands and the glistening waves crowned with diamonds that the endless, dark blue waters would send to the shore. He would keep playing and singing until the disc of the newborn sun crawled slowly upward once more into the face of heaven. This moment arrived with the tramping around him of feet whose owners he would not permit to share in his private world that he had had all to himself for hours. Then he would take up his oud and leave.

Except for one night—or more exactly, very early one morning—when he was alone in one of the *cabinas* that only a narrow strip of sand and a paved passageway separated from the sea. The beach was devoid of any sign of life at the first intimations of dawn as darkness still spread like a tent over the scene. A single ray of golden light was able to escape the clenched fist of night; it made the features of the place visible to Daoud, at least a little. He became lost in the music as he flirted and played with the strings of his oud, singing warm words that lapped like waves on the empty shoreline. And between the veils of the prevailing darkness that were wrapped tightly about this spot, the figure of a person enveloped in obscurity approached from the pathway and passed him, heading toward the beach. A few threads of the dawn light fell upon the figure as it stopped, revealing the body of a woman. She seemed to look at him for an instant before turning to walk daintily toward the sea. In that instant, her outer robe fell off and lay heaped beside her. Then, in a diaphanous gown, she stepped forward toward the water. Daoud ceased playing his oud to contemplate the vision before him: the body of the woman against which the sea was pounding, first holding her then releasing her as her sculpted form—its mountains and ravines—was silhouetted by a magical rosy glimmer of the coming dawn. At this moment, the woman rolled playfully into the shallows as the waves broke around her. The flimsy garment drew back from her calves and her thighs at the same time that the rays of dawn started gradually to grow so that her body began to glow as though she were a being of light just emerged from the depths! Daoud sat unable to move, his heart beating ever faster until it nearly leapt out of his chest, what he was watching having aroused his lust in a way he never could have imagined. She truly was a nymph, a *houri* of the sea—the kind of which he always had heard but never seen.

The woman immediately began to sway in the water, dancing within it as she bobbed up and down to its continuous rhythm. She plunged under the surface and then rose to it again, her gown sticking ever more closely to her body until she seemed to be wrapped in cellophane—like a packet of sweets—making her appear even more desirable than Daoud thought conceivable. Just then the woman—or this sweet confection—came out of the sea. With an effortless motion that set her ripe breasts trembling, she neatly shook the water from her hair. Carefully she bent down to wrap herself in a towel that she had brought with her, drying her body off with patience and deliberation. Daoud thought that she raised her head to look his way once again, yet she did not seem disturbed by his presence. She did not act agitated or change her pace even a little. Rather, she continued until she finished drying herself, then dusted the grains of sand from her robe, put it back on again, and walked with carefree confidence—her sandals bouncing to the tempo of her gait as they dangled from the fingers of her right hand—until she crossed the paved pathway. Then, at the place between the *cabinas* where she had first appeared, she stepped out briskly toward the Corniche.

Daoud remained nailed where he sat, trying to discern if this lady whom he had seen come and go in such an extraordinary way was really one of the many women who sneak onto the beach under the veil of darkness to bathe in the sea, far from any intruding eyes. Or was she simply a hallucination of a *houri*, one of those nymphs that have come to him through the grace of the wine at *al-Khawaga* Antonelli's Tavern?

Daoud did not see Gamal Abdel-Nasser again until that amazing day, October 26, 1954. Yet he followed his news in the papers, proud that this man was once his friend to whom one night he had given the magic ring, after which he had succeeded in carrying out his revolution that changed the path of the country. In the following days came Gamal Abdel-Nasser's election as president of the founding body of the Free Officers. At the same time, Mohammed Naguib became prime minister. On July 18, 1953, the press published the Revolutionary Command Council's decision to abolish the monarchy and establish a republic and to grant the presidency of that republic to Mohammed Naguib, who would also remain prime minister. As for Gamal Abdel-Nasser, he took his first public posts as deputy prime minister and as minister of the interior in that cabinet that formed after the declaration of the republic. In the following month, Gamal left the post of minister of the interior but kept that of deputy prime minister. In February 1954, Mohammed Naguib was removed as Gamal became president of the Council of Ministers as well as of the Revolutionary Command Council.

Daoud, his heart dancing in his breast, could not believe that this young officer who had come to meet him in the coffeehouse with Sheikh Hassanein one day nearly five years before had now been made President of the Republic.

After those momentous events had passed, Daoud's days rolled by unremarkably like the calm preceding the storm—and that which follows it as well. Yet Daoud had to swallow the pain of Sheikh Hassanein's estrangement from him and naturally rued the distance that his closest friend kept between them. And he was besieged by the memories of that nymph who had appeared to him that dawn by the sea—she haunted his imagination both night and day. To anyone who saw him, he seemed graver than usual and silent most of the time. He decided to take advantage of these quiet days to spend more time with Elaine and the children. They never missed the chance during that time of the year to go to the beach, all of them together, but he did not expect to meet his *houri* there, in any case. He did not think about himself or express his own desires when he went to the sea with them. But he anticipated neither the measure of happiness that these simple, trivial things brought to all their hearts nor the profound effect that they had on the children, especially. They would remain engraved in their memory for all their lives.

In fact, he suffered from the loss of the income he used to get from his work with Sheikh Hassanein. But he managed thanks to the help he received from his Jewish friends in Moharram Bey. Chief among them was Zaki Fariha, the jeweler who had sold the magic ring to him and who, like him, was too proud to leave Alexandria like some of the Jews who emigrated after the end of the Palestine War in the fall of 1948. Zaki saw to it that Daoud found work immediately by forming a group for him to perform in, specifically to revive the music of the late Jewish artist Daoud Hosni. This troupe met the acclaim of the Jewish community of Alexandria: they began to invite him and his band to enliven their private parties in their homes by bringing back songs like "On his cheek, O people, are a hundred roses." They would also do numbers in the vein of "The dearness of your heart to me keeps growing" or play "The paradise of my blessing is in your love" by Umm Kulthum along with shorter ditties such as "The moon has come out so many nights without minding who's watching."

The moon did come out for Daoud once more, and he did not mind the darkness that surrounded it. Rather, his material situation improved after a brief spell, and he was soon called "The King" once again.

Nonetheless, like most joys that are lacking in one way or another, Daoud's own happiness was not quite complete, for he had withdrawn within the circle of the Jewish people. His sense of isolation reminded him of the feeling of inferiority that had shamed him since childhood. Back then his classmates in the district would huddle in a circle at the entrance of a building, short of breath from running the streets during the long summer evenings, and start to sing as they clapped along laughingly:

Pray, pray, on the Prophet, pray
And read the Fatiha for Abu Abbas
O Alexandria whose people are the best
And all those who do not pray
His father's an Armenian
And his mother is a Jewess.

One morning in the fall of 1954, Daoud and Elaine were returning home from a visit to the Antoniades Gardens in a taxi of the kind equipped with two folding seats behind the driver. With them were Suleiman and Mona, Elaine's two children, and Layla, the younger daughter of the deceased Budur. They loved those seats in that style—the happiness gleamed from their little eyes, and their innocent laughter rang here and there. Daoud was following the scene with pleasure and delight when Elaine suddenly shrieked without warning, "Oh my God, this is the end!"

She struck her upper chest with her hand as she stared along King Fouad Street, which the taxi was straining to cross. Daoud turned around to find teeming crowds of people like waves of the sea, pushing and shoving as they clung to each other only a few feet away. These masses surged like rippling circles, squeezed on either side by two lines of buildings whose windows and balconies were filled with smiling faces, clapping hands, and placards. Elaine was gripped by fear despite the joyful scene, for the very density of the throng filled her with dread.

Meanwhile, in the vastness of that splendid tableau which stretched before him at a distance of about two hundred meters from where he sat in the taxi—at the very axis of that jubilant humanity—Daoud saw a gleaming, shiny black Cadillac, its top open, come to a halt. In it was Gamal Abdel-Nasser—yes, *him*, in person—with an officer on either side of him, greeting the crowds swarming around his motorcade. All that Daoud could do was to shove not just his head, but the whole trunk of his body, through the taxi window and wave both his arms aloft wildly as he shouted with all the strength that he could muster.

"Gamal, I'm over here! This is *al-Khawaga* Daoud! I am here, son of Abdel-Nasser Effendi! My brother!"

But his cry was lost in the immensity of the din surrounding him.

CHAPTER SIX

THAT EVENING DAOUD LISTENED ON the radio to the speech of Lieutenant Salah Nasr, head of the secret police, followed by that of Sheikh al-Baquri, the minister of religious endowments. Afterward came the oration of President Abdel-Nasser, celebrating British Withdrawal Day at Manshiya Square, still surging with thousands of Alexandrians who massed automatically around their leader. Daoud wished that he was not only among them but at their forefront, as Gamal regaled the teeming throngs—for he knew he had been one of the soldiers of the movement from the start.

"Citizens, we celebrate today together," Gamal began, motioning with his hand toward Daoud, who imagined himself standing before him in the front row. Everyone looked to where the president was pointing, for they all understood whom he meant by "together." (Daoud daydreamed that "together" meant the President and himself—and the rest of the crowd, of course.) "Together we celebrate Withdrawal Day, the feast of freedom and the day of dignity . . . "

Daoud heard a loud cracking sound like fireworks of the kind called "the children of Ali Bamba"—*traak traak—taak taak tik tik taak*—yes, that's how it sounded. He smiled to conceal the anxiety that came over him. Next a momentary silence fell until Gamal's voice again issued from the radio, and Daoud had the feeling that he was surrounded by alarm.

"Men, everyone stay in their places! Men, everyone stay in their places! Men, everyone stay in their places!" Scores of times the call was repeated to Gamal's fellow officers around him, to the seething crowds in front of him, to all of Egypt gathered by their radios, telling them that the president was unharmed—that the attempted assassination had failed. Daoud leapt to his feet as tears flowed down his cheeks once more.

Two days passed and Daoud not only refused to leave his house but barely ventured out of his room due to the anxiety and depression that afflicted him, whose hidden meaning he did not understand yet, and to which he surrendered meekly. The time crawled by slowly, made heavier by a strange stickiness that had clung to every second that passed by and from which only a miracle could help it break away. He spent the first hours of the day sprawled on his bed, staring at the ceiling or burying his head under the pillows as he tried to block out the familiar noises of the street. These sounds included the cries of those selling vegetables or yoghurt, the bells of passing bicycles, the calls of the neighbors back and forth through their windows or on their balconies, and that rare, piercing sound at the entrance of houses: "So-and-so, you've got mail!" From the street there came the sound of the radio broadcasting patriotic songs extolling Abdel-Nasser's revolution. Daoud felt a sense of pride that he had shared in that nationalist work. Then he remembered the wounding words of Sheikh Hassanein, and his heart shrank in his chest, writhing in pain all over again. He surrendered to another wave of the tearful despair that he had felt until he had been surprised by the face of the child on the seashore, telling him that men don't cry!

Yes, men don't cry; even when their friends doubt their loyalty to their country, they do not cry. Even when their livelihood and that of their children is cut off because of their religion and nothing more, they do not cry. Even when the people of their own hometown, Alexandria, are called "*khawaga*"—foreigner—all

54

their lives because they don't follow the faith of the majority. Or when the same people call the immigrant arriving to the country, be they Turk or Levantine, as "*Hajj* (Pilgrim) So-and-So" or "Brother So-and-So"—so long as they are Muslim. But what did he care? Men do not cry.

And why do men not cry, as Daoud had? Because they are strong, of course. That is, not only are they the example and the model, without any doubt, but the clay from which they were molded seems to be different from the clay that had formed the rest of mankind—or so he understood that class of men. They do not cry!

Daoud recoiled in fright from a series of knocks on the apartment door. They grew louder, seeming to fill the house. In moments their echoes filled the entire apartment with what sounded like the beating of a drum rattling the walls of the room. This set everyone in motion: the children scurried from every room to the large parlor in the apartment's center while even Elaine stuck her head out the door of the kitchen, an anxious look on her lovely face. Yet she hesitated to leave her place lest the food she was preparing burn.

Elaine made clear she was there by shouting, "Oh Virgin! Someone open the door, children and see who it is—Oh St. George; Oh martyr! All is well, God willing!"

Daoud moved to open the door, and there was *Sitt* Umm Lutfi in her usual, traditional black body wrap. In her hand was her young infant peeping out at him curiously, his tiny thumb, on which he sucked continuously, in his mouth. Her other hand still banged on the door hysterically, even after it was opened.

When she finally saw him, as it dawned on her that he was standing right in front of her, she wailed through her tears, "Save me, *Khawaga* Daoud! Save me, people—they have taken Sheikh Hassanein!"

Daoud's eyes bulged as he grasped in an instant the secret of his isolation and depression that had led him to submit to being held captive in his room for two days. Without saying a word, he gestured to *Sitt* Umm Lutfi to enter, the child gripped in her hand still staring at him, a pair of wide eyes in a honey jar-shaped head. At that moment Elaine scrambled from the kitchen, thumping her chest to show support for the woman as she worried over the fate of her husband. Daoud seized upon the distraction of Elaine's coming to hide the sarcastic smile that had begun to override the serious expression on his face when he saw the child's protuberant head, which confirmed for him secretly that he didn't look anything like his mother.

Daoud ducked into his bedroom to change his robe, returning very quickly as the *Sitt* Umm Lutfi recounted to Elaine all the details of what had happened. When he returned to the living room, the two women were reciting their stories to each other in turn within his hearing as he finished tying his necktie and sipped his last cup of coffee. He learned from the women that some men in civilian clothes who had appeared to be informers had visited Sheikh Hassanein's apartment the night before—or, more precisely, in the first hours of dawn today. They took him away in an uproar after they had turned everything in his flat upside down.

This despite the shrieks of *Sitt* Umm Lutfi as well as from the neighbors gathered on the apartment's doorstep and all down the stairs, right to the door of the building. They shoved him into a police paddy wagon without replying to any of his questions: where were they taking him, and why? In an instant they vanished with her husband, heading toward the main street and leaving confusion and fear in their wake, the neighbors milling confounded around the house's entrance. In a matter of moments, the family's condition had been turned topsy-turvy, as though a tornado or one of Alexandria's February storms had attacked and destroyed it.

The woman in tow, Daoud wandered all the streets of Alexandria to no avail. He started with a young sergeant from the police station in the Moharram Bey district, then an officer from the Bureau of Investigations, then the chief of the precinct. Finally, he searched the whole security department, every floor, passageway, and lobby to find him. In every case, the answer was the same: "We don't have any information about this Sheikh Hassanein al-Basri. There must be some sort of error." Daoud was perplexed about what to do, having spent the day without accomplishing anything while the unfortunate woman did not stop crying.

Clouds gathered menacingly, the road darkening as the sun disappeared. The air reeked of cold dampness mixed with salt and iodine effused by the seaweed heaped haphazardly on the sands of the empty beaches as arms of light occasionally reached down from the sky between the angry clouds. All ran to their homes, their windows closed tight while street signs and traffic lights danced with the feverish gusts of wind that warned of the approaching storm. Meanwhile, Daoud and Umm Lutfi kept wandering the streets and sidewalks, to no avail.

Suddenly there was a torrent of rain, as if the heavens had parted: in an instant they released all the water they stored. Water everywhere! Not only running over them, before them, and behind them, but under their feet as well. The waters plunged to the pavement, then splattered back at Daoud and Umm Lutfi from below. With agility and skill gained from experience, Daoud jumped up and turned on his heel, clinging first to a wooden door under the entrance of one of the houses ahead of him while Umm Lutfi lagged a step or two behind.

That was all it took, because he then saw her coming toward him to seek refuge from the downpour as he had in the covered doorway. It was as though a great vessel of water had been overturned on her head or a wave from the sea had washed over the Corniche and caught her by surprise. Her clothing clung to her body, and not only her face but all her form stood out before his eyes for the first time—and he was vanquished by what that revealed. Daoud looked at her perhaps for the first time—not since meeting her, but since he realized he was looking at *her*: at the young woman weeping in front of him rather than the wife of Sheikh Hassanein. There loomed before him an image that had not left his imagination since his eyes first fell upon her—since the dawn of that day when this seductive *houri* had bathed before him on the seashore. The same features and the same spirit that had delighted him, as if they had never left him, ever.

Yet this fleeting glance conquered him. His heart overflowed now, tears nearly welling in his eyes when he saw this amount of sadness afflict her. But the sight of the bewitching *houri* still beguiled him and awakened his feelings. Umm Lutfi remained nailed in place beside him under the roofed entrance, drawing close to him in the confined space until her breath beat on the back of his hand as it played with his necktie.

Daoud tried to put her at ease, so he began to talk to her in words meant to calm her. He then readied himself to take her and squeeze her in his arms but then resisted the impulse. He was about to address her by her name, but realized at that moment he didn't know her real one. She was always Umm Lutfi to him. Yet the sadness in her eyes gave her a weakness and fragility that drew him toward her as happens when a woman whom that man must protect weeps in front of him— he is obliged with all his manliness to stop her tears. At the same time, her tears and her overwhelming helplessness lent her a fragile, enticing beauty. Her frail femininity leaped out unexpectedly before him, wrestling with him in the guise of a pale, delicate woman who needed his protection and guidance—and so she overthrew him! Without warning her status changed from Umm Lutfi, the housewife he had always seen her as, to the enchanting woman before him whose clothes embraced the body of the seductive *houri* so tightly. Struck by an astonishment that felled him, he was just as suddenly transported back years in the past, and his impulsively chivalrous manhood immediately rushed to defend her.

Daoud saw her for the first time as a young woman—ripe as a tantalizing fruit, her figure well-wrapped and her skin as pure as the light of dawn. A lock of her hair, golden as the sun, showed from under her headscarf, flowing defiantly over her forehead and falling down the right side of her face. It danced over her green eyes as she sobbed. He imagined that, through her tears and the strands of her hair soaked by the streaming rain, she was looking at him with the same amorous rapture and wonder with which he was looking at her. A wind blew down into their faces, and as he drew closer to her there came a scent like roses. Once again, Daoud wanted not only to caress her shoulder but to hold her in his arms. And yet again he took hold of himself—with difficulty. After he had vanished into those thoughts that had suddenly seized him like a cyclone—those thoughts that had made him ashamed—he changed the direction of his feelings, praying that the woman had not noticed his scandalous emotions toward her. Trying to sound serious and sincere, he asked, "What is your name, Umm Lutfi?"

The woman raised her eyes toward him—and he withdrew into their green depths, disappearing into the abyss of a new world he hadn't known before. She stifled her tears with the hem of her blouse, amazed at his words and his glances toward her. Then she dried the hair spread over her face, and—as though she were putting up a barrier to hide it from him—replied like one caught by surprise, "My name is Qamar, *Si* Daoud—why do you ask?"

He smiled and answered with embarrassment, "I just realized I didn't know your name. You know that my second wife, may God have mercy on her, was named Budur: 'Full Moon.' Like your own name, 'Moon.'"

Daoud laughed. Qamar, however, didn't understand what he was getting at, so she kept quiet. He looked at her face. She had stopped her crying and sobbing; her gleaming white skin and the spherical drops of her tears and of the rain flowed down her cheek to gather on her upper lip, lush with the vivacity of youth. She licked these drops away unthinkingly with the tip of her tongue, her green eyes peering at him questioningly. He was taken with the sheer excess of her beauty and natural attractiveness along with the wetness that covered and flowed over her, imbuing her with a certain radiance and lending her ordinary humanity the enchanting quality of a female genie. He felt she was unique, a new woman—an Eve created for just him—when she emerged from the waves of the sea to accompany him through life. To hide his embarrassment at the impact of her beauty and femininity upon him and to bring his mind back to where they had been in their conversation, he said, "I'll talk to *al-Khawaga* Zaki on the telephone—he'll get some important people we know to help us."

The rain stopped as abruptly as it had begun. The clouds dispersed and the sun burst forth brilliantly, its rays filling the sky once again while a coolness clung to the scattered gusts of wind. Daoud looked at Qamar and smiled sympathetically at her soaking wet clothes. He suggested taking her back to their house so that she could change clothes while he made some phone calls, and she agreed. They walked side by side silently, all the while his thoughts revolving around how he could ask her about the nymph that appeared to him that day on the seashore and turned his being upside down completely!

But he deemed it wise to remain silent, for she might feel ashamed if her secret was exposed. Or perhaps she wasn't that gorgeous apparition after all, and she might not only deny the question but even consider it insulting. Deep inside he rejected that possibility, for he was sure in his heart that she was his *houri*.

In the afternoon, the two of them met again. Daoud went with her to the palace of Binyuti Pasha, where he entered with the woman, now blossoming in a black dress tinged with red roses wrapped delicately around her glistening white skin, her hair bound with a red kerchief. Hanging from the scarf's golden edges were red and black threads that shook in time with the vibration of the multilayered golden earrings dangling from her ears with each step she took. Qamar was dazzled by the trappings of power that filled the palace overlooking the sea while the refined sound of Beethoven's Moonlight Sonata floated from a piano. It seemed to come from the area opposite the salon toward which the servant was guiding them.

A few minutes later, they encountered the pasha in that daunting salon adorned with antiques and paintings scattered here and there, the fumes of his fat cigar floating ahead of him as he walked. Reproach that Daoud had brought this lower-class woman to his house showed on the pasha's face. Yet Daoud's obvious seriousness in requesting his help, which involved Sheikh Hassanein, arrested his interest more. Because of the special esteem that he harbored for Daoud, the pasha immediately ordered his servant to bring lemon juice for his guests and to get the notebook with telephone numbers from his office room.

After speaking for several minutes in a whisper, the pasha put the phone back on its receiver. Meanwhile, Daoud had been sipping his lemon juice, the tinkling of the piano still reaching his ears. The pasha took another puff of his cigar, and—after exhaling—he proceeded to rebuke him, the smoke rising from his mouth like steam from a locomotive with every word he spoke.

"*Khawaga* Daoud Effendi," he said, "shouldn't you have told me that this friend of yours belonged to the Muslim Brotherhood? Why did you hold this back? And why, my brother, did you mix with the likes of him?"

There came an audible gasp—no, rather an abrupt wail—from Umm Lutfi, as Daoud speedily put his hand over her mouth before she could utter a word that would offend

His Excellency the Pasha. He felt her lips trembling under his hand while her eyes promised him she would keep silent.

Daoud lifted his hand from her mouth. But then, anxious for more information, he spoke himself.

"I'm sorry, Your Excellency. Sheikh Hassanein has been my friend for ten lifetimes. I beg you—if you can only tell me where he is now?"

The pasha stood up to indicate the visit was over.

"Your friend was sent to Cairo two hours ago," he said. "This information came from high up—from very high up. Do you understand, Daoud Effendi?"

Daoud felt a vacuum around him. As he sat on the train heading for Cairo, he was alarmed by a sense that he had left something important behind him or that he'd forgotten something. He started searching in his pockets and taking off his *tarboush* and putting it back on his head while looking at the handkerchief in his vest pocket before restoring it to its place.

This went on for several minutes until he remembered that he had left his *oud* behind in his house on purpose. He wasn't used to being separated from it. He looked out the window, struggling to resist the overwhelming feeling of loss that gripped him. The vision of Qamar gazed at him with her lovely, gleaming white visage, her full lips quivering under his hand pressed against them. Then he quickly shook his head, turning away from these thoughts, appalled at even having them about the wife of the friend that he swore not to return to Alexandria without. He diverted himself by reflecting on the expanse of greenery on either side of the train tracks— that still, silent, flat, sempiternal vista. He forgot his thoughts about Qamar by following the distant line of palm trees, unbroken as far as the eye could see, that preceded the train as it flew toward Cairo.

He remembered the day his father, Issa Effendi Abdel-Malek, went with him to Cairo—his first time—to attend the wedding party for his maternal aunt's daughter's son, Yusuf Qitani Pasha, the famous millionaire. The night was enlivened by the singing of the young Mohammed Abdel-Wahhab, who later became of one of the greatest stars in the artistic heavens.

At that time, Daoud was no more than nineteen. It had been his first trip outside of Alexandria. He recalled very clearly how he awoke that morning at four o'clock. Daoud and his father left the house as darkness still covered the streets of his city. How his mother's hot tears flowed as she bid farewell to him on their apartment's doorstep—as though he would never return!

"How many days have passed," he reflected to the monotonous clattering of the train's wheels, "and how times have changed. Father and mother have both left this world, and you, Daoud, are destined to become a grandfather!"

"The important thing now," he continued, "is to find a way to bring Sheikh Hassanein back to Alexandria."

CHAPTER SEVEN

As soon as he stepped into the square around the central
station, people coming and going all around him, he awoke
to that feeling of strangeness that usually afflicts Alexandrians when they visit Cairo. The capital was jammed with
humanity, with buildings, with all kinds of cars—with black
and white taxis rather than the orange ones of his city,
horse-drawn carriages with fold-down tops, and with little
horse-carts. Also, with emigrants from the neighboring vil-
lages and people gathered around wagons selling koshari,
chewing their food in cowed silence amid the crowds of the
massive metropolis.

Daoud flagged down a car for hire and said to the driver,
"Let's take off for Manshiat al-Bakri, to the house of Gamal
Abdel-Nasser."

The driver glanced at Daoud in the rear-view mirror
and nodded his head, wondering who this well-dressed, middle-aged man who still wore a *tarboush* in this new age in which
it was banned by the order of the president, along with the
titles of "pasha" and "bey." The man had no sooner stepped
out off the train when he hailed his cab then sank into its soft
back seat as he headed off to meet with the president himself. Despite his curiosity, the driver did not utter a word the
whole way there. Overcome by fear, with difficulty, he barely
accepted the fare for the trip. And to Daoud's astonishment,
the driver not only insisted on going around to open the car

door for him but seemed to be hurriedly fleeing from some crime he might have accidentally committed.

At the entrance, an officer was sitting behind a small wooden desk inside a checkpoint with high stone walls, which were adorned—out of an abundance of caution—with a sign that said "Office of Security." The room within it was small with but one tiny window that looked out on the street. Next door was another room—or more accurately, a cylindrical little cell barely large enough to hold a single person. Inside it stood a soldier, a rifle with fixed bayonet at his shoulder. Daoud advanced past the soldier after waving a greeting to him, to which the sentry did not respond. Approaching the window, he saw a soldier sitting behind a desk. He then tapped lightly on the glass pane, and the soldier motioned for him to come around to the door of the room on the far side, hidden from the street.

Daoud followed his instructions and entered, saying, "Good morning, officer sir. I want to meet President Gamal, if you please."

Daoud spoke spontaneously as he pulled out a handker-chief to wipe the dust from the seat of a wooden chair facing the office while preparing to sit down on it.

The officer smiled in amazement at his elegant appear-ance. Behind his sarcastic veneer, he feared that perhaps this strange visitor would turn out to be an important person, and how many important persons there were these days! He sat all alone in that little room void of ornament but for a picture of President Gamal Abdel-Nasser—a huge smile fixed on his face as he peered down from the wall behind the officer—and some papers scattered about the desk. There was also a black telephone without a dial, meaning it was only for receiving calls and for communicating with others in the building, rest-ing on a stand perpendicular to the desk. Beside the telephone was a teacup, empty but for old, dried-out tea leaves hang-ing from its rim, a fly or two buzzing above it. The walls, the desk, the telephone, the stand, and even the teacup were all coated with grayish dust, perhaps from the room's proximity to the main street, from which blasted out the sounds of car horns and people, plus the din of the horse-carts and the stray dogs and cats that jammed it—this noise which engulfed him during the whole encounter.

"Why, sir, do you want to see the President?" asked the officer as he began to take down the information from Daoud's identity card, which he had demanded. In his mind, Daoud thanked Sheikh Hassanein, who had advised him to go and obtain a certificate of Egyptian citizenship more than twenty years before. At that time, most Egyptian Jews did not hold proof of Egyptian nationality. He was fortunate to have been carrying a personal identity card since precisely that day and especially to be carrying it now when he requested to meet the President of the Republic.

"I wouldn't ordinarily request it," Daoud replied, "but this is a personal matter. If you please, inform the President that Daoud Abdel-Malek has come from Alexandria and asks to meet with you; I mean, to meet with you, *sir*."

The officer wrote what Daoud told him in the visitors' notebook, then leaned over and lifted the telephone receiver before pressing down on its top several times in succession, looking up at the ceiling as he waited. Suddenly he sat up in his chair and informed the speaker at the other end that there was a visitor who wanted to see the President, repeating what Daoud had said, then replaced the receiver. Once again smiling, he looked over the notably refined Daoud Abdel-Malek, who wanted to meet the President of the Republic, sitting in front of him. In but a few moments the ringing of the telephone burst through the uproar from the street. Daoud started in his seat with terror. As for the officer, who was used to that sort of ringing, he calmly turned and lifted the receiver again. Then his face suddenly furrowed as he abruptly stood up straight.

"Yes, *Effendi*, right away," he said. "Thank you, sir—good-bye, sir."

With the utmost politeness, he motioned for Daoud to follow him inside the building. There another officer met him and ascended several steps with him as the first officer returned to his station in the security office.

President Gamal greeted him standing, his face beaming and his arms outstretched, ready to embrace him. Daoud responded to his invitation cautiously due to the terror that normally surrounded the person of the head of state. He took the required steps but, as it was not fitting to hug him with the vigor demanded for two intimate friends, he settled for getting so close that their chests nearly touched. Yet all this lasted but a moment. Daoud's nose filled with the scent that was without a doubt unique to Colonel Gamal. That scent from the day he met him in the Khalil Agha Café—that blend of lemon and burnt sugar that he at first reckoned came from someplace in the café itself. He did not think it would have been Gamal's scent as it was not familiar to him at the time.

Gamal patted the top of his shoulder. He seemed to Daoud to have grown both taller and wider since their last time together.

"Welcome! Welcome!" the president greeted him.

Gamal took Daoud, walking beside him unhurriedly with his arm on his shoulder like old friends as they crossed the vast room, toward a set of green leather-upholstered seats scattered around the far side of the Persian carpet. He had never seen one so large or magnificent before, despite having frequented many palaces of the rich in his life. The president sat down facing him, not only with a relaxed smile beaming on his face but sometimes with a silent chuckle that revealed his gleaming white teeth.

Daoud looked at him, seeing him for the first time without his military uniform. He was wearing a white shirt with the sleeves rolled half-way up over gray pants over sandals, with no socks. This dress displayed how brown his arms and ankles were—those previously covered by his military clothes. Gamal's torso was thrust forward, his arms resting on his thighs and his hands folded in front of him at ease: Daoud felt no tension or awe of where he was.

To begin the conversation, Gamal said—his broad smile filling his tawny face as he gestured with his hands to the flow of his words—"Where have you been, *Khawaga* Daoud? By God, I've missed you a lot. I know I'm in your debt. But, by God, there are many distractions, as you must know very well."

He chuckled for a moment, then added in his shrill voice that did not match his giant frame, "Actually, this job turned out to be a gag! What I mean is, this is the first time I've been President of the Republic—ha ha! The most important thing now is what will you drink, Daoud?"

Gamal laughed again. His easy manner with Daoud lent the place a relaxed, laid-back atmosphere. Daoud quickly felt a wave of lassitude wash over him as he reached out his hand and removed his *tarboush*. He placed it on the stand in front of him and stammered, "No need for anything, sir. Only if it's possible—that is, if it's not any trouble—then a cup of Arab coffee with medium sugar."

Laughing again, Gamal commented, "Man, I thought you were going to ask for a tough one—a cappuccino, that is, when you stuttered like that."

He was still laughing when he pressed an electrical switch next to him. In came a Nubian servant in a white turban and a shiny blue uniform, his vest embellished with gold thread and an apron of elegant gold-colored fabric around his waist like the stewards in the lobby of the Hotel Cecil in Ramle Square. Gamal asked him with profuse politeness, "If you please, *ʿAmm* (Uncle) Bashir, bring us two coffees with medium sugar. The special blend, not the regular Mahmoud al-Gayyar brand for the sake of this man, who is a coffee pro and dear to us. It would be a scandal if we gave him anything else."

'Amm Bashir smiled as he bowed silently and departed. Daoud's courage grew owing to that relaxed atmosphere Gamal brought to their encounter. Clearing his throat, he said, "Mr. President, I came from Alexandria to ask for three things from your Excellency."

"Three at one time!" Gamal interrupted. "First of all, before you say anything, this belongs to you. We took it for a ride, and it brought us much luck, for real. But now is the time for all things to return to their owners."

He said this as he removed the silver ring from his finger and reached out to give it to Daoud, who took it with joy and excitement after their separation.

"Actually, I don't know what to say, Mr. President," he said. "Really, I, I . . ."

Gamal stopped him again.

"Hey, what's wrong, Daoud? What 'actually' and what 'really' do you mean? What are you saying, man?"

"I didn't come just to talk, Mr. President," he answered. "I came especially for Sheikh Hassanein al-Basri, sir."

Gamal's face darkened as he leapt to his feet, looming like a giant in front of Daoud. Reaching his hand into his pocket, he pulled out a packet of cigarettes and lit one of them. He blew out the smoke as his lips tightened at the mention of that name, which he had expected Daoud to bring up sooner or later—and which he wished Daoud had never mentioned.

He resumed talking as he watched the clouds of smoke floating toward the ceiling, "Those are dogs!"

"Don't be upset, Mr. President," interjected Daoud. "Not all of them are like that. Sheikh Hassanein . . ."

Gamal cut him off for the third time. "He's a dog too. They're all dogs. They respect neither honor nor religion—they are working against me."

He fell silent for a little, then resumed, "Me, Daoud? After all we've done for the sake of Egypt?"

He turned toward Daoud to see the upshot of his words.

"I am loyal to you, Mr. President. So is all Alexandria, I swear to God. And Sheikh Hassanein is loyal to you too. It's not possible, I mean, it wouldn't get to that point . . ."

"What are saying?" Gamal stopped him, immediately seizing on his slip of the tongue. "You still don't know if it would get to that point or not? Whether he was involved—or not? Then, you come to me without even knowing if he was involved or not? When was the last time you spoke to Sheikh Hassanein, Daoud?"

"It's been a while, Mr. President. I'm sure that Sheikh Hassanein is a good man, as you know, of course. You know this better than anyone. Whenever anyone says anything to him, he immediately believes it like a little child. But he is naïve, Mr. President—really naïve, by God. His intellect is limited and he has many little mouths to feed. What's more, the man is an old fighter, as you know firsthand. That is, the bit of insult and detention he's been through is more than enough for him. It will serve as a lesson that he'll never forget for the rest of his life. And he would be under my guarantee, Mr. President."

Daoud did not wish to approach the hidden wound inflicted by Sheikh Hassanein's words of approximately a year ago, which he had blurted to him having considered neither whether they were factual nor their likely effect on his lifelong friend. Rather, Daoud laughed and giggled to himself when it occurred to him that the position he was now in was the greatest proof of his profoundly Egyptian character. You could not find a citizen of any country, having any other kind of loyalty in this world to the same extent who would do what he was doing now—unless he was an Egyptian, son of an Egyptian! For here he was, meeting with the head of state to entreat him to set free a person accused

of attempting to kill him. Yes, to kill that president personally. And to release him on his personal responsibility—that
being the same person who had previously accused him of
treason, of being a foreign agent—and who had denied his
faithfulness to his country. Moreover, Hassanein had effectively cut off his livelihood. Never mind this growing feeling
in his heart toward Qamar, the sheikh's wife! I swear to God
no one would do all that but a true Egyptian! Crazy, like
him—exactly!

He jumped at the sound of the president telling him
firmly, "Alright, *Khawaga* Daoud, but let me think about this
question." Gamal said this, wanting to close the door on this
subject that so angered him.

But Daoud then retorted, "As you wish, Mr. President, but
I am staying here in Cairo until the order is issued to release
Sheikh Hassanein. I won't go back to Alexandria without his
hand in mine. You know, Mr. President, that I couldn't look
his wife—whom I promised that I would not return without
him—in the eye unless I do so."

"Are you twisting my arm, Daoud?"

"I seek refuge in God, Mr. President. Could I even do
that?" answered Daoud. "I swear by God Almighty, this is my
only choice."

There was a moment's silence.

"Fine, buddy—he'll be out today," said Gamal. "Are you
happy?"

"Thank you, Mr. President! Thank you!"

Daoud's spontaneous look of gratitude made Gamal step
toward him and pat him on the shoulder, commending his
friendship with the sheikh. His friendship with the sheikh! The
pain had begun to weigh on Daoud's conscience due to those
burning emotions that that he had started to harbor toward
Qamar, his friend's wife. He resolved to himself to cut off
these feelings, to cleanse himself of them—and to never go
back to thinking those thoughts again.

Here Gamal's desire to end the meeting slipped out, which drove Daoud to appeal to him again as he prepared to walk away.

"There was one last thing, Mr. President," he hurriedly added. There followed another moment of silence as Gamal peered at him curiously while they strolled together side by side toward the door to the room.

"Very well, *Khawaga* Daoud," said Gamal. "What is the other thing?"

"I want to see Abdel-Nasser Effendi and to sit with him again."

The president gave a nervous laugh. The fear that Daoud's request would go beyond that had left him.

"Okay, Daoud, that is very simple," he replied. "You have my father with you all in Alexandria: go and visit him. I am quite sure he would be very happy to see you. I'm the one constricting his life. For my own peace of mind. I dislike being indebted to anyone; to put my mind at ease, I don't want to have any issue with any person. You know that people's eyes are upon us these days. I'll give you the address."

He stopped by the office jammed with papers. He then folded a tiny slip of paper on which was written the address of Abdel-Nasser Effendi and gave it to Daoud.

At this, Daoud left him.

Within a few hours Daoud sat playing with the silver ring that he had fixed on his finger. He didn't find anything to say to the sheikh sitting beside him, with whom he didn't exchange a word or even a glance. Musings and daydreams guided him to scattered places but for one that he kept heading back to, yet which he insistently refused to get near even for a moment.

Meanwhile, Sheikh Hassanein sat beside him, withdrawn into himself, shaking in his seat on the train taking them both back to Alexandria.

CHAPTER EIGHT

SHEIKH HASSANEIN PULLED THE KEY to the flat out from his outer robe's pocket with difficulty, then quietly turned it in the lock and opened the door, trying not to wake anyone in the house. His limbs shook from the cold and the intense fear that gripped him. The back of his head and neck hurt from the number of times he had turned to look behind him along the entire darkened route to his doorway. He had returned to meet with the Brotherhood as soon as he came back from detention, and they had given him the reception that his heroism deserved. Meanwhile, his zeal to complete the path that he had begun only increased.

Daoud's effort on his behalf did not revive their friendship, which had effectively withered and died that day they met by the sea more than a year ago—though he knew that without him he would not have been released. He had just finished a two-hour meeting with Sheikh Foda, who had survived internment and its hardships due to his relation to one of the Free Officers. With a group of other activists from the organization, they had inquired into the fate of the rest of their colleagues held after the failed attempt to assassinate Gamal Abdel-Nasser, who was the obstacle still standing between them and the seat of power. Fear continued to stalk them while the desire to rule by themselves still drove them on.

They met in one of the warehouses belonging to one Sayyed al-Damanhouri, the merchant of manufactured goods.

They gathered after the evening prayer in the Shabrawishi Mosque, having dispersed after they agreed to assemble at the warehouse. They slipped, one after another, through a side door of its unlit hall. Guided by burning matches, they each made their way to a windowless room within, its fixed-tile floor covered with a thick folksy rug and a gas light gleaming from one of its walls. They talked for a while, the discussion growing furious at times. But the men decided not to meet again for a period of six months after that night—until things cooled down and they could resume their activities.

Yet Sheikh Hassanein was one of those who opposed the idea: he had felt drawn to secret political work since becoming acquainted with it alongside Daoud before the Revolution. Yet he was compelled to consent in the end when the only one to share his objection was Master Mohammed al-Buri, an Arabic language teacher and graduate of Dar al-'Ulum secondary school who, like him, pushed for the completion of the jihad. From a purely religious standpoint, he believed in the superior claim of religious authority to the seat of power until the secular system is brought down and governance is set again on the straight path at the hands of the Brotherhood. It was known that some of the Free Officers were still loyal to its political program within the regime. That even included its leader, Brigadier General Mohammed Naguib, who was said to be among the most fervent supporters of the Islamist political movement.

Thus, with the passage of time, as Sheikh Hassanein grew more enthused with a particular idea, it would not only intrigue him but completely dominate all his thoughts and actions. A similar inkling made him admire Sheikh Mohammed Abduh, whose life story he had heard when he was in the full bloom of youth, enrolled in al-Azhar University. He was unable to complete his studies, given the time needed to plan his life with his first wife, Zaynab Sharbat—a lady of the night that he had gotten to know in the side alleys of Clot Bey Street during his stay in Cairo. In a blaze of passion, he resolved to marry her to rescue her from the grip of sin there and then. Within a year, he had, of course, divorced her—after she bore him his first born, Mohammed, about whom he had since learned nothing.

Calmly, he crept toward the bedroom where Qamar was lying on the far side of the bed facing the wall, fast asleep. Sheikh Hassanein hastily changed his clothes as the dampness inside the stone-built apartment penetrated every inch of his body. He took off every piece of clothing, then put on his woolen robe. He rubbed his palms, blowing on them quietly, his teeth chattering.

"I seek refuge in God! What's with all this cold? Why has February come on so hard this year? Have mercy, Oh Lord!" Then he lifted the coverlet and slipped under it, seeking the warmth of his wife, whose backside stuck out toward him.

Within minutes his limbs had warmed. His hand slid inside Qamar's robe as he pulled her toward him, thrusting his manhood inside her. As he did so she gasped for an instant as she woke from her sleep, and just as quickly he had discharged that which he needed to. He then turned on his back and stared at the ceiling for a moment, his snores soon floating up to it. Qamar put on her underclothes before falling back into her very deep slumber.

She awoke to the cries of her son Lutfi, who had wet his bed as usual and was huddled in his stinging hot covers, wailing. Pulling off her own covers, she sat for some moments, her thoughts balanced between the snores of her husband beside her and the shrieks of her child. The latter summoned her to pull him out of the bed, remove his clothes and wash his soaked body over the bathroom sink while he wailed even more, as she knew he would. She then turned on the gas stove and made breakfast. This was followed by the rest of the household chores: heating water on the stove until she was able to crouch over the tub in the bathroom to wash the dirty bedsheets and underclothes, then spreading them over the balcony before the morning sun disappeared behind the building, when the laundry would not dry.

These were the typical thoughts with which she began her day. And every day until that in which she went out to bathe in the waters of the sea, as she always used to do, before the eyes of dawn awoke But on that day, precisely at dawn, she heard the sound of an oud and mournful singing coming from the direction of the *cabinas*. In a fleeting glance she saw the shape of a man crouched in the gloom. She immediately realized he could be a drunk or a criminal—and that they were hidden here, far from the eyes of the nightly police patrols. The voice continued to chant with a captivating warmth that removed all the dread from her heart, perhaps because it awakened some sense of familiarity or prior acquaintance with its owner.

How strange! She was resolved to do what she had always done before she married Sheikh Hassanein, the presence of this unknown man arousing no fear in her. It would not prevent her from enjoying the waters of the sea cleansing her body of the hardships of life. Rather, because of his being there, and perhaps from a hidden feeling that this man was Daoud Abdel-Malek, whom she had heard singing from the balcony of their apartment before, she felt a growing confidence that he was sitting there to protect her from the evil of the voyeurs.

The sense of his watching over her filled her with an elation she had not felt before: she relished bathing that daybreak more than any other time in the past! The same feelings gripped her and thrilled her heart at the boldness of his gaze when she went out with *al-Khawaga* Daoud to search for her husband in detention. To this moment she does not know what happened to her that day, and yet she had grown sure that her life had not been the same since. This was due to the power of the amorous love and tenderness that showed in his eyes as he asked her for her name; that heat radiating from his body, and his burning breath, as he stood beside her under the covered doorway; the cold and the wind had perished in the fire of his presence beside her; and what he did to her by pressing his palm on her lips to stop her from shouting to confront the pasha that day. She had not felt that wave of femininity that seized her from the top of her head to the soles of her feet except one other time before. It was the day after her wedding to Sheikh Hassanein after he came out of the hashish-induced stupor that had filled his head the previous night. Her beauty and womanhood did not stand out in his reality except on that morning, when he looked at her and his eyes, which gleamed like lightning, seemed to devour her completely. Then he made love to her, and for the first time, he was bewitched by her—a feeling never repeated after that day until she saw the same expression in the eyes of *al-Khawaga* Daoud.

Daoud was joyful as he ascended the staircase leading to the apartment of Abdel-Nasser Effendi on the second floor, clutching his oud in his hand, a wrapper full of *kufta* dangling from a ribbon tied to his fingers. In his other hand he held two cold bottles of Stella Beer concealed in a paper bag; these he longed to imbibe in the company of his old friend. With difficulty he pressed the doorbell, wishing to spend a delightful spring evening party reminiscing with his ancient companion about their shared memories together.

Abdel-Nasser Effendi greeted him gladly and anxiously, taking the packages he was carrying and placing them on the table in the center of the reception before embracing him with pure affection, the two of them kissing each other on both cheeks as long-time companions do when they meet. Daoud was taken aback by the signs of aging that showed on Abdel-Nasser Effendi's face, realizing how many years it must have been since they last saw each other. At the same time Daoud grasped the inevitable change that he must have suffered as well. He was satisfied, perhaps, with the comparison, because

Abdel-Nasser Effendi was more than ten years his senior. Between bites of *kufta* and sips of beer, from which Abdel-Nasser Effendi politely refrained, keen not to hurt Daoud's feelings, they exchanged words of affection. The two of them brought back the bygone days and nights and the memories they shared together.

Daoud sang a song by "The Lady," Umm Kulthoum:

You renewed your love, why? / After the heart had healed
Shame on you to keep it / neglectful of what had gone
You abandoned me when I was close to you /
I had hope you will come one day
But your distance from me / keeps the heart deprived.

Abdel-Nasser Effendi told him that night that his son Gamal had contacted him by phone some days before and spoken of Daoud's visit to him, expressing a lot of warmth and respect for him. Daoud was quite moved to hear these words about the feelings of the President of the Republic for him—and he felt very proud as well.

In the middle of the day, while she was busy as usual in pursuit of the affairs of the house, Qamar was surprised by a knock at their door. She hurried to wake her husband, who was still immersed in sleep. Meanwhile, the child Lutfi ran, also as usual, to open the door. Then he stood in front of it staring wordlessly at the man who had knocked, for the child was later to speak than others his age.

The sheikh was in motion, rubbing his eyes sleepily and calling to his son from the bedroom, "Who is it, Lutfi boy?"

The sheikh knew very well that Lutfi did not talk, but his question enabled him to buy some minutes in which to change out of his nightclothes into his robe and turban, items he would not meet a stranger without wearing. As he did so, Qamar disappeared into the bedroom— according to the new instructions—until her husband could look over the person at the door. It would be determined by him whether it was "lawful" for the man to be viewing—yes, simply viewing—his wife or not. Qamar was beginning to feel uncomfortable with these new constraints added to the hardships of a life that was already difficult, the dull days growing ever duller from the tight grip of scarcity on one side and the isolating confinement to which she had been sentenced, without having committed any crime to deserve it, on the other. To further this despotic detention, he did not permit her to leave the apartment except for reasons of utmost dire necessity. Adding to her hardships was her cohabitation with a man nearly thirty years her senior while all other men were forbidden to glimpse her, be they the people of her district, her neighbors, or *'Amm* Sa'id the doorman. Indeed, this included all the men she was accustomed to seeing throughout the years of her marriage and even before that due to their being neighbors of hers—and this was without any of them intending to incite the sheikh's suspicion toward them or herself.

From behind the door, Qamar heard the sheikh invite the stranger to come into the sitting room. It was obvious from the hesitation in his voice that the sheikh was surprised or annoyed at the man's coming—that he was *persona non grata* at his house. Her curiosity aroused, she angled out a little to see if she knew the guest, who was hidden away with her husband behind the door that was closed firmly on them both. The man was a stranger; she had not seen him before. He was in his mid-forties and tall, with a distinctive appearance: broad-shouldered but leanly built, and dark complexioned, his expression not just serious but depressed—a look intensified by his thick, black-rimmed eyeglasses and blackish beard, which rendered his dark complexion even darker. He wore a frayed gray suit and shoes coated with dust from the street, leaving a filthy smudge on the gleaming tiles that Qamar had taken such care to clean to a shiny brightness to impress her female neighbors. That was, in addition to her tyrannical confinement behind the door of her room, a reason for her disgust with him and with his visit to Sheikh Hassanein—her husband—in the middle of the day like this. She found herself comparing this stranger with his depression to *al-Khawaga* Daoud with his elegance, his familiar footstep to which she had grown accustomed when he used to visit them, and that perfumed scent he used to exude when he passed through the vestibule that lay between the entrance and the sitting room. The scent would linger in the apartment until he left with the sheikh, as was their habit. Her thoughts ran away with her as curiosity overcame her about the reason for Daoud's absence from their apartment all this time, including since Sheikh Hassanein had returned from detention. She dared not broach the subject with her husband so as not to incite him against her or against Daoud.

She shut the door and turned toward the bed, pulling back the coverlet to shake the dust from it. Then she smoothed it back over the sheets as she sang:

I will meet him tomorrow / and the day after tomorrow
And the day after that / and the day after that—
I will meet him, I will meet him, I will meet him tomorrow.

Behind the tightly-closed door, words flew in whispers between the two men—Mr. Mohammed al-Buri and Sheikh Hassanein: whispers that were like shouts, setting their conversation alight. The banner of Islam must once again flutter on high; the rule of God is better than the rule of the people, no matter who those people are; it was the Muslim Brotherhood who made the revolution succeed first and last, and they would not sit back with their arms folded. They would not stop seeking the return of their right from this handful of officers whose back ends had hardly touched the seat of power than they had betrayed their mutual pact. Sharp, angry words, like a fistful of nails, they threw at each other in handfuls, savoring the pain of

gripping them in their fists while also scorning that same agony
for the sake of reaching the higher goal.

In those days, Alexandria seemed more gorgeous than ever,
her golden hair—the far-reaching sands of the beaches—
stretching to the highest heavens, where its locks gather to
embrace each other until they become a golden disc that fills
the world with its light. Ah! How beautiful life is!

The relationship between Daoud and the world of
Binyuti Pasha became strong after Daoud's return from his
visit to Cairo, when he came to the pasha's palace specifically
to thank him for his help in his mission to find Sheikh Hassanein. There was nothing the pasha could do but receive
him as a conquering hero, particularly when news reached
him of Daoud's encounter with Gamal Abdel-Nasser in all its
details—from his coffee of the special blend to his triumphant
return at the end of the day with his friend from the Muslim
Brotherhood—which he had heard from a friend close to the
leadership of the Revolutionary Council.

Daoud was astonished by the way the pasha treated
him, not only when he asked him how solid his relationship
with Gamal Abdel-Nasser was but also when he expressed to
him—immediately and without hesitation—his desire for him
to join in his formidable commercial and industrial works.
Daoud would be his powerful outside façade and a shield pro-
tecting his mighty wealth from the ruthlessness of the officers
of the revolution, who had begun to confiscate the money of
the rich—especially among the Jews—which had led many of
them to flee the country. Indeed, just a few months later, when
he was sitting on the balcony, cradling his oud and crooning
a song by Sheikh Zakariya Ahmed while sipping his morning
tea, Daoud was surprised to see that Binyuti Pasha had sent his
personal secretary in his black Packard car—which blocked
the road underneath the modest building in Moharram Bey—
to find him. Daoud peered down at him from over the balcony,

searching curiously for the source of the uproar that filled the street. In moments, the driver was rapping at the door of their apartment to ask Daoud to accompany him to meet the pasha in his private office at Ramle Station.

The days of her life passed, each like the other, with a crazy speed.

Elaine sat peeling zucchini from a tray on the round dining table in the middle of the salon, empty chairs arrayed all around her. Daoud had scrambled outside urgently as ordered by that strange man who wore a policeman's uniform mixed with that of the elevator boy at Cicurel department store. Although she did not understand the reason why, in reality, she was not worried about it at all. For some time now—she did not know how long—she had ceased to follow his comings and goings. Not just his but anyone's, including even those of Layla, daughter of the late Budur, or even of Suleiman or Mona, her own. She let them go in and out as they wished.

Rather, she started to ask them to leave the flat's door open. She did not even pretend to take the trouble to leave what she was busy with to open it for them on their return from wherever they had gone for their business, whatever that business was. She did not doubt the innocence of what they were up to—God forbid! For they had been children together, in any case. It was not possible to imagine that what they did would be so corrupt that they could arrive at things she or their neighbors in the district would find unacceptable.

But she suffered from the apparent indifference that had forced itself upon her since the death of her youngest, Makari. Afterward her feelings hardened toward everyone—herself included. She no longer found anyone around her who made her happy or even got a little close to that gray wall that surrounded her life. So, she succumbed to a reality in which she spent her days monotonously, her feelings swinging back and forth between sad and not sad. But in any case, joyful news would not dare get near her—not even a bit. The burning flame of joy was extinguished in the depths of her spirit.

Food she made her only exception, for in it she discovered her sense of pleasure. She did not cease her untiring efforts to try to get more out of it, or in any case to sate herself. She became addicted to its drug-like qualities in its many types, shapes, and forms with all her capabilities—mental as well as physical—yet she could not truly be satisfied let alone delighted by it. Therefore, she fruitlessly tried to fill the vacuum inside her by marshalling all kinds of food to her cause.

As would be expected, with layers of lard assailing her one after another, the shameful gluttony showed in her physique. In just a year or a little more, she became a fat lady for the first time in her life. Naturally, she did not achieve the desired satiation or regain even a miniscule part of the carefree spirit that had always lit her being. Yet nature not only endowed her with a gracefulness to compensate for her obesity but also made her even more beautiful in a manner befitting her age. And thus, she became the Lady Elaine.

CHAPTER NINE

DAOUD FELL INTO A STATE of reflection that absorbed him at critical moments like these. He was sitting in the big car behind the driver who, dressed in a black tuxedo with gold buttons and a cap with a shiny gold rim, had rushed to open the car's back door for Daoud as soon as it pulled up at the entrance to his home. Daoud's bewildered neighbors and the owners of nearby shops looked on; this was not only the first Packard but the first privately owned car whose tires had trod their street. Women returning from their shopping turned their heads and one of them nearly ululated, but embarrassment stifled the ululation on the tip of her tongue. The action of buying and selling came to a halt as boys on the street stopped kicking their football back and forth and girls halted their hopscotch game, whose squares were drawn with chalk on the asphalt. Daoud not only exchanged embarrassed glances with them, sharing their perplexity about what had happened to him and to them, he practically shouted an apology to them for that magnificent event which took their district by surprise, wrecking the turning wheel of their day.

He sat in the backseat and began to toy with the silver signet ring on his finger, staring at the multitudes of people around him through the shiny window glass as the car headed down Fouad Street toward the Corniche, the road lining the Mediterranean shore. Nothing had changed in the area, either before the Revolution or after. With the same boundless joy, the huge crowds still hurried toward Alexandria to spend the summer months in flight from the humid dog days of Cairo. They did so with the same striving for life that he had always observed in the faces of the summer vacationers, the same bare feet prancing toward the boardwalk overlooking the seashore. The same oblivious gaze toward the broad horizon at the very moment a child slips his mother's grip to head crazily, heedlessly, toward the long procession of cars propelling down the Corniche. Nothing interrupted the monotonous flow of events but the prolonged hiss of the car's tires on the asphalt, which would cease suddenly when, at the last moment, the car stopped before crushing the head of that errant child and the voices of all the unshod onlookers would rejoice, shouting, "Praise be to God! Praise be to God!"

Then Daoud contemplated the reflection of his face on the car's window while the images of the people behind his own changed to fleeting phantoms—phantoms that brought him back from his musings for that moment to wonder where this trip was taking him. Yet he soon found himself distracted by thoughts of Qamar, with her radiant, comely face, her green eyes, and her golden hair. He imagined her sharing this cozy back seat in this massive car, her delicate hand between his palms as he rode with her about Alexandria's streets packed with people. She would be sitting beside him, smiling contentedly, proud that she was privileged over the pedestrian hordes thronging on the other side of the car's window.

Daoud snapped out of his reverie when he suddenly realized he was enjoying these inappropriate thoughts, which he had deemed inappropriate when they had seduced him before. Except now he blamed them on the continued harshness of Sheikh Hassanein toward him even after he had sought his release from detention. Therefore, he counted that fantasy—shamefully—to be the least he might do in revenge for what Sheikh Hassanein had done to him.

Daoud went into Binyuti Pasha's room on the fourth floor of the building facing the deep blue sea of Alexandria. The pasha, with his hulking body and gleaming hair, was sitting on a plush, wine-colored leather chair behind a sturdy, massive ebony desk, his huge face flushed red from the effect of wine. A refined and elegant man took shape before him on the chair facing the desk while melodious Western music whispered faintly in the background. The two men were smoking Cuban cigars that Daoud knew by their fragrant aroma. They were laughing together—in a dignified way—when Daoud entered the chamber. The wind blowing from the verandah attached to the room played with the cigar fumes when the brilliant brass doorknob turned, the waves of smoke dancing before Daoud's eyes, adding an air of surrealism. It was as if he were drawing close to the movie screen in the Alhambra Cinema on Safiya Zaghloul Street as it showed the film *Casablanca*, which he had seen more than ten times. For a three-piastre ticket, he had watched it three or four times in a row. He drew still closer and closer to the two men until he was treading upon the edge of the carpet spread on the parquet floor.

Daoud twisted his body and nearly fell as he suddenly found himself inside the scene, but he righted himself before falling on his face. He tottered forward, unusually hesitant and distracted. He did not understand the mortal distress that afflicted him despite the relaxed spirit that enveloped the place. Then the private secretary followed him bearing a neat leather bag full of papers. He opened it, putting it down in front of this peculiar man. Then, with considerable courtesy, he made a little bow toward Daoud without uttering a word before ushering him to take the seat next to him facing the pasha's chair.

"What will you drink, Daoud? Would you like to take some cognac with us?" the pasha launched the session with the expected prologue. He beckoned to Daoud who, appearing tongue-tied, half-rose from his chair, then half-turned forward, touching his chest with his palm in a gesture of gratitude, to immediately and silently announce to those present the lowness of his status and his smallness, of course, faced with the abundant nobility of the pasha. But the pasha was not pleased by this defeatist behavior on the part of Daoud—who was his friend—in front of him, especially when he had known him to be proud, strong, and steadfast. Indeed, this diffidence on Daoud's part fit matched what the pasha had resolved to discuss with him later and drove him to say, "What's wrong with you, Daoud? Aren't you feeling well?"

"Not at all, Pasha, your Excellency," he replied. "There's nothing!" Daoud blurted, his gaze wandering around the corners of the vast room, its high walls and gilt-framed paintings peering down at him. He found himself wondering what had brought him to this place. The pasha shifted in his seat: he decided to get down to business straightaway, perceiving the path that Daoud had chosen to tread.

"Good, as you wish, then. I would like to introduce the Honorable Sinut Qiryaqus, the famous lawyer and my business manager here in Egypt," he said. Then he turned toward the other man in introduction.

"Master Daoud, Sinut." The pasha elaborated, "The man you see, sir, who claims such modesty, is the same fearsome man who dealt with the issue of the boy from the Brotherhood that I told you about, on a little trip to the great man. During it, His Excellency took care of every issue and returned with his friend on his arm as if it were nothing. By God, it was just as I'm telling you."

As he said this, Sinut swiveled his gaze between the pasha, with whom he was conversing, and Daoud, back and forth in succession as he shook his head, amazed at Daoud's ability.

"Welcome, welcome, sir," Sinut Qiryaqus said with courteous humility as he extended his hand to greet Daoud. The distinguished lawyer stood trembling with admiration as he realized that the scope of Daoud's influence reached even to the head of the nation. Then he said, in a tone conferring great status, "Hello, Mister Daoud—you've honored us."

The words "Mister" and "Excellency" and "the fearsome man" rang in Daoud's head from one end to the other, from high and low, reverberating successively, continuously resounding louder and louder, repeating inside him. His head swelled so big it nearly filled the room. No longer able in his turn to sit upright in his seat, he sank into his chair, weighted down by his heavy burden, his arms crossed on his chest, his fingers intertwined before him, waiting for the storm of exaltation that buffeted his being to pass away until he was able to speak intelligibly to the two prominent men sitting across from him. No sooner had the servant brought him a glass of cognac than he gulped it down quickly. Its effects sped through his limbs, soaking them like water piercing the dryness of the thirsty earth, and thus refreshing it.

"Look, Daoud," said the pasha, "I will get right to the point. First, because I am a man of business—of work—who knows the value of time, and because I am first and last a Jewish man. Yes, indeed, a Jew, and I know the meaning of this word very well. I can rely on my brother the Jew—and am sure he'd stand beside me." He uttered the word "Jew" strongly twice, then brought his glass to his lips and sipped from it as he steered his eyes between Daoud and Sinut, gesturing to the attendant with his finger to fill Daoud's glass again.

Then he added, "I decided to invite Master Sinut today because I want to transfer the ownership of the new factory in Dekheila to your name, Daoud."

The pasha fell silent as he watched the effect of his words on the two men's faces. Sinut shifted in his seat as he pulled together the lapels of his jacket and stroked the knot of his silk tie, waiting for Daoud to comment.

"Very well," Daoud asked, his embarrassment and stammering returning. "Perhaps I could know why, Pasha?"

"Don't you live in this country, Daoud?" the pasha replied. "If I didn't put your name on this factory today, your friends in Cairo would lust after it tomorrow or the next day, while you too are one of *us* and belong to *us*. Even if you robbed me, even if you did that, my brother Daoud, you would still belong to us. It would still remain in *our* hands and those of *our* children after us. Isn't that so, Sinut?"

Naturally, Sinut did not answer. He knew very well that his Highness the Pasha did not ask him to come to seek his view or consult him in the matter. His presence was for the purpose of carrying out the decision that the pasha was determined to take, whatever it might be. His long experience in dealing with Binyuti Pasha inclined him to keep completely quiet even when asked to speak, including precisely when requested to render an opinion. But that did not prevent his wondering to himself whether from the pasha's side it was best to hand the ownership of a factory worth a hundred thousand Egyptian pounds—that is to say about a quarter-million American dollars or more. Sinut put a business-like smile on his face, and, instead of answering, moved to pull out the papers and documents from inside the leather bag and place them on the table in front of him. As for Daoud, he could not bear to wait any longer.

"But your Excellency, I don't understand anything about factories or about iron works," he declared. "I'm an artist; I play music and sing. My voice is fine—there is nothing like it. But the iron industry? I wouldn't lie to you—I wouldn't know how."

"Listen, Daoud," said the pasha. "I want to transfer the title to the factory to you as soon as possible to save it from being lost, not to waste it! In the hands of those riffraff, it would soon disappear—do you understand? The factory is running at its peak, and those inside it run it like clockwork one hundred percent. The whole story is that if it stays in my name or those of my children, it will go. Get it?"

The effect of the second glass spread through Daoud's mind and body and he drooped in his chair. A smile rose on his face, in whose folds there was neither happiness nor joy—only surrender and the certainty that the matter was out of his hands. The decision was made by the pasha long before Daoud came. Daoud gave in to the reality and smiled broadly at fate, which had given him wealth, reputation, and fame without calculation and without his having to strive for prestige or money, in a single day. He kept playing with the silver signet ring encircling his little finger between the moments he bent down toward the stand in front of him to put his signature where Sinut indicated, the smile still drawn on his lips, which it refused to leave.

Daoud was sitting on his balcony, noisily slurping a cup of tea while smoking a cigarette after waking up from his siesta a short while before, when someone knocked on the door of his flat. He had not yet recovered from the shock of what had happened to him during the past weeks but was still pondering the meaning of all that without finding an obvious answer. He had transformed without rational reason from merely an oud player and crooner—even the king of kings of all troubadours—into an actual king possessing both money and power. Between these thoughts, the insistent knocks on the door came again, and he returned to the reality of his situation.

Who could it be? Elaine and the kids are not here.

The factory's ownership had not been transferred to Daoud for a week when he was surprised by Binyuti Pasha's secretary rushing to him to say that His Excellency had asked him to come quickly, for he had decided to travel abroad. The pasha met him at the palace in a state of urgency, the servants and family members scurrying up and down the marble staircases without cease, racing against time.

"It's finished, Daoud," the pasha said. "Your friends have bought weapons from the Communists' arsenal. Of course,

Israel and the West will not be silent. It's over—our days here are done. It's no longer a matter of being rich or poor; everything has changed. We have to leave as fast as possible."

Quickly the pasha proposed to Daoud that he buy the palace and all that was in it on the spot for a total of ten thousand pounds in cash, but he would have had to go and get the money from the factory's safe in less than an hour. Daoud agreed to bring the requested sum from the cashbox at the new factory to the pasha as he boarded a ship leaving Alexandria harbor in the next few hours. Daoud truly did fly in the pasha's car to Dekheila; he met the head of accounts at the factory and asked for the sum in question. The man received him in a very friendly manner, but he told him that the bank deposits had just been made and only three thousand pounds remained for the workers' salaries due the next day. The man gave the three thousand pounds to Daoud, vowing to replace them the next day along with the balance of the sum demanded, which he would send when the bank opened its doors the following morning.

When Daoud returned to the pasha's palace and told him what the man had said to him, the pasha surprised him by taking the money and signing the bill of sale, making Daoud Abdel- Malek the new owner of the imposing mansion.

"Take care of the factory, Daoud—I'll get in touch with you when I'm settled," were the pasha's last words to him.

The next day, Elaine moved into the palace. Daoud remained in the apartment in Moharram Bey until the final arrangements for the shift in household were made.

At the thick wooden door of the palace, custom made for His Excellency the Pasha with trees from a Polish forest, the servants of the house were lined up to receive Elaine and the children. The child Suleiman leaped from the car's door into the passage that ran between the gardenia beds and fragrant jasmine shrubs then flew errantly over the steps of the marble staircase and finally through the servants' ranks and into the palace. There he continued up the stairs one after the other until he opened the last door and found himself on a terrace overlooking the sea stretching endlessly before him. He propped his elbows on the railings as the breeze caressed him, playing with the locks of hair on his head. Soothed by the pleasure of the beautiful view and the smell of the sea, he clasped his two hands under his chin.

The person at the door resumed their rapping. Daoud got up from his chair to close the door's two-part screen to block the burning rays of the sun, then went to open the door.

Qamar!

Yes, she was standing before him in the flesh. In his pajama bottoms, undershirt, and bare feet, his half-drained teacup in hand, he stared at her in confusion. He looked her up and down, not believing it was really her. Her uncovered golden hair flew above her forehead while her eyes—oh, such green eyes wrapped in those clouds of sadness, her cherry lips promising hidden treasures, and her cheeks—by God!

But, what is this?

Red and blue marks showed on her rosy complexion— bruises. It hurt his eyes merely to look at them. His eyebrows knitted and face muscles tightened, yet he still could not express what was in his breast. His heart grew sad; he frowned, yet he could neither weep nor protest.

"Will you leave me standing at the door like this, *Si* Daoud?" said Qamar, standing posed in front of the apartment door as a cloud of grief engulfed her.

"Elaine and the children aren't here, Qamar," he said.

"But I came to see you, Mr. Daoud."

"My heart has felt the same way, too," he told her as he withdrew from the front of the doorway to beckon for Qamar to enter. His eyes hugged the ground, following her footsteps, blood seeping from her open heels as she walked. Qamar stopped in the middle of the salon, then turned toward him, not knowing if he would permit her to sit down.

He felt that he wanted to take her in his arms and let her cry on his shoulder as she complained to him of what time had done to her. Yet he thought it wiser to settle for motioning for her to have a seat. He ducked into his bedroom, put on his pajama top, and returned. Qamar buried her face in her hands and began to sob.

"What's wrong, Qamar?"

"He beat me, Master Daoud," she wailed. "He's broken me with his beatings because I fear for him and his son." Then she vanished once more amid her tears.

"Calm down, if only for my sake, and tell me what's happened," said Daoud. But she kept on crying, and he replied emotionally, "By my life—that's enough!"

Qamar lifted her face toward him where he sat across from her, not believing what her ears had just heard. All this tenderness coming from the man who enjoyed so much influence and ability that he brought her husband back to her in just a few hours.

She dried her tears and called out helplessly, "What can one do when one fears for her home? Every other day this man named Mohammed al-Buri comes to us and sits there with him, and they whisper secrets to each other behind the closed door for hours. With my own ears I heard them talking about the President—they want to kill him. When I complained to my husband, he beat me up. I mean, does he want me to wait for when they come and arrest him again?" She realized her voice had risen higher.

"I put in my two words with him, Mr. Daoud," she continued. "He cracked down on me with slaps to the face, then went to get the rod he keeps to teach me manners. Why, my brother? Is it that I'm so lacking in manners?"

Qamar went back to sobbing, then stopped suddenly. She raised her head, saying in a defeated tone, "I took the boy

Lutfi to Umm Ihsan, then I came to you right away. You must find me a solution, Mr. Daoud. I am from a good family, and I am not this pathetic thing that I seem to be now."

She began crying again.

"Enough weeping, Qamar," he said. "Is that, too, any way to behave? Can anyone treat a grown woman this way?" he added, clenching his fists as he spoke.

"I'm not going to say I'll just hit him back because he hit you," declared Daoud. "No, that's enough. But if you'd like me to kill him, then I'd do it to stop your precious tears!"

Then he turned his face away from hers and avoided looking at her directly.

He spoke so earnestly that he frightened her. She gazed into his eyes, probing them to see how serious he was. Her eyes dried suddenly as she contemplated his words. Yes, she would rather a thousand times that Hassanein al-Basri die and disappear from her life and that his place be taken by Daoud Abdel-Malek—with the power and influence he wielded despite his delicate feelings and ebullient emotions— rather than her enduring more of Sheikh Hassanein's tyranny toward her, even if she had to share Daoud with Elaine.

Qamar stood up, resolved to see the matter through to its end. She walked around the table that stood between them until she came face-to-face with him; she reached her hand toward his palm, then raised it to his lips. She kissed the back of his hand admiringly, then his palm lovingly, as warm feelings flooded his heart and his whole being trembled. In return, he stretched forth his other hand and it encircled her waist until he enfolded her and drew her toward him forcefully. He lifted her chin a little and pressed his lips toward her. His eyes closed bashfully as he tasted the most beautiful nectar he had ever known. She savored her first real kiss and melted in his arms. With the deliberateness of a fifty-year old, he gently drew off her outer clothing and covered her body with soft kisses. Her feelings flared and she met him love for love.

She rose again and moved toward the oud leaning on the back of the chair facing her, gripping its neck and giving it to Daoud without uttering a word. Daoud began to stroke its strings, then played and sang the same song he had done for his bewitching *houri* on the seashore. The melody penetrated Qamar's body, making it sway with ecstasy and delight. She removed the strap of her inner blouse from her shoulder, and it fell to her feet as she kept moving to the music. Then her brassiere and underclothes were gone, and she turned around, gleaming in all her beauty.

Next his own clothes came off, and they both stood naked in the middle of the salon. She stood like the statue of Venus de Milo, her eyes closed in reverie as Daoud kissed her all over, still playing his oud as though he were the sculptor Alexandros of Antioch when, with his fingers and his soul, he created his most famous figure. The light of the setting sun streaming through the balcony's shutters moved in stages up her figure and stirred her with its blaze. Qamar became a mass of light that Daoud fluttered around like an amorous moth robbed of its will to which it could only try to cling. He felt a lust consuming his whole being such as he had never felt before. It brought back to his aging body the tensions of his youth—his vigor and his strength, which he hadn't experienced for some time before that day. That day, which he would regard thereafter as having separated his life before it from what came after.

Daoud and Qamar lay on the bed, their eyes closed, bathing in the sea of their intoxication. He lit a cigarette and watched its smoke climb to the ceiling. Several quiet moments had passed when Qamar leaned on one hand to raise the upper half of her body, and gazed at her companion. Clutching the coverlet to her breast with the other, she said to him, "I have to go now. What time is it? I must go and get the boy Lutfi from Umm Ihsan's place."

"And then what, Qamar? What do you want to do about your husband?" he asked her between puffs on his cigarette.

"I don't have a husband," she answered hurriedly. "I must divorce him today, not tomorrow."

Daoud turned toward her, trying to gauge how serious she was, and queried, "And what do you want from me? I told you I could kill him for your sake."

"Then you'll have to kill him—if you can!" she blurted coldly, shifting her body in his direction while lifting her eyebrows in challenge.

Daoud stared straight ahead and muttered as though addressing the unknown, "A little trip to Cairo, which will bring about your death, Sheikh Hassanein! You got out of detention on my responsibility—and when you carry on your wicked ways, you'll harm me personally! Your end will come at these hands of mine." He held his palms in the air as though in prayer, looking at them not only in confusion but in disbelief at what he had just resolved to have the audacity to do.

Qamar stood up and in moments had left the apartment. Daoud stayed by himself in the darkened room, futilely puffing cigarettes for hours as one gnaws at a delicious pear bursting with exquisite sweetness, savoring the pleasure. Until, that is, without intending it, you bite on its bitter seed. Yes, the bitterness filled him, and he could not get rid of it despite the cup of tea with three teaspoons of sugar that he gulped without even tasting it. A heavy feeling of guilt gripped his heart, and he donned his clothes in haste. Wanting to flee, he went down to the street and strolled past the closed-up shops and the cafés full of people out for the evening as they are in spring in Alexandria. The storms that come in regular succession in winter had cleansed her streets, and the people had come out at night again after a long absence. He headed down Market Street to the sea, whose delights, he thought, might be the cure for his bitterness.

Until he crossed the Corniche, the air was filled with the fragrance of smoldering waterpipes and the laughter of those out for the evening. The aroma mingled with the cold zephyrs bearing the scents of the sea and the scent of ears of sweet corn spread by street vendors over burning coals. In his dismay, he pictured himself twisting like the corn over the fire as he would in his punishment in the afterlife—that consuming fire of which his family and his people in Alexandria had long told him. That would be his just deserts—not only for his ugly deed but for what he had decided to do to his friend Sheikh Hassanein. He found himself staring at the sea, with its dark, vague expanse and silver waves ever coming in, and he muttered, "O God of clemency, O God of forgiveness!"

But it was Qamar.

Yes, she tempted him with her beauty, her youth, and her tyrannical femininity! Then she came to him—without his invitation—to his house and cried. Imploring him not only to rescue her from her predicament but to avenge her, as well, unto death, from that stupid man who had beaten her. How could he possibly gaze at that comeliness without kneeling before it in worship?

It was Sheikh Hassanein.

Yes, he is the culprit. He deserves the chastisement that will visit him.

No, it's not his own fault—or hers. Sheikh Hassanein is the only one to blame. He truly merits what has occurred and all that is going to happen to him.

The blackguard beats her! He must be blind, groping in the darkness, not knowing where to go. From al-Azhar to hosting parties, from Zaynab Sharbat to Qamar. Then he comes to me, his friend and companion on the road of life, and tells me that I should leave my country! He trades me for Mohammed al-Buri! That scoundrel whom he had met once or twice before and who sometimes called himself an artist and a painter and at others a politician and a socialist, then he turns around again and now he's a Muslim Brother. A clown frolicking with an elephant under the Big Top of a third-rate circus. He truly must be blind: he can't make out what's in front of him. He will soon fall into the first hole he comes to. Yes, it's definitely Sheikh Hassanein!

There was no way to avoid the comeuppance for his disgraceful misdeed.

CHAPTER TEN

THE SUN RETURNED, RISING ONCE again as it did yesterday and as it had a month ago and since the beginning of creation. Its rays streamed through the gaps in the shutters on the room's high windows in the upper level of the house. Elaine awoke from her interrupted sleep, anxious over her son Suleiman huddled beside her. He had spent the whole night shivering from the heat that lit his body like a fire. So, she had moved him to her bed to pass the night with him. As for Daoud, he had traveled to Cairo to buy some items needed for the factory. That day was the first they had been apart since the first time they met in Moharram Bey. She muttered her prayers as she fixed her eyes on the face of her sleeping son. Beads of sweat collected like pearls on his forehead. She wiped them with a damp cloth at times and with the palms of her hands at others as tears flowed down her cheeks. Her lips still mouthed prayers she had learned by heart as a child and teenager in the orphanage. Flights of memory seized her and took her back to where her son Makari—the younger brother—had been lying on her bed in their first apartment in Moharram Bey as he quickly melted away in her arms, due to the amount of vital bodily fluids that he was losing.

Elaine had been totally overcome, unable to do anything but wash his skin drenched with diarrhea and vomit that never let up, day or night, limitless until they did away with him. She did not stop crying for long months afterward, and she still cries for him sometimes. She stopped singing completely afterward.

Singing was her whole life—the sign of her presence wherever she was. Even Daoud, her man, she no longer desired or wanted to be close to as before; she found herself avoiding him even in the bedroom. She began sleeping in the children's room hours before he would come back from his nights out, and in the morning—or rather in the middle of the day, when he awoke—she would distract herself from him with affairs of the household and of life. When Daoud did not forbid or object to that, she attributed his acceptance of the new situation to his advancing age. That problem did not affect their relationship since neither of them brought it up in the years following. They each remained silent about it so as not to hurt the other's feelings—because it was not only one's own problem, but also the other's.

The smell of sickness filled the room. She rose from her bed and threw open the windows, letting the delicate breeze of the sea wash away what clung to the air from the breaths of last night. She fixed the sleeping youth with a sympathetic stare, which was all she was able to give him. The deep feelings of love had fled from her—even those toward her children—ever since her son Makari had returned to dust three years ago. As for Suleiman, he was delirious from the heat and blurted in his sleep, "I am Suleiman, son of Daoud, son of Issa: stay away from me, all of you! Keep away, or else!"

The fever had taken him away to those sprawling deserts where malicious youths wanted to tear him apart, though he did not know them or why they were lying in ambush for him. So all he could do was to lunge suddenly toward a young man among them who stood facing him. Suleiman signaled to the youth with his hand, his father's signet ring flashing before him with its red stone burning like a naked flame as his footsteps pounded the sand with surpassing speed. He was still advancing swiftly as though his toes barely touched the ground beneath him as he started to rise in the air gradually until he flew toward the disc of the sun, passing over the youth confronting him. Then he was propelled upward by the wind, though he could not bear the heat of the sun. He opened his little eyes to find his mother in front of him, looking sympathetically upon him as he raved with fever.

He begged her, "I'm thirsty, mama—I want to drink. My mouth is so dry. Imagine—I dreamt I was flying toward the sun!"

Daoud returned at noon to find Suleiman ill and bedridden. Elaine was crouched in the corner of the room, crying without cease. But he was annoyed that she had not thought to get a doctor or even to give the boy a tablet of aspirin. Within an hour the driver was on his way to the pharmacy to bring the medicine prescribed by the physician Daoud had summoned urgently. He felt as though a punishment from heaven had descended upon his house in payment for the grave offense that he had committed. Yet he felt even greater grief when he did not find anyone to complain to about his catastrophe and to beg for guidance as he was used to doing with his only friend, Sheikh Hassanein—the man he had brought back from Cairo—particularly after he had completed his mission today, pounding the last nail into his own coffin. Daoud went up to the roof of the mansion facing the sea and stopped in its center, bathing in the view of the pure blue sky of Alexandria and the dark, mysterious blue of the sea. He shouted as loud as he could, "O God of forgiveness! O God of pardon!"

He spent the rest of the day between going down to the bedroom to check on the youth's condition and up to the mansion's roof to scream and weep from the pain that wrung him like a winepress.

In the evening, Daoud remained vigilant on the roof, alone among the watchful stars scattered like diamond seeds in the glittering Alexandrian sky but for the diaphanous gown of clouds enshrouding the deep, magical night. Daoud kept pacing the roof from one end to the other, his eyes raised to the heavens, then toward the sea, whose darkened waters stretched outward until they met with the blackness of the sky at the horizon under the concealing wing of the night. Then back to the sky again, in wonder and supplication: *Oh Lord! How long will these feelings of guilt last?* Sorrow and dejection enfolded him, his tears glistening along the corners of his mouth. Daoud was unable that night and until the end of his life, no matter how much he tried, to rid himself completely of the stain of what he did with Qamar and of his betrayal of Sheikh Hassanein.

Yet it appeared that heavenly justice sided with Suleiman. When the sun rose the next morning, it was clear that the son did not inherit the sin of the father. The youth recovered his health despite the immense outrage his father had committed. Daoud rejoiced, as we all would, for it seems that among us, justice is the exception, not the rule.

Suleiman continued to grow more and more attached to his father as the degree of affection he showed him was greater than that he gave to the rest of his siblings. These feelings compensated for the ongoing aridity between Suleiman and his mother. Elaine did not neglect him as a mother, but her maternal feelings had seemingly dried up. Yes, they had dried up to the point that she no longer went beyond the limits of motherly responsibility in looking after her children and husband, a responsibility discharged with an obvious aptitude that everyone witnessed. As for love, she had been stingy with it—without meaning to be—toward them all since the death of Makari, as if he had taken her heart with him into the depths of the grave when he passed away. Nothing remained for her or for them but her mind, her native instincts as a mother, and her duties as a wife toward Daoud and as a mother toward the children.

After her husband's detention, Qamar sought immediately to divorce him. Instantly upon her divorce, which she obtained in record time due to the determination of those in charge to act against him as a member of the Muslim Brotherhood in deference to authority, the way looked clear to achieving her dream of marrying her beloved Daoud. Yet two obstacles stood in the way of her sweet aspiration: her friendship with Elaine and the difference in religion between her and Daoud. She grasped right away that if Daoud converted to Islam, he could solve both problems at the same time. While Qamar seldom gave much thought to anything, when an idea occurred to her that might solve one thing or another, it was usually the most extreme one conceivable. And if the solution to the particular problem seemed mad at times, she was prepared to carry it out without knowing how the idea had occurred to her in the first place. If she had thought on the problem for a hundred years, this solution would not have come to her. But it would be hard for Daoud to be satisfied with conversion to Islam, and she was unable to find another way out of their dilemma nor an easy way to introduce the idea. So she decided to leave the matter to resolve itself when she met him. She thought about these things while gazing on her own beauty and her svelte shape in the mirror as she pursed her lips, thinking in horror about Sheikh Hassanein, who did not acknowledge her true worth. Not like Daoud, who melted with passion whenever he found himself near her.

Qamar went out to get oil and sugar for the house, leaving her son Lutfi with the neighbors to play. She was struck with a feeling of freedom that she had missed for a long time. She walked down the narrow street between the same houses attached one after another. The same houses that had surrounded her home since her childhood, though their façades had peeled due to the salty air and humidity. The same neighbors' faces and the same storefronts stretching along both sides of the road. Their owners and businesses themselves had changed, for Hamid the clothes presser's was now Hussein the coffee seller's; Abbas the butcher's was now Lawandi the watchmaker's. The rest had maintained their original trades but had exchanged fathers for sons within their same crafts and businesses, young men and women filling the street with life—playing, shouting, laughing, crying, and running about everywhere.

She went into Rizq's spice shop. "Welcome, *Sitt* Qamar, rose of our neighborhood." Qamar smiled as piercing scents gushed from the array of stacked bags packed with seasoning seeds and spices. She stretched the tips of her fingers to gather leaves of mint, flowers of sweet basil, anis seeds, cumin, and fenugreek, and rubbed them between her fingers for no other reason than to bring them close to her nose and breathe in their fragrant scents. She let her eyes wander among them, appraising them, and bought half an ounce of nutmeg to grind with roast coffee beans to prepare Daoud's coffee in the way that he loved. She also bought paper cones of fenugreek and aniseed.

Was she still really the rose of the district? If so, was she that in his eyes? Qamar remembered her childhood, those days that did not seem so far behind her—how she had constantly led her peers in play and how she had been in the forefront whenever they met to have fun, especially during the festive nights of Ramadan. She had been at the head of the caravan of the district's children going around the houses with their lanterns that were lit with burning candles. They collected sweets and pastries, delicious almonds and nuts, while they sang their Ramadan melodies.

She passed the home of Amina Hilmi, with its old and cracked yellow walls and its complete calm and serenity. Amina was her childhood friend and her departed darling. She asked God to have mercy upon her, recalling the painful sting to her heart from the tram accident that had killed her. How sleep quarreled with her for months on end after that frightful event, especially since she had seen it with her own eyes as the two of them had been playing together—they were fourteen years old at that time—just before Amina had crossed the tram tracks in haste (May God have mercy on her) before she realized the tram was coming. That seemed long ago now. But in the end, Qamar was strong, enduring the catastrophe with her perseverance and stubbornness.

She grew to be a girl of proverbial firmness and commitment. The world also endowed her with a rare beauty and a comely figure; she became an object of desire for all the young men of the district.

Yet Sheikh Hassanein captured her at the threshold of her youth, encouraged by his connection to her father—may God have mercy on him—who leaped to marry her off to him owing to the dangers he saw coming in the gazes of the young men around her. Sheikh Hassanein married her when she was still a girl of sixteen, he in his mid-forties. From that day, between the walls of his house, she became merely a piece of the furniture without an opinion or a word to say; she was powerless. Qamar the intelligent leader vanished behind the walls, then lately behind the new barriers of clothing and veils whenever she emerged from the prison of their apartment. And he dared to strike her as well? It's not possible! She didn't want—nor was she yet able—to celebrate it, but still she praised her Lord that divorce had divided them forever.

One day, Daoud agreed to spend his evening in his flat in Moharram Bey. Qamar realized that quickly when she passed in front of his residence on her return from the market. She found the windows open. Glancing around furtively to be sure that no one saw her, she walked through the building's entrance without hesitation.

Three light raps on the door and she found herself in front of him. She fell into his arms in a warm embrace, and when Daoud tore her from him gently, he was in agony.

"I cannot, Qamar," he told her. "My sense of betrayal tortures me."

"It's over, *Si* Daoud," she informed him. "I'm divorced."

"Is that possible?" he asked her. "That quickly? How?"

"Through good people!"

"Through good people?"

"It's over! The past has gone where it belongs."

"So soon, like that? To become something in the past? How could you . . ."

"Say, how could he? Was it so little, what he did?"

Daoud bowed his head in silence. For a moment, he did not press her for an answer. Then he resumed without agitation.

"Right," he said. "Was it so little, what he did!" Then he vanished into an impenetrable silence.

Qamar did not cease contemplating his quiet. That silence enveloped him with an increasing fineness of feeling that revealed a new dimension to his manliness, which elevated and exalted her. It inflamed her emotions until she was unable to control her passionate feelings toward him. She rushed to throw herself again into his embrace, burning this time with desire to join completely with his body. Their oneness now had become complete, unhindered by fear of anyone, suspicion of betrayal, or torture of conscience. Since her feelings were truly decent, and she was innocent of the least bit of falsehood, her contagion spread—like a fever—to Daoud's body and into his heart. And thus, all resistance left him; at the same time, the happiness of ecstasy dissipated all doubt that what was between them could be treachery or sin.

She told him about her entire life, of her childhood and girlhood, about Amina Hilmi and Sheikh Hassanein, of anything and everything. Then, as love made her lips tremble and as if the earth swollen with molten lava was no longer able to retain its heat or stop itself from bubbling up from inside, the volcano erupted. Her heart burst with its blaze, and she could no longer remain calm.

"I can't do it!" she shouted. "I'm not able to describe to you how I feel! How I need you! I belong to you, Master Daoud—do with me what you will!"

Her green eyes overflowing with passionate love, she added, "It's up to you. With a single sign from you I am ready to live under your command for the rest of my life."

"I seek refuge in God, Qamar!" he exclaimed. "Under my command, how? When you are the greatest of ladies?"

"I don't want you to get me wrong," she explained. "But Mrs. Elaine, is, after all, like a big sister to me. I wouldn't wish her any ill, ever."

"I don't know what we'll do with this unfortunate one," he replied, "who all her life wouldn't hurt an ant! My God, she didn't deserve all of this!"

"Enough, then. Let's get married, Daoud—even in secret," she urged. "I am willing." Then Qamar fell silent, embarrassed that she had hurried to say these things, wondering what he might think of her—that she wanted to steal him from his wife.

After a moment, she continued, "In any case, whichever way you see it, Daoud."

"We get married? How's that? Aren't I married to Elaine, and not permitted to get married again? And what's with you? I tell you we don't want to upset her, then you want me to divorce her?"

"Who said anything about divorce?" said Qamar. "What we're doing now is called—I seek refuge in God—'betrayal,' Daoud, my sweetheart. That's what wears on your conscience with respect to Elaine. But if we got married, even in secret, then there is no betrayal or anything."

"Again, Qamar, you tell me, let's get married. But how, then?"

And here Qamar grasped that the decisive moment had come. In all innocence and trust, she had led him to it. Without prior planning or maneuvering on her part, it came. From her side, she had seized a unique opportunity. She leaned toward him, pressing her feminine charms strategically against his gray-haired chest, at which she played with her fingers while he laid on the bed next to her.

"Look, Daoud, my sweetheart," she whispered, "There's nothing for it but that you go to al-Azhar Mosque in Cairo and convert to Islam. Nobody but me would know, and later maybe we could marry privately—in Cairo also, because that would help keep it secret. That is, the contract—a mere piece of paper—would be just between you and I. To certify that we are married before our God, which would make it right. And I would be your wife and your servant all your life. And you could stay married to Elaine without feeling you are betraying her while you're with me."

Qamar thus laid all her cards on the table—without malice or ambiguity. Yet what she asked of him was hard for him to do—or at least not as easy as she suggested it would be. Moreover his worries were more difficult to dispel quickly.

"Again?" he thought to himself. "Should I rush down that road once more after all these years have heaped up behind me? Truly, I have never cared about that word, written on some piece of paper, in the line for religion. Really, my faith and my belief are engraved on the walls of my soul in letters of gold drawn on the innermost part of my body—the part that eyes never see, except the eyes of my heart."

"I thought," Daoud continued to reflect to himself, "that I had reached the end of that road because I had run through water and fire and experienced the fullness of life. I thought that I finally would find some rest! After my first two wives and their departure from me, then the responsibility for the children that Elaine had borne for me. And my livelihood—even the income that Sheikh Hassanein had cut off from me; the money came back, and its doors opened up for me!

"But could I really do it all again for the sake of another woman? A Jew, then a Christian, now a Muslim? And they all suddenly become my family and my people? What a farce! But I—who am I? What am I to them?"

*

Despite the beautiful clear weather in Alexandria's wonderful spring, the season of love and flirtation—the origin of life— he spent the day withdrawn into himself in his apartment, perplexed to his soul. In the midst of troubles, real feelings tend to go astray. He wondered if he really loved her or if it amounted to no more than a fling. Images of their past rendezvous appeared to him, and their memory kindled the thrill in his body all over again. At his age? Was it just the physical pleasure, then? No doubt his lust was the greater part of his attraction to her at the beginning of their relationship. How he longed to be near her—not only then, but now.

But is that all that was drawing him to her? These ideas raged madly within him. He could not make out the path before him. Thus, Daoud chose silence as a refuge and a stronghold in which to seek protection while he organized his thoughts to reach a decision.

CHAPTER ELEVEN

THE COLD OF NIGHT IN the desert is of a peculiar kind. There is no cold like it and no pain rivals it. It pierces the pores of the skin like a dagger, then gnaws and twists and settles not only in the flesh, but in the bones down to the marrow. Painful, cruel, without mercy.

Mohammed al-Buri sat alone in the tiny cell. His feet dangling over the edge of the iron bed frame, he leaned against the coldness of the cement wall and raised his crossed knees. He clutched them in his arms to his broad chest, trying to lighten the pain that pervaded his whole body. A sad spirit enshrouded him that he was unable, no matter how much strength he exerted, to remove. Tears streamed from his eyes as he stared fixedly at the vacant bed across from him—for Sheikh Hassanein had departed this world today, right in front of him.

No one noticed his death, as though he were a bug crushed underfoot or a lifeless beast. He was not so fortunate as to receive from those around him a hint of compassion or a feeling of guilt. Neither from the brutal guard nor from his bosses did the sarcastic smiles vanish for an instant except when these men slurped successive gulps of tea, only for the smiles to dance again upon their coarse lips while their curses and abuse pursued the rest of the prisoners.

The whips and clubs in the hands of the soldiers still burning its bodies with the fire of hell, the herd scattered to the ends of the yard, and Mohammed al-Buri scurried through throngs of prisoners, dazed by what was happening. Whiplashes chasing him, he lifted his glazed eyes toward the sergeant, who was forcefully gripping the back of Sheikh Hassanein's neck. He tried to get closer, but the bodies of the crowded prisoners, plus the guards and their sticks, prevented him. Shoving at the bodies around him with both hands to no avail, he screamed, his eyes fixed on a single object: the sheikh's head. With cruel brutality, the sergeant bashed it again and again against the building's cement wall, then let the sheikh fall to the ground, a motionless corpse.

That was all Mohammed al-Buri could see. In those moments, the yard, the soldiers, and the prisoners dissolved into nothing. All disappeared before him, yet he could still make out the face of the sheikh—his bulging eyes, the white of his skin, the red of the blood that had not yet dried, and the blue tint of death mixing with the cement wall's dust that covered everything, its presence pervasive. He stopped motionless, surrendering to the lashes of the whip as he cried in silence. Afterwards they brought a truck and carted Sheikh Hassanein's body outside the walls of the prison to bury him in the open desert around them. The pain still tore Mohammed al-Buri apart in his cell as the screams of torture came from every direction.

Fear gripped him as he muttered, "Nothing is fated for us but what God has written."

He had not forgotten his fright as he had sat, grimacing, in front of Sheikh Hassanein in the vehicle they were shoved into the back of at dawn a few days before. Surrounded by soldiers bristling with arms, they were both on the road to Cairo. There, the two of them were led to the governorate building first, then to the Interior Ministry, where they took their statements before driving them to what was termed "the Foreigners' Prison." They did not exchange a single word all the way due to the terror that seized them both. Despite the nearness of Sheikh Hassanein's scheduled release from detention, nonetheless, Mohammed al-Buri was gripped by a definite feeling that the trip would lead to evil consequences.

First, they were terrified by the sight of the frightening black gate. The car passed it on the way inside the walls of the prison, and a wave of anxiety struck them as they saw the prisoners—some fleeing and some falling to the ground—in their underclothes, whips in the hands of the soldiers who relentlessly pursued them without mercy. Mohammed did not forget the face of the aged Sheikh Hassanein at that moment: his terror had transformed into anger and agitation as he scowled ever harder, his face reddening until his eyes almost popped from his head. What could Mohammed do then but to try to calm him with soft words, as if he had foreseen the consequence of his anger and what had lain hidden from him in the following few days.

After his encounter with the officer in charge and the taking down of his personal information, Sheikh Hassanein was startled when the officer ordered him derisively to take off his clothes in front of everyone. When it became clear he was serious, he complied, revulsed and trembling with anger, never even having undressed in front of his wife in the privacy of their bedroom before. How could he order him to carry out that shameful deed in front of scores of strangers—and why? What crime had he committed to deserve such a punishment? He had not the slightest idea that what awaited him later would render this curse into a blessing and a fine welcome from his lordship, the officer!

The day started with a gathering in the prison yard. The prisoners—all in their underwear—were ordered, without regard to age, to run in columns, then to stop suddenly. Next, Sheikh Hassanein had to race, then squat before standing, and so on, in rapid succession. Violators were punished instantly by flogging at the hands of the surrounding soldiers. Then the music began with the chanting of a song by Umm

Kulthoum: "Oh Gamal, Oh example of patriotism". The officer commanded Sheikh Hassanein to stand indecently in front of the hundreds present—and take the microphone himself to sing that Umm Kulthoum song. Because the sheikh was a melodious Qur'an reciter who performed at parties, he was forced to entertain the Muslim Brothers held there together with his beautiful voice—or else. Meanwhile Sheikh Hassan al-Hodeibi, the Supreme Guide of the Brotherhood, was compelled to stand alone, clothed in blue, in the center. In his hands he held a stick, which he waved in front of him like an orchestra conductor, adding to the humiliation. After the singing of one verse, a debasing embarrassment settled over the Brethren. Muttering rose among them until one of them called out, "No reactionism and no Ikhwan! No trading of religions!"

Then, "Hassan al-Banna and Hassan II: they took a path against humanity!"

No one knew who called out this way, but all were forced to repeat the chant by order of the officer commanding the ranks. And here Sheikh Hassanein made the mistake of his life: he asked the officer seated in front of him, coarsely and sarcastically, just who was this Hassan II?

And what else would the officer do then but get up, raise his hand, and strike the massive man's cheek like a lightning bolt? But the sheikh's age had overtaken him: he staggered and nearly fell over. The officer leered in his face mockingly.

"You don't know who Hassan the Second is, you son of your mother? Come here, boy, and take down a written statement from this brave lad! The 'Second,' you innermost soul of your mother's heart, is Hassan al-Hodeibi. Do you know him—yes or no? Speak up, boy!"

Then the officer sat down again, fixing another sardonic stare upon Sheikh Hassanein.

"I know him, sir," the sheikh declared, his palm still raised over his cheek, which contempt had touched, whose stain he sought to remove. He was overcome by anger as his face still burned with the blow that he had received in front of all those present.

"Stand at attention, inmates! Name, age, and address." The sheikh's hand fell to his side, and he recited his answer dejectedly. The officer leaned back in his chair, crossing his arms over his chest, and questioned him mockingly.

"What is it you know, Hassanein, about Hassan al-Hodeibi?"

"He is the Supreme Guide of the Society of the Muslim Brothers, sir," the sheikh replied.

"And he is the one who killed the then-prime minister, al-Nuqrashi Pasha," the officer taunted, "after he came down from your mother's place, isn't that so?"

"No, sir, not him!" the sheikh stuttered as he rushed unthinkingly to respond. "I mean, I wanted to say I don't know. But Sheikh Hassan al-Hodeibi is a pious man, a great Islamic scholar. He has nothing to do with killing or anything like that."

"He is the one who tried to kill President Gamal Abdel-Nasser the night of 26 July," the officer taunted, "after he finished with your wife, Hassanein—isn't that right?"

The blood boiled in the sheikh's veins, but he took hold of himself at the last moment, answering excitedly, "If you please, sir!" (Silence.) "Stop it!" (Silence.) "Sir, Counselor al-Hodeibi is a great man. In my opinion it's not possible he did that!"

Enraged, the officer screamed in his face, "You think you're going to tell me your opinion on the subject, you son of a bitch?"

Sheikh Hassanein's anger was truly inflamed. This time he lost all control of himself. In an unexpected and hysterical movement, he launched his huge body at the officer without warning, knocking over his chair and throwing the man onto his back, his feet raised to the sky. The officer then summoned the soldiers around him, howling at them to grab that "son of a bitch" who dared to aggress against him while the prisoners laughed uproariously at the sight. One of the soldiers then pounced upon the elderly sheikh and carried out the deed to uphold the honor of his superior by satisfying his wish, a contented smile on his lips, as befitted any solid citizen who had executed his duty to the fullest extent.

This is how Sheikh Hassanein died, and in front of all those prisoners. With him perished their laughter, which suddenly fell from their faces, and all their dreams were murdered together. When the lowly soldier smashed his head, the triumph over the sheikh killed them all along with all their laughter and all their hopes. The power of the authorities had vanquished them—they were helpless in the face of it. Sheikh Hassanein had never been a boss or leader in his life, but his death elevated him to the stature of a hero and martyr to them. Despite their belief in him and his stance and though they had enfolded him in their embrace, he had passed away from them forever, none of them able to do anything about it.

Mohammed al-Buri wondered, under the thick darkness of his cell and the coldness of its walls, if he was now prepared to follow in the footsteps of Sheikh Hassanein should he be asked to do so.

Elaine insisted on enrolling Suleiman in the Saint Mark School in Chatby—a private Catholic school with high tuition. Daoud had now become wealthy, and it was right for him to give his son the best possible education. From his side, Daoud did not object, as he remained distracted by the idea of travel and departure from the country, perhaps to flee from his story with Qamar, which seemed to harass him, pressing down like a mountain on his chest. He was unable to sleep or preoccupy himself with work. Even the oud, singing, and serenading stirred no desire in him. Elaine noticed the change, yet she was used to not involving herself in his affairs if he did not open up to her first.

She deemed it wise to leave him and his business alone while she faithfully handled the affairs of the children and supervised the servants, from Abduh the cook to William the driver, and from 'Amm Hassan the gardener to Mrs. Nargis, governess or director of the household—she didn't know for sure—and wife of Mr. William! Despite the fact that she did not normally handle any of the household chores after she moved to the palace, she not only found that there wasn't enough time to take care of her daily concerns but also found herself spending less time with the children and with Daoud. In her new home, she felt like a lost woman, wandering daily from room to room or among the servants to tell them what to do or not to do while she searched for something—for the children or for her own self, which she had left in her old apartment or with Makari there in Moharram Bey.

And if she did meet one of her children, they would exchange words in the flush of coincidence in some hallway between the rooms on the upper floor, for example, or on one of the balconies, or in the great hall on the first floor as they came from outside or left the residence. Then they would trade disconnected words and incomplete sentences she would forget—and they would disremember with her—later to complete them during their following chance meetings. Meanwhile she grew more and more isolated, more and more stout, and even more apathetic. Gradually she lost her active nature, spending most of her time in her room on the upper floor, gorging on pastry and listening, on rare occasions, to songs on the radio by Umm Kulthoum and Abdel-Wahhab, and some by Abdel-Halim Hafiz. And she prayed that He might grant her peace and joy again.

But she did not forget the shelter of the Virgin that had witnessed the days of her childhood and youth—the days of real joy flowing within her heart and of true peace of the soul.

So she made cash gifts to the shelter and rendered it other aid in secret, that is, without revealing her identity. She feared embarrassment should they see her reveling in her fortunate circumstances, and perhaps that they would envy her easy lifestyle. Or—and this might have been closest to reality—perhaps she could not convince herself that she truly deserved this magical change of existence, especially as she did not gain happiness from it for herself or anyone else. Thus, she decided to send Suleiman to Saint Mark School and Layla and after her Mona to the E.G.C. School, otherwise known as the English School for Girls (which later changed its name to El-Nasr School for Girls). Her discrete donations to the shelter were perhaps the hidden cause—a secret enfolded unto eternity under the Divine Will—that had turned their lives upside down.

Sheikh Hassanein left a fatal vacuum behind him—a hole in the life of Daoud Abdel-Malek that neither work nor the affairs of life, like the running of the factory or shepherding of his family, could distract him from. It was as though there was a hole in the wall around his self through which the reasons for his happiness had leaked out. As a result, his heart now was never filled with joy nor his soul with contentment. He lit a cigarette as he walked, thinking that he still missed the friendship around music and late-night conversation that used to bind the two of them in work. He missed even the delight of carefully rolling a hashish cigarette, of which Sheikh Hassanein was a master. He produced them most beautifully—but also in competition with those of his rivals, during their nights out together. The sheikh had boasted proudly as he stood among them at their gatherings, holding the cigarette up between his fingers with love and tenderness.

"Make way, you brave ones, for 'The Bride!'" he would say—to be compared with the famous "Gray-Haired Lady," "Limping Lady," and "Sad Lady" that others ventured to roll in his presence.

Daoud found himself carrying his silent oud under his arm, heading toward Mahmoud al-Qirsh's café that Thursday to buy a piece of "hash" that he might use to fill the void that had come into his life, or perhaps he would chance upon Sheikh Hassanein sitting there once again.

Truth be told, they received him most beautifully. Indeed, Mahmoud al-Qirsh cried out to ask his serving boy, al-Hunn, that he put the chairs back inside the café to maintain their high spirits! *Al-Khawaga* Daoud showed up right on time as the people of taste, art, and leisure gathered in the café. He sat down with them, a smile painted on his face. He did not find his absent friend among them, so he began to fiddle with the silver ring around his finger. Then a voice issued from the radio in the heart of the coffee house, announcing the monthly performance by Umm Kulthoum. Daoud could not believe it had escaped him that today was the first Thursday of the month—the day on which she always promised a new song. Its opening verses were as follows:

The setting sun gilds the / Leaves of the date palms, O Nile
A work of art painted / On your surface, O beautiful one
The flute on the riverbank sings / And the figures sway
With the blowing of the wind / When it rolls gently

The voice of "The Lady" overwhelmed his being and cleansed him of all trace of his troubles. He soared high with her, then extended his legs beneath him and felt the ground beneath his feet once again. Once more, he felt empowered to cope with this life with all its contradictions—even if he acquired them all on his own.

Day after day passed by, yet she did not hear from Daoud. A feeling deep within her warned he would not return. Again and again, she passed by his house and gazed with passion toward his apartment; perhaps she'd catch sight of him. Or perhaps she saw a light emanating from within that brought hope back to her. Wrapped in a deep black shroud, the end of her relationship with Daoud loomed over her insistently while the gloom of her life kept growing. The idea of death appeared to her—from where, she did not know—over and over again. She proceeded slowly as she crossed the road. Perhaps the car coming would end her torments, but the blaring of car horns always frightened her, and she jumped away in terror at the last moment. However, she stopped one day over the tram tracks, confused when she glimpsed the ghost of her friend Amina smiling at her, waving her hand. The prolonged clanging of the tram's bell awoke her, and she scrambled for safety moments before being mangled under its wheels.

Yes, as the days went by, the same insistent thought continued to grow—that perhaps Daoud would never come back to her.

CHAPTER TWELVE

TIME WRAPS ITS FINGERS AROUND us, bringing friends together at times and splitting them apart at others. In Manshiya Square, too, in the middle of summer 1956—precisely on the evening of 26 July—a gentle breeze lightened the heat and added an element of gladness to the crowd. They had gathered here again as they had for the past two years—invited in advance this time along with select prominent individuals spread from government agencies, companies, and factories, spread throughout the crowd. In their midst was Daoud Abdel-Malek—yes, in reality this time, not in a fantasy like the one that had afflicted him two years earlier.

They assembled in the same square to receive their leader and commander, who would deliver his much-awaited speech on the twin anniversaries of the Revolution and the withdrawal of English troops from Egypt. Daoud had received an invitation from the syndicate representing labor in the person of Abdel-Hamid Mustafa, president of the Union of Young Workers, who worked in Daoud's factory. He always reminded Daoud of his son, Fouad, who had abandoned him for Israel years before. He no longer heard from Fouad, who had left behind him heartache over his absence, confusion, and mystery surrounding what had happened in his life. Gamal arrived in his splendid procession, surrounded by a storm of applause as he advanced toward the dais amid the loud cries of the masses. He began then to speak about the changes that had taken place in Egypt in recent years.

Daoud reflected on the changes in his personal life that had pained him during those same years. He thought about the people around him, seeing in their eyes that same joyous gleam that they all shared. He delighted in being among them, sharing with them that historical moment, as he later recognized it to be. At the end of his speech, Gamal announced the nationalization of the Suez Canal to turn it into an Egyptian company, to even louder cheers—but not from Daoud. For despite his personal admiration for Gamal, he was not able to prevent the lump in his throat when he thought about the likely revenge from France and England and where that revenge would lead this Revolution, which was still taking its first steps in running the affairs of the country. As Daoud stood up to clap with the others, he feared for the Revolution and its survival. He feared that the nationalist struggles in which he had participated with Abdel-Nasser Effendi and Sheikh Hassanein—for Egypt's sake—would fade into nothing. Perhaps this caused an inner tension within him because he applauded with less fervor and shouted with a lower voice than the rest of the crowd around him.

Next, Daoud was surprised by two bodyguards in military dress, walking side-by-side, as they approached him immediately after the speech ended. They flanked him by his shoulders, and one of them whispered in his ear that he should follow them. He walked obediently without hesitation and filed behind them in silence, not even wondering what he had done wrong because he doubted—or, rather, was certain in the bottom of his soul—that he indeed did not truly welcome that decision as he should have done. Yet he asked himself whether his conduct might have exposed his displeasure. How easy was it for them to train men like these to such a degree of competence that they would be able to detect the most trivial behavior revealing the ideas spinning in the heads of citizens? Alerted suddenly that they perhaps could now tell what he was thinking, and increase his punishment accordingly, he suddenly stopped his rumination.

They went into a room in an ordinary building in one of the apartment blocks surrounding Manshiya Square—or Mohammed Ali Square, as they then called it. Daoud entered first, then one of the two guards who had come with him entered while the other remained outside. It was a room in a medium-sized apartment, simply furnished as though it were that of a minor lawyer or public accountant. Darkness enfolded most of it. At the desk sat an officer, a lamp burning in front of him with a halo of light—the only source of light in the room—reflected on a sharp-featured face. The officer was writing on a big notebook in front of him. At first it appeared to Daoud that he knew him or had run into him before. Giving him a military salute, the guard that had come with him went out. And indeed, when the man seated before him stopped writing and raised his head in his direction, he recognized him immediately: Kamel Fayyad, Gamal Abdel-Nasser's friend whom he had met in San Stefano—that officer whom Gamal had introduced to him before the Revolution as head of the movement in Alexandria and Lower Egypt, as he recalled. He smiled a little, realizing how easily he could convince this man of his goodwill, affection, and respect for the president—which he had personally witnessed during their first meeting—even if Daoud indeed had refrained from clapping with the appropriate enthusiasm for the decision to nationalize the canal.

Daoud stopped in front of the desk, awaiting his invitation to sit on one of the wooden seats arrayed around him that appeared to be the kind rented from a consignment shop that specializes in weddings or funeral services. Their look made him remember his friend Sheikh Hassanein, whose shadow loomed before him. He wondered what his condition was in that moment. When the officer finally raised his head, turning toward him with a phony smile, he gestured to him, saying, "Please sit down, *Khawaga* Daoud."

He pressed a button in front of him, and the sound of a ring filled the room completely. The door opened, and Daoud was surprised to find out that the person whom the officer invited to enter was none other than his own young employee Abdel-Hamid Mustafa, the very one who had invited him to attend the President's address. As for Abdel-Hamid, he greeted the sitting officer with a military salute as well, then nodded gravely to Daoud, owner of the factory that he worked in, without opening his mouth to say a word. Afterward he took the seat across from Daoud and sat silently, gazing distractedly around at the officer, the papers in front of him, and the walls of the room. However, he avoided looking Daoud directly in the eye. A relative silence spread over the chamber for a fleeting instant but for the roar of the crowd coming from the direction of the square—until it was interrupted by Kamel Fayyad, who spoke in an official tone and aimed his words at Abdel-Hamid, who sat before him like a faithful dog facing his master, gazing at him in wait for any sign or gesture calling him to move from his place.

"We are very thankful, Abdel-Hamid," he said. "His Excellency Colonel Farouk al-Tabi'i will be in touch with you in two days to inform you of *al-Khawaga* Daoud's decision. Now you may take your leave. Go with safety." With that, Abdel-Hamid rose from his seat and saluted again, then turned to go out, also without looking at Daoud. The other officer again busied himself with writing some words in his notebook as the silence returned, which put Daoud on his guard. But its weighty continuation made him cut it off.

"What is the decision, your Excellency, that you mentioned to Abdel-Hamid?" he asked.

But Kamal Fayyad remained preoccupied briefly until he lifted his head from his notebook and said with a broad smile, "Your decision, of course, *Khawaga* Daoud!"

Shaking his head malevolently, he went back to his notebook. Daoud had wondered if the matter had anything to do with his feeble applause regarding nationalization. He continued wondering, filled with curiosity.

"Yeah—with respect to what, sir?"

Kamel Fayyad answered him immediately, as if to change the context of the conversation, "You don't remember me, Daoud?"

The man giggled with a high rude laugh, stood up, and walked around the desk until he came to the chair in which Abdel-Hamid had just sat. He sat down on it, still laughing as he directed his gaze toward Daoud, who was wearing a smile filled with confusion over what had prompted levity in the despicable words the man had been speaking.

He jibed in reply despite himself, "Of course, I remember you, sir. Lt. Colonel Kamel Fayyad, or now you might be a regimental commander. Very impressive!"

"Major General Kamel Fayyad, *Khawaga* Daoud," he answered. "'Regimental Commander' and 'Lt. Colonel' were the titles in those days, which are now over—aren't they?"

Daoud felt as if he were submitting to an officer conducting an investigation—unofficially, of course—for the functionary who normally would record what was said in interrogations was not in the room. But that sense of conflict and supremacy and an investigator's air of hostility filled the place, as did a feeling of impotence on the part of the accused that normally accompanies an official enquiry. He pulled out a package of cigarettes from his vest pocket, and—extending his head forward—asked with a look if he was allowed to smoke. But the man said with finality, "No, forget it. I actually have a cold and can't take the fumes."

Daoud noticed the cigarette pack thrown on the desk next to the ash tray filled with butts. He realized the matter was personal—that the man sought to incite his feelings and tighten the noose around him. But he refused to let him do that. It was thus an elaborate game, and he had to play it with skill, or lose! He wondered whether his disinterest towards the canal's nationalization was worth all that. But he remembered the question the man had posed to him before and calmly put the cigarette pack in his vest pocket, answering with a happy smile.

"Of course, Major General sir, those titles are from long ago. All of them have the odor of the past—they're all gone! Let's be done with the old days! They're all past and done! Because of that, it's called the Age of Extinction. The important thing is that we return to today. You haven't told me, your Excellency, the reason you have invited me here this evening nor what the decision I will tell Abdel-Hamid is all about?"

"About you, of course, *Khawaga.*"

"You call me—Daoud—that, sir? I am no foreigner."

"But everyone knows you're a foreigner, Daoud. Isn't that so, *Khawaga* Daoud?"

Recognizing the inflammatory intention behind his words, Daoud immediately chose to be silent and smiled. The subject was not the nationalization of the canal. Rather, Kamel Fayyad was laying a trap for him. He was putting pressure on him and his fellow Jews who remained in the country to leave. The confrontation between Egypt and Israel was getting closer, especially after the arms deal between Gamal Abdel-Nasser and Czechoslovakia. The presence of Jews in the land of Egypt had become a threat to national security due to the possibility of their recruitment to Israel's side. Especially after the famous Lavon affair—Pinhas Lavon, the Israeli Minister of Defense—which had filled the public's ears and the newspapers' headlines for days when bombs blew up at several branches of the post office in Alexandria on July 2, then at the American Cultural Centers in Alexandria and Cairo on July 14. Then followed the arrest of Philip Nathanson, an Egyptian Jew, after a bomb exploded in his pocket by mistake. It was revealed that Israeli intelligence undertook the operation with the help of Jewish Egyptians who were recruited particularly to carry out this operation. Immediately afterward, Lavon resigned from his position as Minister of Defense.

But in any case, neither did his Excellency Major General Fayyad nor any of the leadership taint that pressure with any hint of violence out of consideration for the Revolution's public image. As Daoud Abdel-Malek in particular was a friend of the president and of the president's father, it was necessary to treat him with all care and caution so as not to bring matters to a head. Hence, he said to him reprovingly, "You're angry—why? I'm just kidding you, man!"

This answer just incited him more, and he felt that the man was more adept at managing the game than he had calculated. Daoud followed then, agitation marching across his face.

"Isn't it easy to say?" he pressed him. "You can't even say my name—Daoud—without sticking 'Khawaga' in front of it. Honestly, sir, is this the face of a foreigner?"

He grabbed his own cheeks, squeezing them in his fingers, adding sarcastically with an irritable calm, "Look carefully and judge for yourself, your Excellency. I'll be satisfied with your judgement! Seriously, is this the look of a foreigner?" Yet Daoud grew more agitated from what he saw as the absurdity of his position.

The officer Kamel Fayyad, who had now become a major general in the Egyptian Army, laughed nervously, for he could not allow this human bug to behave this way in front of him, even if he were a friend of the president! He laughed again in the same high, harsh manner adulterated with the aroma of the countryside, of clay, of the dung of beasts—the laughter of the broad, open fields. This laughter danced over them until it faded in the distance, no echo returning from any wall surrounding them.

"Look now, Daoud Abdel-Malek," Kamel Fayyad replied, "you're an old man, my father's age. In all honesty, I want to help you—it's not easy for me to see you maltreated. If you want to leave the country as your relative, Binyuti Pasha, left it, maybe I can help you sell the factory in

Dekheila, the villa, the car—at a very good price. I can also get you passports for the whole family—except for Qamar (of course)—so that you can exit respected and honored, with your money in your pocket, able to live like a king outside of Egypt!"

He resumed his excited guffawing, its vile clamor filling the room, as he alternated between shrieking laughter and a melodious stammer.

"But only without Qamar! What is the night without Qamar! You, who left the stars of the world because of Qamar!"

Finally, Daoud understood the rules of the game: They wave before him their knowledge of all his affairs, both public and private, and they wrap it in an undertone of not only threats—but scandal! If only he would not insist on opposing them and submit to their wish that he leave the country! But what drove them to do something so disgraceful, and why insist that he go away? He did not know.

First, Sheikh Hassanein and the Muslim Brotherhood, now Kamel Fayyad and officers of the Revolution? It could not be possible that this decision came from Gamal Abdel-Nasser personally, for Daoud knew him well, and he would never approve of such a thing. No doubt he would have to confront him in person to know his opinion of the matter.

"Okay, give me a moment to think, Effendi," pleaded Daoud.

"Is a week enough?"

"A month, your Excellency Major General. It's not an easy matter at all. That's a difficult decision that requires a lot of planning. My destiny and the destiny of my children depend on it."

"And Qamar?" Kamel Fayyad resumed. "I mean, Mrs. Umm Lutfi. By the way, I'd like you to inform her that her husband, who divorced her—your friend, Hassanein al-Basri—has passed away."

What did he say? He died? But how? And why? It was as though Kamel Fayyad had read his mind while he continued his emotionless narrative as though recounting a story from a serial he had watched on television.

"It happened while he tried to escape from prison. The boys guarding the prison shot him dead. My condolences," he added, with a malicious smile and a sardonic wink. He then added ironically, "May your days be an extension of his," as he stood up and paced around his desk once more before sitting behind it to confront him again.

"I'm also told that Sheikh Hassanein was buried there in the desert at the government's expense, old boy! Go tell his wife at your convenience before she receives the letter we sent her in the mail. Alright, *Khawaga* Daoud, you have a month to think about it." He placed his palms down on the desk to indicate that his speech was finished and their meeting was over.

He died? Just like that wondered Daoud. *May God have mercy on you, Sheikh Hassanein, and on all your days too.*

Daoud asked leave to withdraw, holding back his tears as he exited lest they escape in front of this strange man. He fidgeted angrily with the silver signet ring on his finger, pondering whether it had lost its magical potency.

He died?

On the darkened stairs, Daoud—unable to suppress his feelings any longer—found himself sobbing, the tears flooding his face. He cried for Sheikh Hassanein, who had abandoned him. Then it did not take long before he cried for himself, for they had resolved that he, too, should go away.

The term of their sentences in Tora Penitentiary after judgement was passed against them was done. After the execution of a group of their leadership—Ouda, Farghali, and Hindawi—whom Daoud knew personally, his friend Sheikh Hassanein, and others whom he did not know, Mohammed al-Buri wept for them all for many long nights, feeling the

133

fearful void left by their departure from this world. He was then told that he and the other prisoners would be transferred from Tora to Kharga Prison in the middle of the Western Desert. Despite its being located in the wilderness nearly 240 kilometers from the city of Assiut, it was nonetheless considered an easy place from which to escape, being only a collection of tents surrounded by a barbed-wire fence. So, they had to be moved again to the high-security prison at Qena, like a herd of animals being driven from one slaughterhouse to another, waiting for their time to be butchered.

"Long live the Revolution!"

These thoughts distracted Mohammed al-Buri as he sat in his jam-packed prison cell, his entire body sticky with sweat. He squatted in a corner, eyes fixed on the only window in the crowded ward, his vision passing through its black iron bars toward the clear blue sky behind the prison building's walls. Every possible blemish that might have marked the sky was steamed away; any group of clouds fled northward from its scorching summer airs toward his splendid, beloved city that he sorely missed—Alexandria! There were his wife Zeinab and his three children—Mohammed, Mustafa, and his youngest, Mai. He smiled despite all the circumstances surrounding him, which not only weighed on him but also drove him to weep and become depressed, or even—God forbid—to seek relief in suicide. Regardless, he smiled when he thought of Mohammed, his oldest son, and what had happened to him before the officers had brought him here. He craned his neck and looked around him, as though selecting from among the prisoners the man who would savor it with him when he recounted his story with his eldest son.

But he had not found that chosen friend since Sheikh Hassanein had departed from him, leaving him alone: there was no one with whom to share his thoughts or meditations. He could do no more than to shut his eyes and daydream about what had happened when he had called his son Mohammed to follow him into the salon one morning as Eid al-Adha drew near. The feast sheep was penned in on a balcony attached to one of the rooms, munching its clover calmly as it awaited its fated end. The boy had come obediently to where his father was sitting on the gold-colored couch in the salon and sat down next to him. He patted his son on the shoulder, saying to him smilingly that he had enjoyed a luminous vision last night. The boy's eyes widened in astonishment even more as his father spoke of a brilliant winged angel sent by God— may He be exalted—who had visited him in a dream that had seemed to be a message from our Lord.

God had asked the father to sacrifice his son as he woke up in the morning. Therefore, he had invited young Mohammed to talk with him in the salon. His grin broadened when he recalled how his son withdrew from his seat with him, wondering innocently about whether the angel had told him exactly which of his sons he was to slaughter. He had answered immediately that it was his first-born son, of course. The youth had withdrawn further until he clung to the armrest of the couch, asking if the angel had mentioned his name directly. That is, had he really uttered the name Mohammed? Or maybe had he rather meant for him to slaughter Mustafa, who was always causing problems and angering his father? A broken laugh escaped Mohammed when he recalled how the boy had jumped off the couch when he had told him the angel had demanded that he slay Mohammed. The youngster had pushed open the door and left the salon. His wife, Zeinab, later told him that the boy had run toward the bedroom screaming in his little brother's face to get up immediately and follow him outside since their father had seen a vision to slaughter them both! Himself first, Mohammed had explained, "but inevitably he would butcher you too Mustafa, after me, because you are basically a demonic child—your mother's pampering has corrupted you. It seems as though the man has gone mad!" he had told him.

The two of them leapt up together and in the blink of an eye had left the apartment, disappearing into the surrounding streets, far from their father's knife, with which he had been ordered by his Lord to butcher them both. They did not come back to the house until *Usta* Salim, the clothes-presser, met them as he returned from delivering work on al-Kafahani Street and as they stood on the sidewalk watching a game of football being played on the street. Mohammed al-Buri smiled, thinking: What devilish children! By comparison with the little angel Mai. And what eyes Mai had! Her hair blowing wild as she ran from room to room with tripping, innocent steps in their apartment in al-Hadra, filling the place with mutterings of obscure words that only her brother Mohammed understood. Mohammed al-Buri smiled and smiled, then guffawed, the eyes of the brothers around him followed him, amazed at his laughter amid that despair that enveloped them, beseeching with their prayers that the High and Exalted One preserve him from madness.

It had all vanished entirely as he shook from his mind the rotten smell of the bodies around him, which had not been washed or even near water for three days. Those blue overalls distorted by circles of sweat rimmed with white fringes of dried salt; those faces, eyelashes, heads, beards, and bodies clad in dust, which settled over them as their sluggish steps on the barren desert ground raised a squalid halo of dirt around them—the dirt over which they were driven throughout their arduous journey, including during the transfers between trucks and trains, over the last twenty-four hours. With the power of the creative artist, he replaced it all by imagining the sand and dancing waves of the beach at Sidi Bishr that he loved so well, its breezes bearing the bracing scent of the sea in their folds, which flowed over the dancing waves at sunset as he stood with his brushes in hand, painting and painting and painting, his nose and chest filled with a long breath of fresh air. It all ended suddenly with a sharp wave of coughing combined with a feeling of nausea that brought tears to his cheeks.

He decided to revolt against that reality: to do the most he could do to change it, without exposing himself to the violence and brutality of the jailers. He decided to resume his painting! Though he was not able to get closer to the dream himself, it was fitting for the dream to come to him at the spot where he huddled. Even in Qena!

"Mail!"

The roughness of the cry accompanying the knocks at the door distracted Qamar from slicing the onion in her hand. She wiped away the tears caused by the radiating smell with the tail of the house gown she wore and headed toward the door of the flat to investigate. Just as we sometimes sense fear we do not understand regarding some incident or encounter, Qamar felt an unease that seemed normal at first but which grew to torment her. But she had mumbled to herself for the past two days, saying "Well—may God make it all well!" with each knock on the door and each cry of the children playing in the street in front of their house. Each time she heard the noise of a car backfiring from the direction of Market Street or the sound of its wheels screeching over the road, she would sigh and say, "May God make it all well!"

Last night had been filled with disturbing nightmares that made her cry out in bed many times over. She had blamed that on the plate of okra sprinkled with garlic that she had eaten just before going to sleep despite her mother's warning about eating it then and despite that inner voice that kept repeating its warning to her, which she did not heed! Not yet ready to ask this question of herself she also wondered about Daoud—why did she no longer hear from him? For a week or more she had not seen him or any sign of him— not even a light in his apartment when she passed it tens of times on her way to buy her household needs over the past few days—until she nearly went mad! But perhaps because nothing had happened to confirm her apprehensions over the past two days, Qamar told herself not to pay attention to those voices of the whispering devil in her head as she wiped her hand with her robe then stretched out her hand for the doorknob, as she kept saying in a frightened tone, "Well! May God make it all well!"

"Good morning—Mrs. Qamar Hassan al-Sukkari?" said a tall, thin young man with a pleasant smile that lent a humanity and grace to his official uniform; his cap, with its cheap, shiny plastic brim, was pushed back on his head. Indeed, he looked more like a train conductor than an officer from a police station. He carried a leather bag full of papers and letters pressed in a binder: its sides gleamed when he opened its folding flap to pull out the wide, tattered notebook covered in a tall, expansive script, then a sheet of black carbon paper, which he placed with intense care between two pages of the notebook.

"Yes, brother, I'm Qamar. Is everything alright?"

He handed her an envelope covered in stamps and official seals. It was as if the authorities had determined they could get nothing more out of concealing it any longer and had finally decided to give it to her.

"Please sign that you received it here," the man said. "Or do you want to place your fingerprint instead?" He pointed to the bottom of the page and the end of a line, at the start of which Qamar read her name. She grasped the pen and wrote her tripartite name (given, father's, and grandfather's). Then he took the notebook back from her and asked for the number of her identification card, but she did not carry one. He inscribed that information in his notebook and replaced it in his bag, first putting back its cover and closing its two sides with deliberation before patting it twice gently, announcing that his mission was completed. He smiled cautiously, but when he realized he would not be rewarded with a tip, he turned about and descended the stairs, hurrying to carry out his next assignment.

She pulled out one of the chairs arrayed around the dinner table at the opposite side from where she had been sitting as she had chopped the onions and sliced the vegetables to prepare food for lunch. She sat down to open the envelope with the letter, shuddering as she muttered, "In the name of God, the Beneficent, the Merciful." Slowly and silently, she read each letter of the missive addressed to her from the Interior Ministry, which bore the signature of Major General So-and-So, chief of the Prisons Authority, offering condolences with all regret for the death of her divorced husband, Sheikh Hassanein.

"He died? No—rather, he was killed. Sheikh Hassanein would never flee, ever. They killed him! No one killed him but me. I am the one who killed him. Me! I am the one who pushed al-Khawaga Daoud to complain about him to the government because he had beaten me!"

These thoughts overwhelmed Qamar's mind—she could not control them. In the flood of depression in whose depths she swam for days, she did not dare defend herself against the charge of murder but rather surrendered to an overwhelming current that was sweeping her to an unknown fate. She cried and cried and cried until her tears dried in her eyes. First, she cried for Sheikh Hassanein, because she had killed him! Yes, she had killed him. A black cloud descended, and it felt as though the sky had wrapped itself around her from the top of her head to the soles of her feet. She could not escape its grip. An extraordinary sadness seized her spirit and she cried again: she found she could not stop. A whirlwind of weeping and sadness took control of all her feelings. Rather than regaining her composure, she found herself not only suddenly slipping but surrendering herself to a swift descent into that deep hole toward which she had begun to incline. She began to summon the face of Amina Hilmi, her lifelong friend, as Qamar had followed behind her, screaming for Amina to stop—to turn and notice the coming train—screaming and screaming. Meanwhile, Amina was flying like a madwoman toward an obscure cry that urged her *not* to stop and rather look at the iron wheels with their metallic clatter. Meanwhile Qamar's screaming drove Amina forward, her beautiful face turned behind her. Looking backward but frozen in place—fixed with a magical force like a magnet pulling Amina toward it, wearing that ambiguous smile that she had directed toward Qamar as if promising her that their secret would remain hidden forever!

Yes, their secret, which had for so long deprived them both of sleep! For how can one of them face the normal life expected of her while she pines away for the other? After all the kisses and touching and embraces and quivering of fever-ish love that had afflicted them for so many years whenever they were alone together, for long hours and nights. They had pledged to one another amorously, time and time again, that their love would remain secret for eternity.

A frightful feeling had afflicted them—a combination of the fear of scandal, if any part of their secret leaked to their families or their neighbors, and the torment of the Hellfire to come. That was the least of what they had anticipated from the One Almighty God's anger in view of that sinfulness and debauchery they were engaged in. On the other hand, their secret, free-spirited, unique, impetuous emotional relation-ship granted the two teenage girls their only emotional outlet. It began suddenly, their hearts trembling with love, and that brought with it the ecstasy of being near the beloved—the yearning to meet her—but also the tension and anxiety over her absence and estrangement. Such emotions were impossi-ble for them to share even with a youth of the opposite sex, given the solid sense of propriety that both their families shared. And with their increasing closeness, as they explored the consequences of playing with fire, they were completely engulfed by it. Their feelings turned into a mad, raging love that roiled both their lives. Qamar was certain that burden had weighed heavily on Amina's delicate heart. She could not bear the life hidden within her any longer! Yes, their secret was engraved in their hearts, yet it remained concealed from the rest of the world for eternity. Still, Qamar, despite all those years that kept passing, could not forget Amina's face imprinted with that dear, inviting smile, the smile when her time stopped and all was surrendered.

Qamar was never able to erase the crime. That pang that she felt at the time and that afflicted her now had come back to her repeatedly over the years—the pang of her responsibility for the death of Amina, her sweetheart. She likewise felt the same pang over the death of her husband, Sheikh Hassanein. She had killed Amina at the time that she had loved her and bewitched her with her burning emotion. At the time Qamar shouted to her to watch out, Amina had turned toward Qamar's voice instead of looking at the train coming in her direction, instead of surviving! Then Qamar had killed her husband by asking her lover to kill him for her. And so, she was his murderer, first and last—for Daoud would not have wanted to harm him but for her. She had killed him! If she kept on this way, how many more victims would she have? Wouldn't she have killed Mrs. Elaine, the benevolent princess to whom she was attached and felt affection for but whom she had humiliated by snatching her husband from her, and Lutfi, her son, after she had thrown his father into ruin—then left him, too, in search of a new husband.

Murderess! Murderess! The killer is killed in the end!

Those voices echoed in her head without cease, without mercy or sympathy.

Abruptly Qamar leapt up from her chair, pushing it behind her with the back of her thigh, and it fell over. She headed toward the kitchen, then bent down on her knees below the sink and lifted the cloth curtain around its base and withdrew the brown bottle of phenol she used for cleaning. She grasped it with all her strength, then stood up again.

She remained standing for some moments like one in a trance, then turned and left the kitchen. She went toward the bedroom where her son Lutfi lay napping on the edge of the bed next to the wall. She leaned toward him and kissed him tenderly so as not to wake him. Qamar sat at the end of the bed, surrendering to the clouds of oblivion that enveloped her—a wave of pleasure with which that oblivion swathed her and that she made no effort to avoid. She was not thinking of anything in particular. She no longer saw things around her clearly, as if a cloud of mist had enveloped the room. Without warning she brought the bottle to her lips and swallowed all of it to the last drop as if it were a bottle of carbonated soda. Then she firmly replaced its cap before putting the empty bottle on top of the nightstand next to her. She looked at it questioningly, then lifted her legs, swiveling them over the bed to lie next to Lutfi. Gazing at him one last time, she attempted a smile, and closed her eyes.

A tall building appeared to her. She hurried toward its entrance, then strolled submissively and began to mount the marble staircase. Marveling at its grandeur, she was amazed at the high spiraling structure in the middle of the building. Suddenly the electricity in the area was shut off and darkness fell everywhere. Qamar clung with her hands to the railing, climbing in complete darkness, unable to see any of the features around her. She began to feel fatigue mixed with despair that she would reach the end of her ascent until the face of a woman appeared, its surface just about illuminated with the light of a candle that danced in her hand. She opened the door of an apartment on one of the floors that she passed on her way up. The lady, whose familiar features looked so very like her mother's, though she was much younger, stepped forward. She stretched out the hand that held the candle and gave it to Qamar. She smiled but did not speak. Yet a draft blew out the candle, extinguishing the light reflecting on her face, and she vanished. That sight was enough to reassure Qamar as she continued to ascend. She had ceased to feel tired, so she raced up the stairs, driven by a childish curiosity to learn where this spiral staircase led. The sound of Daoud's singing and oud-playing flowed whispering from afar, and she thought the electric current returned to light up a lamp hanging from the highest point in the building. She lifted her head toward it, but she could not make out its details as it was still too far away. Yet the reflection of its calm light on the walls was reassuring as it spread confidence and peace in her heart, encouraging her to continue to ascend towards the lantern suspended from the building's summit. The nearer she came to the top, the sharper was the edge of that dazzling circle of light from whose singular brilliance and luminosity she was unable to escape, and the more could she make out the features of her surroundings.

Perhaps these vague scenes were the last thing to stick to her memory.

CHAPTER THIRTEEN

GRAY SKIES RETURNED TO ALEXANDRIA, warning of the end of summer—its sweltering hot days and fresh, delightful evenings—at the advent of autumn. But this year the fall had a very special flavor: a tightly-woven blend of colocynth and honey just as the warm days were followed by cool ones, clouds gathering and winds coming from the north.

From the north came a new disaster as well.

Squadrons of British and French planes soared in the sky over the area of the Suez Canal. At the canal's head, a hail of soldiers with humungous parachutes hovered in the heart of the sky, expelled from the bellies of giant aircraft circling above the city of Port Said. Meanwhile, from the east, Israeli soldiers and tanks marched onward, spreading over the Sinai desert supported by a curtain of aerial bombardment, the two advancing in tandem until they covered the whole of Egypt east of Suez. A catastrophe! No—rather, an international farce in the guise of a military operation of great magnitude in response to Gamal Abdel-Nasser's heroic step in nationalizing the canal. The bitterness of the colocynth . . .

What about the honey, then?

The honey came in the death-defiance of the people of the city of Port Said. They rushed to the defense of their country with sticks and bricks, with hearts full of love for their nation, with bravery and heroism from which only death would deter them. Yes, such a spontaneous movement of popular resistance naturally has the taste of honey! It was not the purest of honey, to be sure—they did not achieve over-all victory by any means. Instead, the newspapers and radios extolled the struggle and the stubbornness of the people of Port Said who had beaten back the attack of the aggressors. For it is not really courage at all when the mouse confronts the lion, hoping to savor his reward afterward.

The passing days showed that Daoud was right to fear the punishment for the decision to nationalize the Canal that Gamal had announced at Manshiya and that would imperil the revolution and Egypt. None of those who died in Port Said at the hands of the French and the English or in Sinai at the hands of the Israelis deserved to perish that way. The death-defiance of the rest of them did not bring the war to a halt: it only ended with the personal inter-vention of Eisenhower—the American president—who ordered the allies to withdraw immediately. He did not do so because he was a man of great principles but rather to prevent the spread of communism in the region, which had already begun in earnest with Bulganin's threats to France and England. But in any case, that crisis was the first confir-mation of the growing popularity of the Revolution and of Gamal Abdel-Nasser—its leader and commander—in the hearts of the people. The battle of Port Said had succeeded in demonstrating that success.

These thoughts had wandered through Daoud's mind during his walk when he snapped out of them to realize he had not spoken to anyone for four days. Yes, the last time he could remember saying a word was the previous Monday. He smiled at the thought. Then he thought of Qamar and reproached himself because he for two weeks had not asked about her nor had he gone to his apartment in Moharram Bey.

What could be going through her mind about me now? he won-dered. *A man like other men; he takes what he wants from a woman, then gets rid of her.* But he was not like that—he was not like all other men. He would go to her and explain everything until she understood his point of view.

Daoud Abdel-Malek continued to wander aimlessly down the Alexandria Corniche on that warm autumn morning. Autumn was the dearest season to his heart, when his city shed its summer garments and returned to being a quiet, enchanting coastal town after the uproar and hubbub of the summer revelers subsided. He had not gone to the factory for four days—since the visit of Abdel-Hamid Mustafa in his office last Monday. Daoud had completed his meeting with the head of accounting, who had informed him that profits had started to rise after they had declined with the transfer of management from the pasha's hands to his. Through his persistence and intelligence—and the help of a handful of his faithful friends—Daoud had seen the reasons for the drop in production and grasped them quickly, and the rate of payments and their returns had risen again. Then came the sound of knocking. Peering through the door that stood ajar was the face of Abdel-Hamid, who no sooner had seen that Daoud was alone than he immediately entered the office and closed the door behind him.

He said he was carrying a message for Daoud from above! Daoud looked derisively toward the room's ceiling and asked Abdel-Hamid about that "above." He answered haughtily and with disdain that he was sent by Major General Kamel Fayyad personally. That was exactly as Daoud had expected. When he asked what the letter contained, the youth replied—insolently this time—that the major general himself wanted Daoud to finally give up his ownership of the factory in the interest of the Workers' Committee. Daoud smiled at their shared insolence—the major general dispatching the message, and the messenger delivering it—and he then asked sarcastically, what would oblige him to do that? To which Abdel-Hamid responded confidently that the factory did not belong to him in any case. Rather, it was the property of the people since the glorious 1952

Revolution had ordered the cleansing of the national finances of the feudalists and the return of their property to the people. As the factory had belonged to Binyuti Pasha, one of the feudal lords of the country, it therefore followed that their possessions belonged to the Revolution and the people.

Daoud replied, exerting every effort to maintain his calm and composure, that since Binyuti Pasha had sold the factory to him in a binding contract, he was its real owner—and given that he was not a bigshot feudal lord, they did not have the right to demand it from him. Daoud believed that his answer was appropriate since perhaps his Excellency the Major General who had sent the messenger did not know that his ownership of the factory was backed by a reliable bill of sale. Yet Abdel-Hamid surprised him with a level of insolence he had not expected when he asked about the source of the money that Daoud had used to buy a factory valued at LE 50,000. Or had someone been interested in loaning him the amount with his position as security, for example? He said this as he chuckled sarcastically—the same laughter that his boss the major general displayed to Daoud the other day. Abdel-Hamid asked about the number of weddings, birthdays, and christenings at which Daoud had to perform to enable him to gather the money. Or whether he was forced to pawn his oud and with the profits had bought a factory for LE 50,000! Insolence and rudeness without end! As Abdel-Hamid's impudent guffaw filled the room, Daoud promptly leapt up from his chair and threw him out of his office—after he gave him a message to his boss: "Tell his Excellency the Major General, for the sake of his health, to stay out of my way. Instead, he should look for someone he can actually boss around." He was daring him to do whatever he could to him.

Yet that encounter really affected Daoud. His patience in waiting for another meeting with Gamal was almost exhausted. Those words had been the last he uttered before his four days of silence.

During his walk on the Corniche, Daoud began to suspect that there were footsteps following him. They came up behind him, falling in rhythm with his own. He paid them no heed at first, ignoring them completely and forgetting them amid the crowd of thoughts raging in his mind. But the insistence of the steps and the way they closely followed his began to annoy him, so he decided to quicken his pace. He hoped that his speed would divert his companion, but he kept up. Then Daoud stopped, wheeling about defiantly, and found a young man standing in front of him. He did not know him, and the youth did not display any emotion toward him. He was nearly featureless and impassive as if he were a ghost or a figment of the imagination. The young man stood facing Daoud in silence, without turning away in avoidance, as if he had been ordered just to follow Daoud but those who did so had forgotten to tell him what to do when he caught up with him.

When he remained mute, Daoud asked, "Yes? Can I help you?"

It occurred to him that these were the first words he had uttered in four days. The youth did not answer at first, but after a few moments, he seemed to suddenly remember the message he was carrying.

With a hollow, hoarse voice like that of a youth on the verge of adolescence, he blurted, "Sheikh Foda requests to see you."

Daoud remembered the name right away. He was the man who caused his friend Sheikh Hassanein to lose his direction, leading to prison and death. This thought made Daoud shudder, so he asked, "Why does he want to see me? And who are you, anyway?"

Here the youth was emboldened, his raspy voice rising as he seemed to find himself treading familiar ground.

"Who I am is not important, *Khawaga* Daoud," he rejoined. "You may regard me as the sheikh's messenger, sent to deliver a message to you. But if you'd like, I could maybe tell you that

I'm Maged Abdel-Hamid or Gaber Mahmoud Ateya or some other name. It would make no difference because the message is always more important. As for your question—why Sheikh Foda wants to see you—what's between the sheikh and you is too big a subject for me, a mere messenger, to know about."

"Alright then, that's enough," answered Daoud. "Don't shadow me anymore and let me think about it. I'll find a way to reply to Sheikh Foda."

He drew a pack of cigarettes out of his pocket and lit one of them.

"You'll think about what, *Khawaga* Daoud?" the young man shot back. "Our master Sheikh Foda wants to meet with you right now. He sent me to get you and bring you to him. Sheikh Foda is a man who is all blessing: his acquaintance is a gain, not a loss. Just put your trust in God and come along now!"

"Good morning children, my name is Monsieur Nathan, your class teacher this year. I will always be at your side like a father you can turn to at any time. Perhaps you'll find my language strange. But it is our Arabic language that we will speak during the Arabic language period until we learn its correct grammar, just as we speak the French language in other class periods so that you may learn it too. And now we will begin our first lessons in the Arabic language with its first letter: the *alif.* It's made with a vertical stroke, like so," he said. Grasping a piece of chalk, he drew an *alif* on the surface of a green writing board.

The child Suleiman threw a fleeting glance toward his new friend, Yusuf. These strange words falling upon him had aroused his curiosity, and he found that Yusuf, like himself, was trying hard to stifle his laughter. He turned rapidly forward before his laughter escaped despite himself. He may have deserved the anger of *Monsieur* Nathan, who went back and forth waving a long stick in his hand in front of him. Its length, crookedness, and pitch-black color made it resemble a crime boss's cudgel. It seemed out of place next to his elegant English wool suit and vest, from which hung a gold chain that ended with a watch that fit into a little pocket. He pulled it out many times to look at it as he addressed them. He spoke in this formal Arabic language, which differed completely from that with which his mother, William the driver, Abduh the cook, or Hassan the gardener spoke with him. A language new to his little ears and a new world in which he was taking his first steps, filling him with a passion to discover that world's secrets.

"We will begin with three words beginning with the letter *alif*," said *Monsieur* Nathan. Then he wrote as he spoke each word he was writing: "*Aqra'u* (I read), *afhamu* (I understand), *a'malu* (I work / I do)."

"The letters of the alphabet are the keys to the language: they beckon you to enter their world by reading them," *Monsieur* Nathan explained. "It must be accompanied by comprehension of what you read until you are able to reproduce what you have read. Understood? And now, who among you is able to present us with another word that begins with the letter *alif?*"

This is how Suleiman spent his first day in the School of St. Mark. A beautiful child, he had inherited his mother's looks and clear skin; he had inherited his intelligence and rapid intuition from his father. On his sweet face, there were the lines of a pleasant smile as his wide, honey-colored eyes roamed silently in that new world he was thrust into. He did not cry as did the rest of the children when their mothers dropped them off at the school's iron gate. Rather, he felt a pleasurable sense of curiosity and desire for discovery.

He was drawn to that huge number of children, whose crowdedness and tumult when they gathered on the school grounds for the first time in their identical uniforms reminded him of his family's old apartment in Moharram Bey. They were scattered around at first, then at the frightening ringing of the brass bell, they filled the square, through which passed instructions in a loud voice coming from loudspeakers in an unknown place. Suleiman walked on the tiptoes of his tiny feet, trying again and again to pinpoint its source to no avail. Therefore, he thought at first it was the voice of God, through which He had spoken to Moses on Mount Sinai, as his father had told him about—that divine voice of legal authority and influence, directing them however He willed. Then that huge assembly of children surprised Suleiman by beginning to move automatically to carry out the instructions to the letter. These strangers differed so in color and features that he doubted they spoke the same language: Suleiman was dazzled that they had organized themselves into columns under the influence of the voice's magical power. At the head of each stood the teacher of that class, carrying a colored emblem; they distributed a sign of the same color to all their pupils. Still that loud voice resounded, then it began to speak in a very strange language. Suleiman knew afterward that it was French—even the Arabic the voice had spoken at first was sometimes difficult for him to comprehend as some parts of words were missing. Meanwhile, the voice's echo rebounded from the giant walls of the school that surrounded the grounds like mausoleums waiting in silence for the moment when they might gulp all the children, with their innocent faces, into their belly. His eyes grew wider and wider and gleamed brighter and brighter as the smile broadened on his face, the rays of the rosy morning sun beaming on both his cheeks.

It was nearing 7:30 in the evening, and the cell was lined with oil paintings set on the floor, leaning against the walls in despair; in the paintings were the sad eyes of the sellers of oil-cooked broad beans, of children playing, of a man crouched on the Corniche behind a fishhook whose tip was immersed in the sea as he awaited its bounty. Eyes and faces that looked out from every corner, inquiring about their fate. Mohammed al-Buri sat on the edge of his iron bed searching for answers, his thoughts confused. He rose from his seat and spread a piece of cloth over the floor of the cell. He placed it in the direction of Mecca and prepared to perform the sunset prayer. He would carry out the ablutions before prayer once per day in the few moments granted them to use the sole bathroom on the entire floor. Afterward he was keen to avoid touching anything the whole day to preserve his cleanness so that he could perform all five prayers without needing to repeat the ritual beforehand. This practice alone occupied a great part of his mind and, as strange as it sounds, he considered it a great help in passing the time—the utmost punishment that pained his soul while in prison.

Time stood before him, like one of the great stone blocks on the beach of Sidi Bishr. He struggled from the first rays of the sun in the morning to the last in the evening to move it in his cell—a life and death struggle that sapped every drop of his vitality. All to shift that stone of time. A journey that began when he opened his eyes before dawn and did not end until he dropped down to sleep at the end of the day, only to recur again the next. With the repetition of the task and the numbing sameness of the days, he lost his sense of time. Perhaps he did so to avoid going mad!

He heard a light knock at the door, which was then opened to reveal the face of Sergeant Higazi, who announced, "You have guests, *Si* Mohammed."

He withdrew from the cell's entrance to clear a path for a strange man to come in and closed the door behind him—a prisoner, like himself, dressed in blue overalls. He was tall, with a bald head and a well-trimmed beard and mustache, plus an imposing nose that filled his entire visage. On it rested a thick pair of glasses that a less daunting structure might not have supported. He entered preceded by a hand outstretched in greeting, his belly shaking before him, and what looked like a smile on his face.

"Good evening, Mister Buri," he began, "I am Rashad Fikri, your fellow inmate in the wing next door. Since I am a writer and a poet, as you may know, sir, the others have told me about your paintings. I have come over to get acquainted with you and your work."

He heard the man talking to him, but—since he was still trapped in obliterating despair—the words passed him by without effect. Not finding any desire to comment on the man's words or even return his greeting, Mohammed remained silent, though he still took the man's hand to shake it in turn with an involuntary movement devoid of any feeling. The one called Rashad Fikri kept roaming around the cell, his arms crossed over his chest, nodding his head thoughtfully at the paintings lying quietly on the floor. He stopped in front of some of them, his fingers stroking his beard, muttering unintelligible words, then resumed his tour, going around again and again. He did this several times until he had examined each one four or five times. Sheikh al-Buri stared at him without even trying to stand up out of respect. Then Rashad Fikri spoke in his deep, quiet voice.

"Beautiful—everyone should see this work, Mister Buri."

Despite the fact that autumn had arrived—officially, at least—Qena was still languishing in the dog days of summer, as attested by the sticky heat and humidity that surrounded them. Yet despite the frigid winds blowing inside him—from where, he did not know—his soul and spirit had caught fire within him. The words that fell on his ears aroused him, if only temporarily, from his dark mental absence. But with all that, he wondered suspiciously about just who was this Rashad Fikri could be. And why did he call him "Buri" and not Mohammed al-Buri like everyone else?

CHAPTER FOURTEEN

DAOUD WALKED NEXT TO THE peculiar young man in silence. He watched him out of the corner of his eye as he turned from Fouad Street to a narrow street branching from the main road. Daoud still wondered what motivated him to follow the stranger to this unknown place surrounded by a suspicious hush. And who was guaranteeing his safety during this journey toward a mysterious goal? Yet he was curious to meet Sheikh Foda and to know why he had asked to see him in the first place. Clouds gathered overhead, laying a dark gray color over the people and things around him, increasing his apprehension. Midway on the route, the young man went ahead of him a couple of steps, then ducked into one of the shops.

"Peace be upon you!" he said, laughing. "The entrusted delivery has arrived!"

Daoud followed him inside the shop. The youth's voice echoed in its emptiness as he sat down in a wooden chair placed next to a green wall, the center of which was decorated with a Qur'anic verse in gold script that read, "Surely, We have granted you a clear victory."

As he stood there, Daoud quickly saw this was an apartment broker's shop. Two men were discussing a three-room apartment that one of them wished to rent. Then a young man came in, greeting those present, and they all muttered their replies.

Stretching his hand out to shake Daoud's, the youth said

confidently, "Let's go—the sheikh is waiting for us."

Daoud looked toward the young man who had brought him. With a wave, to him, the lad rose suddenly from his chair and headed back to Fouad Street. Meanwhile, the newcomer's gaze fixed on Daoud as he inspected him with a smile. Then he resumed speaking.

"Shall we go?" he asked.

He was a pleasant young man, younger than the first one, and his wide, dark eyes gleamed with an intelligence that distinguished him from his colleague. He was, also unlike the other, talkative. They had hardly left the shop when he said, "Is it true, *Khawaga* Daoud, that you are a Jew?"

Daoud looked at him, smiling at his bluntness in posing the question.

"Very well," he answered. "Aren't you going to start by telling me your name?"

"My name is Hadi Mustafa Darwish," he answered. "Of course, you're going to say, as people always do, that I don't look *hadi* (quiet) at all. But that is my name. Anyway, most people call me Dido."

"And how old are you, Dido?" asked Daoud.

"Nineteen, sir. And you?"

"I'm about fifty-two and a bit," answered Daoud. "Do we have much further to go?"

The pair had already crossed Cairo Station Square and turned toward a narrow street lined on both sides with old houses displaying ornamental fixtures above their entrances. They had layers of plaster with fading geometrical patterns on their trim and flowers around their windows, revealing their old-style grandeur—the glory that had been. But they were elderly now, standing attached side by side as though leaning against each other to remain upright. Their paint had worn away, and the naked stone at their foundations had begun to show their age. On the other hand, modern houses, which would replace those old houses too weak to endure, had started to appear, with their fine red brick between reinforced cement columns that lacked the beauty and solidity of the ancient stone.

"Aren't you afraid, *Khawaga* Daoud, to meet Sheikh Foda?" asked Dido maliciously. His smiling eyes had widened as he looked at him.

"I'm not afraid of anything. So is Sheikh Foda that scary?" Daoud answered, laughing.

Dido didn't answer the question, but said instead, "I long to know the extent of your relationship with the great man. Sheikh Foda says you are a man who has very high-level connections. Is that true? Is it true that you, sir, have met the president himself?" The youth asked the question in a voice dripping with admiration and flattery.

"The whole secret is this," Daoud lifted his finger, pointing at the magic ring. "That's my secret, Dido. This ring is the face of good fortune. It always opens the door to good fortune before me. I'll tell you the story."

Although he did not know why he was doing it, Daoud began very spontaneously to tell the tale of the magical signet ring which, before he had worn it, had drawn fame and fortune to Sheikh Sayyid Darwish al-Bahr and Gamal Abdel-Nasser. And finally it had done so for Daoud Abdel-Malek, and would do so, too, for his son Suleiman after him—at the end of a long life!

At the end of the street stood a distinguished old two-story building surrounded by ancient oak trees. Between the posts of its iron fence were branches of clustered sweet basil bushes clearly untrimmed by human hands for many long years. Surely it had been the residence of someone grand in the past.

Dido pushed open the iron gate, its rusty hinges creaking loudly with an ugly screech. Then with small steps he proceeded within, followed by Daoud. Dido closed the gate behind them. The signs of neglect were obvious: the wild branches of shrubs covered the meandering passage to the main entrance and a dried-out marble fountain crouched in the center of the garden under a thick layer of dust and cobwebs and an infernal canopy of leaves. Meanwhile, the squeal of the iron garden gate as it opened alerted those inside the house. A huge wooden door atop several steps opened, and a face peered out from behind it, then a hand beckoned them in.

Daoud could hardly keep his customary composure as he stepped over the uneven, time-worn marble steps, his heart pounding like a drum and his instinct urging him to turn around and go back the way he had come while his feet—and his curiosity—led him to proceed wearily, with tiny steps, to a gloomy reception hall behind the door. As his eyes were still adjusting to the darkness of the place after the bright daylight on the street, he was surprised by hands thoroughly searching his clothes—not only around his torso, but down his legs as well—for a concealed weapon. At the same time, melodic Qur'anic chanting, coming from far away, gradually grew louder in his hearing; his sharp ears might have identified the source as Sheikh Mustafa Ismail. Then a gruff voice spoke from behind him.

"No offense intended, *Khawaga* Daoud, but caution is required," it announced to Daoud, the young man, and the sheikh's other minions around them. Daoud could not tell where or how many of them there were in the darkness.

"Clean as jasmine," the voice declared. "Okay, men, let him in!" came the verdict.

Indeed, Dido led him into a long hallway at the heart of the residence. The hallway ended with a room whose door was ajar; a light radiated from behind it. He strode through the door to find an Istanbul-style couch with a plain white coverlet and a cheap, folk-design cotton rug laid in front of it. The room was devoid of any other furniture; it had an austerity not in keeping with the grandeur of the building—or, at least, its grandeur of old, once upon a time. A sheikh who looked about seventy sat cross-legged on the couch, fingering a rosary. He had a venerable white beard and lusterless gray eyes, and he was clad in a white robe and a warm woolen cloak, as is the custom of the elderly, even in the height of summer. The gaunt sheikh, thin as a desiccated tree, greeted him with a tattered, artificial smile that revealed his few remaining teeth. In a feeble voice, he said, "Welcome, *Khawaga* Daoud. Praise God it was written that I should live long enough to meet you, man."

Dido leaned into Daoud's ear to alert him that Sheikh Foda's eyesight was weak. Though he could hear fairly well, one had to get close so that he could catch everything that was said. Daoud nodded as he took several steps until he fully faced the sheikh.

"Peace be upon you, Sheikh Foda," he hailed.

The aged sheikh shook his head from side to side, reacting angrily and replying, "No, by God! Again, you salute me with the Islamic greeting. You, insolent man!"

The sheikh coughed repeatedly due to his sharp agitation. If this was just the beginning, what would the ending be like? Daoud thought of getting up to leave, but he was afraid. Yes, he feared the result of the man's anger and that of his help-ers spread everywhere throughout the place—the same way that Sheikh Hassanein told him he had feared him on the day they met with President Gamal Abdel-Nasser for the first time. Hence, he remained silent. He had not told anyone where he was going or where he was now, so if something bad happened to him, nobody could even imagine where he was, and no one would rush to his rescue. Therefore, he would have to see for himself how things turned out. All he could do now was wait.

He did not know if he should sit down next to the sheikh or remain standing where he was in front of him, so he did not move. For his part, Dido stepped forward and kissed the sheikh's hand, bidding him farewell as he departed, thus increasing Daoud's embarrassment and sense of isolation. Minutes passed in a heavy silence that killed any spontaneous conversation that might have buzzed between the pair of them. Daoud continued to study the deep lines and wrinkles of the sheikh's face and was struck by a sense of compassion for him that made him forget his own situation for a moment. Then the sheikh wriggled up straight in his seat before he began to speak.

"What's your story, *Si* Daoud?" he said sarcastically. "Tell me honestly, what do you want from us, exactly?"

"Me?" answered Daoud. "I should ask you, Sheikh Foda, what made you ask me to come to speak with you. In other words, it's not me who wants something from you, God forbid."

"I'm going to tell you straight what I need to say to you for Our Lord's sake," said the sheikh. Clearing his throat, he continued.

"You befriended Sheikh Hassanein, then sold him cheap to satisfy the dogs that bought you. And so, he died, may God have mercy on him. Then you played with his wife, *Sitt* Qamar, to the point that she, in turn, committed suicide and so ended up damned forever because of you. Then . . ."

Daoud cut him off sharply.

"What are you saying? Qamar is fine—I saw her just a few days ago. She was perfect."

The sheikh stopped him by coughing again.

"No, Mr. Daoud, Qamar died nearly a week ago. Moreover, I helped bury her with these two hands. When she got the news about Sheikh Hassanein, she drank a bottle of carbolic acid."

Daoud was struck!

What was happening around him, and how did the passing days lead to this descent, from which there was no survival? There had got to be some secret behind it. And he had to know it—now! This blind sheikh huddling in front of him was not as feeble as he seemed. But he had to find out from him the hidden truth of what was happening. There was no doubt he had a hand in what was going on around him, for catastrophes do not come about by themselves. There had to be a hidden hand

guiding the destinies of all these people. And Sheikh Foda—
if he were not the owner of that hand—would, one way or
another, point the way to whomever that was. But now he had
to control himself, even if that meant he had to play an act in
that drama. For why, then, did all these winds sweep down on
him without any prior warning? What was the relationship of
Abdel-Hamid Mustafa and Kamel Fayyad with Sheikh Hassanein and Qamar and the senile Satan in front of him who
would not stop coughing? No doubt he knew completely what
started these affairs and thus understood those mysteries!

Hence, as though with a sharp blade, Daoud carved a
smile onto his melancholy face and surprised the sheikh by
saying, "Do I have to keep standing here like this, or what?"

"Go ahead and sit down, *Si* Daoud," he replied. "That is,
do you want an invitation? Your own desire must have led you
here to get rid of me, and to sit in my place!"

"Why this accusation, Sheikh Foda?" protested Daoud.
"Have I, in my life, ever gone after anything of yours?"

"Sheikh Hassanein!" Sheikh Foda rejoined. "That's the
most important one. Then *Sitt* Qamar. I don't want us to talk
about things that don't need discussing."

Then Sheikh Foda knew what was between him and her. But he had
to be careful; perhaps he was throwing out some bait for him to swallow
and reveal a secret whose details he did not know yet. He had to watch
out for that snake!

"Sheikh Hassanein—may God have mercy on him—
was my friend all his life, through the good and the bad,"
said Daoud. "What's more, you must know I was the one
who got him out of detention. So if I had wanted him to
suffer, I wouldn't have gotten him out in the first place. *Sitt*
Qamar came to me to complain that he had returned to
his errant ways after we brought him back. In other words,
he was the one who brought it on himself, and cut off our
relations. As for *Sitt* Qamar, this was the first time—I swear
by my late father's memory—that I heard of her death. May

Allah have mercy on her and be good to her. It's absurd that I would be the one who made her drink that filthy stuff to poison her!"

"Look, Daoud, without any twists or turns, the Jews have left nothing but desolation behind them—from the time they betrayed our Master Muhammad, prayer and peace be upon him, right until today. My good man, you have two options. You either say the twin credos ('I testify that there is no god but Allah and that Muhammad is the messenger of Allah'), and live among us as a Muslim like any other or you can take your wealth and leave this country of your own volition. We are frankly uneasy at your presence in our midst like this. And if you don't do either, you will have brought it all upon yourself."

At that moment Daoud recalled the words of Major General Kamel Fayyad and was amazed at how they matched those of the sheikh. He grew more convinced that there was some secret connecting them and swore to himself he would uncover the hidden reality later, when he was stronger than he was at present.

"Who do you mean that you're uneasy at my presence among you, Sheikh?" asked Daoud, knowing he would not get a clear answer from him.

"We, the Egyptians, *Khawaga* Daoud!" explained the sheikh. "From the Brotherhood to the military itself. Do you have anything more to say, or was that all you've got?"

Daoud promised the sheikh that he would think about the matter—as he had promised Fayyad earlier—then excused himself and left. He found Dido waiting for him behind the door. The sound of Qur'an chanting came to him again as Dido hurried along with him to the iron fence of the residence.

"What will you do, *Khawaga* Daoud?" he asked.

Daoud looked in his direction, contemplating the bloom of youth and innocence that shone in his wide eyes, and replied, "By God, I don't know, Dido."

The sun went down, plunging behind the face of the outstretched sea. Under the strain of exhaustion and the commotion of his feelings, Daoud headed directly to his house. He stripped off his clothes in his room as Elaine picked up each garment behind him, one after the other, folding them with care, and put them in the chest of drawers. He had started to relate to her the details of his meeting with Sheikh Foda and the two choices he had offered him. Elaine remained busy with what she was doing and did not comment on what he said, though her sad facial expressions, which Daoud noticed as he spoke, revealed her feelings. When he finished, he asked for her view on what he should do. Elaine did not answer him: she did not utter a word. She was filled with the certainty that life had nothing in store for them but a series of hardships. That magical ring had brought them nothing but worry and misfortune. And when sleepiness had overcome Daoud and he traveled to the realm of slumber, Elaine slipped out on light feet, taking the ring, which lay innocently next to the wristwatch on the nightstand, and stashed it in her brassiere under her dress. She left the room quietly, closing the door behind her.

Mohammed al-Buri was moved by Dr. Rashad Fikri's enthusiasm for his paintings. He was dazzled that this cultured man, who had obtained a doctorate in literature from Cambridge University, as he told him, had condescended to visit him and contemplate his canvasses, muttering at first, then expressing admiration. Fikri told him he had uncovered many questions in them, mixed with a hidden sorrow that personally touched his heart. He further remarked that, like al-Buri, he had spent his life looking for one clear answer, which he had not found. He promised to speak to the warden of the prison about the paintings the next day and left.

In the killing loneliness of the cell, Mohammed al-Buri doubted within himself the soundness of mind of that "ingenious doctor" and concluded that he himself, the doctor, needed a psychiatrist to find the answer to all those questions! He cast his gaze meditatively on the paintings around him, searching for all those questions of which Fikri had spoken. Not finding any of them, he was assailed by a wave of maniacal laughter. He stood up and prayed the suppertime prayer then burrowed under the wool blanket as his eyelids surrendered to exhaustion.

In the morning, Mohammed al-Buri found himself face to face with Brigadier Rushdi Iskandar, warden of the prison. At his side was Dr. Rashad, with his gleaming bald head and thick, strong eyeglasses, both of which bobbled back and forth from painting to painting for a few moments. Afterward his Excellency the Warden ordered Sergeant Higazi to carefully pick up and move the paintings to a room next to the prison library—and announced that there was to be an exhibition of al-Buri's works!

Al-Buri was bewildered. An exhibition of his paintings! These paltry brush strokes on strips of cloth have suddenly risen to attain this lofty position. No doubt there is some confusion here. Yes, this had to be a ploy meant to do him harm! He should be on guard. Al-Buri thanked them, of course, but he stopped Dr. Rashad as he began to leave. He looked at his face and read clear happiness on its surface. But he probed beyond that, wondering, "Why, Doctor? And just what is happening? But first tell me who you are exactly."

After the others had left, Dr. Rashad let out a juvenile guffaw that filled the void of the cell. "Sit down, Buri," he said.

"Why do you always address me as Buri? My name is Mohammed."

"Okay, sit down, Mohammed!" he conceded. "Look, I'm an Upper Egyptian man. The world has given me a great deal. Egypt brought me up and educated me when I took the high school diploma and later the bachelor's degree and graduated second in my class. Perhaps I would have taken first place if I weren't from a humble family—if my name hadn't been Rashad Fikri Mogahed. It's possible! But I took second, and that was good, too! The important thing is that I was one of the top three to go to Cambridge. That was my dream, and I achieved it—and returned to Egypt with the doctorate! When I returned, Mohammed, I found the Revolution had occurred—and I thought it auspicious. The students at Egypt's national university deserved science and knowledge—of the kinds that I learned, of course. So, where did they appoint me, Mohammed? As an employee of the Ministry of Education in the archive attached to Dar al-Kutub, the national library. I said, of course, that this was a mistake—it wasn't possible that the nation would treat me this way. To spend all this effort, even to get a doctorate, just to come back and work as a mere functionary in the archive! I went right away to the highest person in charge, right to the top of the ladder, to put an end to this matter. And who did I find he was, Mohammed? I discovered he was an army officer. My God, how can I say this—I found he was nothing—an officer with three stars. He didn't have a college degree—the one responsible for sending scholarship students abroad for the doctorate! He said to me laughing, as though it was funny story, that, 'If this doesn't please you, doctor, we'll deport you back to where you came from!' It didn't please me, of course, because I had returned carrying a big dream in my heart and it wasn't possible that I would renounce it. So, I resolved to combat the situation in my own way."

Rashad took a breath and continued, "What I had to accomplish was the dream hidden within my breast, that I locked in so tightly all those years of exile. I found writing to be the only solution: articles, research, studies, and books—on people, on the Revolution, on change, on democracy, on the patriotic work. I preferred to write and write and write, and fill Egypt with writings until they arrested me, and I was dragged in here, Mohammed—Buri. Now I'm standing before you.

Let me tell you how very much I admire your creative art. You are gifted, Mohammed."

Mohammed al-Buri fixed him with a meaningful look as he raised his fingers to his chin and stroked it, which gave him the air of an intellectual. Then he declared with the confidence of one who knows the inner truth of things, "So long as you are locked up for writing, then you must therefore be—I seek refuge in God—a Communist!"

Dr. Rashad Fikri laughed, filling the cell with that childish guffaw once more.

CHAPTER FIFTEEN

ONCE AGAIN, THE COLD BETRAYED the expectation of warmth that comes with the final days of summer. It stole in among the people, who found no escape as each tried to avoid it in turn by curtailing their outings to the alleys, streets, and squares. And when winter finally settled in, with its biting whirlwinds of cold, the roads were completely empty of idlers, for folks did not go out to the streets except to take care of their essential needs before scurrying back to their warm homes once again. The gray stormy days outnumbered the cloudless ones. Their heaviness increased Elaine's melancholy and her isolation in her own splendid prison. Even her visits to the shelter and her joking with the girls there—the one trip that enabled her to move toward her own self, however meagerly, and to feel a little joy—were limited by the piercing cold.

As she sat in the center of the salon one morning, she savored a delectable piece of cake that she had made herself for no special occasion. She had lately started to prepare numerous foods outside their usual seasons when they merely came to mind in her relentless quest for the delight she gained, for example, from their sudden appearance on the dining table. Daoud dropped in on her and a buried sadness crept onto his face. She reflected that no doubt he had looked for her all through the mansion until he found her here, where neither she—nor he—was accustomed to sitting between the walls of this room, with its classical atmosphere. Inevitably then, he had come to her to broach a serious subject that was preoccupying him. He took a chair next to her, but he remained silent. She distracted herself by devouring one piece of cake after another, anticipating he would start a conversation with her, to no avail. Abruptly the bell cut through the wall of silence around them and Nargis hurried to open the door. Who would be ringing the doorbell at this early hour of the day, wondered Elaine? Then they heard Nargis speak.

"Please come in, Mr. Abdel-Nasser. They're all in the salon."

Elaine dusted the cake crumbs and powdered sugar from her dress as she stood up, with her ample form, preparing to greet the arriving guest. Daoud craned his neck toward the salon's door, trying to determine if what he was hearing was true—that Abdel-Nasser Effendi had come by himself to visit them. Meanwhile, with an involuntary movement, he felt for his silver signet ring around his finger—but found it was not there. He held up his hand in front of him to verify the absence of his beloved ring—and confirmed that it was missing. He thought that perhaps—in the crush of events that occurred one after the other—he had forgotten to put it on his finger, as was his habit. The old man came into the room led by Nargis. He was elegantly dressed in a simple style, as was his custom: he wore a full blue suit and red *tarboush*, and leaned on his ebony cane.

"Good morning, Daoud," he said. "Good morning, Madame Elaine. I am sorry to have come like this without an appointment. But by God, I had hoped that between brothers there are no appointments."

"Hello, hello, please come in," Elaine told him, welcoming him with a wide smile. Her eyes stared at the floor as she humbly moved back a step. Though she had never met him before, she naturally realized who the revered visitor must be.

Then she added, "I'll go now and make the tea and fill a plate with cake, so that you can savor the work of my hands,

Mr. Abdel-Nasser." Daoud's face exploded in a grin at merely the sight of his old friend, and he immediately forgot the story of the ring and the rest of the preoccupations involved with it. He rose at once and embraced him even before his wife Elaine's words of greeting had reached their guest's ears.

"Where have you been for so long, man?" Daoud blurted sincerely. "At any rate, you couldn't have picked a better time to come." Abdel-Nasser Effendi removed his *tarboush*, and Daoud took it and placed it next to his cane, which he had hung on an elegant piece of furniture next to the room's entrance. The piece had been made in Italy especially for holding similar items. As Daoud busied himself with that, Abdel-Nasser Effendi moved his lips as though he were mouthing silent words before beginning to utter them. Some minutes passed before he resumed speaking.

"Really, Daoud. There is no time more important than this: that's why I came to you today."

Naturally Daoud grew apprehensive at hearing this, but he invited him to sit down first before responding to him in turn, "All is well, I hope, Abdel-Nasser Effendi. Your words have worried me."

The other cleared his throat in embarrassment at what he was about to say.

"I don't know where to begin, my brother, but you are not to blame. The culpability falls on this gang that took the land and expelled its owners based on their claim to be 'God's chosen people.' Fine—and the rest of the people? What about them? Our Lord created them by mistake? And why didn't He choose them, too? Something truly strange!"

The prologue only hinted at the disaster to come, just as the waves grow higher and the clouds darken the sky and the people of Alexandria know that the winter storm is heading their way and that they are helpless to stop it.

Despite his anxiety, Daoud commented, "Oppression, whenever it happens in any part of the world, must bring ruin in its wake. But the world cannot remain silent about this oppression, Abdel-Nasser Effendi. And I am the one most injured because of it: I have lost my two sons, who have left me to run off to the Promised Land."

"I know, Daoud—you didn't have to tell me that," replied the elder Abdel-Nasser. "But the problem now is that there is a state of war between us and them. They started it in effect by forcefully occupying Sinai along with two of the biggest powers in the world that you say would not remain silent about oppression! The truth is, Daoud, that the world prefers to keep silent, and we alone want to say no to that oppression."

"By God, clearly what you say is true, Abdel-Nasser Effendi, my brother: I mean, we get rid of the English and they bring us the . . ." Daoud stopped before he could finish the word. The old man then picked up where he had left off.

"The *what*, Daoud? Complete that and you'll make my mission easier and shorter for me. I'll tell you myself: we got rid of the English and they brought us the Jews. Wasn't that what you were going to say? Fine, I'll ask you a question: Are you able today to do with me the things we used to do together in our mischievous days—to go blow up bombs or lay a stick of dynamite in the camp of the Jews, like we used to do in the camps of the British? Of course not, since—forgive me—one of your own sons might be inside it. Wouldn't that hold you back?"

Daoud was taken aback by this unexpected twist. But he gathered his courage and said at once, "What kind of talk is this, Abdel-Nasser Effendi? First, we were fighting the English who occupied our country, but Israel didn't occupy our land for us to fight a war with it. Second, if Israel hadn't withdrawn from Sinai at Eisenhower's orders, I would have gone hand in hand with you, Abdel-Nasser Effendi, to fight them—even if, between you and me—I have gotten too old to do such a thing."

Daoud added, to lighten the conversation, "And you too, old man? Isn't that right?"

Abdel-Nasser responded by sharing his laughter. At this moment, Elaine came in accompanied by Nargis, one carrying a tea tray and the other a plate full of cake.

The empty words and tinkling laughs went back and forth between them as they sipped their tea and nibbled on sweets while there appeared in the eyes of Abdel-Nasser Effendi words that occurred to him to say, but the presence of Elaine among them made it impossible to elaborate. Her being there also prompted Daoud to wait for an appropriate opportunity to finish what he had to say. Yet Daoud's mind was not put at ease—to the contrary, for he had preserved the image of his encounters with Sheikh Foda, and, before him, Abdel-Hamid Mostafa. He was preoccupied by them, as Abdel-Nasser Effendi's visit to him today was a new episode in this depressing series of events that had overtaken him of late. As Daoud had expected, Elaine had barely left the salon when the old man shifted in his seat and confronted him once again.

"Actually, Daoud, my brother," he said, "I have something to tell you. My son Gamal contacted me last night about you."

"About me?" replied Daoud. "What about me?"

"Just allow me to finish my piece," answered Abdel-Nasser Effendi. "Major General Fayyad had spoken to the president about the factory and the palace we are sitting in right now. They say that these things are the property of the Jewish millionaire Binyuti Pasha and that they must go to the committee for settling accounts—I don't even know what it's called. And then there is the story of Sheikh Foda and your visit to him: why? Daoud, man, don't you know that he's one of the leaders of the Brotherhood?"

"The president of the Republic spoke to you just because of me?" marveled Daoud. "I must be a very important man, and I didn't even know it."

"Daoud, my brother, it means that Gamal loves you and doesn't want any problems for you. He knows how dear you are to me. He asked me to tell you this so that we deal with this subject in a friendly manner."

"Abdel-Nasser Effendi, the factory and this palace both belong to me, as per sales contracts registered with the property tax office. That's for real!"

Abdel-Nasser Effendi reached out his hand to pat, with sincere affection, the shoulder of his friend seated beside him.

"My dear Daoud," he continued, "those contracts can be debunked very easily, because you can't prove you had the money to cover their value at the time of sale. Also, this is the *government*, Daoud—do you think you can fight the government?"

Daoud was aghast to hear this. He contemplated his friend sitting in front of him and doubted his good intentions. Was it possible they were all conspiring against him, that they would seize all his property from him in the blink of an eye while he stood with his arms crossed? *No, that could never be. He would fight until his last breath.*

"So, what is required now?" pressed Daoud, as though surrendering to his fate. At the same time his mind was burning with the search for a way out of this impasse in which he found himself.

"In my opinion, Daoud," said Abdel-Nasser Effendi, "the only solution before us is negotiation."

The three children gathered on the palace's roof on Friday— their vacation day—playing and relaxing. Suleiman had placed a bedsheet over his shoulders, its two ends knotted in front of his throat. On his head was a crown of gilded leaves from the remains of last New Year's party. He paced back and forth the length and width of the roof, dragging the other end of the sheet behind him. At the same time, he gave orders to his flock—Layla and Mona—who carried them out obediently and compliantly. They prepared the royal meal for him, which was made of colored sheets of paper shaped as little balls in a saucer made from the lid of an empty tin of chocolate.

He said to them—as he had learned from *Monsieur* Nathan at school—that the king must be wise before he can be strong: he must be loved by his people more than he is feared by them. He stood on an old chair they had placed at the center of the roof and called it his throne. He looked around him toward the sea, stretching his arm out in front of him, proclaiming that his vast kingdom ranging before him was the strongest on the face of the earth. All its inhabitants were his subjects and they had to obey him absolutely. In return, he had to bestow on them his wisdom and love. Layla and Mona looked at him and laughed, then suddenly announced that the game was over. Now they were going to play "school," in which they would become teachers of arithmetic and the English language, and he would be their pupil. He, in his turn, obeyed submissively. He got down from the chair and removed his paper crown, then put down the sheet and sat on it, turning in the blink of an eye from a crowned king to a pupil in a school.

After the dawn prayer, Mohammed al-Buri started to wake up Dr. Rashad, his new partner in Qena Prison. They grew accustomed to stealing the earliest hours of the day to converse with each other and trade memories before the rest of the prison woke up and, most importantly, before the scorching, burning southern Egyptian sun awoke. Though Dr. Rashad denounced Mohammed's way of thinking about belief and modes of worship, his openness to discussing anything and everything made their discussions a treasure of intellectual pleasure that he had not experienced with any of his friends before. Mohammed asked Dr. Rashad one day if he would pray with him, but he replied that he did not pray! He said it as casually as though, for example, he had admitted that he would not eat eggplant. On another occasion al-Buri asked him if he was fundamentally a Muslim, and he laughed heartily as though he had heard a rare novelty. And with that he said no more! On another day he confessed that both his parents were Muslims who practiced the rituals of Islam in their entirety, like the majority of Egyptian Muslims.

Mohammed addressed him that morning in a tone filled with sarcasm.

"How, Doctor, can you see the dawn and the sun emerge from it to be reborn, and the sky filled with colors like this before your eyes, without thinking that there is an awesome creator behind it all?"

"Whoever said that there is no creator?" replied Dr. Rashad, "All I am saying is that there might be one, or maybe there isn't. I don't have the proof. Would you happen to have it?"

"The proof is here," answered Mohammed. "Do you need anything more than that?" He pointed toward the sun's rays shyly slipping from the horizon.

"This is proof, my dear," Dr. Rashad replied, "of the earth's revolving on its axis once every twenty-four hours and around the sun once every year, as well. We've known about this for a long time—a very long time. If today you went to the temple of Abu Simbel that your ancestors built three thousand years ago, you'd find that once each year the rays of the sun penetrate an opening that looks down on the royal chamber to illuminate the statue of King Ramses—on his birthday! That has endured longer than the less than 1,500 years your own Lord has been with you."

Mohammed al-Buri trembled in anger and was intending to get up and leave when Dr. Rashad Fikri kept him by saying, "Don't be annoyed—you are right. Sit down and be calm, and let's just talk about your paintings. Do you know how many have been sold to visitors and inmates in the prison so far? Four!"

"This is by the grace of my God," Mohammed al-Buri responded with genuine pride and satisfaction. Rashad Fikri came back with alacrity, seizing on the fortunate opportunity that had arisen.

"No—say it is by the grace of my mind, and you'd be right."

And so each of them pursued opportunity after opportunity to direct his hidden blows at the ideas and beliefs of the other while keeping their sarcastic discussions within the limits of good manners and civility. And they always stopped at the edge of what the other considered a violation of the terms agreed, leaving taboos alone.

He looked for it everywhere.

On top of the nightstand, behind and below it, under the bed, in the wardrobe, in the lining of his suits—all these places—and in the pockets of his trousers. He tried to remember the last time he had felt the ring on his finger. It was the day that Dido took him to Sheikh Foda. Could they have taken it then from his finger when they searched him—when he had felt their hands go up and down on his body in the dark? Was it that man with the rough voice who stealthily—hidden by the fearful gloom—prised the magic ring from him? He didn't recall now having seen the ring afterward. No doubt they stole it! He had told Sheikh Hassanein—may God have mercy on him—about his enchanted signet the day he bought it. And no doubt later he, in turn, must have told Sheikh Foda about it. He had talked about it at length in front of Dido, as well. No doubt their filthy hands had reached out for it, greedy for its magical power.

Despite that, on this very day he summoned Elaine to ask if she had seen it. She denied it and felt at that instant a pang of regret—it was the first time she had lied to Daoud. Yet she insisted that she did not know where it was. She would never reveal the truth to him no matter what, as she believed in the evil portent of that cursed ring! He waited until the children returned from school and asked them, but they did not know a thing about that ring. He was hoping that one of them—especially Suleiman—had taken it to play the game "the king and his flock," just as he would sometimes purloin a *tarboush*, a cloak, or a pair of shiny boots to play with his two sisters.

On the same day Daoud telephoned Sinut Qiryaqus the lawyer and set an appointment to meet him in his office two days later to discuss the palace and the factory. In his office, the famous attorney informed him that he was sending his private secretary to bring a copy of the formal contract from the real estate registry. After a strenuous search, the official in charge, drenched in sweat, apologized to him that the dossier that held his contract—and thirty-two other deeds as well—had disappeared.

A few days later, he received a phone call from Abdel-Nasser Effendi asking permission to visit him again, but accompanied by Major General Fayyad this time, which led him to call ahead of their appointment. Daoud had no alternative but to agree obediently. High walls had risen around him that he was not strong enough to knock down from one side nor was he able to peer over them to see what lay concealed behind them for the coming days. At that moment, he intensely missed his magic ring. A profound feeling assailed him that its sudden disappearance was a warning of trying times awaiting him.

Daoud was nailed where he stood before the blue waters of the sea with its seething waves. He was surrounded by the cold winds, his arms clinging tightly to his trembling torso. He could not overcome the feeling that a powerful lasso held his body in its grip and that the ends were being pulled violently like strings on the neck of an oud. This was at the hands of Sheikh Foda and the man with the crude voice from one side and of Major General Fayyad and his underling Abdel-Hamid Mustafa on the other. He was being pulled by each party in opposite directions, which would lead finally to the same end: he'd either be choked to death or leave. The blustery wind nearly blew off his *tarboush*, so he slipped his bonds and stretched his hand upward to brace it.

CHAPTER SIXTEEN

THE STORM WAS CALLED *AL-GHITAS*, "the Baptism."

January, 19, 1958. A new wave of cold assailed Alexandria, just as storms blast her every winter on their regular schedule. Yet this year they were crueler than ever before. The terrifying breakers even came over the promenade and onto the Corniche. The wind descended with a surging roar as the sky darkened and street signs flew in the air. Not only did windowpanes shatter but doors were ripped off their hinges. The torrential rain fell for three days and three nights without cease as people huddled in their homes, waiting for it to end.

In the evening, a tremor assaulted Daoud. First, he felt that his body had frozen. Next an intense fever overwhelmed him and confined him to bed. Elaine covered his chest with newspapers under his pajamas. She gave him chamomile tea, sometimes mixed with lemon, plus tablets of aspirin around the clock as he coughed and sweated profusely through the night.

That night, in fact, as his body lay soaking wet in bed with sweat caused by the aspirin, Daoud nodded off to sleep. It wasn't the normal sleep that comes from tiredness at the end of the day, or at the descent of darkness, or in surrender to boredom, but the slumber of sickness. The sleep that is equal to unconsciousness—after it you do not feel rested or refreshed but more exhausted than you were before. In that state, suspended between sleep and waking, Daoud had a strange dream. He remembered its complete details when he woke up, telling them all to his son Suleiman since he was involved in it with him. He had seen Suleiman sitting in front of him at the end of the bed when he awoke.

In the dream, he was a king wearing a crown and sitting atop a throne in the center of a grand hall filled to the limit with his subjects. Strangely, he did not look like himself, yet he was sure it was he. His ears were assailed by the strains of dancing music like that scored for Hollywood movies such *Aladdin* and *The Thief of Baghdad*. And indeed, as in those films, blonde and brunette female dancers were swaying to the tunes of the oud and tambourine on the hall floor in transparent silken gowns. The king began to sing amid voices of approval coming from all around him.

Amid this joyful atmosphere, a terrifying man wrapped in a long, black cloak that concealed his whole body—even his face, except for his gleaming eyes—slipped into the room. Taking advantage of the happy throngs singing around him and the neglect of the guards, he moved forward and attacked Daoud, pulling the signet—which in the dream appeared bigger, shinier, more lustrous—from his finger, then vanishing in an instant. Daoud screamed at that moment for the guards to stop the thief before he could get away, but they did not move. In an instant he had disappeared. The music and dancing stopped as confusion settled over the hall.

An elegant young man in gold-colored clothing walked gracefully among a group of youths who were exchanging entertaining evening banter in a corner. Daoud perceived—in the dream—that the young man was none other than his own son, Suleiman—even though he did not really look like himself either. The young man raised a sword amid those present and announced he was going on a quest for his father's ring. He swore in front of them all that he would not come back without it. A feeling of sadness for the loss of the ring struck him, as did the fear that he would lose his son forever on his journey to retrieve it.

In the dream's next scene, Suleiman was locked in combat with a gang of ruffians atop a sand dune in a vast desert, beating them off, one after the other. They fell in succession down the mound, rolling over the smooth sand all the way to the bottom, as in the movies. Afterward, he caught sight of Suleiman kneeling in a dazzling costume. He stretched his hand—bearing the ring—toward Daoud after he told him the story of the exhaustive search, which in the end had led him to meet a youthful fisherman, whom Suleiman had encountered crying on the side of a road. The fisherman had spent the whole night on the open sea, which granted him no boon but one single fish, whose price would not suffice to keep his large family alive. So, Suleiman bought the fish from him for a huge sum out of sympathy for his poverty, sharing it for the sake of the man's children. When he sliced the fish open with his sword, he found the signet within it.

Daoud rejoiced once more and stood in the middle of the reception hall, announcing to all present that he would bestow the magic ring and the throne on his son, who deserved to succeed him.

Elaine could not endure the weight of guilt any longer. Sleep fled from her nights with the torments of remorse. Unable to contain her feelings, she decided to talk. Yes! She had to reveal her secret before the anxiety it caused killed her. How could she forgive herself for lying to her husband that way— for bringing this sense of loss and despair upon his days since he discovered that his ring was missing? Who appointed her to decide between truth and falsehood? Between good and evil? Between right and wrong? Not only that, but who asked her to ponder whether a ring could bring happiness or misery, even to the point where she would deliberately hide it from her darling husband, breaking his heart? And all because she thought the ring to be destined to carry evil within it and become the source of their wretchedness. She thought of who could help her in this predicament, and Father Mikhail occurred to her as the best possible person to speak with in these circumstances. He was a man of God with whom she could no doubt find the answers to her questions and the solution to the dilemma in which she found herself.

At dawn, she went to meet him before he began the prayers for mass. And after she met him inside the church and they had their parley together, he advised her not to confess the truth to Daoud, for the time being at least, in order not to anger him—for his fury might cause him to wreck the house. But Father Mikhail insisted that she return the ring to him in an indirect way, say, by claiming that she—or, perhaps, one of the children—had found it somewhere, or something like that. She replied that she felt that a satanic power emanated from that ring. The priest calmed her by saying that Satan is a spirit who cannot live in a ring—an inanimate object—and there was no reason to fear it at all. Moreover, above all, the Holy Spirit would protect her family and shield them from the power of demons for eternity. But he asked her to remain and pray the mass with them and to partake of the body and blood of the Lord—the greatest defense against these malignant ideas. Of course, Elaine responded to his counsel without hesitation; she truly felt some peace after receiving the Holy Communion. But she kept thinking during the return trip about the best means to give the ring back to Daoud without arousing his doubts, as the priest had advised her.

On her return, she found Daoud sleeping on the upper floor: he was still suffering from the cold that had sent him to bed. Layla and Mona were still playing with their dolls while Suleiman sat on the couch perusing one of the illustrated French children's magazines that he would borrow from the school's library. When he saw her, the boy got up joyfully to meet her, and, aflame with delight, danced around her as he related the details of the dream that he had heard a little while before from his father. Elaine smiled and said nothing, though her thoughts focused on the fish and the ring. She wondered whether she could buy a fish in the market, then hide the ring inside it and announce that she had found the ring in its belly. But she drove this thought away immediately when she realized that Daoud would inevitably discover the ploy—it was so simple—and fly into a rage when he grasped that she had concealed the ring from him, and he would never forgive her for deceiving him.

Daoud recovered after a few days and in time to receive the guests who were coming to visit him. At exactly seven o'clock in the evening, the doorbell rang and Nargis announced that Abdel-Nasser Effendi had come with "some officer" to see him. Daoud received them in the office room that contained a huge desk, shelves crammed with books, and a couch and three large chairs covered in rich wine-red Italian leather—a set rarely sat upon by the family. There, also, was the piano to which Daoud had listened when he visited Binyuti Pasha for the first time, accompanied by Qamar—may God have mercy on her. No one had touched its keys since he and Elaine had moved into this palace. He and Major General Kamel Fayyad exchanged wary looks as they sipped their coffee, which Nargis had hurried to prepare, while Elaine preferred to remain alone upstairs in her room. The silence continued to hang in the air until Kamel Fayyad politely asked Daoud about his health, then launched into a discussion about the intensity and cruelty of the winter storm this year—it had even closed the harbor port for three days. When it became clear to all that those honeyed words were choked with the powerful tension that had settled over the place, Major General Fayyad reached his hand into the pocket of his military tunic and removed a folded piece of paper with care. Without a word he gave it to Daoud, who took it from him. Daoud saw plainly that it contained a letter in the hand of President Gamal addressed to His Excellency the Major General.

Daoud put on his glasses and began to read its contents while he followed—over the rim of spectacles—Kamil

Fayyad's searching looks around the place, taking advantage of his preoccupation in studying the letter like a real estate agent who had come to appraise its value before venturing an offer. Daoud smiled to himself, confirming the first impression about this man that he had formed in the meeting in Manshiya: that he was rude, puritanical, and lacking in decorum.

Daoud continued his unhurried reading. Yes, this was the handwriting of President Gamal—the same handwriting in which his father's address was inscribed on a little piece of paper that he had presented to him on the day of his visit to his office in Manshiat al-Bakri. The text of the letter was as follows:

> *My dear Kamel:*
>
> *I write these words to you about a dear friend and patriotic man who has undertaken great effort in the revolutionary work to liberate Egypt from the British occupation that lasted more than seventy years. I ask that you let him read these words for himself.*
>
> *I think, Kamel, that you know him personally from when we met with him that night in Alexandria: he is Master Daoud Abdel-Malek.*
>
> *The Revolutionary Command Council is keen to revive the principles of social justice in the distribution of wealth from the big industrialists and landowners in all parts of the republic to the rest of the people. Therefore, it has been decreed for all to obey and carry out what is written in the law, without exception and regardless of high station: how often have our people suffered from it!*
>
> *With regard to the properties of Binyuti Pasha, the well-known wealthy Alexandrian who left the country some years ago, they fall under the former law, which was decreed for all to obey. However, I have absolutely no doubt whatsoever in the patriotism and sincerity of Daoud Abdel-Malek.*
>
> *But there is the question of the contract concluded between him and Binyuti Pasha. I want you to respect the special*

circumstances that apply to Daoud. In return, I ask of you—
as a personal request—to consider him the legal owner of the
factory and the villa—and, accordingly, in return for those prop-
erties, it is proper that we should buy them from him in exchange
for an appropriate material compensation that would not be
considered harmful to him or his family. As these properties are
considered their only source of income, I want you to carry this
out quickly to the letter. And, once again, treat Daoud Abdel-
Malek as a personal friend and as one of the trustworthy fighters
with us for the sake of the independence of Egypt.

Finally, accept all my thanks, and deliver my greetings to
Daoud when you meet him—along with this, my letter to him.

President of the Republic,

Gamal Abdel-Nasser

Daoud lifted his head over the paper, folded it silently, and, with a curt nod, returned it to Major General Fayyad, who in turn put it back in his tunic pocket. Here, Abdel-Nasser Effendi began to speak for the first time since he came, trying to lighten the wary silence that encompassed them. As per his custom, he was a man of delicate feeling, very sensitive, and he harbored personal affection and a benevolent spirit toward Daoud. He sensed how much he was affected, no doubt by the occurrence of their visit and the results of that letter, which he had read on the road before they arrived. He felt with his hand the folder that Major General Fayyad was carrying with him to placate Daoud and that he had put on the coffee table in front of them both. He unwrapped it with care, took out a bottle of Gianaclis wine, and then called to Daoud.

"Order three glasses for us, brother Daoud, to warm us up on a cold night like this." In response to his request, Daoud looked toward him with a sidelong glance full of love, then stood up, heading toward the kitchen.

Kamel Fayyad seized the opportunity of Daoud's absence to get up on his feet and walk around the room with his hands clasped behind his back, contemplating the pictures on the walls and the sculptures and antiques scattered here and there above the shelves of the library. Then he commented in a sub-dued tone as though his thoughts were escaping from him, "This money belongs to the wretched poor, all of it. It must go back to them. In twenty-four hours, this palace will become a school in which their children will learn."

He turned languidly to face Abdel-Nasser Effendi, say-ing as he pointed to one of the oil paintings, "For the price of this painting here, a whole family could maybe eat for a full year, Mr. Abdel-Nasser. Or the piano . . ." Abdel-Nasser Effendi smiled, not believing a single word Kamel Fayyad had said. He had perceived—with the accumulation of days—the weakness of the soul that most of these young officers had fallen prey to and the reality of whom these possessions would wind up with. But he cut him off gently, commenting with fatherly sympathy, "Fine—but calm down, Kamel, my son, so as not to annoy Daoud."

When Daoud returned bearing the tray full of empty glasses, a cloud of worry had begun to darken his features. Daoud's aged friend held out a glass of wine to him and joked, "Rise up and fill your glass with wishes before destiny fills the cup of life!"

"And who would be destiny and what would be the cup of life, Mr. Nasser?" Kamel Fayyad asked in embarrassment.

"That was meant to be a secret between Daoud and me!" the old man answered craftily, and finally Daoud smiled. As he began to pour the wine into the glasses, a wave of laughter struck him that swept them all as well.

Half of his judicial sentence had gone by, and Mohammed al-Buri realized that the main reason for the swift passage of days was Dr. Rashad—his attractive presence and stimulating, mostly provocative conversation. Mohammed filled most of his days with his unlimited activities and interests, though sometimes he failed to accomplish all that he intended to. He learned by reading a great deal: literature, history, philosophy, and art—everything in the prison library, which Dr. Rashad had stocked with his own books—in addition to painting, which absorbed his hours and days. He made dozens of artistic compositions, half of which he sold, generating income for the prison administration—and there was no harm in that. But the most important thing was the spread of his reputation until one day a reporter from *al-Jumhuriyya*—*"The Republic"*—newspaper came to them with a photographer. Mohammed al-Buri gave a press interview, which was published with a photo of him amid his paintings, under the headline "From Salafism to Expressionism: Visual Art Liberates One of the Inmates of Qena Prison."

From that time, he felt he had become a distinguished person. He received special treatment, as though he had changed overnight into one of the most famous painters in Egypt. He still kept a copy of the newspaper among the folds of his clothes, and he read it over again every evening, boasting about it to his fellow prisoners. But he kept a wary eye on that brief period remaining: Dr. Rashad Fikri's release was due in less than a week. He realized how much he would miss him, though he was too proud to divulge frankly that he both admired and feared him. At least, until now he had wondered whether those Communist ideas of his had infiltrated his own mind and heart—I seek refuge in God! He would flee into ritual ablution and prayer whenever these ideas occurred to him.

The night Dr. Rashad went out into the world once again, he came to bid Mohammed goodbye. Mohammed did not merely welcome him but took him into his arms and wept, engulfed in emotions he was not able to repress. Dr. Rashad told him that he was convinced that destiny had brought the two of them together in this place for a purpose—it was not by chance. They had to think seriously and clearly about the purpose of that meeting and its meaning. Mohammed answered him that the one who had brought them together was God the High and Exalted, not fate—and they laughed together. Mohammed went on that he believed that their path of mutual friendship was still at its start and that the work of building it that they had started with each other must inevitably be completed after he left detention. Egypt had a claim on her sons, and it was incumbent upon the two of them to fulfill her demands. Dr. Rashad answered that he was happy he had come to *believe* in something! The two of them laughed again.

Then Dr. Rashad said that the true revolution is not based on laws alone; rather, its real power relies on productive, motivated people to move its wheels. Ignorant people are not productive. Thus, their responsibility lies in educating the people and enlightening them so that they are able to bear all the determination and unprecedented effort required for the revolution to succeed. These profound words had the greatest effect on Mohammed el-Buri. Dr. Rashad uttered them with certain confidence and faith. Mohammed memorized them, swearing that he'd focus on them as a goal for the remainder of his sentence—time that would be spent without Dr. Rashad—and pledged to meet him in Alexandria as soon as he was released. But, as the days passed, he found that these words had faded one by one, fleeing from his memory until they were gone completely—along with that close relationship that had bonded him personally to Dr. Rashad Fikri, who nonetheless retained a lofty place in his mind as time went by.

Major General Kamel Fayyad promised to compensate Daoud if he would help him follow Sheikh Foda's trail to his vintage home. The reward did not tempt him, but the desire to fight against the sheikh's tyranny and domination over the fate of worshippers is what drove Daoud Abdel-Malek to guide a police raid on the sheikh and his helpers in the sheikh's house. Thus, one day at dawn, he sat in the back of a car next to His

Excellency the Major General, who was sending a series of instructions to the driver of the vehicle leading a silent convoy of armed troops about the streets of the somnolent city.

The convoy crossed Fouad Street, then the cars headed down a side street past the office of the real estate agent, which, of course, was closed at that early hour. Nonetheless, Daoud was sure they had taken the right route. Then they passed the first cross street, where the old houses were located. Daoud pointed out to Kamel Fayyad the villa crouched at its end; it was swirling in a halo of dawn mist that obscured it even more than the dense thicket of trees surrounding it.

With a wave of Fayyad's hand, the soldiers arrayed themselves nimbly on both sides of the street. In a few minutes the formation had advanced cautiously, with slow steps, toward the iron fence shrouded in the leaves and branches of the trees that clung to it. A rusty lock wrapped in a steel chain embraced a divided external door. The Major General motioned to one of the soldiers, who came forward and broke the lock with a sharp tool. With utmost quiet, he removed the chain, then opened the gate, which grated loudly as it had the day Daoud came to meet with Sheikh Foda. Meanwhile, Daoud prayed—privately—that the young Dido, with his wide eyes and laid-back spirit, was not then at home.

The soldiers made their way with speed and agility down the passage that led to the main door, preparing the path for His Excellency the Major General, Daoud, and the other officers that were following them. They mounted the staircase, and the repeated banging on the door with their palms and rifle butts resonated like the banging of war drums. But when no one opened the door, the soldiers smashed it with their shoulders. They quickly stormed the house, fanning out as they moved, filling the serenity of the place with the sound of their military boots that roved clamorously over every corner—discovering in just a few moments that not a creature was there.

CHAPTER SEVENTEEN

SPRING'S WARMTH AND WINDS ONCE again seized the reins from the grip of the steely winter cold with its despotic brutality that showed no mercy. Electric sparks of love filled the breezes of passion; every living being trembled at their touch with the charge of love. It lit the buds of the flowers with captivating colors, inspiring the birds, one by one, to flap their wings amorously toward branches hidden from sight. The people of Alexandria came out of their winter hibernation to fill the streets and roads, without thought of work or timetables, not bound for schools or markets. They sniffed the pure winds of love that bore the reviving smell of the sea following days of violent rainstorms, one after another. These hidden sparks touch them, and each one wanders in search of their lover.

In that joyful atmosphere, the wheels of a cart drawn by a donkey—its head bowed—rolled over the well-rinsed asphalt, heading with fatalistic determination toward the Moharram Bey district. It carried the personal property of Daoud Abdel-Malek's family after they were forced to leave the palace of Binyuti Pasha. They were returning to where the journey had started: the apartment Daoud had inherited from his father, the late Issa Ibrahim Effendi Abdel-Malek. Where it all began! Where Daoud had had intimate relations with Budur, Sofie, Elaine, and then even with Qamar—may God have mercy on those who have died and strengthen those who remain! And in recalling those who still lived, his thoughts drifted to Sofie,

189

his Turkish wife, who had fled with his daughter Margot, and he wondered how they were doing now in this crazy world.

With whispering quiet, the motor of the black Packard driven by William, the chauffeur, carried the family home. Daoud sat next to him dejectedly, contemplating these things while Elaine and the three children squeezed into the back seat. Happiness began to show on her face for the first time in years. As for Layla, Suleiman, and Mona, they were absorbed in a quarrel about who would sit next to the car's windows; the move to Moharram Bey was not really on their minds. Daoud thought about this strange world, which unexpectedly folds you in its wings and lifts you for a time toward the sky. Then it turns around to eclipse your power down to the lowest of the low while seizing you by the nape. You have no strength, influence, or ability to adjust your path even by one inch. Rather, you must agree to take it all, lest people accuse you of being a rebel, of being defiant or ungrateful, of not bearing up for the long haul for destiny's sake. And he wondered when he would turn around and find that cursed ring once again.

The silent procession entered the narrow street, the neighbors and families of the district greeting them with caution mixed with a hint of derision on account of their failed plan to escape the world of the dim toiling masses for the world of the pampered rich. But, as soon as the black car's doors opened and the faces looked around from it, they rushed forward with hugs and kisses, welcoming their return once again to their family and people—a response owed to that spring and what it created in their delicate hearts. Tears of joy overcame Elaine, while Daoud remained in a daze, unconsciously shaking his head like a defeated prizefighter at the end of a bout, eyes swollen and blinded by too many punches. Then came the greetings and embraces of strangers, their faces since erased from his memory, as he drowned behind a curtain of tears that filled his eyes. At that moment, the children raced along the street, whose inhabitants examined them with innocent eyes. Their memories of the house and the district had all been wiped away in the few years they had spent far away in the palace of Binyuti Pasha.

Daoud embraced the oud and withdrew to his room, locking the door behind him. He sat on the edge of the bed, then his fingers began to play with the strings and he sang a sad lyric by Daoud Hosni in a subdued voice. Next, he called William to the room, telling him tersely that he had resolved to give him the Packard to run as a taxi from which he and his wife Nargis could profit. Then, in a peremptory tone, he asked him to leave, as he needed to sleep for a while. But he didn't sleep. Instead, he lay flat on his bed, fully clothed, his eyes fixed on the ceiling as he reviewed all the stops on his journey. These electric flashes failed to touch his broken heart.

From that day, Daoud stayed in his room, not leaving except to use the bathroom, after which he would return to read and play the oud. Even food and cigarettes were brought to him in his isolation. Then he awoke one day to a voice within himself—from the innermost depths if his heart—urging him to fetch a paper and pen. It was an insistent, compelling voice that he had no choice but to obey. Then the voice began to dictate words—more and more words—to him. When he recited them, he realized they were odes of Sufi aesthetic poetry he admired. He asked Elaine to buy a notebook, blue as the sea at Alexandria, and he collected all his poems in its pages. Afterward, the words began to come in succeeding bursts that gripped him at all hours of the day and night, compelling him to respond. He would sit alone as he wrote them down. Then one day he was overcome by a compelling urge to sing his verses, so he set them to music in the months that followed, singing them to himself. But he never played them in the presence of another person nor revealed his poems to anyone.

As for Elaine, it was as though she had been struck by a magic wand like that which sets the dried branches of trees ablaze with color in the last days of winter and in spring brings forth the season's warmth as limbs sprout gravid with flowers and young fruit—with life! Her return to Moharram Bey had removed her depression and introversion, so she smiled often in the beginning. Then she began to laugh at the antics of the children, and for the first time in long years, she started to sing. Yes—to sing! For when Elaine returned to Moharram Bey, she found everyone around her singing. Yes, she sang with them joyfully about the Revolution, which had imbued the neighborhood and the neighbors with a merry hue that she had not noticed when she was alone in her lavish prison. Her sweet singing voice came back to her. From the flood of memories, she ran through the songs of Umm Kulthoum and Mohammed Abdel-Wahhab, which were buried in hidden corridors. She augmented them with the tunes of the new singers who had appeared on the scene and the new anthems filling the world, praising the popular revolution with new terms that were obscure to her—heavy expressions that she sang with the rest of the people—such as "socialism," "responsibility," and "membership in the Basic Committee"—odd words whose meaning she didn't understand. But the melodies pleased her, especially the songs extolling their famous hero, Nasser—known as Abu Khaled, meaning "Father of Khaled"—and his brethren, the flower of the nation!

Elaine rejoiced in him because she loved his father, her husband Daoud's friend Abdel-Nasser Effendi, and because of his good relations with the head of the church, Patriarch Kirolos the Sixth. She loved him and looked forward to the happy days that awaited her family in Moharram Bey. With a quiet determination, she went to a branch of the National Bank and deposited the entire amount that the Sequestration Committee had paid to them in exchange for the house and the factory—seven thousand Egyptian pounds. That guaranteed that they would live comfortably on its income while their kids continued in their private schools until they finished their secondary education. She had only to economize somewhat to meet household expenses and needs, and she could plan for that.

Time kept on turning, both with and without Dr. Rashad Fikri. The days and nights passed indistinguishably as though they had not passed at all and as though time had stopped turning for Mohammed al-Buri in his prison in Qena. He wondered about what had disabled the passage of time and when the day of his release would come. He did not find an answer. Once again, boredom crept into his whole body, exhausting his senses. He stopped painting, talking about life, or counting the days as they flowed by, no longer caring as he had before. Reckoning that the end was drawing near, he rallied all his forces to keep up the vigil for the day he would leave, rolling up his sleeves eagerly. But he saw that as the anticipated moment grew closer, it seemed to grow further and further away until he gave up looking forward to it. His feet began to sink into the ground beneath them as though he stood on a pile of shifting sand, his every attempt to escape from and survive the depressing reality plunging him deeper and deeper into it. Slowly his body and spirit vanished and disappeared entirely under it. Even prayer lost its earlier effect of making him more confident in his today and tomorrow. Instead, he increased his efforts to thoroughly study how religion deals with what comes after death, and its effects on his own thoughts—the greatest being his despair in life. One day he thought of suicide but quickly recoiled from it due to his fear of the eternal torment that would await him should he do it. Hope was like a mirage that vanished every time he started even to try approaching it.

Not all these musings were phantasms or delusions from his side. By order of the Interior Ministry for inmates who were members of the Society of the Muslim Brothers, the period of his prison term turned out, in fact, to be longer than that handed down in court.

His wife Zeinab and his children Mohammed, Mostafa, and Mai had begun to visit him in his dreams while he slept and while he was awake, sitting atop his iron bed and resting his back against the cold wall for the comfort of its humidity against the burning sun in the yard where the rest of the inmates and prison guards spent their days chatting with each other or playing football.

During his musings, the taste of the freedom he missed so intensely came back to him. He seriously wondered if his persistent struggle, for all these long years, to enable the leaders of the Muslim Brotherhood movement to reach the ruling seat had been worth all this sacrifice.

A wave of horror struck him suddenly one morning at the infiltration of white hairs on his head—age was leaking his days through his fingers. Life was passing him by—and he was oblivious to its advance. Hot tears finally flowed down his cheeks as he contemplated the fact that Mai would not recognize him when he returned to his house in Hadra. If he ever did return!

Despair dug its sharp claws into his flesh, and they sank in. He was not able to pull them out, no matter how hard he tried.

Layla had become not only an attractive young lady but a truly gorgeous one, making her the object of the stares of both boys and men with roving eyes and hearts. She reminded the older men of Moharram Bey of the late Qamar, the most beautiful of women. They feared lovely Layla would meet her same fate. They surrounded her not just with affection and sympathy but with watchfulness over her comings and goings from the house—so no wolf could block her way. But good intentions are always weak before the brutal hand of fate. The thing they tried to prevent happened despite all their efforts. He had followed her on her way to school one day: the engineer Maged Baroudi, a good-looking young man known in the whole district for his adventures with ladies and his obdurate refusal to accept failure in conquering the heart of every woman once he had decided to woo and seduce her with predatory skill. Layla was tempting, easy prey, for she was a student in secondary school, and he was in the final year of his bachelor's degree studies at the College of Engineering of the University of Alexandria. True, this was his second attempt after failing the previous year, yet that did not affect his confidence in his own abilities. Rather, he thought it added to his life experience—especially with women! Yet his greatest motivation, apart from her bewitching body, was that she was Jewish! Yes, for in his tried and true knowledge of women, Jewish women were prized prey, not to be underestimated. They were beautiful, easy, and liberated—always imitating European girls. It had become rather difficult to find one of them in those days after most of the Jews had left Alexandria, particularly following the Tripartite Aggression against Egypt. Thus, when he knew of the return of the family of *al-Khawaga* Daoud to Moharram Bey and with them the young, adolescent girl, he began to study her steps and with patience and skill drew up his plan for her to fall his victim.

Layla responded more quickly than expected, for she was dazzled by his handsomeness. All the defenses she had erected around herself weakened when she caught sight of him following her that morning, his mature good looks crowned with a golden mustache that cut across the middle of his face. He only had to mutter "Good morning, Miss Layla," for her to smile at him with affected shyness. He was taken aback by the splendid beauty of her honey-colored eyes when she turned to look at him: a tremor moved through his body until his knees wobbled so much beneath him that he nearly fell, and he quickly took some small steps that allowed him to regain control of himself with difficulty. He rebuked himself sternly for that disgraceful mishap in the crowded history of his fearless deeds and adventures with women. Yet he was only human! Her beauty and sudden responsiveness stunned him completely. He was accustomed to sly deception, coldness, and contrived stubbornness as the first reactions of countless women and girls who were half as beautiful as she. Would he not expect a superior rejection from a girl with that power and allure?

A strong relationship of intense mutual admiration began. Soon the admiration turned into passionate love, whose coming surprised the man who had launched so many raids. And its fervor shocked the naïve girl. Its advent without guile surprised them both; their nights were altogether sleepless while their days were made happy with trysts stolen for a few moments next to the school, on the Corniche, or at the train station, fearing that the eyes of neighbors—or Suleiman, or any of his friends—would notice them.

And despite that, the delicate breezes and the wings of birds flying in orderly flocks from the sea bore the news of the innocent relationship, and Elaine seized upon it anxiously. She did not hesitate to relate the details to Daoud, isolated in his room, as soon as she reached it, because such issues of honor should not be hushed up nor should there be any hesitance about confronting them despite the appearance of innocence that surrounded such an affair. But they lived in the Moharram Bey district: they were not in Gleem or San Stefano. Then there was the sensitivity of her position as stepmother of the girl Layla. That made some dislike her handling of the matter, exposing her to criticism—especially if it were not seen favorably by Layla or Daoud. In addition to his astonishment upon hearing the news, Daoud was surprised by the girl's sudden growing-up, as though she had become a young woman between night and morning, or so it seemed to him. Yet he did not know for a moment how to deal with the issue, deeming it wise to leave it entirely to the wisdom of his wife to decide it as she pleased.

And with all that, the problem was smoothed out faster than anyone expected with the surprise appearance of Nabil Yusuf Qitani, grandson of the famous millionaire and son of

Daoud's deceased father's paternal aunt, at their own house. He had come to inform Daoud that he and his family were departing for Europe in a matter of days. Nabil's father had sent him specifically to ask Daoud if they wished his family to take Miss Layla with them, her being the last remaining Jewish maiden among Daoud's children from before he had converted to Christianity to marry Elaine.

Despite Layla's opposition—or rather outright collapse—upon hearing the news, her departure from Egypt nonetheless seemed the best thing for her. She was forced to leave for Europe, especially in the wake of the increase in hostility between Egypt and Israel and the fear for Daoud and Elaine in the face of the increased aversion of the Egyptians in general toward the Jews. Under the pressure of the huge media campaign that the state was mounting at that time, Nabil's proposition was naturally an opportunity to interrupt the development of the new emotional attachment without directly confronting it. Layla's traveling away from Alexandria was a great shock to Maged al-Baroudi that led him to fail the baccalaureate exam once again, though he made it through the crisis, obtaining the degree the following year in time to avoid being expelled from the college. The course of his life changed because of that emotional relationship with Layla, which, despite its brevity, caused him to end his pursuit of women out of loyalty to her. He was committed to a platonic bond that he felt for his beloved, Layla Daoud Abdel-Malek, sure that the days would bring them together once more in spite of how they had been split apart.

As for Suleiman, his life had changed completely since his return to Moharram Bey. The decision to return was, relatively speaking, easier for his father and mother, and even for his sister Layla, because they had spent a long time in Moharram Bey before they had moved to the palace of Binyuti Pasha; therefore, their return to slum housing was expected. They had twice experienced the feeling of change, the second time their affairs merely returning to how they had been before. For Suleiman, this was the only change of which he had been aware—an experience shared with his younger sister Mona. This change was the result of the recent move from the luxurious lifestyle in the palace, which had included Nargis, *Amm* Abduh the cook, and William the chauffeur—driver of the big gleaming black limousine—that used to deliver him to the school in the morning and take him back home in the afternoon. It was the first real change that hurt him; since their return to Moharram Bey, it had pained him to have to walk to school all alone each morning and then home again along streets and neighborhoods that were entirely new to him. Yet the years of study passed quickly as he advanced through the succeeding grades with confidence due to his status as an outstanding student who crowned his accomplishments with a certificate of outstanding merit at the end of each year.

But, contrary to expectation, he felt a new kind of happiness that he had not known before—the happiness that comes with freedom. Yes, freedom grants happiness even to the heart of a young man moving curiously through the first sixteen years of life. Even if he had not previously felt that something was missing or holding him down, he realized that during the time he began to spend by himself. Going back and forth between the house and the school every day without being watched or told what to do—as was the case since he was born—gave his life a dazzling taste. Even if it was merely his ability to change course and continue walking on Market Street or al-Halwani Road or Fouad Street, for instance, without the need to consult anyone. Or, for example, he might stop on his return at the window of one of the shops to stare at an orange shirt or a green-tinged picture of the players for the Alexandria Ettihad Club or hobble into a confectioner's shop to buy a piece of *harisa* pastry dabbed with cream on his way home on a Thursday. He could do all of that—or not, as he wished—without needing to ask for anyone's permission. Freedom! How beautiful that was! Being the boss of his own feelings—freely—naturally led to boundless flights of imagination. He would envision himself on a given day as a famous football player, or a movie star, or a successful doctor, as his thoughts led him from one day to another. Freedom!

His eyes grew accustomed to the features of the various roads that he began to traverse during his daily walk, from the drainage holes dispersed on the pavements here and there to the towering stone buildings, especially on Fouad Street, and the neighbors, shop owners, and doormen of those buildings—even the dogs and cats that dashed quickly in front of him at the entrance to a house or in the central courtyard of an apartment block or an alley running next to it. He felt certain that he knew all of them and that they were beginning to know him. He was even able to talk with these animals and prevent them from harming him by virtue of his control over their little minds. And on top of that, his legs had gained strength and his muscles bulged as he grew to a youth in his prime. He inherited his mother's good looks and his father's slenderness, yet he surpassed his father in height and breadth though he was still only sixteen.

In addition to his daily promenade, Suleiman would go out shopping every day as part of his manly role in the family. During these outings, he became street smart, learning many skills, including not only to choose and buy vegetables and fruit but also to compare prices—experiences one could never acquire if you spent your entire life waiting around in Binyuti Pasha's palace, surrounded by a small army of servants. He gained the confidence of some of his companions in the district; they permitted him to share not only in their amusements but also in some football matches that used to take place between the neighbors. Yet these relationships never reached the level of friendship. Yusuf remained his only friend.

CHAPTER EIGHTEEN

SEVEN WHOLE YEARS, DAOUD REMAINED in his isolation, not knowing of world events but for those he heard on the radio. Most of the time, he was not distressed by what was happening. But with the first hints of summer in the seventh year, he received crazy signals and hellish signs that seemed to arrive from a mythical world that had no connection to the real one. They carried irrational meanings despite that they were communicated in actual human voices. He hoped that they did not signify a mental or psychological ailment on his part. But with the passage of time, he realized they were truly mad messages that gushed suddenly from every radio at the same time, all through the city. In a hysterical fashion, they formed a tapestry of emotional music and song mixed with brief news bulletins—military announcements that flowed in an astonishing torrent, delivered in a somber tone and a melodious voice, about the staggering victories that the Egyptian armed forces had achieved—with hallucinatory speed and singular steadfastness—in the face of the Israeli enemy.

Yet the fantastical stream of victories was not believed by everyone, especially after the first hours they were broadcast. As if hidden hands had reached into every part of the land, it seemed that everywhere, radio dials were turning away from the signal of Voice of the Arabs and the Egyptian broadcasting stations to seek the truth of what was happening from the BBC or Radio Israel. That truth had spread like wildfire until it consumed the whole country in just a few moments. The hopes of all Egyptians went up in smoke, their hearts turned to handfuls of blackened ash. The unexpected news—the imaginary and the real, the insane and the logical— spread everywhere altogether: in every alley, every street, and every house. Tears flowed and cheeks were slapped in lamentation on every balcony as cries came from every window. Crowds of people scurried onto the streets, wandering aimlessly as they wept.

Suddenly, in the flood of silence, that he'd chosen to adopt, Daoud shrieked in his monk's cell, "Why have you done this, Gamal?"

How could the leader have let things reach this point? And why? Daoud nervously put on his shirt and pants and threw a jacket over his shoulders. Then he automatically placed the *tarboush* on his head. He went out of the house for the first time in seven years and headed directly to the sea.

At the basement entrance of the house, Hafez the launderer called out to him, "*Khawaga* Daoud! It's impossible—you're still alive! Where have you been, brother, all these years?"

And at the intersection with Market Street one of the youths standing at the corner commented, "Hey gang— *al-Khawaga* Daoud is back!"

A middle-aged man among those sitting in the café remarked, his anger burning with the narghile's fire, "Of course he had to come back. What else would he do? When the calf falls, yet more knives come out for it!" Those words were followed by murmurings from the men around him— sharp, fragmentary, and angry expressions that Daoud found hard to decrypt.

Daoud felt the stares of the people who packed the road around him like a flame at the back of his neck, piercing his body from every direction as if he were responsible for what had occurred. For his part, he continued down his path, oblivious to all—for he had resolved to reach the sea, regardless of all. How you have changed, streets of Alexandria! It was as though he had lost a lifetime, not merely a few years! What are all these crowds of people! Where did they all come from? He remembered a dream that he had had the night before, whose details he could not recall at first, but all of which returned to him then. He was still a small child walking down the same street, holding onto his mother's hand; she had taken him to stroll with her and had bought him some ice cream. He raised his head in her direction after each lick, contemplating the beauty of her captivating face. She looked at him with a reassuring smile as they ambled down the streets, devoid of all human beings. Suddenly his mother disappeared, leaving him all alone. He cried on the deserted road as the rest of the ice cream melted in his hand. Then he awoke, dabbing away real tears that flowed down his cheeks, with a genuine feeling of filth clinging to his hand—so much so that he wiped it automatically on the breast of his robe as he languished between wakefulness and sleep.

A strange voice mingled with those on the street.

"*Khawaga* Daoud," it called.

He deliberately ignored it, as he despised this word, "*Khawaga*."

He realized that his feet were no longer as steady as before his seclusion. Yet, certain that someone was following him, he quickened his pace as much as he could. He made his way through the packed bodies of the crowd with difficulty. But the strength of his legs did not match his impulse to walk quickly, though he was too stubborn to give up. He strained to cross the station square, crammed to the limit with people coming out to the road, gaping with fear at what was happening in the country. It became clear they were not heading anywhere in particular. Meanwhile, the footsteps kept following him. But he did not try to turn and look behind him, as if sparing no effort until he arrived at his intended destination. His longing to behold the sea drove him onward while the weakness he suffered after his years of isolation weighed down his steps, hindering him from reaching the shore where his feet longed to tread the burning sands and feel the caress of the lapping waves. Then the call came again.

"*Khawaga* Daoud." And once more he ignored it.

His heartbeat became audible, and his breathing grew faster as he thought about hurrying at least a little more considering the footfalls that followed in his wake without slackening, the shouts that accompanied them, and that sadness that still wore on him as it had since the noonday after he had heard what he heard. Tears began to flow from the corners of his eyes, then trickled down his sloping cheeks. He wiped them with the back of his sleeve as he hurried on his way without halt or detour. Yet by his steady tread he avoided letting whomever was following him be sure that he knew he was doing so.

He remembered the day of his only meeting with Sheikh Foda and the footsteps of the dogged youth who had pursued him then. He wondered if they belonged to the same man who followed him now. He feared he might try to hurt him—a Jew—in retaliation for what the Israelis had done today. Or maybe to avenge the death of Sheikh Hassanein, given that Sheikh Foda had accused him of causing it when he saw him. Or even the suicide of Qamar, as he had implied as well.

The voice called out to him with a stern, threatening tone: "*Khawaga* Daoud!"

For a few minutes, he managed to hurry his feet, summoning inner strength from his immense fear. The voice continued to call him *Khawaga*, as if he were a foreigner—an epithet that might have been meant metaphorically in the past, but would it be today? What would they do to him after what had happened now? Nothing less than to seize him as prey, than to devour the meat of his aged body with their teeth. He attempted to hurry, but the heat and humidity and the crowded roads were like a screen that he tried to pass through to no avail. He grasped that the mission was clearly impossible. Yet he raised his eyes to look before him, the burning line of the horizon gleaming in the distance. As the sun appeared over the stone wall of the corniche, he stood on tiptoe after each footstep to peer over people's heads, trying without success to catch a glimpse of the sea's edge. He had to get close enough to the Corniche to see the blue of the sea, even as exhaustion finally overtook him.

"Hey *Khawaga* Daoud!" But he didn't reply nor did he look around.

His breaths heaved harder, his heart beat faster and faster, yet he struggled under the burden as he pressed on his way. He knew he had no choice but to reach the sea. The time he had followed the quick footsteps of Sheikh Hassanein— which had been difficult as well—leapt to his mind. That day the sheikh led him to roughly the same place to murder him emotionally by butchering their long relationship and also to urge him to flee his own country—with complete brazenness! But despite that, under his breath, Daoud muttered a prayer for mercy on his soul! His face and body were drenched with sweat. He took off his *tarboush*, pulled a handkerchief out of his pocket, and began drying his head and brow, then put the handkerchief back again, then repeated the same actions, still panting. But this did not stop him from continuing down his path.

"*Khawaga* Daoud!" The cry turned into a shriek, yet even so it melted into the rest of the noise.

The pain began to squeeze his thighs like a neatly tied knot or two sides of a vice gripping the flesh on his weakened old bones. It seemed to him he should stop, if only for a moment, but both his fear of the owner of those footsteps still dogging him and his passionate longing to reach his goal drove him on. Then the pain began to climb from his legs to his thighs until a feeling of nausea struck his gut with a pain that made him stop and gulp a few breaths. But the sense that the footsteps behind him were getting closer left him no choice, so he stuck to his course regardless. Still, he was compelled to slow the pace of his own desperate footsteps at least a little as it became impossible for him—now an old man—to finish with the same strength with which he had begun.

Then for a brief instant, like a flash of lightning suddenly gleaming before him, he remembered his magical ring that had vanished from him so mysteriously. None of the disasters that lately befell him would have happened if it had not vanished. At the same time, it also occurred to him that perhaps if he hadn't taken the ring from Gamal when he called on him in Manshiat al-Bakri—if he had left it with him instead—then what was happening to the country today could have been avoided!

"*Khawaga* Daoud! *Khawaga!*"

He didn't reply or even turn around, fearing to discover the identity of his pursuer. Daoud thought that if he wanted to put paid to him, he would have already done so. If he would not stab him in the back, then perhaps he would not stab him at all if Daoud didn't turn around to confront him. Yet perhaps he wanted Daoud to recognize him first—to watch him plunge the knife in his heart and witness with his own eyes the specter of death as it grabbed him and pulled out his soul under his own gaze.

At last, he reached the Corniche! But a stream of car traffic forced him to halt. Finally, the smell of hot sand and of the steaming salt sea, along with the exhaust fumes from the passing cars, blended in his nostrils! He waited for the opportune moment to take some breaths not impeded by—and not capable of being impeded by—the owner of those footsteps. In fact, Daoud felt as though his pursuer were right behind him, breathing on the back of his head. Moreover, he was preoccupied with that deadly pain that remained like a mountain pressing down on his chest, preventing him from filling his lungs with the air of the sea to which he was finally so near—only a few steps away. Yes, just a few steps away, yet it seemed as distant as the burning disc of the sun in the highest heavens. That distance was the reason for the painful longing that gripped his being! The stream of cars halted at the traffic signal, so he seized the opportunity and exerted the last, slight bit of effort that remained in him. As he made to cross the Corniche, the pain transformed into a terrifying beast that pounced upon him.

Despite that, he dragged his feet onward, propelled by his impassioned body, his clothes stained with rivers of sweat whose swelling waters filled his chest and heart. But he gave all he had in his determination to get to the beach no matter the cost. He paid no attention to the footsteps that continued now as if they were attached to his own. Despite that, he did not turn to reproach the one who they belonged to, even with a glance. Instead, he was overwhelmed by a cloud that fell vaguely over his eyes. His eyesight weakening, things appeared like ghosts dancing and swaying before him, their features obscure. Meanwhile, his pain grew greater, pressing upon his soul. Yet his legs kept moving until he crossed the road, when he lost the feeling of being hunted and relaxed.

Suddenly the image of his father from his shining youth descended upon him: he was taking him to the seashore as he used to do in those days. His feet had hardly touched the sand when he plunged to his knees. In the breathless haste of a boy of five, Daoud took off his shoes and socks, then rolled up his trousers. He steadied himself and rose to his feet, heading toward the placid waters, and with him was the smiling face of his father. His feet touched the cold water, and he shivered all over. Yet the grip of pain on his body lightened a little. Elaine's lovely face came to him, encompassing the smiles of Suleiman, Mona, and the departed Makari, plus the image of Layla, Fouad, Musa, Sophie, and the suckling infant Margo.

He then saw a churning foam atop the waves, and from its agitated heart there burst Qamar—her exciting body wrapped in a gown that clung to every curve of her figure. She looked at him, laughing lasciviously. As he heard the laugh, she stretched her arms toward him as he felt himself striving to get close to her. But his feeble legs lacked the strength to carry him farther.

Daoud dropped prostrate on the sandy beach in submission, the waves lapping at his body. He began to sing mumbled poems to himself as a sense of ease spread within him that he had not known before.

CHAPTER NINETEEN

WHEN THE AMBULANCE REACHED THE French Hospital, Daoud Abdel-Malek was already dead. Someone came to the house to summon Suleiman, who had spent the day at home, as the schools had shut their doors upon the declaration of war, to identify his father. Suleiman looked at him quietly; Daoud's features had frozen into a generally relaxed expression. Despite the restraint he had resolved upon before he arrived, he could not stop himself from bursting into sobs, embarrassing himself by weeping in front of these strangers. Yet all his efforts to stifle his weeping only increased his distress so that he cried even more until he decided—finally—to let himself go. The strangers, in their turn, also went outside the empty room—empty, that is, but for his father's body stretched out on the white metal four-wheeled bed.

Suleiman was astonished when he realized amid his tears that his father had left him forever before speaking with him on many things that he had wanted him to—if only time had granted Suleiman opportunity to ask him about them and to share them with him. At that moment, he wished that he had been able to take advantage of even a few more minutes of life with him. But how hard it is to get back even an instant of time! He laid his head on his father's stiffened chest, vanishing once again into the dark, featureless corridors of his grief. He hadn't known until this moment that all this sadness had lurked inside him. Rather, it struck him that he had not been aware that he harbored all that capacity of feeling for his father, for their relationship—except for during scattered periods—was not so deep as to account for all the tears that drenched him now. He had always blamed that on the great gap in age that divided them, but he realized how wrong he was today after it was too late for regret.

Scenes of them together over the years flashed like photographic images before his eyes. He seemed to have been a mere spectator, as if he had nothing to do with them. But thinking it over, he could see that the sadness that grieved him now was itself proof of the depth of the relationship that had existed between them, without his having realized how deep it really was. But with the passage of time, he had become certain that his father had understood that all along. At the time, Suleiman was convinced his father was a great man, in any case, which reassured his heart, restored his calm, and stopped his tears.

Elaine turned inward and withdrew once again into her sad isolation, dwelling on the memories of death and loss that had accompanied her since the passing of her child Makari. But this time her responsibility for Suleiman and Mona pulled her back out of it quickly. She was not sure, at first, whether she should look for what she had heard was the last Jewish rabbi remaining in Cairo. But she put the thought far from her mind as they prayed over Daoud's body in the bosom of the church. Despite that, she advised the priest of his desire to be buried in the Jewish cemetery next to his father and mother, and his wish was granted. On the third day after his death, Elaine entered his room and felt the weight of its silence. She saw the mournful oud resting on its stand as though complaining of being lonely for the first time. She picked it up and cradled it in her arms with care, wiping away with her fingertips a thin layer of dust that had dared to envelope it since Daoud had gone. Her nose savored the fragrance of the instrument's vintage wood.

She moaned in silence despite herself, then regained control and began to search among his papers in the drawers. She found a group of scattered sheets of different shapes and sizes on whose lines he had traced his thoughts and memories, marked with the date of their composition. They included words from famous songs. Then she found the blue notebook that she had bought for him on their return to Moharram Bey. Elaine sat on the edge of the bed and opened the notebook, wondering about its contents, and found that it was filled to its end with poetry. In the imposing silence she began to read Daoud's poems like one entranced. And from that night that she spent entirely awake, Elaine never ceased reading them during all hours of the day or night until her passing.

Elaine remembered with grief the silver signet ring she had hidden from Daoud all these years. It came back to her that he had urged her many times to bequeath it to his son Suleiman after him. Yes, Suleiman, not Fouad or Musa, even before the two of them had left Egypt. They were his eldest sons and thus first for his inheritance, but he chose Suleiman, her son. Repenting for what she had done against the rights of Daoud all these years, Elaine went to the old wardrobe in which were piled the clothes of the deceased Makari and added to them those of her husband. She stretched out her trembling hand, which knew its way among the accumulated heaps, pressing her fingers over them, then called out in a hesitant voice, "Suleiman! Suleiman!"

She wondered if she was doing the right thing, but her feelings of guilt toward her husband led her to carry out his will. She handed Suleiman the silver ring, then told him the story behind it—the whole story! She made clear to him her intense regret and repentance for what she had committed against his father—even after Mikhail the priest had counseled her to return the ring to him. But she had been afraid—yes, she had weakened with fear. She had feared that Daoud would discover what she had done and would deal with her roughly for his whole life over the right to his ring that she had denied him.

When she told her story to her son, she was filled with a feeling of vileness and selfishness. She wondered how she could be so easily immersed in this kind of cruelty toward her husband for all these years. And how she had not thought to return the ring to him, if only out of sympathy, given that his condition was due not only to neglect and isolation but melancholy and depression as well. She should have considered producing it much earlier, especially as he believed that all these catastrophes had befallen him because he had lost the ring, not knowing that the ring had been hidden only meters from him the whole time. As she was recounting all this to Suleiman, she did not try to diminish the value of the gift that his departed father had bequeathed to him. Just the act of drawing out her story in truthful detail before her son had a soothing effect on her, washing away her feelings of guilt. As for the youth, fittingly for a boy of sixteen, he was dazzled by the tale. Elaine had barely finished her narrative when he put the ring on his right ring finger and was awakened immediately to a strange feeling of power that he could interpret in no other way than as the effect of the magical ring.

For years on end, Suleiman felt the power of that ring consuming him. The effect was not overflowing and all-engulfing—or rather a torrent of overwhelming leaps in his life, changing its course—as his father before him had believed. It came to the son as a continuous drizzle, not like a drenching though intermittent flood, and in the end, it had an equivalent impact on both their lives. For while Daoud had felt that the enchantment had led him to meet Gamal and Binyuti Pasha, and that later its absence had led to the collapse of his wealth on his head, Suleiman sensed a running stream of wisdom and sagacity in dealing with the people around him. With all people, but especially the members of the gentler sex—not a girl or woman could resist admiring him! That included

Najat, the young stunner of the quarter, whose beauty melted everyone. Even Maged al-Barudi could not satisfy her, and she fell in Suleiman's net. Hence he became a legend among his companions, who all dreaded his might and huddled away from him in fear for their young sisters. One day as he walked to his house, he chanced to turn right onto their street and passed by the café on the corner. Sitting in it was a laundry boy called Namla* whose real name was Mas'ud. He earned his nickname due to his slight, delicate frame. Namla bent down to the ear of Houda, his friend the bicycle repairman, when he saw Suleiman coming, and Suleiman heard Namla whisper to Houda: "Let's take it easy with them! This Suleiman is dangerous, man. By the Prophet, maybe one day you'll find him passing over your house, crushing you and your family, coveting your young sisters."

He then smiled at the two of them without saying a word.

But the reaction to his fearsome reputation did not prevent him from maintaining his daring and boldness all the years he was studying until his graduation from the College of the Humanities, Department of Philosophy—with the grade of "Good" despite his having been distracted most of the time with romantic adventures. He deemed Mariam Doss' family's rejection of his relationship with her to be his only failure. They had shunned him despite the young girl's passionate love for him when she told them of her wish to get engaged to him

---

* *Namla* is "ant" in Arabic. *Sura* (Chapter) 27 of the Qur'an is entitled *al-Naml* ("The Ants").
Verses 18-19 tell the story of Suleiman (In Jewish tradition, King Solomon) and the ants. Verse 18 says, "Till when they came to a valley of the ants, (and) one of the ants said, "O you ants, get into your houses, lest Sulaiman (Solomon) and his armies will crush you without even knowing it." *English Translation of the Message of the Qur'an*, trans. Syed Vickar Ahamed, 2nd ed. (Lombard, IL: Book of Signs Foundation, 2006), 209. Translation approved by al-Azhar.

because—as far as he could judge—of the great social gap between her family's wealth and his own modest background. And though their relationship continued in secret for two whole years afterward—despite her family's opposition—because of her contempt for their attitude toward him, she finally let go of her attachment to him in the end. This had a deep impact upon him that he could not overcome for years. In any case, he had considered her intense devotion to him to be among the gifts brought to him by the enchanted signet. As for his feelings, he considered his relationship with her to be a kind of challenge, as though experimenting with the effect of the magic ring in the face of the unbending laws of society. Yet, in the end, the real motivation behind his pursuit of her was that his love for himself was greater than his love for her.

The days passed tediously, one very like the other, with nothing memorable about them, gathering in the pouch of time as an empty ennui. None of their details stuck to the memory of Mohamed al-Buri as he huddled in Qena Prison, patiently waiting—patience being his only solace—for the day of his release.

It did not come.

He awaited it every sunrise and every night when the moon emerged; at the coming of winter with its icy slap and its flowing floods and at the arrival of every summer with its burning hellish days and the dryness of its winds. Still, it did not come.

Until . . .

Until the tyrant died at last.

Yes, he finally fell, after destroying the most beautiful years of his life and those of the rest of the Brotherhood behind prison walls, bringing them to the lowest of the low. They turned into dwarfs bounded by those high fences and the sands of those vast deserts around them—which sealed them off from any trace of life—and the broad expanse of oblivion that separated them from their families, from humanity, and from the country. Then, finally, Gamal Abdel-Nasser died, after laying to waste everything with his presence over the years. He had ruined the country with his presence, and these Communist atheists—his comrades, the Officers—had alienated the people from the worship and authority of God and His Holy Law as they clung to the likes of Khrushchev, Mao Tse-Tung, Tito, and Castro. So, the nation and its people had plunged down the drain of defeat and destruction. Mohammed would never be able to forgive him for what he had done. Clouds of hatred covered his memories and anything that revived them in any way.

In the first half of his sixth decade, when Mohammed al-Buri had lost hope of a way out, the new president, Mohammed Anwar al-Sadat—may God lengthen his life—who had succeeded the buffoon, ordered his release. Naturally, at first, Mohammed al-Buri had cheered the decision. Then he realized with a shudder that it might be too late for him to catch up with the wheels of time since they had run so long without him. Yet he was convinced that the experience—with all its hardships—demanded that he plunge into it without reserve, and he resolved to hold firm amid its clamor, come what may. What was there left for him to lose after what he had already lost? He muttered at the gate outside the prison, "God suffices me; I place my trust in Him, the Lord of the mighty throne."

He wept when he arrived at Misr Station in Alexandria. He could not bear all those feelings he had kept pent up in anticipation any longer and thus released a flood of tears that flowed down his wrinkled cheeks. He smiled with a strange, child-like naïveté as he turned toward all those around him, embracing them with his eyes after having been absent from them for eighteen years. He was supposed to get off the train at al-Hadra Station, but he didn't recognize it until the train had moved on. Or perhaps it had not stopped there in the first place: he did not know. When it brought him to the last station, he disembarked. When he went out into the massive square, he was taken aback by the crowds that filled it completely—a huge number of hawkers, beggars, and men strolling and wandering about selling lottery tickets, their cries rising here and there. A layer of mud covered the ground so that one could not tell the concrete tiles from the asphalt. Women selling vegetables paved the square with their filthy baskets. No doubt some momentous event had taken place—surely, he would learn its full significance in time. Until, with the curiosity of a child running away from his parents into the crowds of the city, he stopped and stared at the scene around him, amazed, then stretched out his hand and gripped the shoulder of one of the peddlers carrying a great tray with baked *semeet* bread, cheese, and boiled eggs held by a strap over his neck, and asked, "What's it about?"

"What's what about? What do you mean, old man? Go on—may God smooth your path."

Mohammed al-Buri called to another peddler seated on two cement blocks and stretching before him a carton bearing an assortment of hair combs, knives, spoons, paper napkins.

"What's the story, son?" he asked. "What are all these people doing here?" The man looked at him in amazement, but he did not reply.

When Mohammed realized that his silence could not stand, he asked him, "Then, if you please, how do I get to al-Hadra?"

"Take the tram that goes to al-Nuzha and get off at al-Hadra. Don't you also want money for the ticket? Go on, old man—place your trust in God and leave, so we may see to our work."

The man looked Mohammed over, took him for a beggar, and turned away. Maybe he thought he was deranged? Mohammed stood aghast, realizing that his appearance had no doubt provoked disgust even in the eyes of this reprobate, so he decided not to speak with anyone until he arrived peacefully at his house.

He carried the parcel full of his clothes slung over his

shoulder and continued walking cautiously toward the tram bound for al-Nuzha to get off at al-Hadra as the man had advised him. He didn't know the price of the ticket these days and was embarrassed to ask the conductor, so he gave him ten piastres. That was all he possessed after having purchased the ticket for the train from Qena to Alexandria. He hesitated as he waited for the man to give him back the change, so he turned to look elsewhere and saw a beautiful girl sitting with her mother, her small hands crossed over her mother's arm, her head bent toward her a little. Mohammed thought she might look like his daughter Mai. The conductor elbowed him and handed him the remaining piastres he was owed. At Kabo Station, carrying his bag, he passed through the bodies packed together as he went down. On the platform, he stopped, nailed to where he stood, the whistle of the tram bidding him farewell. He turned around, asking himself about the way to his house. It struck him how much everything had changed—so much so that he no longer knew how to return to his home.

He thought to ask one of the people packed on the station platform next to him, but the experience at Misr Station made him wary of plunging into such danger again. No doubt he looked strange as he continued to stand in silence on the station platform as such, and the people passing around him began to cast suspicious glances his way. Children at first began to walk around him in silence, then their naughty hands, fingers, and laughter began to reach toward him, exploring whether he was sane like most people or a crazy man who had descended on them from the tram for their pleasure and amusement. It was clear to him that he was viewed doubtfully by all, so he hoisted his parcel over his shoulder once again and moved on.

What had happened? How did all the landmarks change so much? And who were all these people that filled the streets around him, none of whom he knew, nor did they know him? Mohammed crossed al-Hadra Street by a miracle after a passing car almost wiped him out. The features that used to guide him on the way had vanished, and none of the shops he used to see were still there. He did not find *Usta* Kamel the tailor nor Abduh the grocer. Nor did he find the industrial warehouse of *al-Hagg* al-Damanhouri where he had met with the Muslim Brothers after Sheikh Hassanein had gotten out of detention. Where had all these people gone, and from where had all the other people come who filled up the streets and roads this way?

There was no doubt there was some secret behind this that he did not know, for there was no other way to interpret all these changes over the years he was absent. He picked up the pace of his steps toward his house. He passed the high wall that surrounds the school for the deaf and dumb, and seeing it made him realize that it was still standing, praise God. If not for that, he would not have realized that he was close to his home. He then slipped into the first blind alley, contemplating the old apartments on both sides. What frightened him were all the hidden piles of trash at the bottom of each, from which rose loathsome smells. But he endured them stoically as he recognized the passageway leading to their ancient residence. He stepped inside to escape that feeling of estrangement that possessed him. He mounted the well-worn stairs to the second floor, staring at the graffiti about rival football clubs daubed in red on the dingy wall that ran alongside it.

"*al-Ettihad: 2, al-Ahly: 0.*"

"*We'll go to war.*"

Mohammed al-Buri stopped for a moment to catch his breath in front of the door and to prepare himself to meet his family. He recalled how each of them looked, trying to imagine what the days had done to them. Softly he tapped with his fingers on the glass between the iron bars that covered the upper half of the apartment door.

CHAPTER TWENTY

NO MATTER HOW HIGH DISTRESS rises and how far it reaches, there is no doubt that, with the passage of time, sorrows will dissolve and disappear in the rolling streams of forgetfulness. Especially when those streams meet the path of a human being in the act of surrendering to the course of life and its destinies. Despite all her strength in the face of sorrow and separation from her loved ones, Elaine had submitted at last to her fate. She threw off the weight of her own grief over her husband's departure even faster than expected until she suspected that this change in her emotions had been interpreted, in the view of some, as unfaithfulness to her husband's memory: in less than six months after his death, she had finished with all the depression and isolation that still lingered in her life. She had believed that the honest wife must clothe her existence in those sad, broken feelings until the day she meets her husband's soul, or at least for the years remaining after his death—and not merely for half a year! Yet despite the depth of her affection for Daoud, she found herself directing her feelings toward his memory into a new, different channel, or even unto herself, turning to the care of her children to the best of her ability in order to glorify his memory rather than remaining weeping and sorrowful. It was as though she had taken it upon herself to pass on his guidance after his death so that neither she nor the children would feel any want in his absence.

Rather, she felt that Daoud had not died and left her, for his ghost remained wandering around her, his memory determining for her how to proceed on her path. She understood that it was always he who was guiding her through his special route to that goal, as when he left the money from the factory's sale and the palace at her disposal before and when he instructed that the magic ring, as he saw it, be left to her son Suleiman, snubbing the rest of his sons. After his death, she felt his eternal presence in their midst when she read his poems, which had seized her innermost heart since she read them that first night. Daoud's ideas gleamed through them—his thoughts, his legacy, and the essence of his heart and spirit.

Elaine continued her effusive giving that astonished everyone. Even she was amazed by her own exuberant energy. Suleiman graduated from the College of the Humanities, and after him Mona graduated from the College of Business of the University of Alexandria. Through her careful planning, she was able to provide Mona with what she needed for her dowry and to furnish a suitable apartment for when she got engaged to her colleague from college, Nader Abdel-Masih. She did so again for the couple's move to Cairo after they married and began the journey of their life together without help from his father, who managed a branch of the Bank of Alexandria. Her heart broke first for the departure of her daughter, of course. But the transformation that had befallen her since their return to Moharram Bey had given her a rigidity that, with the passage of time, was difficult to change on her own.

A touch of diabetes was the cost of her excessive weight, which Dr. Riyadh Shukri—the handsome doctor that she had wanted for her daughter before she had gotten engaged to Nader—had advised her to reduce, but her old age was nonetheless relatively comfortable. She divided her time between the prayers of the mass and studying the catechism two days a week in church as well as between her monthly visits to the Sanctuary of the Virgin and her visits to her daughter Mona in Cairo during holidays and events, averaging two or three times each year. Yet she was uneasy about her presence in Nader's house and in his company generally even though he always treated her—as God was her witness—in the best possible way. However, she could not get over the feeling that he had kidnapped her daughter from her embrace and from all Alexandria, taking her with him far out of her sight to Cairo. Other than that, she had taken to listening to the radio during the day, then reading religious books and Daoud's poems at night. As for Suleiman, he lived with her as though in a hotel. She saw him only rarely, at the moments of his coming and going, and it was also rare that he spent time with her. He didn't allow her to talk to him about what was happening in the world around the two of them. Nonetheless, she was completely content with the stable course of her life, isolated from the world and its many worries.

In April 1968, a glorious event changed the order of her life and brought her a joy and anticipation that the passing days had blotted out for quite a long time. The church in Moharram Bey had announced that members of the congregation would travel to Cairo to visit the Church of the Virgin in Zeitoun to confirm the clamorous news of the miraculous apparitions of the Virgin Lady Mary over its domes. The first to see her had been humble workmen one evening at the bus station next to the church. They had been startled by a phantom of a woman walking over the church's roof beside its domes, and they rushed to inform the guard. Soon a priest came along with a crowd of people fascinated by how the woman was bathed in the light emanating from her body, which made clear to the priest that this was the Virgin Lady. The others thought she was someone trying to take her own life.

Then suddenly the woman vanished within her own light. The news spread with astonishing speed after repeated appearances witnessed by hundreds, and then by thousands, of the area's residents and from the neighborhoods nearby in the beginning and then from everywhere, later. Even her daughter had gone there with her husband and seen it herself: Mona told her about it by telephone the next day. At her insistence, Suleiman agreed to accompany Elaine there with the rest of the church's congregation. In the bus that brought the two of them down from Alexandria, her heart was nearly bursting to behold the light of the Virgin Lady.

Down the length of Tuman Bey Street, thousands were gathered, covering the asphalt—along with throw rugs and newspapers at times—or sitting on the beach chairs that they brought with them, or standing the whole night transfixed and glued to the spot in terror and longing, facing the silent domes surrounded by the buses at the station from which the workmen had seen her for the first time. At one-thirty in the morning, the light began to radiate over the southern dome amid the cries of the crowd. It lasted for a few moments and then disappeared.

Then around two o'clock, the Virgin Lady appeared over the dome in a noble, ethereal light that Elaine had never seen before. The shouts rose in a surging roar from the thousands assembled as the scent of incense and roses spread with tremendous speed. Then, after roughly twenty minutes, the light and the Virgin Lady were gone and so were the lovely fragrances. It was as though an electrical switch was pressed and they were there, and when it was pressed again, they vanished. Afterward the square was filled with a shout and a cry here and there, attesting that miracles had indeed occurred, or that a heavenly, overpowering joy had delighted them, or that there were people present all the time who never saw a thing the others saw. And to her astonishment, Elaine learned that many of those who saw the apparitions and recognized that they were miraculous were Muslims who had flocked to the place after the papers had begun to write about the miracle. As for herself, she enjoyed a happiness and peace that she had never experienced before. And on top of all that, the Virgin

Mary had granted her the miracle of curing her sugar diabetes, as Dr. Riyadh informed her later.

As for Suleiman, his days were filled with romantic adventures and his new work as a philosophy teacher in the literary department at the Saint Mark School from which he had graduated. But in a hidden place, secluded from the events of his life, his thinking was always occupied with the idea of the miraculous visitations and whether they contradicted the views of science and logic. In his opinion, the light of the Virgin over the church's cupola in Zeitoun was the main reason he started to have these doubts in the first place. Before the visitations, the term was meant figuratively. When he said the word "miracle," he thought of a day when he arrived at the university on time before Dr. Saad Madkur had closed the door and begun to scold the students who came late to his lecture. Suleiman thought that he must have lived in a different country than they did, not seeing the serious problems with public transport and traffic that overwhelmed their daily lives.

It was a "miracle" when Suleiman won the heart of Najat over all the other youths around her—even over the handsome, young, and respected engineer Maged al-Baroudi. But the miracle he saw atop the Church of the Virgin was different. The miracles of the former kind obey the known laws of nature and science and are only called as such by way of exaggeration. Yet the appearance of the Virgin over the dome of the church in sight of thousands of Christians and Muslims together day after day in the Zeitoun district and as he personally witnessed there on Tuman Bey Street conformed neither to nature nor science. It neither resisted them nor opposed them, but rather fell under the classification of being outside the understanding of science, logic, and their laws. After all, the laws of nature dictate that no other influence affects their application—even the supernatural, as he was taught in the Philosophy Department at the college. For example, the law of gravity was not rendered invalid when he stretched out his hand yesterday and caught a ball that was falling to the street after it dropped from the hand of a child playing on a balcony as he was walking by the house. Yet extending his hand had prevented gravity—in keeping with the laws of nature—from making the ball fall to the ground, just as the hand of God— the supernatural—that night, before the eyes of thousands of people, had challenged the laws of nature that dictated the diffusion of darkness over the cupolas when there was no sun to illuminate them, causing the miracle to happen.

Rather, what demonstrated it had occurred was the consensus of its manifestation among the multitudes who gathered to see the visitations despite differences in their religious beliefs and their reasons for being in that place. For example, Suleiman was one of those who came to prove the phenomenon was "unscientific" in its basis. When he engaged in these philosophical debates with his college professors and study mate Yusuf Tahir, despite the strangeness of the idea, he was surprised by their approval of it. So he proposed that they meet periodically for discussion to examine subjects both public and private concerning intellectual, philosophical ideas. They would meet to discuss these topics and any others they found acceptable in the "The Association of Free Thought," which Suleiman headed. They adopted the idea, and one of the professors in the Philosophy Department provided an apartment on the first floor of a high-rise building in the Ibrahimiya district, which the professor's father had used as a law office before his death, as a place for their meetings. On the ground floor—the floor below that former office—there was a sort of café where young people congregated until the crack of dawn. Its owner had bought it from a Greek, who had run it like a tavern that had also received its patrons until dawn. But Suleiman never knew that the owner of this tavern had been *al-Khawaga* Antonelli.

*

The door opened, and a beautiful, brown-skinned young woman—tall and slender—blocked the way with a broad smile. Mohammed al-Buri stood still, his tongue tied with surprise when he saw that perhaps his journey of return had ended at last and that this teenaged girl standing before him was his daughter, Mai. She was amazed by this old man who knocked on their door then stood mute in front of it, wondering if he had the wrong address. The situation became even more complicated when the strange old man began to shed silent tears. At that, moments passed in which she could not send him away and close the door. Rather, she remained frozen in front of him, waiting for him to speak, the smile vanishing from her face. Then the old man finally spoke, haltingly.

"Are you Mimi?"

The ringing tones of his voice reverberated in the deep recesses of her heart and mind. She could not place it at first but realized that, despite everything, it was not only familiar, but intimately so. Especially that her nickname Mimi was restricted to a very limited circle of those who knew her. That this strange man called her by it aroused her curiosity. It also prompted her to gather her courage to answer him confidently.

"Yeah, I'm Mimi. Who are you, sir?"

"I'm your father, my daughter," he said to her in a trembling voice. Then he rushed toward her, opening his arms to enfold her in an embrace. She stayed glued where she stood, terrified by this sudden surprise. Then he removed his arms from her as she remained nailed to the spot. He paced around her as she placed her palm over her mouth in disbelief, and Mohammed al-Buri stepped into the flat, asking, "Where is Zeinab? Where are Mohammed and Mustafa?" he pressed her. "Zeinab!" he called out. "Where are you, Zeinab?"

A joyful shout resonated throughout the humble apartment jammed with furniture that stood in the same places he had left it eighteen years before. Its walls had acquired a new coat of pistachio-colored plaster. Zeinab came scurrying out from within, not believing that she was hearing the voice of her man filling the place once again. Her bounding ecstasy preceding her as she entered the salon. Her fingers extended over her nose, her palm stretched over her mouth and her tongue dancing within it, she let out a series of ululations as she came to a halt in front of him.

"Praise God for your safe arrival, my man!" exclaimed Zeinab. "You light up our house! Thank God that you are well!" she added. She had blurted many similar phrases before at times. She had thought of saying these phrases at other times, though the joy had not gripped her enough then to utter them. He noticed how she looked and was taken aback by what the passage of time had done to her, though he intended to keep his reaction to himself. She too was astonished by how much old age and frailty had ravaged him—mirroring his impression of her—though she too avoided any comment in order not to disturb his feelings.

"So—where are the boys? I mean, the men? How could I call them such, after seeing you, Mimi?" Mohammed wondered aloud, looking at his daughter Mai, who smiled for the first time as he proceeded to enthrone himself in his favorite place on the couch in a corner, its back to the wall below the window that looked out onto the building's central open shaft under its skylight. On one side of the shaft rested a tray bearing two water jugs of clay, the same as he had left it eighteen years before.

He looked around to peruse every part of the place, and—praised the Lord—there was still one thing that had not changed in this new world. Zeinab's head drooped over her breast a little, although her eyes remained fixed upward on his as she said with sadness, "The priest ran away to America, but Mustafa is well. He's working at the Bata factory, and he'll be coming back for lunch soon." Having said this, she fell silent, turning her face away to stare into the distance so as not to

226

show the tears that had begun to run down her cheeks.

He noticed her tears, and—to change the drift of the conversation—he mused, "America right away! *Oh Morsi—Oh Abu al-Abbas*! What is the story with this priest?" he demanded, giggling. In Alexandrian dialect, it had become common for locals to call a wicked person a "priest"—a sarcastic allusion to their cowardice and cunning. He thus succeeded in relaxing the atmosphere, while Zeinab responded, aware that her husband had been absent from his home for all those years.

"The fact is, *Si* Mohammed," she told him, "Umm Gaber, the owner of the house, was standing on the building stairs one day, watching a fight between her son Gaber and his brother Hussein with the sons of *Usta* Hassouna. The blood was—you don't want to know this—up to the knees. Then, my dear, your son Mohammed arrived and mounted the staircase, carrying his books, and—and he passed right through them as if nothing was wrong at all. For he was never into fighting or that sort of thing. *Umm* Gaber called out to her sons, saying, 'Be careful: your blood might soil the priest's shirt.' From that day onward, he was called by that name."

He then smiled at the thought that he had passed eighteen years in prison because he belonged to the Society of the Muslim Brothers and then was released only to find that his eldest son had emigrated to America after *Umm* Gaber had made him a "priest!"

CHAPTER TWENTY-ONE

LIKE THE PROVERBIAL CONJURER'S BAG of wonders out of which comes a speckled serpent whose swaying movements he controls with a flute, a gentle dove that does a fluttering dance high in the air, kerchiefs dyed with vivid colors, or a frightening black bat—its features tinged with those of Death—beating its wings, zigzagging madly over the heads of the onlookers, so the days flow by in an onrushing stream, smiling at us malevolently as they reach into their bag to toss strange events and disasters in our faces at times and gifts and bribes at others. For while Suleiman strolled confidently toward his quiet destiny during his years of study, moving like a butterfly from flower to flower, the country was boiling around him, burning with the fire of grief and frustration imposed by defeat, dejection, and the occupation that cut off the eastern side of the Suez Canal up to the borders between Egypt and Israel. In addition, there was the wavering of the ruling authority between austerity and forbearance. Then there was the "Year of Decision," a decision for which everyone waited but which never came—though they said it was imminent—until it seemed like a mirage that the wanderer in the desert cannot quite reach: the more he rushes toward it, the more it draws further away.

One midafternoon near the end of summer, Suleiman awoke from his siesta and was sipping his tea on the balcony, seated on the chair that had supported his father. As he thought about what to do with himself that evening, there came a knock on the door. His mother came to him to say there was a young man asking to meet him and whom she had sat in the guest room to wait for him. Quickly he changed from his pajamas into a shirt and trousers and hurried outside, engulfed in curiosity about this visitor. He turned the doorknob and entered and—lo and behold—there was the Engineer Maged al-Barudi, the handsome young man, sitting meekly with his red face and his golden moustache. Maged smiled at him as he entered the room, stretching out his hand in greeting and welcome as Suleiman tried to parse the reason for this visit.

"Will you drink tea?" Suleiman asked in a familiar tone. Maged smiled and nodded his head a little, then answered hesitantly.

"No reason not to," he said. "That is, if it would be no trouble, I'd like to." He smiled again, adjusting his position on the gilded chair with the uncomfortable, lumpy seat. Suleiman went out for a moment to ask his mother to make tea. When he returned, it appeared that the handsome young man—who had moved forward in his chair until he was on the edge of his seat—was prepared to start the discussion. He could not guess the secret behind the visit until Maged probed him by asking, "In truth, Suleiman—would you permit me to call you Suleiman without honorifics?"

Suleiman gestured affirmatively and continued to nod his head up and down encouragingly throughout the conversation.

"In truth, I don't know how to start," he continued. "That is, I'm really very nervous. I am quite embarrassed to come here this way, without an appointment—but the subject is important—I mean, it's important to me. I don't want to take much of your time, Suleiman. You know that I am now in the Engineering Corps. That is, I had to join the army after finishing my bachelor's degree. In just a few months, they made me an officer. Owing to my qualifications, they attached me to a unit in the Engineers Corps. I'm sorry to repeat myself, and to annoy you: I am truly sorry, by God. I'm a little tense—no, it's not a matter of being tense. In fact, I'm scared. I'm sorry to have come all the way to your own home to say this to you! After all, why should you care? I'm sorry Suleiman, by God, I didn't mean to bother you." His words came out piecemeal, scattered, like bits of glass from a tumbler that falls to the ground and shatters.

Suleiman cut him off with some soothing expressions, such as, "No need to apologize," "We are brothers," and "There's no formality between us." These calmed him down a bit. He would not have settled down, though, if not for the entrance of Elaine, bearing a tray of tea, which restored harmony to the room.

"Go on, drink, Maged Pasha," Suleiman invited him, trying to break the edge of the tension. Maged stretched a tentative hand toward the tray, picked up the glass, and quickly brought it to his lips. With a slight shake that had gone unnoticed before he took two sips of tea from the tumbler shivering between his fingers, he then put the glass back on the tray, announcing suddenly, "In all honesty, Suleiman, I am scared of the war."

Suleiman didn't grasp the hidden meaning of this sentence or what he was trying to say. Was he afraid of war breaking out? Of the losses from war? Of dying in war? What did he have in mind, exactly?

"What war?" asked Suleiman. He raised his voice as though to scold him.

"What do you mean, *what* war?" Maged replied. "Our war with Israel, of course!"

He means the war that's coming, thought Suleiman. He settled his back in his chair, saying to dismiss the idea, "Oh, man, you believe all that? There is no war, nothing." He said this smiling as he tried to put Maged's heart at ease.

"No, it's real, Suleiman!" he rejoined, bowing his head in silence and clutching it with both hands as he concentrated, propping his elbows on his thighs while his eyes bored into the dingy carpet in the salon. Silence ruled for a moment, then he finished by saying, "There are intense preparations, and things are happening all around us. I can't tell you about its details, of course—but the situation is serious!" Then the silence returned.

"Never mind that," Suleiman assured him, attempting to instill some confidence in him, without success. "Every so often they make these maneuvers in order to convince people they aren't standing still."

"Your friend Yusuf Tahir is with me in the unit," Maged said. "I have spoken to him about this fear I have, and found him very calm. He approached the subject with the utmost simplicity, despite the fact that, like me, he sees it as of greatest importance."

Here he laughed hysterically, then jumped to his feet suddenly and began to pace quickly around the room, his arms crossed behind his back. He kept going back and forth, all the while emitting that nervous, broken laughter. And exactly as he had quickly stood up, he abruptly stopped and sat down, then settled onto the edge of his seat, squeezed his palms together, and repeated, "Yusuf Tahir told me about that ring of yours. He said it was a magic ring. Its power definitely descends from the days of Sheikh Sayyid Darwish, may God have mercy on him, until today." Here his voice began to quiver from the extremity of his emotion.

But he took hold of himself as he added, "I wish, Suleiman—I beg you: I want to borrow the ring you inherited from your late father. I beg you! A loan for a fixed period, nothing more. By God almighty, I wouldn't keep it an hour longer! I feel I would die if I went to the front without it—and I'm leaving at dawn tomorrow! I know it's a difficult request, but I'm afraid, Suleiman—I'm terrified. I beg you!"

Suleiman could find no way to avoid responding to Maged al-Baduri's request. He knew that the whole affair would not last more than a few days, after which Maged would come back when he realized he had read into things too much.

Later, when he discussed the affair with his mother, she was amazed at his disdain for the protection of his own property. Especially that this was ring his dead father had bequeathed him.

"You're wrong, Suleiman," she told him. "How do you know he will give it back again? Wasn't it Maged who also wanted to steal your sister Layla from our midst, if she hadn't traveled abroad?"

Then she added with emotion, "I wonder how are you doing nowadays—Layla, my daughter?"

This is how Suleiman always was, treating all his affairs with a reflexive naivete; his insistent desire to please others constantly drove him in that direction. Yet just a few days later, everyone—and especially Suleiman—was surprised when the truth of what Maged al-Barudi had predicted became clear. War did break out between Egypt and Israel, and the Engineering Corps played a prominent role in the Egyptian forces' crossing of the Suez Canal, breaching of the Bar Lev earthen barrier, and returning to parts of Sinai—the land that the Egyptians had lost for more than six years—beyond it. Then three months after the war began, the engineer Maged al-Baroudi knocked on Suleiman's door, embraced him, and gave him back the magic ring as he had promised. He informed Suleiman that, with the exception of the two of them—that is, himself and Yusuf Tahir, who was stricken by a small piece of shrapnel that wounded him in the thigh—every other member of his unit, be they enlisted man or officer, was martyred.

Mohammed al-Buri returned once more to organized prayer.

Moreover, when he headed for the mosque near his house for the final prayer one evening, he was met by the worshippers there—especially the elderly ones, when they recognized him—with enormous joy: they gave him a tremendous reception. He began to attend all five daily prayers there after finding all this welcome from them. The young people began to flock around and envelope him, especially after he began to speak about his experience in prison. His body began to reanimate slowly, as if time had gone back ten years—particularly after Dido came to see him.

Mohammed met him in his flat one night while Mai had gone to work for her evening shift as a typist. Mustafa had gone out with a group of friends in a car belonging to one of them whose father worked in Kuwait and had bought him a Fiat 124 to compensate for all the years that he spent without a father to raise him.

Dido told him that a friend of his named Abdel-Hamid Mustafa worked in the secret police. He had met him and told him that the regime had decided to release the Islamist groups so that they could operate with complete freedom to help contain the Communist-Socialist movement that had spread like a plague, especially among university students. That friend not only had told him of their release, but he had urged Dido to come to him so that he could deliver the pleasing news.

Dido also told Mohammed about the death of Sheikh Foda approximately two years before, nearly a year following his return to his apartment in Moharram Bey after he'd lived like a refugee, fleeing far from the eyes of State Security by moving between various provinces. He told him, too, about al-Hagg Sayyid al-Damanhouri, trader in manufactured goods and an old member of the Brotherhood. Dido said that he had been stricken with paralysis, spending his days laid up in bed, unable to move, attended to by an elderly female servant after his also-elderly wife had left him to live with one of her daughters in the Sidi Bishr district of Alexandria. She was not strong enough to take care of him—she needed others to take care of her. He seemed unable to recognize anyone around him, including even his own sons. They had stopped visiting him, too busy for him with their own lives after they had cleaned out his business and split up his money between them according to Islamic law, as though he were dead already.

It was clear to Mohammed that Dido, the tender young man whom he had left eighteen years before, had now become a leader responsible for the movement, pursued by the men of the secret police who were surveilling the movement's political activities. He had come intending to compel Mohammed to take over its leadership once again. Mohammed al-Buri was convinced on that day that the responsibility had then fallen on his shoulders since the leadership had vanished from the arena. He was the only one left from the original group. So he praised his Lord for the long years in prison that had preserved his life in preparation for this day on which it was appointed for him to revive the Muslim Brotherhood movement in Alexandria—and by direct order from the regime, under the shelter of their protection.

The mission wasn't as difficult as it had been in the fifties, when they would meet under the cloak of darkness, looking around in fear at the mere barking of a dog they passed on the road. The question of recruiting new members had become extremely simple due to widespread frustration among the youth, especially the half-educated among them. Like fishing in murky waters, as they say, when the prey does not sense from whence peril approaches, so the people could barely see the coming danger. Even as President al-Sadat himself proclaimed 1972 to be the "Year of the Fog," the mosque pulpits and corner places of worship spread everywhere, cloaked in a mist of their own. They did so to the point that all Mohammed al-Buri had to do was launch his call to join among a handful of disciples to start with, then turn them loose among the rest of the worshippers to carry out the rest of the work in his place. As a result, the group's membership grew so quickly that it confounded Mohammed personally. So too, at first, did the number of bearded young men without mustaches roaming about in their robes on the streets of al-Hadra, Maks, and Dakheila, all working-class districts. Then they spilled out into the the areas nearby until they reached al-Muntaza and Abu Qir. But what amazed him the most was their congregating at the major mosques, such as al-Shabrawishi and Morsi Abul-Abbas, without any fear or caution and within the sight and hearing of official guards and even government informers. This is not what he had been used to before.

After the outbreak of war, a rumor arose among the people that soldiers from heaven, dressed all in white, were fighting side-by-side with the Egyptian Army and that the resounding cry "God is most great!" was the real cause for the success in crossing the Canal. And in truth, Mohammed al-Buri rejoiced enormously at what he'd achieved and what he had started. However, he had not expected it to help spread his pronouncements and ideas everywhere this way such that they were now embraced by the majority, shaping public opinion all over the country. But he retained his modesty, always telling himself, "My success is all due to God."

After the president's famous trip to Jerusalem and its resounding consequences for Egypt and the rest of the Arab countries, Dido one day began to question him about his feelings toward al-Sadat, who had ordered his release. He answered that, while he wasn't ungrateful, the one whose hand had shaken that of the Jew—even to seek peace, as he claimed—was decidedly not one of us, as our glorious Prophet, the best of prayers upon him, had taught us.

As the passing days turned into years, she began to notice a trifling change in the way her neighbors greeted her. In the beginning she ascribed it to her aloofness and self-isolation. But in time she felt that the merchants in the market as well as her female friends, both in the building and in the district as a whole were increasingly cold and dry with her. At roughly the same time, she noticed that she was no longer greeted in the shops or on the streets; some even turned their faces away when they met her. The phenomenon of traveling to work in Saudi Arabia, Kuwait, and the other oil-producing countries was proliferating. Among the neighbors, a goodly number of the men disappeared, leaving their women and children behind.

When the immigrants to distant shores returned on their vacations or at the end of their contracts, they had become inculcated with new cultures and ways of thinking foreign to those of the local people in Egypt. A mosque, big or small, sprang up on every street without prior notice. Preachers, men of religion, and lay proselytizers of novel Islamic principles appeared on every corner. Some examples of these principles included wearing wedding rings of silver rather than gold and men's beginning to wear their watches on their right wrist rather than their left and to wrap themselves up in Arab caftans on the street. And gradually, though within a short time, most of the women around Elaine began to cover their heads and necks until showing one's hair on the street became a sign of one's religion. Long gowns covered their bodies completely until only their eyes at times showed. Her withdrawal into herself and her self-seclusion—at which she had become quite skilled, and which she indulged in more and more as pure religious practices in compensation for all she had abandoned of life—filled up her days, or nearly so.

In her serene isolation under the shelter of the surrounding darkness, Elaine sat on the edge of her bed, reading the Holy Book one evening in silence. She wasn't hungry and thus had not left her bed from when she had taken to it at three o'clock in the afternoon until this moment, at which she raised her head toward the picture of the Virgin Lady hanging on the opposite wall. It seemed as though the Virgin smiled at her. She trembled where she lay, then quickly threw off the bed covers and stood up, wanting to get closer to the picture to understand the reality of what she saw. Her eyes remained fixed on the picture as her feet searched for the slippers under the bed. Then a light emanated suddenly from the face of the Virgin and crossed the room until it reached where Elaine was and engulfed her entirely. Next, the scent of roses and blooming flowers, the likes of which she had never smelled before, surrounded her. She was not able to estimate how long it all lasted, though to her it seemed more than ten minutes, after which the scent evaporated and the light faded away.

Those heavenly apparitions continued repeatedly in her room afterward, and she no longer felt the terror and fear that she had at first. Yet she did not confide their occurrence to a living soul—not even to her children for fear they would doubt her sanity. Then, for her own protection, they might force her to move into one of their homes. But she kept on praying and reading religious books and Daoud's poems all the time. Elaine enjoyed these apparitions from the other world that hovered over her life and quelled her loneliness. She began to follow the incidents with ardent zeal. She was content at first just to contemplate them and savor that radiant light and the heavenly scent. Later, when she became more accustomed, she began to interact with these manifestations of the Virgin and address them, as though in a state of prayer. Elaine would ask her questions and listen to the answers expressed in words that resonated inside her—within her depths, her soul, her heart—as though they were thoughts. But they were words she could hear in a conversation with a real, tangible person standing in front of her and talking with her directly.

One day Elaine told Suleiman that he should marry. He wondered if it was wise to be in a hurry to do so at a time when he was enjoying his life as it was. He had at that time been dreaming of marrying Mariam Doss, but the same week he met Amani Saad and married her with a speed that perplexed everyone—including Amani. Elaine felt that it was a matter decreed from above. She dreamed at another time that Mona would bring her her first grandson, and Mona contacted her that evening to tell her that she was pregnant. And a third time, long afterward, she dreamed that the Virgin Mary was weeping. A few days later, President al-Sadat declared the removal of Pope Shenouda III from his seat and ordered that he be confined to a monastery. This upset Elaine to the point that she could never forgive al-Sadat to the day of his death. She spent the rest of her days completely engrossed in prayer, worship, and those light-bringing encounters that filled her days and nights.

She didn't emerge from her flat even to go shopping. Hamdi the doorman took care of that. *Usta* William was keen to buy meat and poultry for her every so often. He would bring them to her apartment in Moharram Bey in exchange for a meagre sum of money that he claimed was the price, wherein he would pay the difference out of his own pocket in gratitude for the courtesy of Daoud Abdel-Malek and his kindness to him. His wife Nargis came to visit Elaine once each month, seizing the opportunity to clean the apartment, open the windows, wash the clothes, and cook her a number of dishes. She would keep them in the refrigerator that Suleiman bought for her as a present for a holiday.

Thus Elaine lived cut off from society, alone in her very private world between the walls of her old, quiet, calm apartment overlooking a side street in the heart of Moharram Bey, which was never quiet, night or day. There she was content to observe her supernatural routines—which, on the whole, were enough for her to face those natural changes surrounding her life.

CHAPTER TWENTY-TWO

SULEIMAN ROSE FROM HIS PROSTRATION, his eyes flooded with tears from the excessive passion of his prayer. He wiped his brow with his shirt as he cleared everything else from his mind. Next, he turned around slowly and cautiously to behold his wife Amani, who had sauntered into the room as he prayed. She stood behind him, sorting at the foot of the bed the pile of clean clothes that had been hung out to dry on the line that stretched in front of the balcony railing. She paused in her dingy rose nightgown, gazing at him with her constant, enigmatic smile, which had become a part of her face.

Serenity and calm enveloped the room—the majority of the district's residents quietly enjoying their siestas—except for faint noises coming from the living room at the center of the apartment, where the children were watching television. Suleiman smiled vacantly at his wife Amani with a grin like her own. He did not trade looks with her but fixed his eyes on the mirror hanging on the wall behind her, examining his face and the simple attire over his still-slender body. It did not take long for him to compare his athletic shape with his spouse Amani's backside reflected in the mirror in front of him. He was pained by her flabbiness as he played with the silver ring around his middle finger—next to the golden wedding ring on his left hand—between his index finger and thumb. He stepped beside her silently, heading toward the door of the room, followed by his fat female cat with its sleek yellow fur.

How beautiful were the humble, silent prayers he was accustomed to completing with repeated prostrations, expressing love of God and begging His pardon and satisfaction, that he had learned as a child from his mother and that she in turn had learned from Mother Irene during her upbringing in the Asylum of the Virgin. How sweet is God's compassion, His mercy, and His limitless forgiveness! How beautiful You are, O Lord of Lords! These thoughts filled his massive head, which still retained its handsomeness, inherited from his mother. His white complexion was crowned with hair of the deepest black that he let hang naturally long and loose, in the fashion of these days. It enhanced the fine features of his face, which was streaked with lines, sublimely handsome in a way from which the years did not detract. He crossed the parlor leading to his favorite chamber: the guest room—his monk's cell.

He pivoted to the right and looked at his three sons sprawled about on the living room floor. Completely absorbed in a TV program, none of them paid any attention to him. He tottered with difficulty into the salon, followed by his faithful cat. He was hindered from opening the door by the great pieces of furniture that covered every centimeter of the room's circumference, fitted together in a square shape with the exception of a rickety desk that occupied a small corner next to the sole window, which was always covered by drawn curtains that were once a feathery white. He pulled a cigarette from his shirt pocket, locked the door behind him, and sat on the wooden chair padded with an old yellow seat cushion behind the desk, which was on the left side of the room, to which he would retreat at the same time each day. He lit his cigarette, still wearing that same smile that he had when Amani appeared in the bedroom, except that his thoughts had now led him far away from her and even further from his meditations on the mercy of God and His forgiveness. For no sooner had he closed the door of the room behind him than he found himself immersed once again in going over the details of his last meeting with Lady Benhar.

Despite Suleiman's departure from the room, Amani kept smiling as she thought how much she loved her husband. Beautiful—she once was that, and the remains of her beauty still clung to her frame despite the passage of years as they squeezed the nectar of blooming youth from her veins. She continued folding clothes and stacking them in little piles on the bedspread according to the order in which she would carry them to place them on the private wardrobe shelf of each of the five members of the family. Slowly, she folded each piece with professional precision, just as she habitually took care of her home in all respects, big or small, and had since marrying five years before. She still remembered the details of their first meeting as though it were yesterday.

As per her custom, Amani had gone to visit her friend Mona at her apartment in the poor, jam-packed Dar al-Salam quarter of Cairo. It was a Friday at the end of winter 1974. A beautiful day, the warmth of the sun still touched her body as she walked eagerly on tiptoe over the rough spots on the street running next to the tracks of the Helwan metro. Along the tracks, the rainwater that had fallen intermittently the previous day, pooling to form a little pond dotted with dry islands. Most of them were formed naturally, according to the uneven nature of the ground itself. But some were made with a piece of brick or a wooden board here and there by the hands of good people. They closed the gaps between those islands, linking people's footsteps so their feet would not sink into the muck of the pond that had fallen from the sky. Amani was tiptoeing on those stepping-stones with her only pair of shoes and the speed and skill of a ballet dancer. She was used to slogging through the winter roads of Cairo, which she had done for all her twenty-six years—years that weighed heavily on her as she waited for her bridegroom to come. As did her desire to visit her girlfriend in her new marital home, especially as she looked for Amani's help in enduring her brother Suleiman's—the bachelor's—coming from Alexandria to visit her at the same time to spend a day off.

The rotten smell that lingered down the length of the route could not wipe the smile from her lips. The road was filled with a disgraceful din, like the drone of a wasp's nest, which did not let up, but rose sharply to an explosive roar with the passing of the Helwan train going north or south every few minutes, its whistle warning of the approach of the iron serpent and its fearful traversal of the entire district. It shook the overcrowded houses with a rippling effect as they looked with sadness on the impoverished and solemn scene as if they were tombstones in a cemetery crammed with the dead. Despite her perpetual smile, in the depth of her heart, Amani hated that needy life of poverty with all her might.

The two of them got to know each other that same day. Within a few weeks, Suleiman stood in the churchyard and signed the marriage contract while she sat next to him quietly in her white dress, smiling, anticipating that a carefree life awaited her.

He drew on a cigarette and held the smoke in his chest, reluctant to let it out—or perhaps he forgot to do so as he thought of the meeting with Madam Benhar. She had bewitched him today with her magic powers as she had when he had first met her some four years before—on April 6, 1976, to be precise, at her husband's villa in Agami. Suleiman had been introduced to her husband in the apartment of *al-Hagg* Murad al-Uwayqi nearly a week earlier. How could he forget this date if he lived to be a hundred!

As was his habit, he had gone to spend some time in the company of the well-known merchant surrounded by that vast, shameless wealth that had fallen from the sky—he did not know its actual source. The world appeared with a different face, its warehouses full, thanks to "the decisions of *al-Infitah*"—al-Sadat's open door to foreign investment. So the merchant had bought the Mercedes, or "the Crocodile," as people called that model. He had finished building and refurbishing that high rise in the sophisticated San Stefano district, and he lived now on the top two floors, which he had kept for himself and his family. He had ridden the wave of the *al-Infitah*, which had brought back his good fortune in business with millions, so he changed in a few years from a small dealer of manufactured goods in the Alley of the Ladies to what he was today. He had become among the largest cloth merchants in Alexandria: he owned an elegant shop on Saad Zaghloul Street and another on Fouad Street—al-Horreya ("Liberty") Way, as it is called today—where there are miscellaneous warehouses. Wholesale trade would land him decent profits.

Al-Hagg Murad was used to inviting to his house, approximately each evening, a regular group of his friends and followers made up of a merchant from the western Alexandria suburb of Maks, a certified accountant, a famous dentist, and Suleiman Daoud, teacher of philosophy and the head of the Free Thought Association, to which most of the invitees also belonged. They would gather for sarcastic discussions, witty remarks, and conversations about politics as well as cultural dialogues through which *al-Hagg* Murad sought to shed light on current events, with prestige and power on the one hand and intellect and a cultured appearance befitting him as a prominent member of the new society on the other. The evening session finished with cigarettes wrapped with the finest kinds of hashish and a bottle of aged whiskey procured by one of his friends working at the customs service. Suleiman met him that night for the first time, recognizing him as Lutfi Hassanein—procurer of the quality whiskey for the evening entertainment of *al-Hagg* Murad al-Uwayqi—who came that night to take part with them in the session for the first time. And despite his insistence that everyone call him *al-Hagg* (Pilgrim), he did not fail in competing with—even surpassing—them in addiction to whiskey.

Suleiman was dazzled by the nonchalant personality of Lutfi Hassanein and the signs of success that radiated from his whole being. The sleek black hair, the golden eyeglasses, the decorous mustache, the confident, resounding laugh, the gleaming blue jacket, the red silk scarf askew, his hands that never stopped moving—up and down, right and left—their coarse fingers loaded with at least three gold rings, constantly clenching and unclenching with the gestures of his hands, calculated and in harmony with his words and his laughter as if they were the hands of a professional magician hovering with conceit over everyone's head before saying the famous word, "abracadabra," to change the rose into a dove fluttering above them. He enchanted all present with his jokes, stories, and nonstop laughter. Thus, Suleiman was sure that very night he was a professional con man.

Lutfi surprised him the same night a short time after they got to know each other by asking him if he had read the latest book by Dr. Rashad Fikri. From Lutfi's appearance, Suleiman was astonished that the former had even heard of Dr. Rashad. But Suleiman replied that Dr. Rashad was a close friend of his, a regular attendee of the Association of Free Thought, to which he belonged. He did not want to say that he headed the Association—not out of modesty, but rather out of the need for caution on his side due to his perpetual doubt about people, even after he had drawn the opposite conclusion about them. Suleiman might very well have inherited that whispering doubt from his mother. He was suspicious of that man who broached the subject of Dr. Rashad Fikri without a clear reason—that thinker known for his opposition to the government and its move toward the new Western capitalism and for his attacks on the prominent men of the media for their shameful flattery of the members of the government and its leading figures. Not to mention his public criticism of religious leaders and of Islamist groups that filled the world these days with their ideologies against all of society. And, to be precise, against Dr. Rashad Fikri and his critical writings on their fundamentalist leanings as well as those like Dr. Rashad among the veteran Socialists and other secular opposition movements—the deviant legacy of the age of Abdel-Nasser, the Brotherhood's implacable enemy.

And so, danger surrounded the subject from every direction. The influence of the high-quality whiskey and the fancy cigarette brands Suleiman had just finished had definitely soothed his nerves enough to complete his discussion with that flawed man without straying into forbidden topics. Completing the mutual introduction with scrupulous civility, Suleiman leaned toward him and asked, "Where are you from originally, Lutfi Bey?"

"From Moharram Bey," he replied. "And you?"

"From Moharram Bey, too."

They exchanged names of friends, neighbors, acquaintances, and schoolteachers. Then Suleiman realized that Lutfi was none other than the son of his father's friend, al-Sheikh Hassanein al-Basri. And Lutfi realized that Suleiman was the son of *al-Khawaga* Daoud Abdel-Malek, whose role in the events that led to the killing of his father in detention everyone knew. Both were amazed at the coincidence that brought them together that night.

Adding to the strangeness surrounding Lutfi Hassanein, the man stopped in the middle of the hall at the end of the gathering. The attendees had gotten drunk, hitting the peak of intoxication. Lutfi announced with youthful exuberance, in speech saturated with the effect of drink and the influence of drugs, his invitation to all those there to honor him by spending the night of the Shem al-Nessim spring holiday in his modest villa on the beach at Agami until dawn, listening to the singing of "the Nightingale," Abdel-Halim Hafez. He said that he might also surprise them with the famous singer's presence if he managed to come after his concert in Cairo. Hafez had promised him personally to do just that roughly a month ago when he had come to recuperate in the villa next door.

Then Lutfi, stepping unsteadily, leaned into Suleiman's ear and asked him to invite Dr. Rashad Fikri so that he could personally acknowledge that extraordinary man, for whom he harbored all respect.

As a representative of the Brotherhood, Sheikh Mohammed al-Buri's stock in the realm of political work rose high. He was surprised at the invitations that showered down on him, asking him to speak at associations and conferences as well as at the meetings of various labor syndicates and unions. Then his connections to businessmen from all over began to come through. Many of them answered his invitation to take part in funding the movement; they converted their capital into a small fortune sufficient to underwrite a committee of three men specialized in economics and trade—among them a university professor—to administer their affairs. His disciples and followers grew exponentially, especially when the returnees from the Arab countries flooded them with payment of their *zakat*—the Islamic tax to help the poor. This was directed toward promoting stricter religious belief and bettering living conditions for all to be more like those of the Arab countries from which the returnees had come after settling in them to make money.

One day Dido opened a peculiar subject for discussion. He told the sheikh that it would be proper to for him marry once again, and that he wished him to marry his own younger sister Marwa. Dido had been thinking about all the torment that Mohammed had inevitably suffered after spending all those years in prison, only to get out and find that *al-Hagga* Zeinab had grown old and given up on marital relations. Dido added that, despite his constant labor and ceaseless occupation with shepherding the group's affairs, the sheikh's body truly had claim upon him. He—that is, Dido—had noticed Mohammed's

248

attentive glances, which he quickly concealed out of courtesy, when he met with the young ladies of the movement. Then Dido told him, out of his genuine affection for him, that he had been thinking about which woman deserved this honor, and had not found anyone better or dearer than his sister to give to him—and at the same time he would keep this private matter secret. He finished these words with a firm smile on his face, for he fully anticipated the impact of his talk on the sheikh. And from his side, Sheikh Mohammed al-Buri gazed at him sympathetically, patted him affectionately on the shoulder, and said, "Let me think about it."

During one of the Friday sermons, Mohammed al-Buri was sitting next to the revolutionary preacher Sheikh Abdel-Rahman al-Damanhouri, listening to him stir the anxieties of the Muslims about the defense of their pure religion from the atheists and lax believers, whom he declared apostates in order to further the Islamic jihad. Mohammed al-Buri was startled by Sheikh Abdel-Rahman al-Damanhouri, who belonged to a group that called for terming all of society entirely infidel; when he declared that the blood of all those infidels was thus deemed permissible to shed publicly, to the astonished cries of the congregation. Moreover, he fanned the flames to intensify the conflagration, finally setting off a ringing explosion when he ranked Dr. Rashad Fikri, author of the book *Between Enlightenment and Excommunication*, as the head of the enemies of Islam whose blood was lawful to shed as shouts of "God is Most Great! God is Most Great!" rose all around.

CHAPTER TWENTY-THREE

AMANI WAS STILL BUSY DOING nothing, something she had grown used to since their return from their annual Easter visit to Elaine, Suleiman's mother, in Moharram Bey. They had moved to the Cleopatra's Baths district after spending a few months with Elaine in her flat, but Amani could not relax while living with her mother-in-law. Small differences between the two women grew larger, so Suleiman decided they should move far away to save what was left of the affection between them. The salary he received the first of every month was enough for them to live on their own after Yusuf Tahir found them a low-rent apartment. It was also enough to buy a red 128 *Nasr*—"Victory"—car, the Egyptian-made Fiat, on install-ments to take Suleiman to the school every morning and to gather the family to visit Suleiman's mother and spend the day off in one of the public parks or recreation grounds.

Upon their return from Suleiman's mother's after the Easter holiday, he invited Amani to spend the eve of Shem al-Nessim in Agami. But she begged off on the excuse that she preferred to go to bed early after such a full day rather than meet strangers from the wealthy class, who would feel she had strayed from her place in society, reminding her of the days of real poverty that she tried as hard as she could to forget. And so, her days were confined to pursuing a mirage of happiness that never materialized physically. She thought that her move from the poor people's economic apartment blocks to relatively luxurious quarters, caring for her house and children to the point of excess, or praising her husband Suleiman whether appropriate or not would grant her a glimpse at happiness. But how preposterous it would be to find the fruits of happiness around her, when she had never had the chance to plant their seeds in the first place.

As for Suleiman, he leapt under the refreshing shower, restoring his vigor. He put on a sky-blue shirt and white trousers, filled his palm with cologne, rubbing it first on his other palm, then spread it over his face, his shirt collar, and his chest. He then combed his hair with extreme care as though heading to a romantic rendezvous.

All along, he was never able to overcome his passion for women, despite several attempts and abrupt decisions that always ended in failure to the point that he blamed those failures on the effect of the magic ring, which he believed deprived him of control over what happened in his life. And the overt piety that he displayed so strongly and that appeared to be so deeply ingrained was contradicted only by the way he looked at an attractive woman, even in the hall of the church. It compelled him to immediately start to play his favorite game of becoming a professional "hunter," laying traps for his pray to fall into. And after he finished with his game, he would fall prey, in turn, to intense attacks of conscience. He would bow down on his knees to worship the Singular Creator, praying He would enfold him in His forgiveness and redemption. He would not rise from his prostration until he was engulfed in boundless feelings of peace. Then he would feel absolved until the next victim would pass before him and that compulsive conduct would overcome him yet again, as if he were powerless to resist, and he would fall all over again and get up again in turn.

Thus, his life became a consistent confection unadulterated with falling and rising, with mockery and seriousness, with belligerence and reclusion. Those around him did not understand him; those within the familiar circle that he had allowed near the details of his life did not know how to evaluate him or deal with him. Was he a mystic aesthete wandering in the desert of life, touching the divine self and clinging to it, or a wolf prowling the same desert searching for the first prey its trained eyes would encounter, tearing at its flesh? As for him, he always answered their queries with a broken smile or a shrug of his shoulders, or sometimes with humility while saying it was all absurd.

On the way to Agami, he took the Corniche, driving fast as he passed the vehicles around him with skill and dexterity. He loved driving fast, especially in the spring, before the streets were filled with the cars of summer vacationers. The wind from the Corniche buffeted his face through the open car window as he sang, "*Coupable*" (Guilty), by Jean Francois Michael, which the Lebanese composers, the Rahbani brothers, adapted afterward into the splendid song by Fairuz, "*Habbaytak fe'l-sayf*" (I Loved You in Summer). The scent of spring's newborn flowers in bloom—flowers peeking down obstinately from the walls around the few remaining villas lining the Corniche road—filled the air with the perfume of love. He burst out singing in French:

Guilty am I that I taught you love.
And lit in your body the blaze of desire.
While I became a specter that stood between you and him
Guilty am I when I have forgotten you.

He drove the length of the Corniche until he crossed through Maks onto the coastal road heading west to the city of al-Salum on the Libyan border. He craned his neck toward the windshield and lifted his eyes to the sky, contemplating the new full moon. The sting of the desert cold came to him, so he closed the side window as he thought of what the night would bestow on him in the company of Lutfi Hassanein and his friends—who would not at all surprise him if he found them stranger than himself.

*

He was speechless when he heard the resounding response of those present when Sheikh Abdel-Rahman al-Damanhouri legitimized shedding the blood of Dr. Rashad Fikri, again at the end of his excellent sermon. His position would be jeopardized if he defended the man whose prospective killing had met such approval from those huge crowds of young people he had worked diligently to recruit under the banner of Islam and for the sake of the dream for which he had sacrificed the best years of his life—the dream to bring back the rightly guided Islamic state to his dear country. In any case, what could he say to them? Could he ask for clemency for Dr. Rashad because he had encouraged him to paint during the days of detention? Or because of his tendency to believe in humanity more than in God Almighty—to believe in the created being and not the Creator?

No—I seek refuge in God!

Dr. Rashad Fikri most definitely deserved their resentment of him. And if he did not deserve it—and only God knows matters from within—he would become a martyr for the Islamist movement, whose wheels had begun to turn. His destination would still be heaven, without his knowing it!

Mohammed al-Buri did indeed marry Marwa in secret, and he discovered hidden powers that he did not know an aged man like himself could have. Dido came to him one night after the evening 'Isha prayer to sip a cup of tea and talk with him. Mohammed al-Buri had grown used to Dido's company, and he had become a friend and a counselor for his decisions. Dido told him that Suleiman, the son of Daoud Abdel-Malek, possessed a magic ring whose secret his father had divulged to him before he died. Dido had tried personally to get the ring from Daoud—even if by force—when he came across him walking aimlessly one day; he had followed him until he reached the seashore. But it happened that the old man fell down unconscious there on that day, so he approached him and inspected his fingers and his pockets but did not find the ring. So, he left him sprawling on the sand and hurried away to call an ambulance. But later he learned that he had died, and no doubt had bequeathed the magic ring to his son Suleiman after him.

With difficulty, al-Buri recalled the face of *al-Khawaga* Daoud, the one he'd met once or twice in the company of al-Sheikh Hassanein—may God have mercy on him—while Dido regaled him with this strange story. He surmised that the ring had a hidden power that bestowed pride and glory upon its owner. He remembered how *al-Khawaga* Daoud had gone to Cairo and in only one day was able to get Sheikh Hassanein out of detention and bring him back to Alexandria. And how, on a similar trip to Cairo, Daoud succeeded in pressing the arm of death around the neck of his friend the sheikh, not letting up until he fell lifeless, a stiffened corpse before his eyes. He recalled as well how, seemingly overnight, he had become a rich man who owned a factory, a villa, and a Packard car with a chauffeur. What Dido said had to be true then—the ring had to hold such magical power that impelled its wearer to fly over the clouds.

"Imagine, Sheikh Mohammed," said Dido, "if we had this ring, what kind of shape the Brotherhood would be in then?"

They were still sipping their tea when Mohammed al-Buri's thoughts wandered, shimmering over an imaginary sea.

Suleiman preferred to park the car far away and walk to the villa so as not to squeeze the car in between the other vehicles, which would result in his inability to take off if his companions annoyed him and he wanted to make an early exit. He cast a final glance at his face and smoothed his hair with his fingers in the rear-view mirror. He was overwhelmed by the purity of the air and its fragrance issuing from the bushes of ordinary and Arabian jasmine blooming in the miniature gardens surrounding the scattered villas, mixed with the breeze from the sea, whose waves he heard breaking on the shore. From the many glowing lights, he recognized his destination. He strolled from the outer gate whose guard—a brown-complexioned young man with a shaven head and simple shirt and trousers rather than the typical robe—stood trembling and greeted him with a military salute.

It was an elegant stone building with a modern design marked by straight lines and sharp angles, and it was surrounded by a cultivated little garden with fig trees and some rose bushes. The main doorway, hemmed by a trellis of jasmine flowers, stood open as he was met by a din from within. At the entrance leading to the reception hall stood a statue of Venus in the center of the marble floor. He stepped through the hall to where the invitees gathered, men and women mingling together; the spacious salon was jammed with them. Most of them flocked around the long table straining with a cornucopia of the most tempting foods. The aroma of grilled meat mixed with the scent of whiskey, cigar smoke, and women's perfume here and there. On the opposite end the bay window was open to breezes from the sea just meters away. To the extreme right stood a rather tall stand on which various brightly hued bottles containing a variety of spirits were arrayed. Behind it stood a thin man with glossy hair who wore a white shirt with a red bow tie. He was preparing the drinks and presenting them to the invitees on request. Voices and laughter rose all around as Suleiman lingered alone for a few minutes—enough to sweep the place with his scrutinizing eyes.

He caught sight of the oil painting, hanging on the wall, of that enticing *houri* reclining in surrender over the sand on the beach, her ample breasts bared, exciting the viewer. And there were two plates of hammered copper, one on each side of the painting, displaying two women bathing. Nude statues in bronze, wood, and marble and of differing sizes were scattered around. Suddenly there came Lutfi Hassanein's giggling laugh. Suleiman was not able to rid himself of the thought that assailed him out of the blue that this Lutfi was not a man in the meaning of the word. Yes, despite every appearance of virility in which he wrapped himself, Suleiman felt it was nothing more than a façade behind which lay weakness and flaccid, impotent laxness. None of that blatant propaganda— the posters for cheap movies, and pornographic books laid out on the sidewalks, their covers deceiving you with a lot until you swallow the bait in all innocence, surprised afterward with the extent to which they were empty of all their promises— could conceal the flaw in Lutfi's masculinity from Suleiman's eyes. Thus, these superficial attempts failed to erase from Suleiman's searching look that reality that he witnessed now with the insight granted him by that magical ring. He was astonished by his close-to-certainty that Lutfi Hassanein was feigning this virility; he was really nothing more than a man suffering from sexual impotence, trying desperately to hide behind all those shameful lies. He raised his left hand as he blew gently over the four red stones mounted on the signet, then wiped it with his shirtsleeve. He grinned victoriously at the audacity of this wicked idea that had come to him sud-denly. His features softened, his mind at ease, and he began to wander among the invitees, trying to find his companion for the night. Without warning, he found her.

His eye had not fallen on beauty to equal hers: hon-ey-colored eyes guarded by dark, languid lashes with droopy eyelids—weighted with an air of sadness that did not escape him with his deep experience of women—hanging over them quietly, plus clear skin with a reddish tint, as if it were sun-burnt. He noticed her on the side facing the hallway and felt that she, too, was watching him, casting questioning looks from across the room among all the guests. He rose from his self-immersion to prepare a plan to overcome this new chal-lenge when his shoulder was gripped by the hand of his host, who had come from behind him.

"Welcome, welcome to my childhood friend!" he said.

Suleiman spun around with a sarcastic smile that concealed his thoughts. Especially when he found Lutfi embracing two female guests that were accompanying him.

"Hello to you, Lutfi Pasha!" he replied. "How handsome and awesome you look, man!" He stressed strongly on the last word as though to observe the reaction to it. His last laugh was fake with exaggeration.

"Where's the wife?" asked Lutfi. "Weren't you going to get her so we could get to know her?" He laughed again—to himself—as he turned in delight toward the two women, as though he had brought the latest joke.

"Sorry," answered Suleiman. "She wasn't able to come with me tonight because she was tired from the holiday and staying up late yesterday in the church overwhelmed her." He added, "But there probably will be other chances in future."

"Of course, of course, there will be other chances in future, naturally," agreed Lutfi. He laughed loudly again. It was obvious he had started drinking early.

"What is it, man?" he added. "You want an invitation, or something? My house is your house. Let's go and get you something to drink, and I'll introduce you to my wife."

He did take him to the bar and ordered the man with the red bow tie to pour him a glass of whiskey. Then he turned toward him, still hugging the two women as though they complemented his clothes or were tokens of elegance.

"Ice?" he asked.

He motioned to Suleiman as he contemplated the two women that flanked him on either side. They both surrendered to their role completely as though they perceived—as Suleiman also did—that their owner was tame, his claws removed, and thus harmless. Lutfi handed him the glass, took one for himself, raised it before him, and cried out suddenly, "Good health of the spring holiday! Shem al-Nessim!"

He laughed with a giggle as usual; Suleiman laughed amiably with him. The two women let out wanton laughs that filled the salon, and the others there turned toward them to discover their source. With a theatrical gesture, Lutfi shoved the two women's hips, pushing them away.

"Go on, my pretties," he said, "and celebrate Shem al-Nessim far away from me—hahaha!" Then he turned in Suleiman's direction and wrapped his arm around Suleiman's shoulder as he walked him across the grand hall in the direction of the sea.

There, the beauty with the sad, honey-colored eyes was still staring at him, and his nose was filled with the odor of drink wafting from Lutfi's mouth when he asked him, "So, when is Dr. Rashad Fikri coming?"

Suleiman remembered then the necessity to invite Dr. Rashad; he had forgotten. Or he had pretended he'd forgotten, for he did not find it appropriate at all to invite the notable thinker to spend an entertaining evening in the house of a strange man—still a stranger even though his acquaintance with him had begun thirty years before. Even at this moment, he was still making up his mind about Lutfi.

Yet he answered, saying, "He must've travelled to Cairo. Or gone with one of his acquaintances to spend Shem al-Nassim on a farm or whatever. I mean, I have no idea where to find him." Suleiman kept walking with him, slowly due to the crowds of guests in the salon. They stared with probing eyes as the pair cut a path right through them, breaking through their ranks, Suleiman's host Lutfi Pasha's arm around his shoulder. Suleiman wondered whether he was mistaken in his analysis of the sexual leanings of Lutfi Hassanein. His face blushed with embarrassment at the way the guests looked at the two of them, and he wondered about the meaning of those smiles.

They kept getting closer until he found himself standing face-to-face with the beauty of those sleepy eyes.

"Here is my wife, Benhar," Lutfi said, in a tone filled with pride.

"Ben-who?" Suleiman stood aghast. So, the beauty is his wife! He tried to mask his bafflement by feigning a casual air.

"Benhar—Benhar, my brother—she's my wife. The name is Turkish."

"Ah, Turkish! Welcome, Madam Benhar. I'm sorry, I mean. That is, you are the first Benhar I've met in my life," he laughed. Then, gathering his courage, he added, "I'm Suleiman Daoud, teacher of philosophy."

"Philosophy on demand!"

"On demand!" he mused. He contemplated her comeliness, not believing he was speaking with the owner of those captivating eyes.

"Fine—what's the opinion of the philosopher then about one who crosses the sea without getting wet?" She gave a giggling laugh then fixed her husband with a wanton look, before excusing herself to leave the two of them. Suleiman considered what the woman meant by her question. His eyes began to follow her chestnut hair that flowed over her naked back as she walked away from them, toward the terrace overlooking the seashore. How gorgeous! Yet the idea of crossing the sea without getting wet—what did she mean?

Lutfi interrupted his chain of thought by saying, "Madam is originally from Cairo. Her father had the rank of bey; her grandfather was Khourshid Pasha from the notables of Luxor. And her mother, my dear sir, was Turkish. By God, she was Turkish. She didn't speak a word of Arabic."

"Extraordinary!" said Suleiman. "That's great! What do you think the story about crossing the sea without getting wet is about?" he asked slyly.

Lutfi truly stammered his denial, claiming he only understood half of what Benhar said, as a rule. Then he added jovially, "Isn't that the case with you as well? That is, you understand just half of what your wife says?"

"Of course not!" he replied. "On the whole, she doesn't talk to me at all. She just smiles."

They laughed together for the first time.

One of the guests broke in. "Hey y'all, why don't you let us in on the joke?" said a middle-aged man—of middling intelligence, middling elegance, and three times average weight.

"I present to you Mr. Hamdi Murad, owner of the famous poultry farms," said Lutfi, introducing his amply proportioned friend.

"Pleased to meet you! I'm Suleiman Daoud, owner of the question, 'Which came first—the chicken or the egg?'" he answered, laughing.

"Suleiman Pasha has chicken farms as well?"

"Suleiman Effendi has nothing but philosophy," interjected Lutfi.

"Philosophy?" said the man. "Does that mean you'll philosophize for us this evening, on demand?" The two men exploded in laughter. Suleiman decided to play along and laugh to flatter them.

Their conversation was interrupted by a voice coming from the main room, crying, "Hey everyone, hey people—gather 'round: Abdel-Halim is going to sing!"

The masses moved toward the television, drawn to the al-Masseyah Troupe's playing of the intro to the song. Suleiman turned around looking for Benhar and spotted her sitting by herself on a seat on the terrace, gazing out to sea. He whispered into his host's ear, "Your wife . . ." but the obese man broke in.

"Do you know—your Excellency—this Ahmed Fouad Hassan?"

"Who is this Ahmed Fouad Hassan?" grumbled Suleiman.

"Suleiman Bey, sir, he is the head of the al-Masseyah Troupe that is playing now. Did you know he was married to Nagwa Fouad?"

"Nagwa Fouad? What's the story, exactly?" Lutfi interrupted again.

"The story, sir," the large man recounted, "is that his daughter by the artist Nagwa Fouad, a truly beautiful girl, was my daughter's schoolmate. She was always coming over to visit us. One day . . ." Suleiman stopped listening as though unable to hear more. Then he nodded his head while preoccupied with preparing the next gambit.

Finally, he took him off guard by saying, "And from that time, we haven't seen her."

"Wow—dear God, that's amazing! Extraordinary!" said Suleiman.

The band was still playing as his mind remained focused on the terrace where Benhar was sitting. Meanwhile, that man's strange tale had made him apprehensive. He turned once again toward Lutfi as he toyed with the ring on his finger, looking for a way out of the predicament into which he felt he had plunged. So, he said, "I see that your wife is sitting alone on the terrace: don't you have to go and see . . ."

Lutfi interrupted him, absorbed in the music blaring from the television.

"Okay, Suleiman—why don't you go see what's bothering her. In the meantime, I'll get you a magnificent cigarette!" Suleiman took off toward the terrace before Lutfi had finished speaking, fearing that the poultry man would come back and try to enthrall him with his foolish chatter.

The appearance of the moon startled him as it spread a diaphanous gleaming silver gown over the surface of the water, flowing to infinity behind where Benhar was sitting. Viewed from the rear, she appeared to be sitting in front of a flattering mirror. He walked lightly around her chair until he faced her, but he was surprised to find her turning her head far away from him, and he began to wonder if she was crying. He lifted his gaze toward the room and noticed that everyone was raptly following the concert. Encouraged, he went down on one knee in front of her as he clutched an armrest of the chair in which she sat.

"Why are you sitting by yourself, Madam Benhar, and abandoning your guests?" he asked. She swiveled toward him and started to reply, but the words caught inside her despite herself. She chose to prolong her silence, turning again to contemplate the waves breaking on the silvery sands of the beach. He continued his abasement in front of her as she remained mute, and the teardrops flowed down her rosy cheeks once again. Her perfume's scent filled his nostrils while he, gathering all his boldness, stretched his hand out toward her, gently running his fingertips over her face with affection.

A baby-like smile appeared on her face, every part of it crinkling—then she burst into a childish laugh. She bounded out of her chair as he stood facing her. His heart was burning as he went to press a kiss on her lips, heedless of the consequences. But she leaned away from him at the critical moment, as though she had read his thoughts, saving him from a fall through bad behavior. She turned around to look inside at the guests assembled to hear Halim's singing. Suleiman stood behind her, reflecting on the beauty of her form wrapped in a tight, shimmering turquoise dress that began at the ends of her flowing hair, encircling her body and embracing her charms, extending until it almost touched the stone slabs of the flooring beneath her. She surprised him by saying, without glancing at him, "You didn't answer my question."

He immediately saw what she was tossing his way, and replied, "Ah—'who crosses the sea without getting wet.' Like the hungry man who is still hungry though he lives his whole life in a restaurant. The food comes and goes in front of him while he cleans the tables. Or the woman who sells tickets at the movie theater though she'd never in her life seen a film, or likewise, a woman married to a man who didn't know . . ." She burst out with a long, giggling laugh, so that the invitees noticed her and turned in their direction, smiling with curiosity. They soon, however, left the two of them once more to

263

savor the melancholic emotional melody wandering through the voice of Abdel-Halim: "the Nightingale."

"Why don't you come,' said Suleiman, "and we'll walk a little by the sea."

They took off their shoes at the end the terrace and in a few steps reached the smooth white sands of the seashore at Agami. They walked side-by-side until they arrived at the silvery waters, which flowed with the moonlight upon them. A nearly full, orange-colored moon appeared bigger than usual. It seemed to melt with longing in the waters of the sea, which it pulled close to itself sometimes and at others drew near them, pouring a libation of its voluminous nectar over the surface. Benhar feared that the tail of her dress would trail in the water, so she held it up above her knee as she stepped agilely over the spreading, glistening, silver waves. Her marble-white thighs appeared to Suleiman amid the waters like two columns of light, their reflected illumination dazzling his eyes. He retreated two steps in shock until he nearly fell on his back.

CHAPTER TWENTY-FOUR

THE SUBJECT OF DR. RASHAD Fikri continued to keep Mohammed al-Buri awake, day and night. He was a man of faith and
of principle who did not forget a good deed. What Dr. Rashad
did for him in the most intensively painful days of his life was
a favor that would weigh upon him for all his days. The saying goes that close comradeship is only trivial to bad people,
but he was not one of them. Rather, his loyalty to Islam and
the Muslim Brotherhood movement was stronger and more
important, more overwhelming and enduring. For what could
he do as a single individual—even as one of its leaders—
against the wishes of all? Only one solution remained to him
between his decent impulse to save Dr. Rashad from certain
death or to submit to the will of the membership of the Islamist group that was now planning to assassinate him—a last
chance to prevent his killing, notwithstanding the determination of the rest of the brothers and his holding to his own line
in opposing their wish to liquidate him.

A repentance session!

Yes, if Dr. Rashad recanted his view—the Holy Law dictates that, before a man is declared an apostate from the One
True Faith, he must be allowed to repent before he is punished.
How easy it would be to speak with him logically and convince him to reconsider his hardline view against Islam, which
could give him a new lease on life. That is, if he announced his
repentance publicly—he, the famous writer and thinker—it

would provide a clear victory that would raise the cause of the movement to the highest horizon on the one hand, and gain it wider popularity on the other. The idea pleased him—so, based on the Islamic principle of consultation, he mentioned it to Dido, who approved it in turn. The sheikh resolved to arrange the meeting with Dr. Rashad.

Dr. Rashad agreed—on condition that the discussion take place in a public venue where others could witness it, leaving no confusion or doubt about the result. He proposed that the encounter be held at the site of the Association of Free Thought in Ibrahimiya the following Thursday, June 12, 1981, the time of his monthly lecture at the center. On this occasion, the subject would be the establishment of the religious state. Yet the scope of the lecture would be restricted to merely a proclamation in which he would express his point of view on the topic, which he would then open for discussion by those who wished to take part. At the head of these, of course, would be Sheikh Mohammed al-Buri. Dido presented him with the doctor's response. He thought for a while, then gestured with his head, saying, "If you are decided, then put your trust in God."

Two days later—on Wednesday, June 11, precisely— Mohammed al-Buri donned his Islamic robe, which reached just below his knees, flowing trousers, and an embroidered skullcap, egg-white in color. This was the new attire he had assumed, a change in which the leadership of the movement and its elite had followed him. He was preparing to go out to visit Marwa, his young wife who had restored to him the youth that he had lost between the walls of Qena Prison. Then the doorbell of the apartment door rang with unusual insistence, and he grew unusually fearful. It was afternoon, and all had left for their work. Even *al-Hagga* Zeinab had gone out to take care of something or other. There was no one left in the flat besides himself as he made his way slowly toward the door to answer it while his heartbeats sped up. Dido normally visited after the dinnertime prayer to drink tea with him; *al-Hagga* and the kids had the key to the apartment, so they would not ring the bell. And at that thought exactly, it rang again with greater urgency.

"Okay, God willing," he called out.

He stretched out his hand and opened the door—and standing silent in front of him was a tall young man with bushy hair and eyebrows. He wore a brightly colored shirt, and next to him on the doorstep lay a traveling valise. The youth seemed surprised, as though he had not expected him to open the door—an aging, brown-skinned giant with a white beard, wearing strangely-styled clothes and with a white kerchief on his head. Who could the young man be?

"Alright, my son, who are you?" the old man asked. "Whom do you want, I mean?"

When the young man heard him, he could not believe his ears. That voice—that tone, which pierced the wrinkles and scars of time—even in these unfamiliar clothes. He opened his arms and bounded toward him, squeezing him in an embrace as he whispered with emotion, "Papa, Papa, Papa!"

Mohammed al-Buri sat him down next to him on his favorite couch and leaned toward him lovingly, not believing that he was sitting with his first born, Mohammed. His son told him how he had alighted in various American states until he settled in California, where he obtained a scholarship that ended with his acquiring a bachelor's degree in political science at the university in Berkeley, where he was now preparing to study for a master's in human rights at the same university next fall. He had seized the opportunity to visit the family in Alexandria before he was busy once again with study and work. The sheikh felt an unequalled pride, but was conquered by his apprehension that his son was lost to him in that amazing world. Then his son, with sympathy, asked him in turn about the years in prison, and about Mustafa, Mai, and his mother, checking on each of them. Then, laughing, he asked him out of curiosity about Mohammed's peculiar garb. The sheikh answered that the *Sunna*, the Traditions of the Prophet, had said to dress like the Prophet (peace and prayer be upon him, as well as his Companions), at which his son shook his head.

The two of them talked about everything. The hours passed as they sat on the couch until Sheikh Mohammed forgot his rendezvous with Marwa.

Suleiman drew a last drag on the cigarette before stubbing it out in the ashtray on the desk in front of him. He was still sitting, smoking, and remembering the details of his last time together with Madam Benhar. During the relations between them, the degree of their intimacy and her closeness to his heart surpassed his sentiment for his wife Amani, with whom he had been for all of five years, in which she had produced his three children. He and Benhar met approximately every Tuesday afternoon in the little Swiss Hotel in Ramle Square that was managed by Madame Suzanna. She was an old Swiss woman, one of the remnants of the foreign communities that had inhabited Alexandria before the Revolution. Suleiman was an old patron of hers, who had been coming to the hotel since his university days. He had also been a friend of her husband Robert before lung cancer had killed him in the early 1970s. Suzanna had become a friend to the two lovers since they began to meet at her place.

Suleiman was surprised by the peculiar mixture of sophistication and crudeness, romanticism and eroticism, and sublimity and baseness, in Madam Benhar's personality. He had never met a woman like her! She knew exactly what she wanted, and her mind would not rest until she had it. The closer they grew together and the more their relationship developed, the more Suleiman noticed her husband's interest in him, born of curiosity—or rather, suspicion—and the more Lutfi questioned him as he invited him to an evening's entertainment here or a luncheon there. Suleiman confided his thoughts to her one day, and they wondered if her husband suspected their involvement with each other. Benhar rejected this vehemently, saying that Lutfi was crazy, and that if he suspected—merely suspected—what was between them, even a basic mutual attraction, he would not refrain from getting a thug to teach Suleiman manners or kill him in cold blood. She finished by saying, "You don't know Lutfi. He's gone over the top."

Yet Suleiman had never been at ease in his relations with Lutfi Hassanein al-Basri. He always felt Lutfi was hiding a great deal behind that painted-on smile, well-groomed hair, and magician's fingers laden with gold rings that he played with in front of him whenever they met. Was he one of the thieves that filled the country these days, gathering all this money and status by illegal means? Or was he working for state intelligence, for example? How else had he become so well-to-do? And what about the tension that surrounded Lutfi's appearance in wherever he happened to be, and his continuous casting of doubt on things? But Suleiman managed never to let this tension impact the relationship that joined him to Benhar and that grew firmer and advanced further with time. On the evening of Wednesday, June 11, his suspicions were confirmed by Lutfi's behavior when the pair spent the evening together at the bar of the Cecil Hotel in Ramle Square. As the wine played with Lutfi's head, his voice began to grow louder as they discussed the students' demonstrations in and occupations of the universities and the government's reaction—with the president describing their movement as "the thieves' uprising."

"Those guys are sons of bitches!" Lutfi shouted. "We're the ones who brought them in and planted them among the students. We gave them heaps of cash to block the Communist delegates in the universities—and they go and bite the hands that feed them!"

"Who do you mean by 'we,' Lutfi?" Suleiman asked with scandalized innocence.

Lutfi answered immediately, "Are you going to play dumb?"

Suleiman laughed from the bottom of his heart as he twisted the ring on his finger without thinking. Then he asked, "Okay, but why did you all let them get so big?"

Lutfi answered him, muttering drunkenly, "Who said we are letting them? That's this democracy—may God curse its father too. The more we want to accomplish something great, the more they regale us with the story of democracy, so we keep quiet. What have we got to do with democracy? By the Prophet, does democracy work for those people? They only respond if you beat them with shoes!"

They both laughed until Suleiman interrupted, "All you did was let the genies out of Aladdin's lamp. Aren't you the ones who kept on rubbing it until you roused the genie that Abdel-Nasser had locked up inside the magical vessel? Well then—deal with it!"

"We will, of course! We're not asleep on the job. Of course, we aren't!" The effect of the wine had brought the two of them to the limit—or at least, so thought Suleiman, whom drowsiness had begun to overcome in turn, and he made a sign that the hour was getting late. But Lutfi provoked him by saying the encounter the next day between Dr. Rashad Fikri and Sheikh Mohammed al-Buri was fraught with danger, especially for the life of Dr. Rashad. Suleiman was dumbfounded by how much Lutfi knew about what was going on around him, for he had only learned yesterday, when Dr. Rashad had contacted him and told him, that the sheikh would attend the meeting.

He collected himself and asked, "How do you know, Lutfi? I mean, just who told you? Dr. Rashad, for example? You yourself told me you wanted to get to know him. So, who told you?"

Lutfi laughed again, saying, "That's what we do, Suleiman, my brother. I can't tell you who told me. But it's certain
that I know everything about everyone in the country—every
man and every woman." He said this in a new dialect—a
confident, firm, and frightening parlance that seeped down to
Suleiman's heart, which twisted inside him. Did that mean he
knew the details about his relationship with his wife Benhar?
If not, when he said, 'every man and every woman,' what
did he mean? And if he really knew everything, why did he
let them continue their nearly weekly meetings at Madame
Suzanna's hotel? And what did Benhar mean when she said
that Lutfi was insanely jealous, and if he knew something he
would kill him?

Lutfi grabbed his attention by asking, "Where did you go?
Snap out of it and listen well to what I'm saying. Tomorrow
morning, I want you to try and stop Dr. Rashad Fikri from
going to the meeting by any means—for his life is in danger
there. Do you understand what I'm telling you? His life is definitely in danger."

If it was this hot in June, what would it be like in July and
August? So thought Suleiman, bathed in sweat, as he parked
his car with difficulty on a side street near the station. Then he
walked to the headquarters of the newspaper *al-Watan*, where
Dr. Rashad Fikri had his office. He had flown here after finishing teaching his philosophy classes at the school in Chatby
to meet his friend, the well-known thinker, before he left his
office at the newspaper to try to dissuade him from delivering his monthly lecture. Lutfi's words still echoed in his head.
Amid piles of refuse and venders of watercress, watermelon,
and underclothes spread out on the sidewalk, he made his way
as he tried to focus his thinking on what they had talked about
without stumbling over one of these lads carrying lottery tickets, packages of paper tissues, bundles of mint leaves, or dairy
products, their faces blackened by soot from the exhaust of

cars, sweat, and dust from the roads. And those that pushed each other about in front of him on the pretext of buying and selling, when in fact they were wandering around begging or looking for the chance to filch a wallet or snatch a purse or a necklace dangling over a woman's chest.

Gently, he knocked on the door on the second floor of the newspaper's modest building. The doctor's voice granted him leave to come in.

"Welcome, welcome, Suleiman!" he exclaimed. "What is this lovely surprise? You tired yourself out coming all this way; why, man? Aren't I going to see you at the salon tonight?"

He received Suleiman as usual: with his cheerful face, his heavy glasses sliding to the middle of his nose, and his loud, mellow voice. Suleiman pulled out the last paper tissue from his pocket, patting it on his forehead and temples as he replied.

"Hello, great doctor. I came because of this very subject."

"What subject? But first, what will you have to drink?" he said as he pressed the notoriously loud electric buzzer, after which the office gofer—showing old age and malnutrition—came in. Dr. Rashad typically ordered him to fetch a cup of coffee with medium sugar or a glass of fresh lemon juice, or, in special circumstances, a bottle of fizzy soda, which would usually be tepid.

A conversation took place between them in which Suleiman shared the crucial information, which he explained was trustworthy, though, he said, he "was not at liberty to tell him the name of its source." His life was in danger tonight, Suleiman warned him, so he shouldn't show up to deliver his monthly lecture on the religious state in the presence of Sheikh Mohammed al-Buri.

Dr. Rashad laughed at the end, leaning backward until his chair nearly tipped over. In truth, Suleiman was perplexed about what to do. He didn't understand the secret behind this sudden happiness—or sardonic humor—that had settled over his friend. He waited until he finished and said, "What is the story exactly, doctor?"

"The story is, you are naïve, Suleiman," he answered. "You still don't understand the rules of the game—maybe because you are too peaceful. That man of yours wants to buy me, Suleiman. He wants to strike a bargain with you in which he protects me for a price, in return for which I work on their account while I stop speaking out from now on—I give up exposing their continued violations of the rights of women and the Copts, and I become a drumbeater for them. Would that suit you? Would it suit you if I stopped defending your rights, Suleiman, while the oppression and discrimination keeps getting worse and worse? If the Islamists want to kill me—and I'm sure one day they will do just that—would they come to the Association of Free Thought to knock me off while I deliver my lecture? Why not here in my office, or on one of those streets engulfed in the uproar we all must endure? They'll do it where no one will see, and no one will know."

He kept on smiling as Suleiman swam in successive waves of thought. Finally, he concluded, "It appears I truly am naïve, doctor. But can I ask you for something? Maybe it's even more naïve than my first request that you not come to the center tonight. Would you agree to take my ring and wear it until the lecture is over and return it to me tomorrow—or the next day?" He said this as he took the ring off his finger and put his hand out toward his friend. Dr. Rashad stretched out his hand in turn, took the ring from him in astonishment, and began to flip it in his palm as though trying to gauge its weight to guess its value.

Then he said, with words wedged between chuckles, "What's this, Suleiman? Ha ha. This is a ring? Ha ha—or is it an amulet? Ha ha ha ha ha ha. . . ."

"What amulet, doctor?" retorted Suleiman. "What have I got to do with an amulet, or things like that?"

"What's up with you then, teacher of philosophy and president of the Association of Free Thought?" shot back Dr. Rashad.

Finding no alternative, Suleiman told him the story of the amazing ring that seemed to have been the common denominator between the dazzling artistic success achieved by Sayyed Darwish and his father Daoud Abdel-Malek's renown, reputation, and wealth. Not to mention Gamal Abdel-Nasser, whose revolution was saved from failure in a seemingly miraculous manner witnessed by all, and Maged al-Barudi, who rushed off to war and came back without a scratch when everyone else in his unit had either been martyred or wounded. Then there was his own life with its successes and fearless deeds for which his peers envied him.

But the strange thing was that Dr. Rashad Fikri, the man of intellect and the author of numerous publications, advocate of the authority of the mind before everything else, hesitated to curtly reject the hand that Suleiman had reached out to him. Strangely, though he did not seem persuaded by anything Suleiman told him, for his friend's sake he bowed to the illogical implication and put the ring on his finger in the end. This despite his conviction that the ring was devoid of any of the powers claimed for it in the tales of those whose heroic deeds and triumphs Suleiman had recounted. Whatever the alleged benefits of this bit of silver set with lumps of red stone, which to him was worth no more than its value as a piece of jewelry, he was fated to be adorned by it that night as he battled wits with his adversary and friend Mohammed al-Buri at the forum of the Association of Free Thought.

CHAPTER TWENTY-FIVE

THE SPHERE OF LIFE HAD dwindled to just the few steps that she took daily between her bed, the bathroom, and the kitchen. She counted them one day and they added up to seventy-two steps altogether. From that day she had become preoccupied with counting the number of steps she took at any hour of the day and those remaining before she slept. Nothing broke the monotony of her days, which did not want to pass, except the visits of her grandchildren on Fridays or on special occasions and holidays. She used to wonder sometimes to which of Suleiman's sons he had wished to bequeath his ring. She was certain that her daughter Mona was happy in her marriage, as she made her life with her husband Nader—to whom she had not yet warmed. They had moved to the upscale district of al-Maadi and were blessed with their children Mina and Mary. But Suleiman's misery, which he constantly tried to conceal, she always saw clearly with the eyes of a mother that could glimpse the beating of a heart. Hence his palliative, conciliatory gestures did not deceive her. Amani was not the right wife for him—but that's fate. "What God has joined together, let no man tear asunder," is what she told herself every time these thoughts occurred to her.

Awaking at dawn one day, she felt as though a veil still covered her eyes, like a darkness she thought was a remnant of sleep. She rose and trundled with difficulty toward the bathroom, leaning on the pieces of furniture so as not to stumble over them. "One, two, three, four, five," the numbers followed each other in her head as she counted them off in silence. Then she opened the water faucet and proceeded to wash her face and her eyes several times—without the intended result. The veil still hovered before her eyes so that she could not make out anything in front of her. She was wretched and alone, and she didn't know what to do. She returned with difficulty to her room, counting "fifteen, sixteen." Sitting on the edge of the bed, she turned toward the picture of the Virgin hanging in front of her—but she could not see it. She realized that the matter was serious: hot tears flowed from her eyes as she lay down on her back in surrender and began to pray. Hours and hours of deadly loneliness and profound supplication passed, after which she sat on the bed and tried to make out the things around her, to no avail. By chance, Nargis came to check on her.

The doctor to whom Suleiman brought her examined her. Regretfully, he explained that there was a hemorrhage in the eye socket due to a detached retina. It would take a miracle to restore her sight if she did not travel for laser surgery abroad. But for her part, she rejected travel, and rather chose—filled with religious belief—to wait amid her darkness until that miracle that the doctor spoke of occurred.

After sunset, the edge of the heat broke a little, and the sea-scented breezes alighted upon each window and balcony in the city of Alexandria. Its arrival signaled the end of the siesta for which they had waited in their houses. The men then made for the cafés and outdoor restaurants on every street corner while the women went to the windows and balconies to visit with their female neighbors across the streets and roads. The march of a few men also began. Over the past few years, their number had increased each evening. They had bushy beards, white skullcaps, short robes, and baggy trousers, their sandals scraping the asphalt on the road as they defiled to evening prayer in the mosques of the city.

But on that very evening Sheikh Mohammed al-Buri did not walk with the rest of the brothers to the mosque of al-Attarin—the Street of the Perfume Makers—as usual. Neither did he spend his evening wrapped in conversation with his son Mohammed, who had returned from the land of unbelief and disorder, and who had that night gone out with his brother Mustafa. He was aghast at his son and his Western views—those suspect ideas he brought back with him from there about the equality of Muslims and non-Muslims and between men and women. It was as if America had created justice and equality between people, and not God's book and the sayings of the glorious Prophet.

He did neither one nor the other. Instead, he put on his clothes, dyed his beard, and prepared for Dido to come and accompany him in his taxi to meet Dr. Rashad in al-Ibrahimiya at the Association of Free Thought! The association of atheists and the enemies of Islam led by a Christian, whose father was a dirty Jew!

"Oh nation—you deserve to burn in hellfire!" he fumed.

On the way, Dido reminded him of Suleiman's ring, renewing his dream that the Brethren acquire it to fulfill their wishes in achieving their hopes and obtaining what they desire, God willing. The sheikh smiled and asked him about what it would please him to acquire if he had the ring. The man replied as he gazed at the horizon, that there was no end to where they might go if an iron will is married with a sure conviction of the rightness of their demand and the power of their belief in their goal, anchored in the judgement of God—lofty is His majesty—on the earth, and that hidden power which those who had worn the magic ring had seen. There is no limit to their ambition: there will be no stopping them on the path to its achievement. All things on earth are by the will of the Almighty God.

The sheikh's face broke out in a broad grin when he saw for himself the extent of Dido's belief in their noble intentions and his endless enthusiasm for their realization. As for

Dr. Rashad, the sheikh had asked him for a truce in his debate with him. The man was notoriously clever and skilled at aiming his blows, though the sheikh cautioned him against any kind of violence, reminding him that the goal of the meeting was no more than to invite him to return to the true faith. That could not succeed without dialogue in a friendly manner, and in any case the eyes of the media and their backers in the pay of the ruling authority were upon them these days. Thus, it was incumbent upon them to exercise every caution in what they do lest they lose the progress they had made so far. Dido smiled at him, shaking his head—but he did not reply.

When the two of them arrived there, the owner of the café that occupied the ground floor received them in person. Suleiman greeted them in the literary salon that awaited them. He introduced Sheikh Mohammed al-Duri and Dido to the rest of those present and they realized—by how few they were—that they had come early. Their eyes wandered around the place and the attendees: it was an ordinary flat with a high ceiling, from which dangled a single electric lamp that gently shook in a delicate pendular motion with the breezes blowing from the open balcony on the side opposite the high rostrum intended for the lecture. In the meeting room were many wooden chairs like those that filled the café on the ground floor: a simple hall unadorned with pictures or written *bons mots*, its walls painted a pale, off-white color. Wafting from the place was an odor of dampness mixed with the kind of insecticide used in apartments that are locked up most of the time.

The sheikh excused himself to visit the bathroom before beginning the lecture, while the invitees continued to trickle into the hall. When he returned, he found his sons Mohammed and Mustafa sitting with a third young man. He was astonished at the duo's coming, as they were surprised to see him when he exited the lavatory door. They suddenly stood together, rigidly like two soldiers surprised by their commander's arrival at the place. All that was missing was their military salute.

"What brought you here?" the sheikh asked sullenly.

"Nothing," replied Mustafa, stammering with an even, neutral smile on his lips. "We came with my friend Murad to hear Dr. Rashad's monthly lecture, so my brother Mohammed could see for himself that in our country there are also people who can think. And you? This is the first time I've seen you here." The sheikh seized the occasion and called Suleiman to come to them.

"Mohammed and Mostafa, my sons, and their friend, Murad," he said, smiling, in a confident tone that expressed the sincerity of his wish to attend that evening. It also signaled to Dido that he was committed to what he told him on the way.

"Ah, welcome, welcome, Mr. Murad. Welcome to you all—you have honored us," replied Suleiman, who appeared to know Murad and Mustafa from before. "Dr. Rashad is on his way and will be here any moment."

Nearly all the seats had filled when Dr. Rashad Fikri entered the hall and greeted those present as he approached the podium. He pulled out a sheaf of paper from a leather brief-case he was carrying, adjusted the pair of reading glasses he had pulled from his shirt pocket, and cleared his throat to prepare to start the lecture. At that moment four or five men sauntered into the hall: at their head was a man known for his elegance, with his pencil mustache and gold-rimmed spectacles—Lutfi Hassanein—who filled the place suddenly, laughing broadly. He stepped directly to the podium, greeted Dr. Rashad, then headed toward Sheikh Mohammed and Dido while passing by Suleiman, shaking their hands with both of his in contrived intimacy. Suleiman was a little embarrassed when he saw him but instantly calmed this feeling by sending someone to bring more seats from the café. In a few minutes, all eyes in the packed hall were fixed on Dr. Rashad Fikri.

Dido leaned into the sheikh's ear, and whispered, "Dr. Rashad is the one wearing the ring tonight!" The sheikh nodded his head in affirmation of his words.

In brief remarks, Dr. Rashad introduced his lecture on the religious state with a moving quotation about Omar bin Khattab: "You ruled justly, you were true to the faith—and then you slept, Omar." He immediately commented afterward that Omar himself was slain while praying in the mosque, contradicting with his death the principle that justice in rule was enough for amity to prevail. He then went on to say that three of the four Rightly Guided caliphs—the ideal examples for their successors of the most glorious era of Islam—had been assassinated for one reason or another before thirty years had passed after the death of the Prophet. Here Sheikh Mohammed began to fidget in his seat. This caught the attention of the seasoned speaker, who added that what he was presenting in today's talk was a discourse on political Islam, not the Islamic religion, and that the Companions of the Prophet were not immune to error—as all humans by nature are subject to it. He intended to demonstrate that just as leaders erred before them, so too did those who came after them. If you examined the pages of history, the ideal society that all the heavenly religions have called for throughout human history has never been realized. Not in the era when the church ruled over Europe, nor during the Islamic caliphate—not even in their heydays, despite what claims circulate among the leaders of the Islamist movement and their youthful followers today in Egypt and various other Islamic countries.

Then he reiterated that he did not intend any harm toward Islam as a religion, which calls for justice and tolerance and regulates the coexistence between people. But what contradicts this call, he said, is the interference of the faith in the affairs of politics and authority that should be governed by secular political principles, adaptable to local and international conditions. Such a call to religious rule should not go so far as to be a ruse that deceives the minds of the gullible and the naïve. Furthermore, it should not harm the sanctity of the

Islamic religion and its divine teachings by throwing them into the rubbish bin of politics with the antics of politicians.

Then he gathered his papers in silence as some of the fans of his words applauded. They included the young Mohammed Mohammed al-Buri, whose father began to look at him malignantly. Yet the father was not content with that reaction only, but stood up and said in denunciation, "Dr. Rashad, what you're saying is dangerous. First, because it is full of errors. You are the one who deceives the gullible and the naïve," he said, looking toward his son.

"Second," he added, "because you deny implicitly the authentic traditions of the Prophet that tell us about Our Master Omar and two famous incidents in which he was speaking inside the mosque with a woman about dowries and with a man about the length of his robe compared to those of the other believers. That is to say, Our Master Omar was meeting people in the mosque as the house of worship but also using it as the place to administer the business of government. What is your view then, doctor?"

Here his son Mohammed rose and said in his defense, "But the doctor said in fact that this may have happened. Yet this does not mean that Our Master Omar did not also die violently. That is, that the system did not work in the past, even in the era of the Rightly Guided Caliphs, and it likewise would not work now."

"How doesn't it work, Mr. Mohammed, man of culture?" railed the sheikh. "Do you, too, believe that? Fine—then how did the vast Islamic state and the awesome civilization that stretched from China to Spain not work: what were they? Did they happen by chance, or by typographical error?"

Here Dr. Rashad seized the chance to cut him off.

"Sheikh Mohammed, the Islamic empire is a historical fact that no one denies. But what propped up this empire was a mighty army and military leadership, not imams or holy men. That said, what is your opinion of what the Caliph al-Mansur did with the Imam Abu Hanifa? He imprisoned him, had him whipped, and poisoned him to death when he was an old man of seventy because he had refused to be a judge loyal to the caliph. And later, with the Imam Malek, when he ordered his men to scourge him with whips and drag him until his shoulder was dislocated. And Imam al-Shafi'i, who died by being beaten with clubs here in Egypt in a mosque, Sheikh Mohammed. And finally, the Imam Ibn Hanbal, who differed with the Caliph Ma'mun and with al-Mu'tasim after him over the pre-existence of the Qur'an before its revelation rather than it being handed down. He was hauled on the back of a donkey as far as Baghdad, then imprisoned, beaten, and tortured. Then they threw him into solitary confinement for two and a half years. And this was at the height of the Abbasid state, whose glories you were speaking of to your son, Sheikh Mohammed. That is what happened to four of the greatest imams, and to other thinkers and poets, in the most glorious era of Islam . . . What do you suppose, then, happened to the ordinary people, and what is happening now in our messed-up age?"

"Here you said it, doctor!" the sheikh remonstrated. "In our messed-up age, we want to change from the rule of humanity—which doesn't work—to the rule of God."

Here was the first time that Lutfi Hassanein intervened: when he felt that the subject had begun to concern him directly. So, he stood up and declared, "What is more the rule of God than this, Sheikh Mohammed? Didn't the president impose a referendum on the people just last month? Didn't he change the constitution to make the *shari'a*—Islamic religious law—the primary basis of legislation? And isn't this *shari'a* also part of what God told the Prophet—or isn't it?"

Sticking out his chest, Dido stood up and said, "We weren't acquainted with you before! As we didn't know each other from the start, shouldn't we first meet and then debate?"

With this, Suleiman—in his role as director of the salon—broke in before the discussion exploded into something with dire consequences. He turned to face all the attendees together. Running his eyes over them all, he said, "We thank Dr. Rashad Fikri for his valuable lecture and the attendees for kindly listening to it—and also for the fine discussion afterward. We invite you all to grace us again here in our weekly meetings or at least once a month, on the second Thursday, for each of Dr. Rashad's lectures. Now I want to bid you all good night."

The attendees stood up, murmuring, amid the shuffling of chair legs over the tiles, then began to file out of the place one after the other as they wondered who had won the contest this evening.

As for Suleiman and Dr. Rashad Fikri, they remained by themselves. They took two chairs onto the balcony to smoke in silence while the noises from the café—which did not quiet or abate no matter how long the hours of the night dragged on—rose to their ears.

CHAPTER TWENTY-SIX

SUMMER CAME AND WENT WITHOUT anyone savoring its flavor, for worry had spread like a restless wind among the people as unrest and instability settled over all. People filled the streets, wandering like drug addicts in search of the nearest hashish den in which to get more stoned. The police and their informers hiding in civilian clothes, state security, and intelligence operatives proliferated among them until they seemed to outnumber those they were watching. And despite the government's open appeasement of the Islamist tendencies, extremist religious ideas filled everyone's ears, ringing out from every side and direction—from both the large mosques and the tiny ones on street corners. They also filled the newspapers and even radio and television. They filled coffeehouses too, where they spewed from the throats of workers spending their vacations away from their jobs in the oil-producing countries.

The authorities responded violently in September when President al-Sadat issued an order to arrest hundreds of Egyptian leaders of various tendencies and in widespread locations. The crackdown confirmed Elaine's dream of the Virgin weeping after the pope's detention as well. Fear came over hearts once again, reminiscent of Egyptians' feelings during the years that followed the disastrous rout of 1967. The tension continued to rise between the government and the disgraced Islamists, and among the people overall, until the country seemed to be on the verge of civil war. People looked over their shoulders when they walked down the street as their smiles, jokes, and laughter drowned in a sea of gloom.

Dr. Rashad returned the ring to Suleiman despite his insistence that he keep it a short while until the situation calmed. "I can do without this silliness," said Dr. Rashad.

As for Suleiman, following that lecture, his dislike of politics and politicians only increased. The debate had grown more contentious before his very eyes with bewildering speed until he feared that it would lead to physical attacks if he had not managed to intervene at the right moment to prevent it.

But how beautiful philosophy is! How lovely women are! And Benhar was the most dazzling of them all! He was so totally absorbed in his relationship with her that he could not wait for Tuesday to come each week, and she matched him— burning love with burning love. He discovered that, like him, she listened to French songs; hence, he was glued to his radio every Sunday. He would record the European program and present the cassettes to her each Tuesday. They would listen to it together while they made love in the Swiss Hotel under the shelter of Madame Suzanna. Yet he felt he was being watched when he went there every Tuesday, so he parked his car in a different place each time, dawdling around the storefronts nearby until he was sure no one was following him. Afterward he would rush in, and Madame Suzanna would greet him with her wide smile, her ample bust shaking with joy as she would stand to kiss him on the cheek before giving him the key to room no. 8. And on the last Tuesday of September, as the two of them prepared to leave their love nest, Suleiman alerted Benhar that the next Tuesday would be October 6— the anniversary of the Suez Canal victory. The schools would be closed, so they could meet in the morning and spend the entire day together—and she agreed right away.

Indeed, they did meet at 10 in the morning the following week and went down for a hearty Swiss breakfast in the hotel dining room, followed by two cups of coffee. They then returned to their room. These extra little interludes were the active ingredient of the magic between them. They did not hurry anything; they made love with slowness and deliberation that they had never experienced before. He drew her to his breast as he kissed her seductive lips. She moaned, aroused by the touch of his body as he pressed his manhood toward her. Suddenly, there were successive loud knocks on the door. The lovers froze in fear, naked on the bed, as Madame Suzanna's anxious voice came to them.

"Hurry up, and take care, sweethearts! They have shot al-Sadat to death! I saw them kill him with my own eyes! I saw it on television! They have killed al-Sadat! They have killed al-Sadat!"

Suleiman rose trembling from the bed. In a few seconds he had put on his shirt and trousers and sat on the chair nearby, pulling on his socks as Benhar rose lazily, laden with ecstasy and passion. She leaned on her elbows, lifting her torso over the smooth bedding, her prominent bare chest lustful with love.

"Who would kill him?" she asked sarcastically. "The old lady is obviously senile."

"How would I know," replied Suleiman. "I'll go down and see. Today is the military parade as well, so how could they kill him then?" In a moment he was in the lobby watching television with Madame Suzanna, and the cook had come out of the kitchen to follow the events. Suleiman learned that he and Benhar were the only guests in the hotel. Men had opened fire on the president, just as Madame said! But who had carried it out? Soon, Benhar had come out of the room and fixed him with a querulous smile, so he told her what had happened. Yet she did not appear affected by the events. Her thoughts were running their course on a different planet. Minutes passed heavily, everyone on the edge of their comfortable seats arrayed around the television in the lobby, following developments with zeal. Benhar sprawled on her back over the luxurious couch, contemplating her painted fingernails in resignation.

Suddenly the main door opened as Lutfi Hassanein stumbled in, his expression gloomy. He looked briefly at all those present, scanning their faces. It seemed to Suleiman that he nodded his head to greet him but made directly for Benhar and leaned over the back of the couch as though to whisper to her—in a voice plainly heard by all, as if he didn't know how to do it quietly.

"Come on, Benhar," he told her. "We have to go to Cairo right away, to see what we can do in this catastrophe!" He stretched out his right hand over her arm and gripped it to urge her to stand up to leave. In her turn, she responded by rising sheepishly, then quietly preceded him in moving toward the glass door that opened out onto the main street. As he walked behind her, Lutfi turned to Suleiman, fixing him with a look whose meaning Suleiman did not understand.

"I'll phone you as soon as I get back," he said.

She waited until they had left the hotel, then Madame Suzanna asked, "Who was that strange man?"

"That's her husband," he replied.

He smiled a little as she let out a loud guffaw that did not at all match her age. The cook put his palm over his mouth while his eyes danced with laughter.

Elaine felt that al-Sadat had gotten the punishment he deserved after what he had done to the head of the church. Yet despite that, she did not seem overjoyed at what had happened. She was still distracted from the upending of her own reality by prayer and fasting, seeking intercession with God from the saints, to whom she pleaded day and night for her recovery. She began to speak softly to Daoud, whose poetry she was still able to recite after she lost her eyesight. She had memorized some of the poetry by repetition, which interceded like a prayer for her as well.

*

As he was stuffing his bag with clothes and books to travel once again, Mohammed, son of Mohammed al-Buri, asked his father if the thought of slaughtering his children continued to tempt him. They laughed together when the sheikh could not find a way to answer his son. But Mohammed confessed to him that this horrible thought never left his nightmares for years. He beseeched his son for the thousandth time to stay. The son smiled—for the thousandth time also—then pointed at the sky through the open window.

"I will continue to learn from up there until I understand what He wants from me," he said. Pointing upward with his finger, he added, "If I knew that He wanted me to return, then I would—but not before I'm sure."

He asked his father Mohammed if he believed that Dr. Rashad was so bad. His father thought for a moment and said, "Even worse!" The son tried to say more, but could not, so he dropped the subject.

With his strong grip around the handle of the packed bag, he lifted it off the bed and set it down next to him. He embraced his father, holding the aged head with his power-ful hands, before running his palm over his bald head with sympathy and love. His tears flowed as he said, "Look out for yourself."

"Go with safety, my son—there is no god but God." Muhammad the son hesitated since he wasn't yet used to the new Islamist greeting. Then he added the rest of the greet-ing, which is the Islamic credo "Mohammed is the Prophet of God." He did not mean anything in particular by it at the time; he was in fact preoccupied with one thought: that per-haps he would not see his father again after today.

Mustafa and his friend Ziko rode with him in Ziko's Fiat 124 to Cairo so Mohammed could travel once again to catch the first lectures for his master's degree studies at the Univer-sity of California at Berkeley.

*

When Lutfi returned from Cairo, he did indeed contact Sulei-man and ask to meet with him. So Suleiman suggested they dine together at Abu Youssef, the popular fish restaurant, to avoid their doing so in a posh place, mindful of the expected uproar and the subsequent whispering around them. He had become convinced that Lutfi knew of his relationship with Benhar. Why would he have come looking for her at this very hotel on that day to take her to Cairo if he did not know of their trysts there every Tuesday? Suleiman's suspicion that someone was following him to the hotel had been correct. This left him confused: how did Lutfi remain quiet for more than a year if he knew all those details?

He was still absorbed in all these thoughts as he drove his car to the restaurant in Manshiya amid a deluge of cars with which the streets teemed, as though the president of the republic had not been assassinated just a few days before. Sud-denly it struck him that the relationship between Benhar and himself was pre-planned by both Lutfi and Benhar. For some reason, he failed to grasp its purpose now, yet it was obvious from the vague attitude the husband took toward the affair, and from the extreme ease with which the wife fell into that relationship when it seemed that Lutfi had practically pushed him in her direction the night they stayed up late before Shem al-Nessim in al-Agami. Could that really be true? Is it possible a husband would drive his wife into the embrace of a strange man this way? To get what in return? He had to have answers tonight. With an involuntary movement his fingers sought his silver ring as he parked his car in front of the restaurant.

Lutfi still had not arrived when Suleiman did. So he chose a spot next to the big picture windows that looked out onto the crowded street and sat down. The aroma of grilled fish filling the place, his eyes wandered between the people on the street and the entrance to the restaurant as he smoked a cigarette to wait for his rival, who was expected at any moment. He kept thinking about how Lutfi would look when he came: would he be elegant, as was his habit? Would he receive him with a scowl or wear a grin on his well-known mask of a face when he clapped eyes on him? And how would he react to him, as well? Would he exchange banter or pleasantries with him or be tough and violent if he chose to confront him? The minutes passed slowly. A half an hour after the appointment, he became convinced that the delay was intended to wind up his nerves and resolved to leave if Lutfi did not show up in the next five minutes. He decided this while glancing at his watch, and when he looked up there was Lutfi standing in front of him, having popped up craftily like a sprite.

Lutfi pulled out the opposite chair and sat down to face him.

"Sorry for the delay," he said, smiling. "The heavy traffic these days has become unbearable!" A black leather jacket and a gray, high-necked t-shirt: elegant as usual but without affectation; a broad, carefree smile that defied Suleiman's expectations.

"The town really is crowded," Suleiman answered, "and the president hasn't been dead more than a few days. How strange! Remember the day Abdel-Nasser died and how people acted then?" He gushed forth in conversation with him as though to keep the bomb from falling, if only for a while.

"The people no longer have any feeling!" Lutfi lamented. "The man who was terrorizing them, who dictated how and when they could breathe, who brought the shadow of defeat and occupation to the country, was sweet and beautiful. Meanwhile, the other man who fought and sacrificed to the point that he went to Israel to reclaim the land—who brought back the political parties and even allowed any dog to express their own view—is nasty and vile. Let's see what the new man will do."

Suleiman did not want to stir him up further with a political discussion—the end of which he could foresee—so he contented himself with shaking his head in regret for the current condition of the people. Then he raised his hand to call the waiter and order dinner as he asked himself when the talk for which they both had come would begin.

He did not grasp that the words Lutfi spoke were not only at the heart of the subject that had brought him there that evening, but they were also the reason they had met more than a year ago at the soirée of al-Hajj Murad al-Uwayqi, for which Lutfi had prepared for more than six months beforehand to make it easier for him to meet Suleiman Daoud Abdel-Malek, his former neighbor in Moharram Bey and the owner of the magic ring, which he had taken possession of before it fell into the hands of the Islamists. Lutfi looked Suleiman over amiably as he chewed a piece of crab meat that he had just cut.

"I think that you don't need to eat crab like me," Lutfi said, "for your manhood to thrive!" He laughed rakishly.

Suleiman looked up from his food, smiling innocently, and answered sincerely, "I don't understand."

"I mean," Lutfi taunted him, "your powers grow strong on their own. Whoever has your ring doesn't need crab meat or anything else."

He kept on chuckling as he dipped a piece of bread into the dish of tahina sauce that lay between them. Suleiman realized what was being thrown at him. He signaled surrender, asking like a teenager caught by his father hiding a dirty magazine, "But where did you get that?"

"You're still asking?" Lutfi replied. "Didn't I tell you we know everything about everybody in this country?"

Suleiman laughed innocently and quipped, "This country only?" The two broke out laughing as they gobbled up cuts of fish, grilled shrimp, and salad, inserting select sexual comments here and there until they both finished their dinners. Suleiman paid the bill, counting the loss to be much smaller than expected. Lutfi offered that they go to a bar at Ramle Station for him to pay in his turn as they hoisted a couple of glasses to digest all that delectable food.

In the bar, Lutfi threw his bomb after the second drink. He said that he could not prevent Benhar from continuing her relationship with him because she had threatened to expose his impotence if he tried. He was convinced of her ability to destroy him should he not let her continue the affair and that she would carry out the threat. He feared the Turk in her that he had experienced throughout their marriage and that would certainly push her to do whatever she wished, even if that led to his personal crack-up. So, he kept silent as a sacrifice to this situation forced upon him by his point of vulnerability, to forestall the scandal that could befall him if Benhar spoke out. This was compelling logic and a morality tale that Lutfi, with his cunning, was able to recite to him.

As Lutfi spoke, he replied in all humility to Suleiman's expected questions—that would not only have inevitably occurred to him in his place, but would even open the path before Lutfi to reach his ultimate goal. Thus, he asked meekly, "Suleiman, my brother, I am at your mercy. I want your ring—as a loan. I am ready to give you anything for it. Tell me what you want for it—an apartment, a car, a position? A chalet by the sea? All I want is that you grant it to me for one or two months so I can get back my dignity—nothing more." The tears poured from his eyes as he laughed to himself at the gullibility of his rival.

Suleiman's heart fluttered in empathy for him. The veracity of his guess about the man's virility the day he visited him for the first time in al-Agami on the night of Shem al-Nessim was confirmed. He saw that he would not lose much if he lent him the ring for a month or two to rescue this family threatened with destruction. He would feel guilty if they were destroyed because of his selfishness and his keeping of the ring's power to himself. And then, what are two months compared with a friendship that might last a lifetime?

Lutfi noticed that he was absorbed in thought, so he urged him even more to choose the appropriate type of gift—one that he would never forget. Suleiman reflected that he already had a car and an apartment, so the chalet by the sea loomed as the best choice. But didn't his mother warn him before against being careless with the right to the ring that he had inherited from his father Daoud the time he had lent it to Maged al-Barudi? In any case, time had only proven her wrong, for here was the ring with him now, enabling him to guide the rescue of a family from ruin. All he would lose was two or three months at most. Then he began to feel guilty about his ongoing betrayal of his wife. Ah—his wife! He put her image aside, smiling finally when the image of the chalet on the sea that he so loved came to him.

CHAPTER TWENTY-SEVEN

THE MORNING SUN REACHED HIM as he arrived at the stairway leading from the building entrance to the street. Dr. Rashad Fikri raised his hand in front of his thick glasses as a shield against the brilliant light. As usual, he greeted the doorman crouched on his bench to the right of the main door facing the autumn daylight. Ahmed then hurried over to take the leather briefcase from him in pursuit of the twenty-five piastre fee he would take for polishing Dr. Rashad's shabby car and carrying his bag for two minutes. That is, from the moment Dr. Rashad came out of the building's gate until he squeezed his towering frame and full belly into the car, offering his tribute in return for the bag. That had been the customary, mutual agreement between them throughout the years. Except that on that day in particular, something momentous happened that would have a remarkably lasting effect.

A taxi approached at a speed inappropriate for the nar-rowness of the side street that ran next to the building, then slowed suddenly in front of the entrance. In seconds, two men, the lower parts of their faces concealed, appeared through the windows on the right side of the car. Under the armpit of each bulged a short metal barrel. The racket made by the car startled Dr. Rashad and Ahmad, interrupting Dr. Rashad's well-known daily routines as they watched with curiosity the amazing tableau of events unfolding before their eyes.

Even stranger, at the same time the two men suddenly began to shout, "There is no god but God!" in unison, adding their clamor to that made by the screeching of their car's tires on the pavement. As a result, Dr. Rashad found it extremely hard to understand what the two men were saying or what it all meant. Worse, the two did not give Dr. Rashad and Ahmad time to consider what was happening around them that morning. For, in addition to their fearful shouting, the men launched a torrent of gunfire on Dr. Rashad and Ahmed that ripped into their bodies. In mere seconds, the pair fell dead on the staircase, their blood mingling with the papers scattered from the leather briefcase. This happened before either of them had grasped any purpose or significance behind what stormed into their day that morning.

"We've got to get hold of Suleiman's ring—that's all there is to it," Dido said to Sheikh Mohammed al-Buri. "We'll watch him until the right time to get it arises," he continued, "without attracting the eyes of the security forces. The time for preparation and planning is over. The Egyptian street is readier today than at any other time to carry out the dictates of the sage book in their entirety. In any case, these are the orders of the all-powerful and glorious God, and there is nothing for us but to heed His command, may He be praised. In any case, the rulers of the Persians are not better than us—they have exchanged the orders of the tyrant and his helpers for the rule of omnipotent God and stuck their fingers in the eyes of the infidel West. No one can push them from the straight path of truth; their people are behind them, extolling the word of their creator over all other speech."

Suleiman walked the length of the Corniche along Cleopatra Beach to Miami Beach. The stroll lasted three full hours as he contemplated the blueness of the endless sea and its weary waves lapping at the edges of the ancient city of Alexandria.

The sea breezes stroked the locks of his hair on that autumnal morning. His mind kept returning to the details of the night he had spent in the company of Lutfi Hassanein. He wondered repeatedly if he had done the right thing when he agreed to that exchange. He thought about what his mother's reaction would be if she heard of it. But he decided not to add to her troubles by mentioning the details, for she still suffered from the loss of her eyesight and spent many long hours in ceaseless invocations of God and in prayer. As for Amani, she was, as usual, distracted from him, absorbed in the details of her monotonous life. He imagined himself sitting among his children as they played around him on the chalet's balcony, contemplating the sea stretching out before him, if the place were ever to become his own. He relaxed at the thought, his face bursting into a grin, and took a deep breath of the pure coastal breeze, encouraged to continue down his path to its end.

At the entrance to Miami Beach, he stopped for a bit to reflect on the glory of the golden sands that stretched to the waters of the tranquil sea—tranquil thanks to the great rock that towered amid the waves, which had guarded the shore since the beginning of time. Suleiman joyfully recalled the day that his father Daoud had accompanied them to the same beach, where the two of them had spent a day, the details of whose events would not be forgotten for the rest of their lives. He toddled down the line of neat *cabinas* to his left, which were as Lutfi had described them to him. There he beheld a captivating sight as he stood dazed as though within an enchanted gateway, transported from reality to an imaginary world. The circular line of closely packed *cabinas* stretched right and left, enclosing at its forefront and beneath the railings of its balconies a paved promenade ending at a stone wall. Beyond the wall, a massive stone block stretched steeply downward until it vanished amid the roiling waves of the sea. In other words, the *cabinas* and the promenade facing them were erected on top of a hill made of a massive rock, its base embraced by the waters and its summit crowned with chalets. There wasn't a sign of anyone around at that time of year, which compounded the magic of the place.

Suleiman continued his stroll until he reached the end of the path. At the next-to-last chalet, Lutfi appeared, sitting in wait for him. Upon his arrival Suleiman was surprised by the presence of Benhar facing him. She was leaning with her back against the wall of the chalet, which had blocked his view of her from afar. Suleiman greeted the two of them together, then sat down on a chair between them, having been in pain caused by the long walk's strain on his legs. Benhar asked if he would like to drink some tea, which she had brought with her in a thermos. He thanked her gratefully and began to sip the tea from the plastic cup she handed to him, savoring it as he drank. A silence fell over them that none of the three of them knew how to break. They traded fleeting glances until Lutfi ventured to end the mounting anticipation.

"What then is your opinion, sir?"

"Beauty beyond description," replied Suleiman matter-of-factly. He wondered if there really was any hope he would possess something like this bit of heaven, or if that was merely a gag.

"Have you come here before?" Benhar asked, joining the conversation to ease the tension gripping him.

"This is the first time, in fact," he answered as he continued to sip from the hot cup of tea.

"So, you must have never seen Masoud's Well then," she added.

"No, I've never seen it," he confessed. "What is Masoud's Well, Benhar?" He addressed her this way—without polite titles such as "Mrs."—as the game's cards had been revealed for all to see. Or so Suleiman thought, at least.

The woman rose and the two men followed her spontaneously as she stepped out of the chalet, her companions still carrying their cups of tea, and crossed the paved promenade.

Then she climbed neatly onto the low stone wall, pausing on top of it as they continued to follow in her wake. She jumped again and landed on the stone block below, and they leaped in turn. She advanced cautiously over the uneven stone surface with its jutting projections, the two of them still behind her, until she came to a hole in the center of the block. The hole was surrounded by a parapet. She pointed toward the depth of the hole, calling out in a triumphant tone, "Masoud's Well!"

Dido and two of his men had followed Suleiman in his taxi to observe him for the length of his march down the Corniche until he entered the beach. They parked the car and trailed him from the boardwalk of the Corniche until he disappeared into one of the *cabinas*, when they immediately jumped over the railing at the roadway, then onto the roof of a neighboring *cabina*. From there they went over the barrier between the building and the Corniche wall that rose over the line of the *cabinas*, proceeding until they reached the ground behind the *cabina* into which he had disappeared. Dido saw Suleiman and his companions heading in the direction of Masoud's Well. But who could they be? One was Lutfi Hassanein al-Basri—no doubt he, too, must be after the magic ring. *One of the dogs in power like Lutfi will get the ring only over my corpse!* Dido thought. He turned toward his men, signaling that they should wait in their hiding place behind the *cabina* until he gave them the signal to start.

A well with a depth of three or four meters in the center of the stone enclosure, its bottom was invisible, covered by the waters of the sea. The waves continued to clash every few seconds in an effervescent whirlpool that rose from its depths, then dissipated once more, revealing rocky outcroppings hidden by seaweed that would vanish yet again in the bubbling churn that came once more to cover the well in an agitated succession of rising and falling waters. Benhar said that the bottom of the well was linked to the great sea through a channel stretching under the edge of the great stone rampart. The waves breaking on the edge of the rampart would fill the channel and then the cistern in turn, and when the waves receded, the level of water in the well would go down too. She added that children and young people would often meet around the well during the summer season. The toughest among them would compete by plunging into the depths of the well when the water rose, clinging to the well's stone wall when the water dropped and scaling to the top of the well until they exited. She added further that a minority of them would compete in leaping into the well then swimming through the channel beneath the rock, emerging from it into the sea. As she pointed, Suleiman followed her words raptly.

He noticed that the pair did not speak with each other at all and wished that his loan of the ring to Lutfi would be a means to forge a rapprochement between the two of them. He also hoped with all his heart that his sharing it would be a way of making them both happy. He truly loved Benhar: in their closeness he felt her misery and depression despite the apparent success and ease of living that surrounded her. Lutfi, too, had been good-hearted but also heartbroken for reasons outside his control. A man incapable of pleasing his woman cannot himself be happy, no matter how much wealth and power or how many friends he amasses around him.

As for Lutfi, in his silence he was reveling in his imminent victory. He had come to the brink of possessing the magic ring that might have saved the life of Dr. Rashad Fikri—God have mercy on him—on the night Dr. Rashad had borrowed it from his friend, and for a few days afterward until he gave it back in his blindness to danger. Thus Dr. Rashad's reserves of strength had been drained from him, and his life ended at the hands of participants in his own program after they had failed to silence his provocative words. They had fired their bullets into him and shut him up forever. The news of his death could not have reached Suleiman yet, and it must not reach him now before the deal was completed properly.

When Benhar had finished speaking about Masoud's Well, Lutfi raised his voice questioningly.

"What do you say, Suleiman? Do you agree?"

"Of course, I agree!" answered Suleiman immediately, stretching out his finger and nervously removing his ring from around it. Lutfi then reached his hand into his pocket, pulled out a folded-up piece of paper with care, and held it out before him.

"This, sir," he said, "is the contract for the sale of the chalet—only your signature is missing!" He extended it toward Suleiman, who took it as he began to hand Lutfi his ring. In that instant, Dido and his companions lurched forward, their eyes fixed on the enchanted silver signet. In the blink of an eye, Dido had shoved his hand forward with lightness and dexterity, eager to snatch the ring from Suleiman. But Lutfi had been waiting to grab it first, and a multitude of hands tangled in a crowded mass to rip the ring from Suleiman's fist. Finally, one of Dido's entourage managed to seize it. In a despairing assault, Benhar dug her nails into his flesh, and the man moaned in pain. Despite himself, Dido's minion relaxed his grip as Lutfi suddenly tried again to seize it, but the man threw it away in the violence of the effort. The eyes of all followed the ring as it flew in the air, its silver band and red jasper stone glinting in the rays of the setting sun.

The ring struck the inside wall of the well, its metallic ping ringing in their ears as they froze in confusion. They watched it tumble before their gaze into the deepest part of the abyss sloping down below them.

Lutfi grabbed Dido's neck and would have strangled him with both hands if the two other men had not intervened to pry loose his grip. Benhar screamed in horror as the men began to fight each other hand-to-hand. They stopped, stunned by her shriek. Suleiman felt a wave of sadness overwhelm him, and he stifled his tears in order not to weep in front of the others as he started to turn away to leave the place. Within an instant, Dido ordered one of his men to dive into the well to retrieve the ring.

The man responded immediately. He stripped off his clothes, and, as the waters swelled, leaped into them in his underwear. Suleiman came over to observe the result of that desperate attempt to bring back his ring. No sooner had the waters, which had turned a shade of red, begun to recede than they revealed once again the back of the man's head, those gathered reckoned he was still searching for the ring. Then the water rose again, covering over the head engrossed in its quest. The waters' redness increased, and all of them stood staring as they waited anxiously for the man to surface at any moment to announce he had found the much-desired object of his persistent search.

Their wait grew longer and longer, and with wave after wave no one raised a hand nor turned their head nor took a breath while the waters returned to their usual blue. No sooner had their hope that the man would find the ring perished than so too did their hope that the diver himself would ever return.

Suleiman stayed looking down at the waters for several minutes, the petrified eyes of the others staring fixedly at him lest he show any sign of movement or turn abruptly toward them. They all realized they could do nothing about what had happened. Then they began to leave, one after the other. Only Suleiman remained. The failed effort—which had led to the death of a man—had increased the weight of his sorrow. The cries of the men behind him rose as they traded accusations.

"You killer!"

"You pimp!"

"You whore!"

Then their tone gradually softened as the shouts transformed into expressions of maturity and wisdom.

"It was his lot."

"It was his fate."

"It was the will of God!"

They said these phrases as they shook their heads and slapped their palms together in despair. But none of them mentioned Suleiman's signet for which they had gathered that day as they left him—and his ring—alone at the well.

Some still come furtively to search for the ring by night, aided by special flashlights. After the diver's body was raised from the deep, an order was issued to place a guard from the security forces to stop people from jumping into Masoud's Well by day.

Meanwhile, it spread among the people that an evil power infested the place and that one day it killed an unfortunate man who had plunged into the well in search of Suleiman's ring.